THE ESTATE

Books by Isaac Bashevis Singer

Novels

THE MANOR

SATAN IN GORAY

THE FAMILY MOSKAT

THE MAGICIAN OF LUBLIN

THE SLAVE

Stories

GIMPEL THE FOOL

SHORT FRIDAY

THE SÉANCE

THE SPINOZA OF MARKET STREET

Memoirs

IN MY FATHER'S COURT

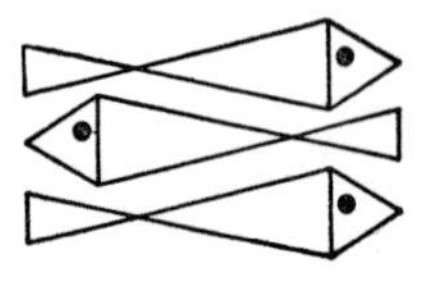

For Children

A DAY OF PLEASURE

THE FEARSOME INN

MAZEL AND SHLIMAZEL
or The Milk of a Lioness

WHEN SHLEMIEL WENT TO WARSAW

ZLATEH THE GOAT

Isaac Bashevis Singer

THE ESTATE

FARRAR, STRAUS AND GIROUX New York

Library of Congress catalog card number: 73–88782

First printing, 1969
Printed in the United States of America
by H. Wolff, New York
Published simultaneously in Canada
by Doubleday Canada Ltd., Toronto

DESIGN: *Marshall Lee*

AUTHOR'S NOTE

The Estate is a sequel to and the conclusion of *The Manor*, published in 1967. *The Manor* begins with the Polish uprising against the Czar in 1863 and *The Estate* ends in the last years of the nineteenth century—an epoch when humanism undertook to practice what it had preached for generations. What happened in the village of Jampol, and what was discussed by a small group of self-educated youths in furnished rooms in Warsaw, became the basis of the social upheavals and the terrible disillusions of our present time. The whole work appeared in serial form in the *Jewish Daily Forward* between 1952 and 1955. Even though *The Family Moskat* was written a few years earlier, it is in a way a continuation of the same saga.

The Estate was translated into English by Joseph Singer, the son of my brother I. J. Singer; by Elaine Gottlieb, the wife of my unforgettable friend Cecil Hemley; and by Elizabeth Shub, who also edited the book before I sent it to Robert Giroux, the editor-in-chief. I thank them all for their most helpful efforts.

I. B. S.

ONE

I

I

Daniel Kaminer was suddenly taken ill. He grew feverish and began to cough. Celina gave him tea with raspberry juice and rubbed his neck and back with turpentine, but it did not help. When morning came, he could not get up. He asked for a mirror. Overnight his face had become sunken, and his goatee seemed to have shriveled up. "Celina, I'm dying!" he said.

Celina began to weep. She immediately sent to Skarshew for a doctor; Daniel Kaminer had pneumonia. He was cupped, and leeches were applied to him, but he grew worse hourly.

His daughter, Clara, was abroad. She had written from Paris that she had quarreled with Zipkin and that he had left her. She had lost money in Monte Carlo. She had made the acquaintance of a Russian Jew, a merchant of the First Guild, who was permitted to live outside the Pale. She wrote short, insinuating letters whose sentences usually ended with rows of dots. One thing was clear to Daniel Kaminer: his daughter was traveling a slippery path. Felusia, whom Clara had left with him, was now a part of his own family. But when you were dying, nothing mattered. Daniel Kaminer had mixed feelings about the next world. There had to be a God, but the immortality of the soul was hard for him to accept. What happened to the souls of dead people? Where did they go? How long could a soul hover over a cemetery or remain in a cold synagogue?

4

Daniel Kaminer had not lost his sense of humor. He groaned and joked. To Celina, who was already mourning him, he said: "Shush! Don't wail! You'll awaken the Angel of Death . . ."

"What will become of us?"

"There are so many widows, there'll be one more."

"What will I, may it never happen, do with my children?"

"Marinate them in vinegar . . ."

Although Daniel Kaminer jested, he worried about his brood. He had accumulated no capital and had had a few bad years. The Russians owed him money, but the dead can claim no debts. Celina had the brain of a mite. She would not be able to collect a cent. His mother-in-law was paralyzed. She could no longer work and had to be supported. What would Celina do with the children? If Clara were at home, he could at least discuss the situation with her. But she was abroad. For hours at a time Daniel Kaminer did not think at all. He lay struggling with the phlegm that filled his throat and lungs. He imagined that if he could get rid of it with one mighty cough, he would get well instantly. But when he tried to cough, he felt a stabbing pain in his side. His head burned, his feet had fallen asleep, his fingers felt numb.

Celina walked around in a soiled housedress, worn-out slippers, and a dirty kerchief on her head. She wept and continuously munched on something. Every now and then she would stop at Daniel's bedside and shake her head in a gesture of grief as old as womankind. It occurred to Daniel that within a year she would probably be remarried. There's always someone to take your place. He hadn't lived right, he thought. He had often heard old people say that if they could live their lives over again, they would know what to do. But what actually would he do differently if he were now forty? Would he become a Hassid and spend his days in the study house? Would he drink more, eat better, have more women? No. One cannot be wiser than fate.

Daniel Kaminer fell asleep. He dreamed that Russia was at

war and that he had been ordered by the Czar to provision the army. The regiments paraded before him, Cossacks, Circassians, Tartars, carrying guns, spears, and swords. They sang a monotonous song, utterly sad and as if from another world. Could they be dead? Do corpses wage war? Daniel awoke with a coughing fit—and a plan. He would send a telegram to Warsaw ordering Sasha to come at once. He was convinced that his grandson was not nearly as wild as he appeared to be. It was true that he had been behaving badly since his mother had left. There had been complaints from the director of his school. But if a boy were left at the mercy of God in a large city, why shouldn't he indulge himself? Daniel Kaminer had long sensed that the boy understood people and that he had a smooth tongue. Perhaps he had a talent for business as well. Sasha took after the Kaminer side of the family. Daniel Kaminer sent for Colonel Shachowsky, an elderly Russian with whom he was doing business. Although the colonel had often disagreed with Kaminer, he was upset to see him so ill and insisted on sending for the regimental doctor.

Daniel Kaminer said: "Your Excellency, I am already as good as gone. My grandson Sasha is my heir."

"Yes, I know him, the handsome one."

"He will take care of my orphans."

Colonel Shachowsky burst into tears. Celina brought him a glass of whisky. He promised Kaminer that he would help Sasha in every way possible. When the regimental doctor came, he again prescribed cupping, but the patient grew worse. His breathing sounded like a saw, his nose bled. A sexton from the Burial Society suggested that the patient make his confession, but Kaminer refused. "One doesn't grow fat from confessing," he quipped.

By morning he was dead. Colonel Shachowsky ordered the military band to play at the funeral. Although the Jampol rabbi declared that it was forbidden to play music at a Jewish funeral, the pharmacist, Grain, objected and called the rabbi an ignoramus. There were by now many enlightened Jews in

Jampol and they sided with the druggist. Sick as she was, Mrs. Frankel came from Warsaw, bringing Celina a hat with a black veil. The Burial Society demanded an exorbitant fee for the plot, but Colonel Shachowsky warned them that he would have them sent to Siberia if they overcharged the widow. The Russians and heretics took over the burial. Mrs. Grain, Tamara Shalit, and Sonya Sorkess sewed a shroud for the corpse. The military band and a company of soldiers followed the hearse, playing military marches. At the cemetery, Grain, David Sorkess, and Colonel Shachowsky eulogized the deceased. The wives of the officers sobbed when they saw Celina and her many orphans, one smaller than the other—like a row of steps. . . . Everyone already knew Sasha. The men patted him on the back. The women comforted him. They all said the same thing: it certainly would have been better had he been able to graduate from the gymnasium and enter the university. But since he had to take over his grandfather's business, they would teach him, help him, and God would protect him.

The officers of the Jampol garrison kept their word. Colonel Shachowsky, who was always late with his payments, covered all his debts promptly. Mayer Joel, Calman's son-in-law, had also become a contractor and had been a competitor of Kaminer's, but now all orders were given to Sasha. It turned out that the boy had the Jewish instinct for trade. He learned so quickly that people were astounded. He even knew whom to bribe. He made sure that both the colonel and General Horne, who had replaced General Rittermayer, received their customary due.

At first Mayer Joel tried to fight back. He held the lease on the estate and was the proprietor of the mill. He could supply products more cheaply than Sasha. He planned to go to Warsaw, pay the necessary bribes, and get the contracts away from Sasha. But Calman intervened. He still had something to say. The lime quarries and the railroad had remained in his name. First of all, he told Mayer Joel, Sasha was not a stranger. He was Calman's son, and Mayer Joel's brother-in-law. It would be a disgrace before the Gentiles for a sister and brother to go into competition. Second, Mayer Joel was a rich man. How much did one need? One didn't take one's money to the grave. Third, Sasha had to support a widow and orphans. Fourth, the authorities were on Sasha's side. Calman saw clearly which way the wind was blowing. The boy spent his days and nights at the officers' club, rode in their sleighs, associated with their wives and daughters. As long as Sasha had studied at Warsaw, he had caused Calman no shame. Now he had come to Jampol to disgrace him. But no good could come from an open rift. If one pushed a boy like Sasha too hard, he might decide to become a convert out of spite.

II

Sonya received a letter from her brother. It was postmarked Paris, and Zipkin had filled four closely written pages:

Dear Sonya:

I have wanted to write to you for a long time, but I didn't have your address. When I left Warsaw, you didn't know what you were going to do, not even where you would be staying. I hear from Mother and Father that you keep changing your address, and in this respect we seem to be alike. In the past few months I have moved in and out of so many hotels and furnished rooms that I'm dizzy. I must tell you immediately that our parents still do not know the circumstances of my trip abroad, despite the fact that Clara demanded that I tell them. Instinct told me that the adventure wouldn't last long. I see from their letters that you have kept your promise and have also not told them the truth. I am grateful to you with all my heart. I was afraid that Sabina might give everything away, but she too has kept quiet. It's good they weren't dragged into the mud with us.

Yes, Sonya dear, you were right, a thousand times right. I

did act like a suicidal fool. I always thought I was the practical one and you a romantic young girl who lived in a dream world. Now I must admit that you understand people much better than I do. I can't tell you, little sister, how much I have suffered. It seems to me that it is years, not months, since I left Warsaw. Kubuś is like a fantasy to me, although I long for him day and night. I see him in my dreams. I know I shouldn't burden you with my mess, but I must tell someone or I will choke. I am shattered both psychologically and physically. Believe me, if it were not for our parents, I would kill myself.

To relate all my experiences and tell you what I had to put up with would take a book, but I'll try to be as brief as possible. No sooner had we left Poland than Clara changed. It was as if the devil had suddenly possessed her. She became dreadfully nervous, complained that she missed her children, that she was ill, that she had done a foolish thing, and so on. In Berlin she insulted the chambermaid. Her behavior was so coarse I couldn't believe my ears. She began to count every penny, argued with waiters, suspected everyone. She reminded me constantly that I had no money of my own. Suddenly she announced that she wanted to go to Monte Carlo before visiting Paris. It was because of a man called Mirkin, a Jew from Russia who lived at our hotel, that she changed her plans. It would take a Turgenev or a Boleslaw Prus to describe him. He'd get up in the middle of the night and order roast duck. He traveled with a male secretary, who was his procurer as well. Forgive my mentioning it, but it's the truth. He had money to burn. He exported Siberian furs to Western Europe and had branch offices everywhere. He also dealt in rugs from Bukhara, and the devil-knows-what-else. He was at least sixty-five years old, blind in one eye, and had a wife and married children somewhere. You should have seen how these two charlatans, he and Clara, were immediately attracted to each other. As soon as they met, I ceased to exist for her. She had once sold herself to Calman Jacoby. Mirkin was even older and uglier, and Calman at least was an honest man.

9

Sonya, you must be smiling as you read these lines. You warned me. If only I had listened to you. I should have spat on her, but I was so beaten and drained that I simply didn't have the strength to make a decision. Like an idiot I dragged along after her to Monte Carlo and suffered the punishment I deserved, even much worse than I deserved. At Monte Carlo the old buzzard played roulette and lost many thousands. Clara tried her luck as well and lost over a thousand rubles. I'm sure she thought she'd take Mirkin away from his wife and become a millionairess again, but he was too cunning a dog. As long as it suited him, he played along with her and plied her with caviar and champagne. Then one day he received a telegram—or pretended to—and off he went. He said he would return to Monte Carlo and even left his secretary, or whatever you want to call him, behind. In the end the secretary too disappeared. What his real intentions were, the devil knows, but he was to have joined Clara somewhere later on. All this, you understand, put an end to our relationship. I saw her at her vulgar worst. You won't believe it, Sonya, but there were days when I actually starved because my few-hundred rubles had been spent on fare. To make a long story short: we said goodbye, or rather we separated without saying goodbye. She tried to ingratiate herself with me all over again. But no matter how worthless I am, I didn't stoop that low. I left cursing not her (scum will be scum) but myself and my disgusting frivolity.

For a long time I dared not write to Sabina. When at last I did, I received no reply, and I couldn't blame her. I had betrayed everything and everybody: Sabina, myself, the child, and all that is decent. I have completely lost all self-respect, and that is the worst of my tortures. It causes me anguish such as I hope you will never experience.

Why do I trouble you, dear Sonya? How can you help me? This is my situation: actually I don't have a franc. I have sold my gold watch and everything else for which I could get money. I want either to come home or to go to America, but I don't have the fare. I owe rent at the hotel. I envy every dog in the street, every cat, every worm. Sonya, you must get hold of a hundred and fifty rubles—although I can't imagine where you can get such a sum—and send the money to me. You once spoke of a dowry that our parents were holding for you. I will, of course, repay you and be forever grateful. I have no one but you. If you too turn away, there will be only one way out for me.

Sonya, don't be angry. I suffer constantly. I never imagined that a person could suffer such hell. There is no heater in my room and it is bitterly cold. My soul feels even colder. I'd like to ask one other favor: Would you see Sabina and talk the situation over with her? I don't want to force myself on Sabina, but I did her a terrible wrong and I'd like to try to straighten matters out. Speak to her, and from what she says you'll know whether she can ever forgive me.

Europe is beautiful, elegant, free. But for me the whole world has become miserable. The Jews here have one good thing: a soup kitchen run by the Alliance Israelite. I eat lunch there, to keep from starving. Yes, your brother has become a beggar. The types one meets there are beyond description. I never knew such freaks existed.

Dear, enough bitterness for one letter! I kiss you a thousand times. If you can't help me, at least write. It will be a comfort.

Your broken ALEXANDER

My dear Alexander, sweet brother of mine, dearest!

Do you remember what I said to you that morning in Clara's house? Whatever happens, I'll always love you.

When I said them, I did not mean my words to be prophetic. Yet I must have had a premonition. I want to tell you that from childhood on I've loved you with a terrible love. It may be a sin to admit it, but I loved you more than I loved our parents. I don't know why. Perhaps because you are so hot-blooded and wild. I remember once when you hit me (how long ago that was!) I forgave you immediately. Well, enough sentimentality!

I didn't reply at once because I tried to find some way of helping you. I did all I could, but here in Warsaw I couldn't raise one hundred and fifty kopecks, let alone rubles. I too have suffered a misfortune. But there is no point in writing about that now. I only want to tell you that Mirale is still gravely ill in the hospital and rumors persist that the person responsible for her illness is her best friend. It makes one shudder to think that such a thing is possible. He denied it vehemently, but nevertheless he found it necessary to disappear. How I have survived all this baffles me. You are an atheist, but I still believe in God, and perhaps that is what has saved me. I'm disappointed, terribly disappointed, not in humankind but in certain people. I still believe that a better tomorrow is coming and that the sun will shine again. If I did not believe that, I could not breathe.

I have a job as a clerk in a store here in Warsaw. Yes, I stand behind a counter in a haberdashery and sell ties, cuff-links, socks, and other such items. I work hard, and I must be there early to open the store in the morning. It closes at seven, but I stay to straighten up. By the time I come home and finish supper it is eleven o'clock. I fall into bed and sleep like the dead.

It's sheer luck that your letter arrived on a Friday, because the store is closed on Saturday. Dearest, I want to tell you everything in proper sequence. On Saturday morning I went to see Sabina. Kubuś is more charming than ever, but Sabina was sour as acid. She didn't want to let me in. She vented all her anger on me, then looked at me with an expression of sarcasm and laughed in my face. If she is to be believed, her only wish is that you send her a Jewish divorce. Obviously her mother is egging her on.

Now would you believe this. I left her apartment and walked aimlessly up Krakow Boulevard. Suddenly someone called me—a woman dressed completely in mourning. I was terribly startled. Who did it turn out to be—Clara! I wanted to avoid her, but she caught me and gripped me so hard that my wrist still hurts. It seems that her father has died. I insisted that I had nothing to say to her, but she begged me not to leave her. She began to cry in the middle of the street, and I was embarrassed. I went with her to a café and there she sobbed and talked continuously for three hours. Fortunately the place was empty. I cried too. The glasses of coffee the waiter brought us filled with our tears. Dearest, what can I tell you? I know all her faults, but she's still not as heartless as Sabina. A vulgar person can also have a soul. I can't tell you everything she said. Essentially, she's sorry. The Russian merchant visited her in Warsaw but she sent him away. She spoke about you as if you were an angel. How strange it all is! She swore to me that she longs for you day and night, and that she is prepared to wash your feet and drink the water (her words). . . . She wanted me to give her your address, but this I categorically refused to do. She wanted to send you money but I knew this would have humiliated you. Instead, I forwarded your letter express to our parents and today (Tuesday) I received a telegram from them saying that they are sending you money. Forgive me, dear brother, for letting our parents know. I couldn't let you die alone in Paris.

Yes, I forgot to add that Clara's son, Sasha, has left the gymnasium and has taken over his grandfather's business. Clara reports miracles of him. Felusia is back in Warsaw with Louisa. Now, Alexander, I want you to know that there is nothing to keep me here in Poland. I can't go home. I'm afraid I'll catch Mirale's sickness. . . . It's going around. Everyone is getting sick. . . .

I needn't tell you that my job gives me little pleasure. I'm also depressed, because I've suffered a great disappointment. I now have only one desire, to go to America. Somehow or other I'll manage to scrape together fare money. But I don't want to go alone. Wait for me, Alexander, and I'll join you. You want to go to America and it's better for us to go together. Answer immediately. I kiss you and hug you to my heart.

Your devoted SONYA

P.S. Answer quickly, for every day counts.

Dearest Alexander!

I wrote you yesterday and today I am writing again. Clara came to see me at the store and begged and insisted that I give her your address. She would not let me work. I was afraid the "Old Man" (that's what they call the boss) would fire me. I did not give her your address, but I promised to send you her letter. I'm enclosing it. Do as you think best. She seems to love you, but as God is my witness, I don't understand her kind of love. I guess I'm just a provincial girl, a "simple miss from Kuniev" as you once called me. . . . Whatever happens, answer immediately. Have you received the money from our parents? Is it enough?

Kisses.

Your SONYA

P.S. If our correspondence should be terminated, you will know that I have fallen sick. . . . But I still hope for the best.

The letter that Sonya enclosed, from Clara to Zipkin, read as follows:

My dear Alexander:

I write and cannot stop crying. Perhaps my tears will be proof that what I say is true. Within a short time I have lost the two people closest to my heart, my father and you, and truly I don't know why God has seen fit to punish me in this way. I have just spent a few hours with your sister and gather from her that you consider yourself completely in the right and blame me for everything. But what you don't seem to realize is that the moment we left Warsaw you changed. It was as if an evil spirit possessed you. I was so happy that we were at last together after so much effort and strain, but you sat in the train silent and brooding and would not even answer when I spoke to you. I thought that for some reason or other you were in a bad mood, and decided to leave you alone (I have some pride too). But your "mood" continued throughout the entire trip. I am afraid that you've forgotten how you behaved, or you've made yourself forget. Your every look cut right through me. You clamped your thin lips together and nothing would pry them apart. You glared at me as if I were your worst enemy. I knew that it hadn't been easy for you to leave your family, but I left children too and, what's more, I divorced a wealthy husband because of you.

I made more sacrifices for you than I have ever made for anyone. And how did you repay me? With scorn and insult. When I struck up a conversation with the lady in the yellow hat, you made remarks that embarrassed me. You didn't even have the courtesy to pick up my handbag when I dropped it, and at every opportunity demonstrated to the other passengers your lack of respect for me. I left our compartment and went out into the passageway to cry—on the first night of our "honeymoon." When we arrived in Berlin, you went off for the day, leaving me in the hotel. On your return I asked you where you had been and you refused to tell me. How a person could have changed so overnight is something I will never understand. The only explanation I can think of is my wicked luck. It has plagued me ever since I was old enough to reason, although I've always tried to be nice to everyone. I know that you disliked my suit and hat, but why wouldn't you go to the tailor with me when I asked you to? You wouldn't even take a look at the fashion book. It was only after I had spent so much money and effort that you expressed your opinion in one word, "vulgar." It was like pronouncing a death sentence. What was so "vulgar" about my costume? Silk, velvet, and ostrich plumes are stylish. Everyone else showered me with compliments. I repeatedly tried to straighten matters out with you, but you have the most "refined" way of ignoring those who are close to you. You literally prevented me from speaking, and whenever I did manage to say something, you made fun of me. You brought things to such a pass that we spent our nights apart instead of being together every moment. You know that what I write is the truth, and if I'm lying, may I not live to lead my Sasha to the wedding canopy. Yes, I'm swearing like a fishwife, as you would put it, but believe me, a fishwife has more heart than you. You were in a rotten mood and you took your anger out on me, knowing that I was dependent on you. Your sarcasm concerning my German was misplaced. How else could I have communicated with Germans? Everyone, knowing we were Russians, complimented me on the way I managed to make myself understood. In a strange city you made me go everywhere alone, and although I took it with a smile, believe me, if you had tasted my heart at that time you would have been poisoned.

Now regarding that old man, Mirkin, around whom you've built a whole nest of accusations. His only sin was that he acted humanly and kindly. He was an old man, old enough to be my father, and he was too worldly and experienced not to sense what was going on between us. To whom else could I have turned when you were so inconsiderate? I have been alone too often in my life. Why should you have objected when an elderly person, and a cripple at that, displayed some fatherly feeling toward me and showed me around a city that he knew well? Even a dog can't always be alone. Apparently you were only waiting for an opportunity to play the jealous lover, although one would have to be mad to have suspected my conduct. Would I abandon my dear children for someone who already had one foot in the grave? And as far as Monte Carlo is concerned, it was your idea to go there, not mine. I wanted to go directly to Paris. But *you* suddenly became enamored of Mirkin. I foresaw that Monte Carlo would be the end of me. You spun such a devilish web around me that even now, no matter how I try, I cannot make head or tail of the whole thing. You seemed to want to drive me into Mirkin's arms. It was quite obvious that he was amorously inclined. You egged him on, and I noticed more than once that you did everything possible to compromise me. I still have not been able to decide whether you planned all this, or whether it just happened. If it was a preconceived trick, then it was the most contemptible thing a person could do. And even if you did act on the spur of the moment, it's bad enough, for it shows that deep in your heart your intentions were far from noble. I swear before God that it was you alone who drove me to play roulette, possibly in the hope that if I lost everything I would commit suicide. God in heaven, is this what you call love? You wanted to destroy me—that's the plain truth. Your eyes reflected such malevolence that the memory of them still makes me shudder. I had even begun to be afraid that you were going to poison me or kill me in some other way. I couldn't stand it any more and I told Mirkin about it. Had he been a stone, I would have confided in it.

It's true that Mirkin attached himself to me and proposed marriage—that is, as soon as he could divorce his wife, from whom he was already separated. Is it my fault that I'm still attractive to men, and especially to someone like Mirkin, who was always traveling and hadn't enjoyed the taste of a real home for a long time? Believe me, old and crippled as he was, he was fantastically successful with women. I myself saw how beautiful women threw themselves at him. He was fabulously rich and clever besides. Despite his grand talk, I never took him seriously even for a moment. I told him that I loved only you. He was sorry, he said, because my love obviously was not returned. He wanted to give me a string of pearls worth twenty-five thousand rubles. I only laughed at his generosity. And all this happened only because you were hiding somewhere and obviously trying to push me off into an abyss. I want to tell you right here and now that Mirkin still hasn't given up. He followed me to Warsaw and I barely managed to get rid of him. He wants to turn over a huge estate to me, and believe me, old and homely as he is, he has more soul than you. If I could only get myself to love him, I would be the luckiest woman in the world. Unfortunately for me, I am not that kind of person. I swear to you by all that is holy that this man has not so much as touched me. It's all the same to me whether you believe me or not. Having survived that tragic journey, I have decided that it is time to stop struggling against fate. My life has been one great disaster, and my father's death has reminded me that I won't last forever. I have put on mourning and I believe that I will never take it off again. I am also not completely well and I have a feeling that it will be—as they say—sooner rather than later.

Your sister positively refused to give me your address, but promised to send you this letter. So be it. I just want to add one thing: Any time you are prepared to admit your mistakes and to come back to me, I will receive you with open arms. Your Felusia is a sweet girl. After my father's death, Sasha took over his business affairs and I can already see that his luck will be better than mine. He is clever, intelligent, and in the short time I was away has grown so much spiritually and physically that I hardly recognize him. He is truly the only comfort of my bitter existence.

Write me before it is too late!

Your CLARA

Dear Clara:

I solemnly swore never to write to you again, but I must reply to your letter. I realize that your words to me were sincere, but I have long since come to the conclusion that sincerity can be partner to the worst kind of falsehood. Your long letter indicates to me that you have no conception of either how you behaved or even who you are. I can only tell you how things looked to me. I may be wrong, but if I can't trust my own eyes, what can I trust? You started on our trip feeling that you were a woman of property and I a pauper whom you were supporting. The tone you adopted toward me from the very beginning was so obvious that I cannot believe it was not deliberate. How much self-deception can a person practice? You immediately began to treat me as if I were your valet. You talk about being conspicuous. No one could have made more of a display of herself than you did. You made it obvious to everyone that you had money, and I had nothing! As far as your clothes were concerned, I can only say that your outfit made you look like a caricature. When I met you at the station, I almost vomited. You wore a hat as large as a washtub, piled high with a whole storeful of feathers. Your suit, with its beaded embroidery, was a model of tastelessness. You had doused yourself with so much perfume that the scent was overpowering. Everyone stared at you. That is the sad truth. How could you be so blind as not to realize how ridiculous you looked? Nor did it end with your lack of taste in clothes. Once on the train, you flirted shamelessly with all the men present, who winked at each other and laughed behind your back. The only explanation I could think of was that you were drunk. The women in the train gave both of us dirty looks. Once we were in Berlin, you insulted the chambermaid, the waiters, even the desk clerk at the hotel. Since we weren't married and were traveling on separate passports, why talk about a honeymoon? Why talk about the children you left behind? Why bare your heart to every stranger? Forgive me for these harsh words, but they are the truth. You developed a shopping mania. You spent seven hundred marks for trinkets and unnecessary things. Your purchases only led to further expenditures, because you had to buy additional luggage to accommodate them. You bothered the help at the hotel to such a degree that they began to whistle under their breath when they saw you coming. When I called your attention to the fact that you were incessantly ringing for the servants, you screamed at me and even tried to hit me. I understand now that the trip must have played havoc with your nerves, but I too was emotionally upset and your behavior drove me to despair.

What you write about Mirkin is a pack of lies, but I'm no longer jealous, and if you two were to marry I'd wish you both happiness. Nevertheless, you behaved wantonly. You write that he never even touched you, yet he kissed and fondled you in my presence. Believe me, I'm not suffering from hallucinations. In Monte Carlo you went completely mad. After the first round you won, you imagined that you could break the bank. Mirkin became so familiar with you that he even visited your room in his bathrobe and slippers. You not only confided in him but insulted me in front of him and that flunky, his secretary. Are these not the facts? Or do you still think I'm making it up? During the day you went promenading with Mirkin; then at night after visiting the casino the three of you played cards until dawn. You drank too. It isn't true that my behavior toward you was hateful and sarcastic. I had paid too dear a price to take our situation lightly. But I was shocked to the core. I have been alone now for many weeks and you'll never know how much I've suffered. I've had time to think, and I still can't find the explanation for what happened to you, or why you shattered our dreams and trampled everything underfoot. When your Don Quixote and his Sancho Panza left to join some other Dulcinea, you returned to Warsaw, where, as you yourself have written me, you later had a rendezvous with Mirkin. You've also been busy arranging a career for your Sasha, while I remained abroad, penniless and hungry. How I was able to go on and not commit suicide is still a mystery to me. These are the hard facts. Because of you, I've lost everything, yet I bear you no resentment. You are what you are, and if I was such a poor judge of character, then the fault was mine. One thing I do beg of you: let me be and let Sonya be. What you and I felt for each other was not love but the basest passion, and such relationships can only end with a hangover.

I won't deny that I still yearn for your body. At the same

time I know that any new encounter would only lead us to catastrophe. Well, enough of that. Forgive me, and kiss Felusia. I will probably be going to America soon and begin what is called "a new life," although I have lost my appetite for everything.

In your letter you invoke God as your witness. I could do the same if I believed in His existence. To my sorrow, I don't —and neither do you. That, I'm afraid, is the reason for all our madness.

ALEXANDER

2

I

Mirale had been arrested for subversive activities; there was word from Otwock that Miriam Lieba was in a critical condition; and Ezriel's wife had borne him a boy. Ezriel had to engage a nurse, arrange for the circumcision, and invite his parents as well as his father-in-law, Calman. All these events presented Ezriel with spiritual and practical difficulties. Circumcising an eight-day-old child seemed to him an act of barbarism. Why stop at that? Why not offer sacrifices as well? It was true that most of the assimilated Jews in Warsaw still circumcised their sons, but where was the logic? Must he, Ezriel, a doctor living in the second half of the nineteenth century, emulate an act of black magic that a group of Bedouins had performed in Asia four thousand years before? But not to have the circumcision was impossible. Shaindel would die of mortification. Ezriel's parents had wept and suffered over Mirale's arrest. This new blow would be too much. And could Ezriel do such a thing to the other grandfather, Calman, whose money had paid for his education? He might even lose his position at the hospital and in the clinic. A Jew who did not have his child circumcised had to be an atheist, and, therefore, politically suspect. Ezriel was forced to find a *mohel*, and invite his parents to his house, although he was ashamed to have his Gentile neighbors see his father in his rabbinical fur hat and his mother in her ancient bonnet. He was ashamed of being ashamed, and his feelings grew even more intense. Although Shaindel kept a kosher kitchen, Reb Menachem Mendel and Tirza Perl had no faith in it. They announced in advance that they would eat nothing in Ezriel's house. To top it all, the infant developed dysentery and there was no certainty that he would survive eight days, and if he did, whether the circumcision could take place on time.

Besides, Ezriel had been foolish. He hadn't told Olga Bielikov that he was about to become a father for the third time. Shaindel's confinement, the complications surrounding the circumcision, and the infant's illness robbed him of the evenings when he would normally visit Olga or meet her at the Saxony Gardens. When he did manage to join her, he appeared distracted, pale, exhausted. It wasn't easy to stroll arm-in-arm with one woman when the other was still recuperating from the birth of your child. Ezriel was conscience-stricken, but at the same time he brooded about whether to give up his Judaism. Why did the Jews segregate themselves? What did they hope to gain? Why all the martyrdom? The Messiah was not coming. The faithful believed in a world to come, but what use was Judaism to someone like Ezriel? Why be a member of the Jewish community, pay them taxes? Ezriel daydreamed about going to Russia with Olga, or of settling with her in France, or in America, where one could live freely, without bearing the burden of generations.

In Ezriel's breast pocket lay a letter saying that his sister-in-law, Miriam Lieba, was close to death. Her husband, Lucian, was still in prison. Her father had disowned her. Her sisters, his wife included, wanted nothing to do with her. At least he should be with her in her last days. But with things as they were, how could he leave town?

He listened to his patients, but he was no less distracted than they. Shaindel's delivery had been expensive. He had been forced to borrow a hundred rubles from a usurer at exorbitant interest. He prescribed all sorts of remedies for the sick: hypnotism, baths, medicine to banish pain, to quiet the heart. But these merely stilled the symptoms. Society itself with its antiquated laws, empty privileges, religious fanaticisms, exploitations, was a fertile soil for madness. What should he do? Wage war against it all, the way his sister Mirale did? History had proved her wrong. Ezriel knew that as soon as one madness disappeared, ten others replaced it. Every revolution had its Robespierre, its Napoleon, its Metternich. Millions of young men had already perished in all kinds of righteous campaigns, but the Bismarcks and the Podbiedonoscevs still ruled. Warsaw was seething over the assassination of the provocateur, Minsky, who had betrayed Maria Bohuszewicz and her group. Kawalewski had just been hanged. The revolutionaries in Russia were divided and had broken into factions. They vilified each other. What would become of his sister? For ten years she would sit in jail and come out a broken old woman. Probably disillusioned as well. Each day in the Shlisselburg Fortress, in the Citadel, in every prison, young people hanged themselves, poured kerosene over themselves and set themselves on fire, or wrote letters of repentance to the Czar. A large number of political prisoners in Warsaw went insane and were sent to him as patients at the Bonifraten Hospital.

Ezriel often discussed these things with Olga Bielikov. She had confided to him that she too had belonged to a revolutionary circle during her gymnasium days. Even now she sympathized with the revolutionaries, but she was a mother. Besides, she had noticed a great deal of egoism and hypocrisy in the rebels. Yes, something needed to be done—but what? What would happen to Natasha and Kolia if she were imprisoned? And how would this help the people? . . . Olga continued to speak about one thing and another. She had nothing to do in Warsaw. She did not feel at home with either Jews or Poles. The Russians who came to Poland were of the worst sort. Her children were lonesome. She had no women friends. Finally she blurted out that she was too young to remain single. Sooner or later, she would have to marry. She made it clear that Ezriel would have to make a decision. What sort of life was this—to hide before a maid, before children, neighbors? What was the sense in sitting in the Saxony Gardens or in the theater when they yearned to be together? He walked with her at night on a dark path in the park and lusted for her. The few times that she had surrendered herself to him in the kitchen or in Kolia's bed had only whetted his desire. She was fiery in a way he had never known. What she said upset him. With someone like Olga, one could travel, enter society. He could even discuss his work with her. But how could he desert Shaindel and the children? Would Olga forsake Kolia and Natasha for him? There was no escape from his entanglements.

In the midst of all these problems, the circumcision took place. Reb Menachem Mendel and Tirza Perl arrived in a droshky. Calman came from Jampol. He was the one to hold his grandchild at the circumcision. Reb Menachem Mendel and Tirza Perl were to be the godparents. A mohel who boasted that he had circumcised the infants of all the well-to-do Jews came and charged a fifteen-ruble fee. Tirza Perl demanded that Ezriel name the boy after her father, Reb Abraham Moshe Hamburg, but Ezriel did not want to handicap his son with such old-fashioned names. Officially, the child was registered as Michael—Misha.

Shaindel sobbed in her bed when she heard the cries of her son. Ezriel stood by with lifted eyebrows. He considered it a foolish act to stamp a child's body with the mark of Judaism at a time of anti-Semitism and pogroms. But he was not the master here. In the living room a chair had been set aside for the prophet Elijah, as was the custom. There were little round cakes on a tray. Beakers of wine had been filled. Ezriel wore a skullcap and recited the benediction: "Blessed art Thou, our Lord, our God, King of the universe, who has sanctified us by Thy commandments and has commanded us to make our sons enter into the covenant of Abraham our father." And the quorum of Jews replied: "Even as he has entered into the covenant, so may he enter into the Law, the nuptial canopy, and into good deeds."

II

Justina Malewska, Wallenberg's daughter, invited Olga Bielikov's children, Natasha and Kolia, to her villa in Wilanow for two weeks. Olga was suddenly free. Ezriel felt that he had to go to Otwock to see Miriam Lieba, who had suffered another hemorrhage and he asked Olga to accompany him. But she was not so easily convinced. They might run into people who knew them. Where would they sleep? Ezriel, who knew Otwock, tried to reassure her. The chances of meeting acquaintances in the stagecoach were small. There was a hotel in Otwock, and the journey would only take about six hours. They would leave at eight in the morning and arrive at two in the afternoon. The air in Otwock was good. Neither of them had taken a holiday that summer. Why not spend a few days in the country? Olga continued to hesitate. She felt that their relationship was sinful. Andrey no longer appeared in her dreams, as if, in death, he were aware of her scandalous behavior. She was not only risking her own reputation but was sullying the names of her children. At first, Olga said no. But finally she reconsidered. She was not accustomed to spending the summers in the city. She longed for trees, green grass, cool breezes, for the smell of field and forest. And she wanted some time alone with her lover. The heroines of the French novels that Olga read did not permit obstacles to keep them from rendezvous in cheap hotels or in the Bois de Boulogne. She, at least, was not betraying a husband.

Everything went smoothly. Ezriel took several days' leave from the hospital. Shaindel obviously could not accompany him. At a quarter to eight in the morning, Ezriel sat waiting in the stagecoach on Gnoyna Street. Five minutes later, Olga joined him, wearing a freshly ironed dress, a straw hat with a green band, and carrying a satchel and a small bandbox. There wasn't another Jew in the stagecoach. Olga sat next to Ezriel. The August day was warm. After crossing the Praga bridge, the coach passed by fields and villages. In a marketplace, peasant women sat beside cans of milk and baskets containing chickens, ducks, mushrooms, vegetables. Jewish women in wigs and bonnets bargained and haggled with the peasants. Officers drilled soldiers in the barracks courtyard. In several of the villages it was market day. A carousel whirled around in a meadow. In front of a church, a band played for a wedding. Twigs decorated the horses' harnesses. The peasants of the Warsaw countryside were not as poor as those in Turbin. Ezriel and Olga passed huts covered with shingles and even roofs of tin. From taverns came the sound of concertinas. In the village stores the shelves were laden with leather goods, hardware, haberdashery, dry-goods. Farther on, there were woods, summer cottages. Polish squires had their villas here. Russian officials came out for the summers. The six hours passed quickly. In Otwock, the stagecoach rolled up to the inn where Ezriel and Olga were to stay. The proprietor requested Ezriel's passport, according to which Shaindel *née* Jacoby was his wife. How could anyone know that Olga was not Shaindel? It went so smoothly that Olga was amused.

They were given a room in the attic, with a French window. It was neat and cool. After lunch, Olga went for a walk while Ezriel visited Miriam Lieba. Miriam Lieba had at first stayed in the sanatorium but now lived in rooms not far from the hospital. Many consumptive women lived in private homes, looking after one another. The winters were severe and the houses were often snowed in. But the air in this season was even purer than in summer. There was always a smell of pine in the town. All of Poland praised the wonders of Otwock. A consumptive could even grow new lungs here. . . .

Ezriel got lost each time he visited Otwock. How could one locate a street in the midst of a forest? Potato fields and pastures were scattered all over the city. At last Ezriel found his way to Miriam Lieba's house. When he entered her room, she was lying in bed. Bottles of medicine stood on a chair. A kitten sat at a window licking one of its paws. One look and Ezriel knew that Miriam Lieba was close to death. Her emaciated face was altered beyond recognition. Gray hairs mingled with the gold. Her neck seemed unnaturally long. Her teeth had changed, protruding in a sort of mirthless smile. Her skin was sallow. Only her eyes remained the same. Ezriel stood speechless a moment.

"Miriam Lieba!"

"Ezriel!"

Then for a long while neither spoke. Afterwards, Miriam Lieba said in Polish: "It's good you came. I'm dying."

"Don't be ridiculous!"

"Look here, he's brought flowers. Put them in water, Ezriel."

As soon as she spoke, Miriam Lieba seemed herself again. She began questioning him about Shaindel's delivery, about the newborn child, about Joziek, Zina.

"How does Papa look?" she asked.

"Pretty well, but his hair is white."

"Do you think he'll observe the seven days of mourning for me?"

Ezriel trembled. "Don't talk such foolishness!"

"Oh, men are such cowards. Mother used to say: 'I'm not an ox. I'm not afraid of slaughter. . . .' "

Miriam Lieba grew silent again. She looked at Ezriel, and her eyes twinkled. Soon she dozed off, seeming to forget her visitor. Quietly, Ezriel began to unpack the things he had brought her: sweet cream, sardines, chocolate, a bottle of cognac. The door opened slowly, without a sound, and Miriam Lieba's neighbor, a yellow-haired woman with the overly red cheeks consumptives sometimes have in the early stages of their illness, thrust her head in. She beckoned to Ezriel and whispered to him that the doctor had been there the day before and had said there was little hope for the patient. She also informed Ezriel that Miriam Lieba's sister-in-law, Felicia, had spent the weekend with her. Felicia was making efforts to get Lucian freed before it was too late. Miriam Lieba had signed a petition to the district attorney requesting her husband's release from prison before her death.

III

It was the first night that Ezriel and Olga Bielikov had spent together. The window was open, and moonlight shone in. Cool breezes blew in from the Otwock forests. Ezriel had looked at death, but his lust for life had not diminished because of it. Too happy to fall asleep, they kissed for hours. Even while possessing each other, their desire increased. If this night could only last forever! If they could go to an island somewhere! If they could forget everything and everybody and merely live for this intoxication! Ezriel had had nights of passion with Shaindel, but his affair with Olga had stirred fresh powers in him. He spoke as the mad do, uttering insane fantasies. They fell asleep at dawn. The sun and the birds awakened them. Warsaw weekdays were prosaic; here in Otwock, nature celebrated a holiday, a lengthy Pentecost, all green and light. Flashes of light danced on the walls and the ceiling, as if someone across the way was playing with a mirror. A bird chirped: "Tsif-tsif." Another gave a long whistle; a third crowed angrily as if calling dire warnings into the thicket of needles and pine cones. "Cuckoo!" a cuckoo repeated again and again. Ezriel and Olga listened and kissed. Ezriel jokingly explained to Olga the philosophical meaning of its call: the world was neither matter nor will but "cuckoo." In the beginning there was "cuckoo" and in the end there would be "cuckoo." All had been created by the celestial cuckoo and his plan was: "cuckoo . . ." In Warsaw one forgot that there were such things as birds in the world. How could mankind have survived all the wars, all the plagues, all the famines and deaths if not for such music?

The chambermaid knocked, asking if the guests wanted tea, coffee, cocoa. She brought a jug of water from the pump. The water was cold, fresh, and seemed full of subterranean secrets. Ezriel and Olga were no longer modest before one another. They washed side by side in front of the washstand. Afterwards, they sat down to breakfast. The poppy-seed rolls were crisp between their teeth. The milk smelled of udder. The cottage cheese was sprinkled with caraway. The coffee was somewhat burned and had too much chicory in it. But it was tasty nonetheless. After breakfast, both of them returned to bed. Ezriel embraced Olga and said: "Now we know each other a little better."

"Yes, but what will come of it?"

Ezriel dressed and went to see Miriam Lieba. Olga was to meet him at the stagecoach. Even Miriam Lieba looked fresher and somewhat healthier this morning. There was a maid there who served both Miriam Lieba and the woman with the yellow hair. Miriam Lieba was in a talkative mood. Could Ezriel persuade her father to come to see her? She wanted to see him before she died. Perhaps Ezriel could arrange for Lucian's release. He had suffered enough for his crime. Why wasn't Ezriel going to visit Tsipele in Marshinov? Was it true that Jochebed was already a grandmother? Miriam Lieba told him that her children, Wladzio and Marisia, had come to see her once. Oh, how handsome they were! Gloriously beautiful, but somehow estranged. The boy still had some feelings for her, but the girl seemed entirely cold. The neighbor fussed about. She apparently wanted to say something to Ezriel. Miriam Lieba raised her brows. Finally she indicated that she wanted to be alone with her guest.

"You come so seldom," she said to Ezriel, "surely we'll never see each other again."

"Don't be a fool."

He raised the pillow and helped her to sit up. He noticed

that she was wearing an attractive nightgown, probably a present from Felicia. She had put on cologne and combed her hair. Even on her deathbed, she remained coquettish.

Ezriel said, "You're still lovely."

"Oh, who thinks of such things?"

Suddenly Miriam Lieba said: "Did you know, Ezriel, that I was in love with you, before Lucian appeared?"

Ezriel paled.

"I've loved you too. All these years."

"Shaindel was jealous. How old was I, anyhow? Perhaps seventeen. Afterwards, he bewitched me. Well, I paid dearly for it."

"Did you at least have some joy with him?"

"Now and then, a day or two."

Ezriel bowed his head. Miriam Lieba looked toward the window. "Ezriel, do you believe in God?"

"What do you mean by God? In a God who acts like a person? No."

"I always did believe. Now it seems to me that there's nothing. The priest will come, and all the rest of it. What shall I do?"

"Don't think about it."

"What should I think about? Yes, I *do* believe. But when the pains come and I can't catch my breath, I begin to waver . . . Ezriel!"

"What is it, dear?"

"Don't betray Shaindel!"

Ezriel could not see the connection between the two thoughts, but he had long ago perceived that the law of association was not as consistent as psychologists thought. The human mind jumped freely from one subject to another.

"Why should I betray her?"

"Oh, you may. It doesn't pay to do wrong."

"Yes, that's true."

"Give me your hand."

3

I

The winter was over. It had been a difficult one. The severe frosts had toppled sparrows from the Warsaw trees. In the fields, the winter wheat froze beneath the snow. Calman Jacoby contracted a stomach typhus but miraculously survived. About to assume partnership in a Lodz factory, Jacob Danziger, Zipkin's father-in-law, had come home at summer's end, jolly and well-fed. Four months later he had a heart attack and in eight days he was dead. He was buried in Gęsia Street cemetery, in the first row. Madame Rosa was a widow. Sabina, Zipkin's deserted wife, enveloped herself in black, her face heavily veiled. The dry-goods business was taken over by her brother, Zdzislaw.

Another who died that winter was Pan Wallenberg's wife, Pani Matilda. She never emerged from the anesthesia after a gallstone operation. She was buried in the Catholic cemetery in Powązek, in the Wallenbergs' family crypt. A famous Polish sculptor made the monument according to Wallenberg's design: an angel with Matilda's face stood on a pedestal. The monument cost ten thousand rubles.

Now it was spring again. Streams splashed into the Vistula. The mud began to dry up. In the synagogues and Houses of Prayer many mourners said Kaddish, for Warsaw had been rampant with typhus, croup, scarlet fever, and all kinds of maladies. In the churches, mothers, wives, and sisters lit candles to the saints in memory of the deceased. Spring had come early. March was warm. Matzoth was being baked in the Jewish bakeries. Jews came to Reb Menachem Mendel to sell the unleavened bread. Reb Menachem Mendel couldn't see to write the bills of sale, and the yeshiva boys helped him. In the Gentile houses, before Easter, a priest came to bless the bread. The janitors and pious women followed behind him.

At the Wallenbergs', Easter was celebrated with great pomp. A bishop blessed the bread that lay on a golden tray. The whole family gathered to celebrate the holiday. But Pan Wallenberg had turned melancholy. As long as Pani Matilda had been alive, no one had been aware that he loved her. He had often been angry with her. She was not as intelligent or alert as he. She had been easy to deceive. When there were no visitors in the house, he used to scold her in the Jewish manner, call her "silly woman," "idiot," and other names. Offended, Pani Matilda would weep. Sometimes he would shout at her using a phrase he had heard from his father and grandfather: "You *beheimah*, you cow!"

Then in apology he would kiss her eyes and promise her jewelry. Now that Pani Matilda was dead, it became clear how fond he had been of this simple woman. When he spoke of her to his children, the tears began to flow. He closed off her bedroom, hired a man to lay fresh flowers on her grave daily. He severed his connections with his beloved *Courier*, though he still put money into the paper. His appetite left him, his stout stomach shrank. Pouches hung beneath his eyes. He even lost his taste for Havana cigars. The doctors felt that a trip abroad would benefit his health, but he refused to go. "Without her," he said, "it would be worse than hell!"

Pan Wallenberg began to write his memoirs, intimating his end was near, but he could scarcely hold a pen. His handwriting was shaky, blotted, and blurred. He wanted to dictate to someone, but his secretary was busy in his office, and, besides, he did not trust her. Intimate things could only be revealed to a person one felt close to. It occurred to Madame Justina Malewska, Wallenberg's eldest daughter, that Olga Bielikov might be just the person. Olga's Polish was adequate and she could spell, had good handwriting, and he would not be embarrassed in her presence. At first the idea did not appeal to Wallenberg, but finally he saw that his daughter was right. He would be more at ease with someone who had suffered a similar loss and could understand his feelings. Olga Bielikov still mourned her husband. She had not remarried.

Wallenberg agreed and Justina arranged the rest. A devoted daughter, she really loved her father, unlike the younger daughter, Pola, for whom pleasure took first place. Justina felt it would be good for her father to have a younger woman around, and it would be a blessing for Olga Bielikov, who badly needed an income. Justina Malewska drove to Olga Bielikov's in her carriage, explained everything, and Olga, as anticipated, gratefully accepted the opportunity. She was somewhat apprehensive about making errors, but Justina assured her that a dictionary would solve most of her problems, and gave her twenty-five rubles in advance. After Madame Malewska's visit, Olga went to Marshalkovsky Boulevard and bought herself a pair of shoes, a hat, and gloves. She could not go to the Wallenbergs' looking like a beggar.

The following day she took a droshky to Pan Wallenberg's villa. He greeted her cordially, treated her like an old friend, even cried in front of her. Then he took her into his office and began dictating the first chapter of his memoirs. He made no secret of his Jewish ancestry. He spoke of his grandfather, who had paid a head tax each time he came to Warsaw, of his grandmother, Beila Brachah, who wore a bonnet and on Fridays brought a pot roast and chicken soup to the poor at the almshouse. Olga was touched by these homely descriptions. It could have been her biography that he was dictating in stentorian tones. Pan Wallenberg paced back and forth in his gaiters, occasionally blowing his nose and wiping away his tears. Olga too felt a tightness in her throat. The recent converts of her acquaintance were ashamed of their Jewish ancestry. Wallenberg called things by their true name. He dictated to her for three hours straight, and although Olga had studied at a Russian school, her command of Polish was such that she was even able to correct a phrase here and there, or suggest the right word. Pan Wallenberg adjusted his gold-rimmed spectacles, read what he had dictated, and nodded his gray head in approval. The chapter had turned out magnificently.

II

The sun was warming everything. In the Saxony Gardens the lilacs were blooming. In the streets, rails were being laid for horse-drawn trolleys. Pavements were torn up. Dray wagons delivered cobblestones and track sections, which were unloaded and neatly stacked, ready for use. Mighty hammers pounded. In Praga, in Wola, in Ochota, even in the center of Warsaw, factories were springing up. From Germany, France, the United States, there came machinery so huge that it was impossible to understand how human minds could have invented it or how human hands could have put it together. On Krakow Boulevard and New World Boulevard the gas street lamps were being converted to arc lights. The banks had more capital: manufacturers and merchants received loans at small interest. The housing authority extended credit and Jews began to build. Land became expensive and buildings soared upward—four and five stories. Rows of houses were erected around two and three connecting courtyards.

The revolutionary circles created by the "Proletariat" party had been dispersed by the police. A new political movement, both patriotic and liberal, a mixture of radicalism and nationalism with a touch of anti-Semitism, had sprung up in Poland. Some Poles, however, still remembered the gallows in the Citadel, the martyrdom of Bandrowski and Kunicki, Osowski and Petruszewicz. Nor had they forgotten the strike in Lodz and the Zyrardow massacre. A second "Proletariat" succeeded the first. In Vilna, Bialystok, Riga, Minsk, the Jewish intelligentsia and workers engaged in socialist activities. There were those who considered themselves "Narodowolces"; others sympathized with Plekhanov, the Marxist; still others were anarchists; and some spoke of forming a Jewish socialist party. Mendelsohn, the son of a Jewish banker in Poland, organized a Polish socialist group in Paris. Farther left than the revolutionaries in Warsaw, he demanded that Polish workers renounce Polish nationalism, stop celebrating national holidays, and become completely merged with the world proletariat. So widespread was socialism among modern Jews that Jewish boys and girls in Vilna, Minsk, and Bialystok sent their Russian comrades money, helped them smuggle banned literature into Poland, obtain hectographs, paper, type, and whatever else was needed to further revolutionary activities. The Russian organizations themselves had a large Jewish membership.

Tragedy struck Ezriel's sister. The women's division of the prison in which Mirale was serving her sentence was called "Serbia." She began to suffer from heartburn, and occasionally vomited. It was not like Mirale to complain or ask for a doctor. Stefan Lamanski, her mentor, had taught her that a revolutionary must suffer proudly and mutely. But the political women prisoners who shared her cell noticed that her waistline was thickening. It was soon obvious that Mirale was pregnant. The prisoners did not know whether to laugh or cry. It was common knowledge that Mirale had worked with Stefan Lamanski and helped him with an underground printing press. There had even been a rumor that they had actually lived together as man and wife. Although Mirale had kept it a secret, the rumor proved to be a fact. Suddenly it was out in the open. Ever since she had dedicated herself to the revolution, Mirale's periods had been irregular. Ezriel had told her it was due to nerves, and prescribed a remedy. It would have been possible to help Mirale if she had recognized her symptoms sooner. Quinine and other abortive aids could have been smuggled into the prison. One of the women was a midwife. But Mirale was now in her fifth month.

In the period of Mirale's imprisonment she felt she had suffered every blow that fate could deliver. She had been beaten, insulted, tortured. She had contracted an inflammation of the intestines and had spinal pains. The district attorney had boasted to her that her organization had been filled with informers. To prove it he had described her apartment in detail and enumerated her visitors. It was clear that there had been traitors among her intimates. But who were they? These *provocateurs* destroyed one's faith in humanity, caused confusion, doubt. As if this were not enough, there was no peace among the comrades in the cell. Women became hysterical, wailed, tried to kill themselves. Some cursed their revolutionary activities. Others fussed about a crust of bread, an article of clothing, a comb, a rag. The discussions and disputes daily grew more bitter. The women argued, formed cliques. Each day Mirale warned herself anew not to be drawn into these conflicts. Outside the prison, reaction ruled. Inside, there were squabbles over words, phrases. One had to be stronger than iron not to become involved. Mirale did her best. She did not speak for hours, read the books that were available in the prison library. She stopped participating in the debates. More than once she stuffed her ears with balls of soft bread to keep from listening to empty words, angry remarks, the absurdities voiced about socialism, the role of the peasant, Polish independence, the place of women in society.

There were moments when Mirale was afraid of breaking down, but she kept reminding herself of Stefan Lamanski. How would he have acted in such a situation? What would he have said? She saw his face, his eyes, heard his deep voice. She imagined him whispering words of comfort to her. Hadn't he suffered even more than she? Hadn't he thrown away a home and a career for the sake of the masses? Hadn't he fought, day after day, against stupidity, ignorance, obstinacy, and even betrayal? Mirale recalled his words: "The revolutionary must be prepared for everything. He must not lose sight of his goal for a single moment. He must rise above mundane pettiness, accidents, weaknesses, errors. He must battle not only the enemies outside, but also the lazy, the incompetents, the windbags, the fools, and the opportunists, within the ranks, who try to exploit the revolution for their own gains. The revolutionary must be capable of compassion and justice, but he must also be able cold-bloodedly to cut away such destructive dissidents as the Tichamirovs, Minskys, Goldbergs—all who, willingly or unwillingly, help the enemy strengthen his position." On another occasion he had said: "If one can't stand the smell of gunpowder, one can't build barricades."

But Mirale was not prepared for what was happening to her now. It was a shame and a disgrace in itself, a slap in the face for the party, a source of comfort to the authorities. When Mirale lay awake at night, her doubts and suspicions bordered on madness.

III

They were doing the wash. In the kitchen there was a tub filled with blueing. A laundry pot boiled on the stove and Tekla, the maid, stirred the linen with a piece of wood. There was a smell of soap, washing soda, and the remnants of supper. Shaindel hung diapers to dry on a makeshift line. Although her hair was already graying, she was forced to occupy herself with an infant, suckle it, rock it, stay awake nights. Ezriel too was constantly fatigued because the child kept them up. He had often said that this was one son he didn't need. But Shaindel wouldn't hear of an abortion. Now she was paying for it. She wore a short petticoat, her bare feet thrust into battered slippers. Her breasts were those of a wet nurse; her eyes expressed irritation. Joziek and Zina sat in the parlor. Joziek had just enrolled in the university as a law student and wore a student's cap and uniform. He smoked openly like an adult. He was not as tall as his father but had inherited his mother's beauty. There was a bluish sheen to his black hair. His face was light, round; the nose straight; the lips full. The dark eyes were serene, preoccupied. This particular evening Ezriel thought that Joziek did not look well. Reading an introduction to jurisprudence, shaking ashes into an ashtray, he kept looking distractedly at his sister, at the window, at the door. Zina, already in her fourth year at the gymnasium, had two golden braids. She resembled Ezriel, but there was also something of Miriam Lieba about her. In her infancy, Zina had been wild, raucous, but now she was dreamy, girlishly capricious, inclined to laugh, to cry, to spite her mother, to nurse secrets. The girls at school often gave parties, sometimes inviting a couple of boy students, but Zina always found excuses for not attending. She seemed to have inherited Ezriel's bashfulness. Joziek was good at mathematics, but Zina could not cope with algebra. Now she wrote out problems, erasing, nostrils quivering.

"Joziek, you must help me!"

"What is it?"

"I'm confused."

"Well, sister, there have been worse tragedies!"

Ezriel came out of his office. He too had been in the midst of reading a book, but now he wanted to take a walk. He did not have an appointment with Olga, but he felt like walking to Zielna Street. There was a good distance between Nowolipki Street and Zielna Street, but he could make it in twenty minutes, perhaps even less. It was 9:30, but Olga never went to sleep before one. He had spent the day among the insane. At night he read about them. He had to clear his head. The nosology of insanity, the etiology, the symptomology, pathology, diagnosis, prognosis, the care—how nicely the textbooks classified everything! How accurately they defined the idiot, the cretin, the imbecile, the epileptic, the hysteric, hypochondriac, and neurasthenic. Instead of admitting that little was known about what went on in the human brain, either healthy or sick, the professors stacked up Latin names. And what was going on in his, Ezriel's own skull? He allegedly cured others, but he himself suffered from all sorts of psychic disturbances. He was obsessed with phobias, worries, superstitions. He wrestled with compulsive ideas. "What would happen if—?" That was his recurring fantasy. If he won seventy-five thousand rubles. . . . If he were to discover a potion for eternal life . . . If he found a way to become omniscient. . . . If he possessed hypnotic power that could control everyone's will—he daydreamed like a schoolboy. Whenever he was alone, he lay on the couch. He wanted only to dream, to ponder. What was time? What was space? What was the atom? What was gravity? Where did the first cell originate? Could life be the result of chemical accidents? What powers were concerned with his deceiving his patients, Shaindel, himself? His parents were both sick, dependent on him, but the moment he decided to go to see them he put them out of his mind. He was haunted by a feeling that his life was nearing a crisis. He would soon have to make an important decision. But why? Why believe in premonition like a servant girl? "I am tired," Ezriel muttered to himself. "I have too many burdens . . . Mirale is still in prison . . . They may still send her to Siberia . . ." Shaindel came in from the kitchen. Zina raised her face from her book.

"Oh, Mother, look at yourself!" And she laughed.

Shaindel grew annoyed. "What is it?"

"You're all smudged."

"Well, what of it? Your fingers are smeared with ink."

"You look so funny."

"When you're busy in the kitchen, you get dirty. Are you going out?" Shaindel said, turning to Ezriel.

"I must take a walk. My head is filled with nonsense."

"Where are you going? You say you're going for a walk and you come back at one in the morning. I haven't been out of the house all day."

"Well, come along."

"You know I don't have the time. You suggest it because you know I won't go."

"Why do you say that?"

"Oh, enough! When will you be back? I'm ashamed to face the janitor. Every night you drag him out of bed."

"You know that's not true."

"It's true. The children know it too. Ask them."

"I won't ask anyone. Good night, children."

Going down the stairs, Ezriel took long strides. He passed the Przejazd, Przechodnia Street, crossed Iron Gate, and soon found himself on Graniczna Street. The scent of trees and grass came from the Saxony Gardens. The streets smelled of horse manure, sewers, rotten fruit. It was a neighborhood of bazaars and inns. In the semi-darkness, carts, covered wagons, and dray wagons were still being loaded. Late stagecoaches drew up, discharging their passengers. On Krolewska Street he suddenly saw the arc lights that lit up Marshalkovsky Boulevard. This section of Warsaw was entirely Europeanized. Open horse-drawn trolley cars skimmed along the tracks, bells ringing, conductors selling tickets. A man wearing a red cap switched a section of rail with a metal rod. Zielna Street was dark and quiet. At the gate of her house, to his surprise, Ezriel saw Olga. She stood there as if waiting for someone.

"Whom are you expecting?"

She smiled. "You, naturally."

"I wasn't supposed to come."

"I know."

"Do you practice black magic?"

"I felt you were coming."

"Are you a mind reader?"

"I always have been."

IV

He looked at her more closely. She was wearing new clothes and appeared youthful, elegant, almost rich.

"What's happened?" he asked. "Did you win the seventy-five-thousand-ruble lottery?"

She smiled mysteriously. "If I wanted to, I could win even more."

"You're speaking in riddles."

"Yes."

For a moment they were both silent. Then he said: "Would you like to walk or go inside?"

"Let's walk for a bit."

She placed her white-gloved hand on his arm, her touch so light that he felt her hand must soon slide away. They strolled along Krolewska Street, passed Prozna Street, and were soon at the Saxony Gardens. Usually they would have had something to discuss immediately, but now they were both silent. "Something has happened," he thought. He felt almost shy. Instead of entering the park, Olga remained standing at the gate, leaning against the stone posts in which the iron railings were imbedded. Here he had a better view of her. She had never seemed so intriguing and mysterious. Her eyes gleamed with joy. He grew alarmed, suspecting he had lost her, although he did not know how.

"What has happened?"

Olga's face became serious. "We must make an important decision today. It concerns you, too."

"What is it?"

"Wallenberg has made me an offer."

"What sort of an offer? Does he want to marry you?"

"Yes."

In the darkness, Ezriel felt himself flush. He felt ashamed, like the betrayed hero in a story.

"How did it happen?"

"Suddenly. I don't understand it myself."

"Oh."

"I must give him an answer."

"When?"

"Tomorrow."

Ezriel did not reply immediately. He moved his arm to free himself from her hand. She held on a moment longer, then let go. He too leaned against the rails, and stared at a house across the street. Now he understood his uneasiness of the past days, his disturbed sleep, and distorted dreams. "Why hadn't this occurred to me immediately?" he wondered. "After all, I knew she was working with him . . ." He stared at a lighted window on the second story, at shadows gliding behind the draperies—male and female. What were they doing? Were they dancing? All at once the woman beside him had become alien as only a person can who has withdrawn all that has been given. He had a sudden urge to run away. He reconsidered quickly and decided to remain calm, proud, and not to make foolish scenes like the patient who had gone to look at his former sweetheart through a keyhole . . . Ezriel had no desire to degrade himself before this woman who simultaneously carried on an affair with him and permitted an elderly millionaire to make overtures to her. All was lost. At least he must retain his human dignity. He even grew lighthearted, as always happens when there is an end to uncertainties.

"Well, why are you silent?" she asked.

"What can I say?"

"Come, let's go. You have a lot to say. You mustn't think that I deceived you from the beginning." She spoke with a tremor in her voice. "I'm not as frivolous as you think."

"I no longer know what you are."

"I'm the same Lithuanian girl." She suddenly said in Yiddish, "Love is no toy for me," and continued in Polish, "I waited for you beside the gate. I hoped you would come. I called you."

"What for? To be best man?"

Olga stopped. "You know how rich he is and the position

he holds. But if you want to marry me, I'll say no to him. He's a decent man and I like him, but I'm yours. Do you understand?"

"Yes."

"For my own sake, as well as my children's, I can't remain someone's sweetheart forever."

"I understand."

"You keep telling me you can't divorce your wife. What's left for me? To live a life of shame?"

"It's not a shame."

"Not for you, but for me. The children are growing up. Natasha understands everything already. How long can I live a hidden life? Even Jadzia guesses the situation. Once she found one of your blond hairs on the bedding. God in heaven, if someone had told me that I was capable of such a thing I'd never have believed it. If someone had told Andrey that I could conduct myself in such a manner, he would have shot that person. It's against my nature, my upbringing, everything I believe in. To share someone with another woman . . ."

"What actually do you want me to do?" Ezriel asked. "My wife won't divorce me. I can't force her to do so."

"I want nothing. Oh, you could manage it! True love finds a way. We could go abroad, to America. One can't hold a husband by force. You even once mentioned converting. In that case, every bond between you and Shaindel would have been broken. I know these are nothing more than words to you, but I say them because I want you to believe that I'm ready for anything. I would go off with you tomorrow."

"I'm listening."

"I'm willing to give up Wallenberg's millions for you, but what are you prepared to do for me?"

"Everything, except murder a human being. As far as that goes, I'm still a Jew."

"Oh, those are empty phrases. You won't kill her. Having survived Andrey's death, I know that one doesn't die of anguish."

"You were young. You're still young. For Shaindel it would be the end. Besides, it would make me a thief too."

"I don't know what you mean."

"I studied on her money. Stealing and killing aren't part of my character."

"Money can be repaid."

"She has a baby as well."

About to laugh, Olga suddenly grew sad.

"A baby?" she asked, astonished. "When did that happen?"

"It happened."

"And you said nothing to me all the while?"

"I had no reason to say anything."

"Well, that's odd. I felt you were keeping something from me. What is it—a boy or a girl?"

"A boy."

"Well, *mazel tov*," she said. For a moment her eyes became merry.

"God willing, the same to you and Wallenberg," he replied also in Yiddish.

"Two children are enough. I once dreamed of having a child of yours, but that's impossible now. What is he called?"

"Misha."

"What else will I discover if I continue to ask questions? Perhaps you have one or two more sweethearts? Well, that's that."

They walked in silence, a bit apart, each lost in thought. They came to Alexander Square and stood there looking at the gas-lit street lamps and the obelisk looming above them against the night sky. The square was empty and quiet as at midnight. Shadows concealed Olga's face.

"When did all this happen?" Ezriel finally said.

Olga shivered. "It was all very sudden. I can't understand it myself. He'd always been so correct. He was dictating. We talked a little. I've known him for such a long time. He was always weeping because of Matilda. I consoled him as well as I could. I really felt sorry for him. We grow wretched in old age. We're wretched when we're young as well. All at once he began talking to me in an entirely different tone. I can't understand it!"

"What about your religion? You'll have to convert again. He'll want you to become a Catholic."

"Yes, he insists on it."

"Well, Jesus won't mind."

"Don't laugh. This is serious."

"What we won't do for a couple of millions!"

"I don't need millions. If I were greedy for money, I wouldn't be pleading with you. All I want is to provide for my children."

"We all say that."

"It's true. What sort of happiness will I have? He's an old man. He has sons, daughters, sons-in-law, daughters-in-law, grandchildren. He's a patriarch, and I'm terrified when I think of it. Justina in particular makes me feel ashamed. All this luxury means nothing to me."

"He'll leave you a fortune."

"Since you don't want me, why be so cruel about it?"

"I do want you. More than you imagine."

"Those words don't mean anything!"

"I can't destroy four people. I can't throw aside my family any more than you can disregard your children."

"Well, then, there's nothing to say."

They stood for a while longer as if searching for something in the gravel at their feet. A breeze blew in from the Vistula. Somewhere a train whistle sounded—drawn-out and sad, as if longing for distances. After a while they started back. Olga clung to his arm as they walked down Mazoviecka Street to Holy Cross Street. In the semi-darkness Ezriel stopped to look at a Buddha crouching behind the windowpane of a store—stout, burnished, naked, with a gem in its forehead. "How can the Hindus reconcile Nirvana with corpulence?" he mused. He tried to read the title of a book, but the erratic light of a street lamp made the Gothic characters illegible. They continued on, crossing Marshalkovsky Boulevard, and were once more on Zielna Street. They spoke in clipped sentences. Just to say something, she commented on a house, a store, a sign. "Warsaw's filthy," she blurted out.

"Well, you'll soon be in Paris," he replied.

"In Paris? What makes you say that?"

"He'll take you on a trip around the world."

"How do you know that? Yes, a trip . . ."

They were now standing on Zielna Street. The branches of closely planted trees on both sides almost met over the roadway. The shadows cast by their dense foliage formed a net on the pavement. Gates were being locked. Window lights went out. A dog bayed. This street, to Ezriel, filled with love, secrets, quiet meetings, late farewells, was like a mysterious garden. It occurred to him that he had never seen it in daylight.

"Well, this is probably our last time together," he said.

"Why? We can remain friends."

"Oh? Well, good night."

"Don't run away. If you want to, come up. Jadzia is not sleeping at home tonight."

"Where is she?"

"Her sister is sick."

"No, Olga, why?"

"I thought that . . . Well, perhaps you're right."

"Good night."

"Don't be in a hurry. After all, you write for Wallenberg's paper and you may be invited to various functions. What I mean is that we won't be able to avoid each other. I don't want to avoid you. We've had happy moments. I'll never forget that night in Otwock."

"What are memories?"

Olga, apparently, was reluctant to let him go, but Ezriel was overcome with impatience. He wanted only to be alone with the blow he had received. Olga made a gesture as if to kiss him goodbye, but he only extended his hand. She squeezed it and he pulled it away, tipped his hat, and walked rapidly down the street without looking back, although he knew she was waiting for him to turn. He had conducted himself with dignity and that somehow eased the pain. At least he hadn't acted like a beggar.

Soon, he knew, the longing would start, the passion, the emptiness, the regret, but of one thing he was certain: he would never cry on anyone's shoulder. As he walked, his face burned. If she put her children first, why shouldn't he? This logic was irrefutable. He was suddenly overcome with a profound love for Joziek, Zina, even for Misha. They were his flesh and blood. He was responsible for them. To Shaindel, on the other hand, he was deeply in debt. He was a psychiatrist, not a madman. There was something else, too. He knew that his firm behavior would hold Olga with a force that no psychology could explain.

4

I

Everything was as it had been. His mother with her wrinkled face and the satin bonnet covering her shaved head; his father in his velvet capote, with the sash around his waist and the skullcap above his high forehead. His mother had no teeth left; her empty gums showed when she spoke. His father's beard had grown white and seemed shrunken. He was sitting in an armchair at the table. Although his father could see little, a kerosene lamp with a milky white shade stood on the table and some books lay open before him. He spoke to Ezriel: "So, here you are. Well, praised be the Almighty that we can see you. I've missed you, missed you badly. After all, you are my son. My only son. No small matter to have an only son. Your mother talks about you endlessly. Since Mirale's misfortune, your mother's love for you knows no bounds. Well, it all comes from above. Mercy too, but we don't always have the power to receive it. The rigor of the law comes from us, not, God forbid, from Him. If a father gives his child a nut and the child swallows it, shell and all—how is the father guilty?"

"The father should have warned him, or removed the shell. You are referring, of course, to our Father in heaven."

"Naturally. He gave man reason so that he could choose. He gave reason and a law which tells what is allowed and what is forbidden. But we refuse to listen—so how can we blame Him?"

"We might listen if we knew they were the words of God. But how can we be sure? Each people has its own religion."

"If man could actually see the workings of Providence, he would have no doubts and, therefore, no free will. This world is based on free choice. Of what can we be sure? Of life? Of one's livelihood? Man must constantly choose between truth and falsehood. If the heavens opened and we could observe the celestial host, then everybody would be a saint. Do you understand me, or not?"

"Yes, Father, I understand."

"Everything is easy for angels. Therefore they have no reward. Man must fight for his faith. Every day, every minute. Even the holiest man doubts."

"Yes, Father, I see."

"What's new in medicine?"

"Nothing much. One has to find out everything for oneself."

"Well, they do find out things. Once there was no hope if you became blind. Today, your good friend, what's his name, told me that now an operation is possible. I need only wait a little while longer. When I can't see at all, when the—how are they called—cataracts become larger, it will be possible to remove them. As it is said: 'Before the light comes, there must be a deeper darkness.' "

Tirza Perl called Ezriel into the kitchen. She stood near him with her rounded shoulders, her bonnet perched on the back of her head. Her glasses, minus one lens, rested on her beaked nose. A book lay on the kitchen table, *The Lamp of Light.* "What sort of misfortune has befallen Mirale?" she asked sharply. "Woe is me!"

"I don't know, Mother."

"You don't know? There was a girl here, a hunchback, one of *them.* The things she said made my ears ring. I don't want your father to know. He has enough troubles of his own, poor thing. What sort of catastrophe is this? I'm afraid to go out into the street. People will spit on me or stone me. Such a terrible disgrace doesn't even happen to barbers and musicians."

"Mother, it isn't my fault."

"What do these people want? It would have been better if she had converted. I'd known I had lost a daughter. I don't sleep nights, Ezriel. What do they want?"

"To redeem the world."

"Such evildoers! They're crazy. Do they think that God Almighty will remain silent? He destroyed Sodom, didn't he?"

"Let Him do as He pleases!"

"What are you saying? Why aren't you more careful? I couldn't understand what she was saying, the hunchback, I mean. My ears filled up with water. My face burned so much, I couldn't see her. I just sat there."

"Yes, Mother, I understand. But how are you guilty?"

"How am I guilty? People curse the parents of such an evildoer."

"Mother, I must go."

"Well, go. Now you see what happens when one forsakes God."

Ezriel went to say goodbye to his father, whom he found dozing in his chair. The old man awoke with a start. Ezriel shook his hand and then kissed his mother. He walked down the dark steps. He had not realized until now that she knew about Mirale's pregnancy. The hunchback had told her. What joy in her old age! At the gate Ezriel collided with someone, a man. Somehow Ezriel sensed in the darkness that this person had a connection with him. Later he thought about this moment. It was one of those things for which there is no explanation, unless one accepts the existence of a sixth sense. "Excuse me, sir, could you tell me where the rabbi lives?" the man asked in Polish.

"Turn to your right. Perhaps I can help you. I'm his son."

"You're Dr. Babad?"

"Yes."

"Doctor, I must speak to you. The janitor is about to lock the gate. Let's go outside."

"Who are you? What do you want?"

"Don't be frightened, Doctor. I'm not as bad as people say. I want to introduce myself to your worthy parents, but since fate seems to have ordained our meeting, let it remain this way. I beg you, Doctor, be patient a few minutes and don't judge me until you've heard what I have to say. That's all I ask."

"Who are you?"

"My name is Stefan Lamanski. I'm your sister's husband."

Ezriel remained standing where he was. "Her husband? I didn't know that she had a husband."

"Not officially, but—please, come outside. The janitor is waiting. Yes, I'm her husband and wish to remain her husband whenever she is freed, or whenever I succeed in getting her freed. I'm in a terrible position, Doctor. I wanted to speak to your parents but knew that they don't understand Polish. That's why I haven't done so before this. I thought of approaching you, Dr. Babad, but was told that you are—how shall I put it—an impatient man, and I need to speak to someone who is both patient and good."

"What's on your mind? Where were you going?"

"I? It doesn't matter. Wherever you are, Doctor. Generally I am a resolute man, but I've already walked past your parents' house many times without going in. I purposely came late today so as not to meet visitors. I'm sorry but I don't speak Yiddish. And here I bump into you. Isn't that a strange coincidence? I'm in such a nervous state that everything seems odd. I'm not well; I have a fever. I shouldn't have gotten out of bed. But the slanderous rumors that have been spread about me and the unfortunate thing that has happened to Mirale have confused me so much that—don't take offense, Doctor—I know I'm not making sense. I really don't know where to begin. I'm accustomed to all kinds of difficulties, but what has occurred is beyond the powers of one person. There are some blows one can't defend oneself against. I suppose, Dr. Babad, that these disgusting tales have reached you too."

"Yes, I've heard."

"Who told you? Well, it doesn't matter. It's a lie, Dr. Babad, a vicious lie. I would swear to it, but we freethinkers don't even have the privilege of swearing by some higher power. All I can do is give you my word of honor that I am the victim of criminal slander. Do you know that there is a price of five thousand rubles on my head? Even my own comrades, for whom I risked my life, are now anxious to get rid of me. I can't leave the house, because I'm afraid I'll be shot in the back. I've told them I'm ready to stand trial before them and if found guilty to put a bullet through my own skull. But even the right to defend myself has been denied me. I mentioned earlier that I have nothing to swear by, but there is the memory of my mother. It is sacred to me, more sacred than anything in this world, and I swear by her bones that everything I'm saying now, Dr. Babad, is the absolute truth!"

Stefan Lamanski covered his face with one hand. This stranger, who called himself Mirale's husband, was crying in the street.

II

Only now did Ezriel realize that they had reached the corner of Ciepla Street. To the left were the police barracks; to the right, the barracks of the Volhynia regiment. It was dark and quiet. Stefan Lamanski took out his handkerchief and murmured: "Please excuse me, Doctor."

In the past months Ezriel had more than once thought about this man, who was accused of being an *agent provocateur*, who had involved his sister in illegal activities. As a boy in cheder, Ezriel had not taken the side of Simeon and Levi, who had slain the inhabitants of Shechem because of their sister Dinah. He had sympathized with Jacob, who on his deathbed had cursed the brothers: "O my soul, come not thou into their secret; into their assembly, mine honor, be not thou united." But of late he had begun to understand the anguish of these men at seeing their sister treated like a whore. Now his sister's seducer stood before him, wiping the tears from his eyes. Her lover, Ezriel saw, was a poorly dressed man. Unshaven and pale, as if after an illness, he wore a cap with an oilcloth visor and carried a wooden box. He reminded Ezriel of an army recruit. He called himself Mirale's husband! In that case he was his brother-in-law.

Ezriel said: "What did you want of my parents? You know they're old-fashioned. A rabbi . . ."

"I know. You mustn't think, Dr. Babad, that I made my decision lightly," Stefan Lamanski replied. "My situation is such that I must leave. It's a matter of life and death. I don't want to be sacrificed to satisfy my one-time comrades' malice. I say malice because our movement has split and the resulting struggle can only help the enemy. Some so-called patriots have infiltrated our ranks and, under the guise of socialism, are again trying to delude the people with dreams of an insurrection. I needn't tell you, esteemed Doctor, how hopeless such fantasies are and how harmful to the proletariat. For wherever the fire of nationalism starts burning, the atmosphere is immediately poisoned by chauvinism, by the hate of brother for brother. Who then stands to gain? The exploiters, of course, who feed off the people! Those vampires have ruled for generations, stealing bread from the masses and collaborating with the enemies of Poland. I needn't tell you what role our last king played; think of it. First as lover of bloody Catherine and later, after he had enslaved Poland, as a sycophant at her court, like those pimps who in their old age carry the chamber pots in the brothels. What did these noblemen do in 1863? They appealed for help to the peasants and workers. Fortunately, the common man understood that a native hangman is no better than a foreign one, and wouldn't have anything to do with their adventures. Understand, the ones who paid for all this were always the workers, for in the final analysis they square all the accounts. Now this nationalistic plague has flared up again. And where? In our own ranks. Oh, I can't begin to explain to you what is going on. These so-called revolutionaries keep speaking about the worker and his situation, but they're really concerned with only one thing—the return of the Polish nobility to power and the taking away from the people of those shreds of rights that Alexander had granted to them. It would mean that Poland would be freed from her foreign yoke, and a native yoke substituted instead. In Western Europe, especially in France, there are groups who understand this danger and continue to warn us against it. Their leader, a young man of superior intelligence, came to Warsaw not long ago—illegally, of course, under another name. Had he been caught, he would have been strung up. He happens to be Jewish, and you would not believe this, Dr. Babad, but the comrades stooped to the lowest form of anti-Semitism. I don't keep my convictions secret, and so much poison has already been generated by my former colleagues against me that they stop at nothing. It is to their advantage to destroy me. In so doing, they overlook the real *provocateurs* within their own ranks. The truth is—they are all *provocateurs*. Because a traitor is a traitor whatever he may be called—but why am I bothering you with all these details? You're certainly not interested in them."

"Why not? I've heard that this division exists among the Russians, but it's news to me that such frictions exist right here in Poland."

"Actually, I shouldn't have told you all this. It's true these are not party secrets and I trust you, Dr. Babad, because you're Mira's brother. Still, they are internal squabbles.

"I've been sick for several weeks, really sick, and my nerves are shattered. I've stopped sleeping and that is killing me. I used to have nerves of steel; now I jump at the squeak of a mouse. I have a feeling that I'm not speaking coherently. You asked me something, but unfortunately I don't remember what it was. This is also due to my nervousness. Oh, yes, about your parents. As I have mentioned, I must go abroad, and I would like at least to have one look at the child. . . . I know how embarrassing it must be for you to hear these words, but still, it is my child, our child, Mirale's and mine, a child of love. I know how the philistine looks upon such babies, but I'm above that, and I am convinced that you, Doctor, are not so fanatical as to be contemptuous of an innocent being just because a formality has been omitted. If Mirale were not in prison and your parents wished us to go through some ceremony, I would do it to spare them unnecessary grief. One has to make a distinction between members of the older generation, who can no longer understand the course of progress, and those hypocrites who wrap their reactionary intentions in revolutionary phrases. . . . In short, I had hoped that they would give me the address."

"They don't know the address. My father, especially, knows nothing at all about it. My mother did hear something but—"

"Well, if that's so, it's a lucky coincidence that I met you, esteemed Doctor. I hope you'll understand how much I'm suffering and what a look at my child would mean to me. This may sound sentimental, provincial, but there are biological processes that—"

Stefan Lamanski stopped talking. They had gone past Mirowski Place and found themselves on Elektralna Street. The windows were dark, the gates locked. Ezriel felt uncomfortable. What if a patrol were to come along and arrest them both? And what if one of Lamanski's fellow revolutionaries was following him? Ezriel had heard frightening stories about the nihilists and their acts of revenge. He had to get away from this person, the sooner the better.

He said: "The child is on Dzika Street, near Powązek. But I warn you, they are affiliated with your enemies. You don't want to walk into a trap, do you?"

"Who are they? I know everyone from that group . . ."

"Their name is Cybula—" Ezriel said. "His name is Jonas Cybula. He is a locksmith."

"A locksmith? Cybula? The name is unfamiliar."

"As far as I know, they're members of the organization. The one caring for the child is a hunchback, but I don't remember her surname. Her name is Edzia."

"A hunchback? I don't know her either. What's the number of the house?"

Ezriel gave him the number.

"Well, I'll go there tomorrow. Does the locksmith work at home?"

"I've never seen him there."

"Thanks, thanks a lot. I don't have to tell you, Dr. Babad, that the whole thing was—how shall I express myself—entirely unplanned, a catastrophe, but it will all come out well."

"What good can come of it? She'll serve in prison for another six years, and afterwards they'll probably exile her to Siberia. What good can come of a child raised without parents?"

"This barbaric order can't endure for long. Something must happen soon."

III

It was already half past twelve when Ezriel said goodbye to Stefan Lamanski and started home. He felt chilled. His head and feet ached. "What's happening to me? Am I getting sick? Despite the past, despite what I owe her, what I have with Shaindel is no life. . . . Everything has become a bore. I don't even have the time to study. Everything is just disgusting routine. I'm an idiot, too. I had a chance to have a career, to have Olga. Actually I sacrificed everything for Calman Jacoby's daughter. Well, those who permit themselves to be destroyed have no right to complain." He had to hurry. He had to be up at seven o'clock, but he walked slowly. "If at least I hadn't brought children into the world!" He was suddenly filled with rage against Shaindel. He had pleaded with her to get an abortion, but she was one of those rabbits that must bear and bear. "Well, I'll be revenged, I'll go away. What would happen if I were to die? She'd live on. She'd probably remarry. Only an imbecile like me kills himself for such parasites!"

He came to the gate and rang the bell. The janitor mumbled something as he opened the gate. Ezriel didn't even have a tip for him. He clattered up the dark stairway. "Demons? If only demons existed! This would indicate that there was something else . . . that creation was not just a Darwinlike charnel house. . . ." Opening the door with his key, he noticed a light in the living room. "He still hasn't gone to bed, the savage!" Ezriel muttered. "Ruining his eyes with all those idiotic books!" The jurisprudence of the jungle. . . . He opened the door and saw Joziek. The boy was sitting in an armchair, without a book, in an unbuttoned jacket, his hands on his knees, hair disarrayed. Joziek, who always seemed calm, with all buttons fastened, now looked disheveled. "What's wrong with him?" Ezriel wondered. "Why aren't you asleep?" he asked. "Why ruin your eyes with this stuff? Get undressed and go to bed."

Joziek did not even stir. "Papa, I must talk to you."

Ezriel bristled. "What about? It's late. Soon I'll have to go to work."

"Papa, sit down."

"What's happened? Speak up."

"I can't continue at the university!"

"What then? Will you sell onions?"

"I'm going away."

"Where are you going? What in hell is wrong with you?"

"I'm going to Palestine."

Ezriel laughed.

"Well go, in happiness and peace. Give my regards to Mother Rachel!"

"Papa, it's no joke."

"What's happened? Did you hear one of the Lovers of Zion make a speech? Did you read Pinsker's brochure?"

"Papa, it's more serious than you suppose."

"What's more serious? What are you babbling about? Either tell me nothing or everything. I haven't the patience to pull the words out of you."

"Why are you so angry?"

"My anger is none of your business. Talk, because I still want to sleep a few hours. Even a horse has to rest sometimes."

"Oh, Papa, I'll tell you tomorrow."

"Not tomorrow, today. But make it short! I'm listening! What's happened? Where do you want to run? What sort of madness is this?"

"Papa, I can't stand it any more."

"What can't you stand?"

"This anti-Semitism. You'll never know, Papa, what I faced in school. I didn't say anything because it wouldn't have helped. Now I must tell the truth. Everyone tormented me: the teachers, the students. A hundred, perhaps a thousand, times a day they threw my Jewishness up to me. You studied alone, at home, but I had to go to school every day. I was beaten too, innumerable times. Now something has happened that I . . ."

"What happened?"

"I went into Lurse's with two other students. We were sitting quietly at a table when two bullies started baiting us. They wanted to insult us. Finally, one of them tore off my cap and threw it on the floor. I challenged him to a duel, but he replied that he wouldn't duel with a Jew. He hit me, too!"

"Why didn't you hit back? You were with two others."

"Oh, he was a head taller than I. The others were frightened. Everyone laughed. Someone poured water into my cap. I came home without it, without my honor too. Papa, I can't stand it any more! I'd rather die."

"Well, we've lived like this for two thousand years."

"That's long enough. A man who can't speak up when his cap is being filled with water is no man."

Ezriel felt his heart pounding. "Yes, that's true. But Palestine won't solve anything."

"What will? I've thought it all over. If I don't go away, I'll have to kill myself. First him, then me. But I wouldn't even recognize him. It's something I'll never forget."

"When did this happen?"

"Yesterday."

"Yesterday? Where were your friends?"

"They sat like little lambs. Jews aren't men. You know that, Papa. We're emasculated."

Ezriel was silent. For a long time he remained standing at the door. Then he entered Joziek's room. He took a book from the shelf, opened it, read a line, and put it back in its place.

IV

"What actually do you expect me to do?" he asked. "The Turks are no better than the Poles or the Russians. Don't be fooled."

"I know, Papa. But it's our country, our earth."

"How is it ours? Because Jews lived there two thousand years ago? Do you know how many nations have perished and assimilated since that time? If we changed the map to what it was two thousand years ago, three-quarters of mankind would have to be moved. And how does it follow that we actually come from these Israelites? Where did I get my blond hair and blue eyes? The ancient Hebrews were all dark."

"How do you know? And then, I'm dark. I can't search through my genealogy."

"What will you do there? Drain the swamps and catch malaria? Is this why you graduated from gymnasium?"

"Papa, I can't stay here any more. I hate this city. I don't want to be pointed at as the one who was slapped."

"A Turk might hit you, or an Arab."

"I'll strike back."

"If you can. We've received blows in our own country too. The Babylonians, the Greeks, the Romans. Poland has been torn as well."

"The Poles are at home here. They lead normal lives."

"You could become a Pole, even a Russian—" Ezriel regretted his words as soon as he said them.

"Is that a solution?"

"No, but—to be free, one needn't begin everything over. You can study in Western Europe. Jews aren't beaten there."

"They are, they are. I read *The Israelite*. 'The Jew is Our Misfortune—' this is the slogan everywhere now, in Prussia, in Austria, in Hungary. I can't take on the beliefs of those who beat me."

"And what do you believe? What do we modern Jews believe? Well, I must go to sleep. I had a hard day myself. It's all a question of names. I'm no radical, but all this nationalism is false. What's the difference between a Prussian and an Austrian, a Dane and a Norwegian? Why did the German states wage war for hundreds of years? It's all madness."

"That madness is the law of life."

"It won't always be like that. What separates them? Not ideas. They all want power. Take America, for example, a thousand nationalities. You can become an American too. All you need is a boat ticket."

"All Jews cannot become Americans."

"Why worry about all Jews? Oh, you're only a boy and you repeat everything you hear. The Jews can return to Palestine as much as the Hungarians can become Tartars. We'll talk again tomorrow. Good night."

"With your opinions, Papa, I'd become a socialist."

"To spite whom? They'd jail you as they did Aunt Mirale. The prison's big enough."

"What can one do?"

"At least not make things worse. How can one fight madness? There's no cure. That is the truth."

"Papa, I want to leave."

"Well, I won't stop you."

5

I

My dear Papa and Mama [wrote Sonya to her parents], Forgive me for not writing in Yiddish. I tried, but somehow I've forgotten too much. I don't remember all the letters, and after all, you both know Polish. This is our fifth day in New York. It's only two months since we said goodbye, but it seems to me as if I've been traveling since I was born. First the trip to Berlin, then on to Paris, to Cherbourg, and later by boat to America. Thirteen days on the ocean. We were in a storm too, and the religious passengers cried, "Hear O Israel" and said their confessions, although there was no danger. You know how frightened our Jews get, especially the women. Almost all of them were seasick. For three days I was ill and, excuse me, vomited up everything. I ate only a few biscuits all that time. Thank God, Alexander was a good sailor. But he was depressed and still is. Don't worry, he'll come out of it. If I had taken this trip without Alexander, I would have died of loneliness. He is such a devoted brother. He was concerned only about me and my comfort. It wasn't very comfortable, because we were traveling steerage. We didn't sleep in beds but in bunks, like soldiers, he with the men and I with the women. I still shudder when I think of how much dirt and boorishness I encountered aboard ship. It was a nightmare. But I'd rather remember the beauty of the ocean, the flying fish and the dolphins that leaped over the waves, dipping and diving. The magnificence of the Atlantic is beyond description, especially when the sun goes down. Once after a rain we saw a rainbow stretching from one end of the horizon to the other. One never had enough of the view. I'd stand by the rail half the days and even half the nights, just looking. How vast the ocean is! How endless! It is astonishing to realize it has existed since the world began. Sometimes, in the distance, we saw the silhouettes of ships. One of the passengers let us use his binoculars. Some of the young people put letters in bottles which they sealed and threw into the ocean. It's funny to think that a person drowns immediately, but a bottle can float for thousands of miles and reach a shore. I enclosed a greeting to you, my dears. . . . There was a group from Odessa and Kiev with us. They were former students, intellectuals, and some workers too. Some of them call themselves Am Olam, people of the world. They hope to form colonies in America and live together, sharing everything. Others are opposed to them, and discussions went on all night. They were so noisy that we couldn't get any sleep. The food wasn't too good. Many ate nothing but potatoes in their skins, and herring, because the food was not kosher. They all had their own opinions and wrangled with each other as though still at home and not in the middle of nowhere. Alexander would not participate in these debates and they resented it, but I wouldn't let them criticize him. Finally we arrived in New York. Long before we reached the harbor, the Statue of Liberty came into view and everyone shouted: "Hurrah!" The officials let us off quickly. Immigrants only have to show that they have five dollars or ten rubles.

Oh, I can't tell you how different New York is from all the other cities! Berlin and Paris were marvelous, but still somewhat like Warsaw and Kiev. New York is another world. It's as if one were walking upside down. It's not as pretty as Paris, far from it! Even ugly. Most of the houses aren't plastered, the bricks are visible. There are no courtyards here either, children play in the streets. I studied French in gymnasium, but I don't understand a word of English. On the ship we all spoke Russian. They gave me an English reader, but Americans pronounce words differently. Even their mouths seem different from ours. Only God knows if I'll ever learn this language. We went to the Jewish section and Alexander immediately disapproved of New York. You know he becomes either inspired or dejected. We rented a room from a widow, who also gives us lunch. The Yiddish here is different from what we speak at home. It is mixed with English. The landlady is called the "Missus," and the tenants, "boarders." It is terribly hot here. Food must be kept on ice. People go around half bare and many sleep on rooftops. The roof of our house is flat, a sort of Oriental roof, and at times I imagine myself in Persia or Palestine. Many Germans as well as Jews who speak German live in this neighborhood. With them one can make oneself understood somehow. (They are called "Yekies" here.) The Americans themselves are unusually patient and polite. When you ask them about a street, they lead you there. The colonies that our young people wanted to go to are somewhere far off, many days' journey by train, and, they say, in the wilderness among Indians. Incidentally, one sees in New York Negroes, all black, as well as Chinese, without pigtails. One meets Spaniards, Italians, and even some Poles. There are iron bridges over many streets, and trains run on them. There are also trolley cars. Everything is so ludicrous. In the trolley you throw the ticket into a glass vessel. Aliens here are called "greenhorns." Yes, I am a "green girl." That's what everyone calls me.

My dears, you needn't worry about us, although it doesn't seem as splendid here as the agent claimed. Many people are out of work. On a street that they call the Pigmarket, workers stand, waiting to be hired. One carries a saw, another the head of a sewing machine, or some other tool of his trade. Along come the bosses or their agents, and the whole procedure resembles a slave auction. One seldom sees a ragged or dirty or barefoot person here. Everyone eats white bread, even paupers, and no one is afraid of saying what he thinks. Women, too. Sometimes I want to laugh at everything. Work isn't considered demeaning. I'll have to work in a factory, or "shop." Alexander will surely find something too, although he talks only about settling in a colony or returning to Europe. He's been very foolish, but why dwell on that? Sabina was distant to me from the beginning. I only feel sorry for the child. . . .

My dears, we think and speak of you day and night. I suspect Alexander will write you a letter full of despair, but don't take it too seriously. Everyone feels that way at first. One is terribly nervous and wanders around as if in a dream. At times, I imagine I'm still aboard ship. Everything shakes—the room, the street, the ground, the sky. But they say one grows accustomed to it.

How are you, my dear sweet ones? I know how you worry about us, and you may laugh at me, but I only want to bring you here, so that we'll all be together. There are many synagogues and religious Jews with beards, although they all wear short cloaks. This crisis won't last forever, and one day we'll still be happy. I kiss you a thousand times and press you to my heart. I hope you will write me a long letter full of details, like mine, because when I write to you, it seems as if you are near me . . .

Your devoted daughter,
SONYA

II

Zipkin's letter to Sabina:

Dear Sabina,

I have already written you twice, once from Monte Carlo and again from Paris, but you didn't find it necessary to reply. Now I'm writing to you for the third and last time, from New York. It isn't in my nature to burden anybody and I don't know how much longer I'll continue to make the effort. Apparently I'm fated to self-destruction. How else can I explain the mad things I've done these past years? I've driven myself into a corner, from which there seems to be no escape. You can probably see the difference in my handwriting. Today from 6 a.m. until evening I stood at a machine making covers for boxes. I've always taken the side of the exploited but never imagined the hell that exists in every workshop or factory—the noise of the machines, the dust, the stink, the insults of the overseer, or, as he is called here, the "foreman." I never understood that a day, an hour, even ten minutes, could last so long. The feet ache, the eyes close, one's head feels as if screws were being bored into it, and all this, six days out of the week, for the miserable wage of five dollars. I step on something called a pedal and this bends a tin sheet. During the morning I think of nothing but the lunch whistle. We eat lunch in a bakery, standing, or sitting on a high stool that only Americans could have invented. Afterwards I begin to dream of the whistle which means the day is done. We live across from an "El." Every time the train passes, our windows and all the furniture in our room tremble. Everyone assures me that one becomes accustomed to it. But it's an insult to humanity just to accept such conditions. Yet it comforts me to know that I am looking at bitter reality.

I could go on forever about New York. This city reflects the chaos in my soul. Everything here opposes our way of thinking. What is beautiful in Europe is considered ugly here. What is comical to us is serious to them. In spite of their democracy and liberty, votes are purchased at election time. Bribes are openly accepted. The butcher, the corrupt policeman, the tavernkeeper rule here. Death has no special significance. Mortuaries stand between barbershops and restaurants. Cemeteries are not fenced in. Beside a stable there's a hospital. Women drink great mugs of beer in taverns. The men speak only of boxers and circus athletes. Negroes shine shoes on the sidewalks. Speakers declaim in the midst of the city. The architecture drives me wild. I try to read the English newspapers. Not one serious word about the world situation—only news about prospective weddings, funerals, amusements. Mister "This" arrived, Mrs. "That" has gone away, Miss "Something-or-Other" has become a bride. The sermons of the priests, ministers (as well as rabbis) are printed as if these people had discovered the North Pole. Everything else is advertisements. Even churches advertise. Spiritualists advertise. The heat too is vulgar. It burns hellishly, and there is a constant clang of fire wagons. I have already visited the famous Coney Island. One takes a long ferry trip to get there. When I arrived, I found the true meaning of the word plebeian. The screaming, the confusion is indescribable. One eats sausages, "hot dogs," gets one's fortune told in cards. In a sideshow one views a woman with two heads, a girl who is half snake, wax figures of kings, presidents, Popes , murderers. Meanwhile one nibbles candy and peanuts. In the midst of this tumult stands a monk, or a sort of missionary, and shouts that Jesus is God and that one must save one's soul. You won't believe it, but Sonya and I, out of sheer boredom, rode a carousel, and I even tried chewing tobacco (yes, the Yankees chew tobacco!).

Well, enough complaints about New York. There are good things here also. There's a socialist paper, printed in German, although its socialism is diluted. Jews play an important role here, especially the German ones. Someone has told me that America must be discovered over again by each person who comes here.

I am writing to you because I've learned the tragic news of your father's death. Sonya told me about it while we were still in Paris, but I withheld my condolences. He was my only friend and protector in the family and it really grieves me to have caused him suffering in his final days. But one need have no regrets for the dead. It's fortunate to be rid of this disgusting world with its useless efforts and empty hopes. What I am going through here I can't explain to you. I'm spiritually paralyzed. The more I think about what I've done and how unhappy I made you, the child, my parents, and myself, the more fantastic it all seems to me, as if someone had bewitched me. At times it seems to me that I've already died, and am in Gehenna. Sonya has told me that you insist I send you a Jewish divorce, and I'll certainly do so, but do me one favor: write to me about Kubuś and send me his most recent photograph. I am his father. When I've received your reply, I'll go to a rabbi (they call themselves "Doctor" and "Reverend" here) and send you the divorce. I hope you'll forgive me for having sinned against you. I want you to know that Clara sent long, apologetic letters to me in Paris and wanted to rejoin me but I never replied. This woman ruined me and has killed my belief in humanity. You may rest assured that I will never marry again. I forgot to add that Sonya is working in a dress factory, learning to sew on a machine (here, she is called an "operator"). Her situation is no better than mine, but she has the humility that makes everything easier. After a day's hard work, she takes classes in English. She also stood in line for half a Saturday waiting to get opera tickets to hear Patti, who, a while back, charmed St. Petersburg. She goes to all kinds of lectures.

I myself have decided nothing. There are days when I'm ready to return to Europe. I only have to save enough for my fare. But sometimes I plan to settle in a colony, deep inland, among forests and prairies, and forever break away from so-called civilization. The Am Olam have founded such colonies here. A few have already failed, but others refuse to surrender. Occasionally I meet young people. In a certain sense, politics is an obession here too, as it is in Russia. Famous socialists arrive from Germany, even the daughter of Karl Marx came on a visit from England. There's great concern about anarchists, particularly those who have been sentenced to hang. But it seems to me (I don't know why) as if everything here is imitation. Something is lacking, I don't know what. The loneliness, naturally, makes me moody. I hope you'll answer promptly, for I may soon be back in Europe, or somewhere in the state of Oregon, near the Pacific Ocean. I'm sure I won't remain in New York. Forgive me and kiss Kubuś for me, often.

Your ALEXANDER

6

I

It was a hot September day. That afternoon, there were only a few patients in Ezriel's office, the usual neurasthenics, each with his or her particular illness and complaints. The man who served tea opened the door to Ezriel's examining room and admitted the last patient. Ezriel stood looking out the window and did not turn immediately. He stared into the courtyard, at the garbage can, at the children playing around it, at the surrounding buildings, whose windows revealed entire apartments, segments of Jewish domesticity. Joziek's trip to Palestine was already a certainty. Shaindel walked around the summer resort with a handkerchief soaked in vinegar around her head, and took sleeping pills. It was a weekday, but it seemed to Ezriel as if it were a Sabbath eve. An inescapable boredom had followed him from Turbin to Lublin, from Lublin to Jampol, from Jampol to Warsaw. Smoke rose from the chimneys. He watched girls sweeping floors with worn-out brooms as they sang old, tired melodies. A golden dust fell over everything. Out of the distance there came a sound that could be either the chanting of children in a cheder or the croaking of frogs in a country swamp. The children in the yard began to play a game of buttons. The janitor's dog sniffed at a stone. "Why do I have to live through all this? How long will it last?" Ezriel asked himself. To go to Falenica would mean to lie next to Shaindel and spend the night explaining that going to Palestine was not the same as dying. To remain in town meant to eat chicken broth and noodles in a dirty restaurant on Karmelicka Street and then to sit at home reading the case histories of more neurasthenics, more melancholics, more paranoics. A phrase in Ecclesiastes occurred to Ezriel: "All things are wearisome." Ezriel, when he turned from the window, was astounded to see Olga standing at the door. She looked pale, though she was smiling. "Is this the way you receive your patients?" she asked.

"Oh, they drive me insane."

There was a pause, then she said: "I have a number like everyone else. Here it is!"

She handed him a blue ticket.

"What's the trouble?" he asked, in a professional tone.

Olga bit her lip. "Oh, everything."

"Nerves?"

"Yes."

Again they were both silent. He saw everything at once: the sadness in her eyes, the trembling of her lips, the new straw hat, the white blouse, the gray pleated dress, the white pocketbook. She had selected the things he liked. Even her earrings were a pair he had admired. She stood before him with an expression at the same time rebellious and humble.

"What has happened?" he asked.

"I've told him the truth."

"Wallenberg?"

"Yes, about you. It's over. I could not love him. I love you."

Ezriel's eyes grew moist. "You're my last patient. Let's go out."

"Don't you have to go home?"

"Yes, but I won't go. They're all in the country."

"Joziek, too?"

"He's spending some time with his mother, before leaving for Palestine."

"Palestine? How odd."

He kissed her on the cheek. She caught his hand in hers and pressed it. He spoke with a tremor in his voice. "It would be better if you waited for me downstairs. I must stop at the administration office on my way out."

"I wanted to write to you, but somehow I couldn't. I'll wait at the Gardens' gate on Ziabia Street."

"I'll be there soon."

He accompanied her to the door, and then went to the office. He passed the door of the dentist, the obstetrician, the surgeon, the pediatrician, and heard a variety of moans. Only the cashier was in the office. He took his hat, gave the girl the patients' tickets, and left, skipping down the stairs. His feet grew light as a boy's. How many times had this happened in his life—resignation, then victory! Everything that had appeared mundane and trivial to him had suddenly grown festive. The sun's rays were no longer too hot. The odor of flowers came from the baskets of women vendors. Racing down the street, he was nearly run over by a droshky. For a moment he could smell the horse's muzzle. At the gate of the Saxony Gardens, near the stand selling hoops, balloons, toy horns, rubber balls, stood Olga. She smiled the shy smile of those who are relieved at having surrendered. They went into the park. He took her white-gloved hand and they walked like a boy and girl on their first date. Though the path was level, they seemed to be walking downhill.

"Why is Joziek going to Palestine?" Olga asked.

"He was insulted in a restaurant, and he doesn't want to serve in the Czar's army, not even for the single year that's required of students."

"Who insulted him?"

"What's the difference? He's become a Lover of Zion. He wants to go back to the land of his ancestors."

"What does his mother say?"

"She's completely broken up."

They looked for a place to sit, but all the benches were occupied. The women's hats were ornamented with flowers and fruit: cherries, grapes, plums. Little boys, mostly in sailor suits, rolled hoops. Girls played ball, danced in a circle, chanted childish doggerel. At the lake, governesses helped children throw crumbs to two floating swans. In the distance an orchestra played and a trumpet blared. It was unseasonably hot. After a while, Ezriel and Olga came out on Niecala Street. They found a café opposite the Brill Palace and sat down at a table. Olga ordered coffee. Ezriel, who had not eaten lunch, ordered new potatoes and sour milk. The late-afternoon sunlight glinted through the separations between the draperies, quivered on the waxed floor, on the tapestried walls, in the prisms of lamp crystals, on the gilded frames of the pictures. Two golden-green flies chased each other around the ceiling lamp. A man with a flowing mustache and a red nose, obviously one of the local landowners, was reading a newspaper and smoking a cigar. The waiter went back to the counter with the order.

"When did all this happen?" Ezriel asked.

"Several days ago. No, it was the day before yesterday. No. Sunday. He asked me and I told him the truth. But I would have told him anyway."

Ezriel lowered his head. "I longed for you all the time."

Olga, who until now had been smiling, suddenly grew serious. "It was more than longing for me."

"What was it?"

"Death. I can't live without you."

Her mouth trembled. She knew that a woman does not admit such things.

II

Everything moved so quickly. Joziek had just been talking about Palestine and now he was leaving, even before the holidays were over. Shaindel returned to the city, fluttering over the boy as if he were mortally ill, pleading and weeping; but he was adamant. With packed valise and no bed linen, he was ready for the land of his ancestors. He was to travel with a group from Lithuania, who had assembled in Warsaw. They sang, rolled cigarettes, and spoke of ships, seaports, the free acreage that Baron Rothschild was granting settlers, and Turkish law. Listening to them, Shaindel cracked her fingers. No matter how often Joziek explained to her how harmful the Jewish Diaspora was, that a people must have a homeland, a language, a worldly culture of its own, Shaindel could not understand. She insisted he was a victim of the Evil Eye. It was madness for a boy to leave his mother, father, and the university for Palestine. There was starvation in the holy cities. The Arabs were still as wild as the ancient Ishmael. The swamps were malaria-ridden, the soil chalky, barren, and rocky. Shaindel knew that one went to the Holy Land to die, not to live. Those for whom the groschens in the almsboxes were collected went there. Shaindel had once studied about Jerusalem, the grave of Rachel, the Cave of Machpelah, but she did not actually believe that Palestine existed. If it did—it was located somewhere at the end of the world, near the River Sambation, or the Tower of Babel. Shaindel cried until she had no tears left and talked until she lost her voice. Ezriel had borrowed three hundred rubles to pay Joziek's fare. Calman had also contributed. But why give him money when the group intended to live communally? Shaindel had met the other boys. They were swarthy, unkempt, with weary eyes and tousled hair. They wore black shirts with sashes, spoke Russian and a mixture of Yiddish and Hebrew. There was a girl going with them who had taken the biblical name of Abigail.

After Joziek's departure, Shaindel became disconsolate. Usually for Rosh Hashana she had prepared challah, carp, apples with honey, and bought grapes to make the benediction, "who hath preserved us in life," as had been the custom in her father's house. And each year she prayed in her mother-in-law's apartment, which was turned into a synagogue on the

Days of Awe. But this year Shaindel spent both days of Rosh Hashana in bed. She did not even go to hear the blowing of the ram's horn. Ezriel urged her to accept the situation. What did one do if a child died? Joziek was alive. They had already received a letter from him, from Constanz. But Shaindel refused to be consoled. Within his own house, Ezriel recognized a classic example of melancholia. Shaindel had all the symptoms: the grief, diminished alertness, lack of appetite, the inability to sleep, the constant repetition of the same words day and night. Ezriel prescribed the usual remedies: bromine and opium. Shaindel slept for a long time but arose empty-headed, as she said. Time stopped for her. Her skin grew parched. She crept from room to room, pale, preoccupied, looking off into space. Although Ezriel knew that Shaindel was sick and not responsible for her actions, he could not control his annoyance. She did not take care of little Misha. Ezriel sensed an element of hostility in Shaindel's melancholia. She wasn't so confused as not to know what she was doing. She had grasped at this misfortune as a drowning man clutches at a straw, blaming Ezriel for Joziek's departure. He had shown his son that home meant nothing. She began to predict that Zina too would come to a bad end. She had no girl friends, spent too much time with books. It was a terrible thing to say, but she was, God forbid, following in the footsteps of Miriam Lieba.

Her words were so full of spite that Ezriel scarcely knew how to answer her. Actually the situation was far worse than she realized. Ezriel was caught in a trap. There was not a day when he did not consider deserting this household that was destroying him both spiritually and physically, even though the ignominy of such an act seemed impossible to him.

The night before Yom Kippur, Shaindel pulled herself together and went out to buy a long, memorial candle. In preparation for the fast, she forced herself to eat a little more. The following evening, in a holiday dress, she took a prayer book and went to the synagogue to pray.

Zina and Tekla, the maid, remained with Misha. Ezriel too left the house. There had been a time when Nowolipki Street had been a Gentile street, but now only Jews lived there. Yom Kippur candles shone from the windows. Jews were on their way to prayer. The men were dressed in white robes and slippers, and wore their prayer shawls under their coats. The women wore beaded capes, silk or satin dresses with trains, and their most precious jewels. In a top hat and frock coat, his beard combed into two silver-white points so sparse that every hair could be counted, an enlightened Jew was on his way to the German synagogue, escorting a woman in a hat trimmed with ostrich plumes. In Wola, the large red sun set among purple clouds, like plowed furrows. All the shops were shuttered and bolted. Even the Gentiles walked by with muted steps. The horse-drawn trolley rode past, half empty. Not far away, on Krochmalna Street, the "Pure Prayer" was being read to Ezriel's father, who had become blind. His mother wept at the lighting of the candles. Millions of Jews in Russia, Germany, Palestine, Yemen, even in America and Argentina, were beating their breasts at confession during the evening services, praying for forgiveness to the Almighty God. In the small towns they were probably still lighting wax candles and allowing themselves to be whipped.

But their God was no longer Ezriel's God, or their prayers his prayers. What meaning did the Declaration of Vows have for him? Nevertheless, he hummed the melody of Kol Nidre to himself. If You are there, God, forgive me. If You are not—what is there? A great pity filled Ezriel for man who must learn everything for himself, must pay dearly for the slightest achievement. Even if God's plan for the world was eventual bliss, man remained His martyr.

III

Shaindel grew worse. She developed a persecution mania and complained that Ezriel wanted to kill her. She refused the medicines he prescribed, because she feared he wanted to poison her. Although Shaindel knew nothing about Olga, she spoke of another woman, whom Ezriel would marry after Shaindel's death. Ezriel was amazed. There was a trace of logic in all her madness. Through what power had she surmised that her rival was a modern, educated woman? "You don't have to poison me," she told Ezriel. "I won't last much longer."

"Shaindel, what's the matter with you?"

"I'm not altogether crazy. I know your tricks."

Ezriel had often discussed hypnotism at home. He had even taken Shaindel to see Feldman, the hypnotist, conduct a séance. Shaindel now accused Ezriel of hypnotizing her. She insisted that Feldman "spoke" to her every night and that was why she could not sleep. She knew that Ezriel sometimes treated his patients with electric massage. He had had a telephone installed in the apartment and Shaindel had actually accused him of electrocuting her with it. Ezriel learned from a Dr. Halpern, a neighbor, that Shaindel had come to him and bared her heart. She had told him that Ezriel had electrocuted her head and left leg and that the poison he put in her food had burned through her heart. He had delayed her period and had contrived a plot against her with their daughter, Zina. The girl laughed at her, mimicked her behind her back. When the doctor asked Shaindel why she thought her own daughter would want to make fun of her, Shaindel had replied: "Because, after they bury me, they want to convert."

"What you should do is eat, drink, and become healthy despite them," Dr. Halpern had advised her.

"No, they are stronger than I. I'll have to give in," she had replied.

What a misfortune to deal all day with the madness of strangers and at night come home to an insane wife! Ezriel wrote a long letter to his father-in-law. Calman came to Warsaw to try talking his daughter out of her delusions, but Shaindel reproved him for conspiring with her enemies. Calman suggested that she come to stay with him at the manor or that he take her with him to visit Tsipele and the Rabbi of Marshinov, but Shaindel had replied: "Father, you want to fool me into leaving the house."

"Daughter, why should I fool you? You're my child. I'm an old man now."

"He has hypnotized you, too."

Joziek wrote often from Palestine. Each letter was more optimistic than the last. It was warm in Palestine. In the morning it rained, but by afternoon the sun shone. The sky was bluer, the stars seemed bigger. Joziek took care of cows and horses, was learning Hebrew, had a dog and a gun, had grown muscular and tanned. He sent photographs of himself—working at a wine press, riding horseback, standing near a tent holding a gun. Although Shaindel's sickness had been brought on by Joziek's departure, she would not read his letters or look at the photographs. She would grimace, as if to say: "I know these tricks."

The news that the doctor's wife had lost her mind spread quickly along Nowolipki Street and the surrounding areas. Although Shaindel had learned to wear a hat when she left the house, she now put a shawl over her head, as she had done in Jampol. She walked about shabbily dressed, in battered shoes with trailing laces. Shaindel's suspicion that Ezriel wanted to poison her affected him strangely. He began to fear that Shaindel might do him bodily harm. Who could say what a person in her condition was capable of? He had heard many gruesome stories in the hospital. Mothers had slaughtered their children, men had set fire to their houses, hacked up their wives. Ezriel slept fitfully at night. He would fall asleep and soon wake up. He began to keep a knife under his pillow to protect himself.

Tekla, the maid, left her job in the middle of the quarter because Shaindel accused her of putting magic herbs into the food. Shaindel now had to take care of Misha. The child became extremely nervous, complained that his mother smelled bad. He was afraid of her and called her a frog. Ezriel realized that Warsaw was a small town. Everyone knew of the tragedy—his patients, the doctors with whom he worked. It was dangerous for him, for the children, even for the neighbors. Olga, who was aware of what was going on, never mentioned it. But she grew more indulgent with him, no longer objected when he was late, or even when he did not come at all. When Ezriel asked the advice of a colleague at the hospital, he was told frankly that Shaindel must not remain at home.

It was easy to say, but where could she be placed? Patients slept in the corridors of the Jewish Hospital. There were private sanatoriums either in Warsaw or its vicinity, but they did not accept Jewish patients. There were also state institutions, but it was questionable whether they would admit her. Shaindel knew little Polish and no Russian. She had grown even more pious, carried her prayer books everywhere, was overzealous in keeping the kitchen kosher, and constantly consulted the rabbi on matters of rabbinical law. In an asylum without kosher food she would die of hunger. Ezriel tried to find a place for Misha, but Warsaw had no nurseries of the kind that were (according to the newspapers) found abroad. There were only the foundling homes where illegitimate children were raised. Despite all the achievements of modern civilization, in a European metropolis like Warsaw there was no refuge for a soul-sick woman and a neglected child.

Olga suggested to Ezriel that she raise Misha with her own children. Ezriel did not know what to say. He was afraid that taking Misha away would throw Shaindel into complete despair. The family would be scandalized. His father-in-law, Mayer Joel, and the Rabbi of Marshinov would discover that he was permitting his child to be raised by a convert. Ezriel explained the situation to Olga. Something climactic was bound to happen. He must wait a little. Events seemed to be drawing him closer to Olga. He longed for her the moment they were separated. She found opportunities to be with him, waited for him at the clinic, left Natasha and Kolia with the maid and joined him at the hospital. She stopped concealing their relationship from the neighbors, the maid, the children. Ezriel knew well that Olga could scarcely wait for the day when Shaindel would enter an asylum. He caught himself too wishing for that day.

7

I

On the Day of Atonement, Calman was at his son-in-law's in Marshinov. The rabbi paused in his discourse before the taking of the scroll from the Holy Ark to quote from the chapter of the Book of Isaiah which is read on the Day of Atonement: "But the wicked are like the troubled sea when it cannot rest, whose waters cast up mire and dirt." The rabbi was referring to the growing number of enlightened Jews. On that Holy Day the rabbi said things that were entirely out of character. In calling the "moderns" to task, he utilized their own expressions. "A wicked person," the rabbi said, "always wages something—war or love. This may seem to be a contradiction," he continued. "War expresses anger; love, kindness. What connection is there between the two? And how can one wage love? The answer is that man is born to serve. If he does not serve God, he serves man. 'The fool hath said in his heart, there is no God.' Since a wicked man does not believe in the Creator, his brain is only concerned with admiring flesh and blood. He extols one man because he is rich; another because he is comely; a third because he is shrewd; a fourth, powerful. Those who think only of material things are jealous. Jealousy brings anguish, and anguish leads to conflict. It is written: 'Jealousy is cruel as the grave.' There is a kind of love that may be compared to death. The love that arises from envy kills. The love of the wicked is as destructive as war. The wicked man wants to take what another possesses. He looks on a woman as booty. Though at first he may treat her gently, once he has satisfied his lust, he will torture her. The love of the wicked is basically violent."

When Calman heard these words, he thought of Clara. She always talked about love but was actually consumed by rage. Her lover, Zipkin, whom she had brought to the estate to tutor Sasha, envied the rich, though he pretended to side with the poor, and what had been the outcome! Zipkin had deserted his wife and gone off to America; Clara was a divorcee, left with an illegitimate child. She had only what her son Sasha gave her. Calman had heard from Sasha that her health was poor. She suffered from stomach trouble and female ailments. One could justly say that she was like the troubled sea whose "waters cast up mire and dirt." Still, Calman pitied her. She had destroyed herself. Had he still been wealthy, he would have provided an allowance for her. But she was to blame for his being poor. Because of her, he had left his business and let Mayer Joel take over. Calman now lived on his son-in-law's bounty, although he still worked a little on the manor enterprises and at the lime quarries, which were almost exhausted. But he was nearly seventy and his strength was waning. Mayer Joel had asked Calman many times to live with him or to rent a room in Jampol. Why should he live alone? But Calman would not leave the Chamber of Prayer he had set up in his cottage on the estate. He had grown accustomed to the quiet of the surrounding fields, to the singing of the birds, the broad sky that extended to the end of the world. Besides, he was his own master. He had no steady maid and prepared his own food over a tripod. He milked the cow, or a peasant girl milked her for him as he watched. He also had a horse and wagon. On the day of the Sabbath eve on which the prayers for the new month are offered, or before a holiday, he would drive into Jampol to pray in a quorum. He had purchased a burial plot for himself in the Jampol cemetery. He wanted to lie next to Zelda, although he was afraid she would be ashamed of him in the other world and would reprove him for marrying Clara . . .

It was a bad winter. The snow lay high, the frosts were bitter, and the peasants predicted the winter crops would freeze. This would be the second year of famine, God forbid. Calman developed trouble with his teeth. He had always had healthy teeth, now suddenly they had begun to hurt. His daughter, Jochebed, urged him to go to Warsaw to see a dentist. But she herself hadn't a tooth in her head. She had become an old woman. Then why should he make a fool of himself with dentists? It was better to pay for one's sins in this world than to wander off to hell or become transmigrated. He had committed enough transgressions, had raised bad children. Some of his grandchildren were Gentiles. Woe unto him, he had left no Jewish male descendant, for Sasha was a heathen. It was an act of mercy from heaven that Calman was allowed to exist. He now fasted on Mondays and Thursdays. He did not touch meat for the entire week. He no longer had new clothes made, but wore his old capotes. In cold weather he remained at home, seated beside the stove, studying the Mishnah, reciting his prayers, even looking into Zelda's Yiddish Pentateuch. His eyes bothered him too, and Mayer Joel brought him glasses that enlarged the characters. Oddly enough, his lust still hadn't cooled. Man apparently retained desire all his life. Although Calman ate simple foods and slept on a hard straw mattress, he still dreamed of women. In his dreams he cohabited with Clara, and even with Antosia, the maid, who had once served him in his hut in the forest. Years ago Antosia had been drowned in the Vistula, near a village somewhere. But the Lord of Dreams knows nothing of aging or death. At times, even while awake, Calman was shaken with passion. Sitting at the Mishnah, a graybeard, his cheek swollen from toothache, with ruined eyes, heavy of foot, he would suddenly have a shameful thought. Calman could barely shake it off.

"Oh, woe is me, Father in heaven!"

One day Sasha entered the Chamber of Prayer. He had his sleigh and driver waiting outside. He told Calman that Clara was in Jampol. She was going to America and had come to say goodbye.

"To America—well!"

"She wants to see you."

"What for?"

"She wants your forgiveness."

"Tell her I forgive her."

"What are you afraid of? She's not going to make love to you."

"I'm not afraid."

"Maybe you can talk her out of making a fool of herself. Papa, how old is she?"

"I don't know."

"She says she is forty-two. She must be at least forty-six."

Calman did not reply.

"A foolish woman. Stupid."

Sasha glanced at his watch. He had neither the time nor the patience for these errands. Once he had only been ashamed of his father, now his mother embarrassed him as well.

II

Sasha spoke a while longer with his father and was reminded by Calman to wear his phylacteries. "Why wear phylacteries if there is no God?" he asked. Then he left. He got into the sleigh, covered his knees with a fur piece, and drove off. Although it was bitter cold, Sasha wore only a short fur jacket, riding breeches, and high, fitted boots. A hunting hat with a green feather in it was set jauntily on his shock of pitch-black hair. He was so healthy, so full of energy, that he had an impulse to leap from the sleigh and tear up a tree by the roots. People complained of all sorts of illnesses, weaknesses, pains, but Sasha did not know what sickness meant. At night as soon as his head touched the pillow he fell into a deep sleep. He ate the heaviest of foods, drank tumblers of whisky without suffering any discomfort. He could walk miles and ride horseback all day without tiring. The officers' wives whispered among themselves about his sexual prowess. He had a straightforward attitude toward women. No sneaky tricks, no bargaining, sighing, or delay. Yes was yes; no was no. He spoke frankly and coarsely. He hated sentiment, indecision, made no secret of his disdain for the sex that was so comically built, weak of character, full of wiles and dodges, always ready to dominate the male and betray him. Not yet nineteen, Sasha had already had the experiences of a thirty-year-old. He had seen women ruin men: they wove a net about a man, entangled him with duties, ensnared him with parasitic children, and finally destroyed him, jeered at him, buried him, and absorbed his inheritance. True, the poor woman herself did not enjoy her triumph. But the instinct of a spider existed in all females, from the court lady to the washerwoman. Sasha had already determined never to marry. In love, it was always best to deceive. For all their cunning, women were inclined to become attached, to lose their reason. They believed in male promises, even if it were the offer of the moon on a silver platter. It was only a matter of how to present a lie, any lie, and it would be accepted. There was no brutality they would not forgive if it were properly explained away. Sasha had read of this in books and discussed it with companions.

He sat in his sleigh, gazing at the snowy fields, at the chimneys of the lime quarries that belched smoke, at the castle where he, Sasha, had been born and where the officers' club was now located, and at Jampol, which was growing before his eyes. A balconied building several stories high had already been erected. In the distance he could discern the contours of the barracks and his Uncle Mayer Joel's watermill. It seemed strange to him that he was part of all this. He was a guest at the officers' club, and was having affairs with several of the officers' wives. The manor and the lime quarries were practically his property, although on paper the estate still belonged to some duke and the lime quarries were in his father's name. Every merchant in Jampol had to come to him, the contractor, to sell his wares. He dealt with the police, with the county natchalnik, with Colonel Shachowsky, with the colonel's wife, his daughters, even with General Horne in Warsaw and with his family. Sasha Jacoby enjoyed the protection of the governor of Lublin, the governor of Pietrkow, the Governor-General of Poland himself. "How can this be?" Sasha wondered. Most young men had no high-ranking connections whatsoever, but he kept making new ones. If things went on like this, he would be summoned to St. Petersburg to the Synod, perhaps even to the Czar. It was all so simple: everyone, no matter how great, needed money, a good word, pull, advice. And it was easy to do favors, for favors paid off. As for women, they could be bought with a smile, a look, a compliment. The main thing was not to be confined to one group, or to pass up any opportunity. Even a squire's lackey had to be tipped; a dog at court must be petted. Of all methods, bribery remained the best. Sasha had not yet met a functionary who had refused one. There must be some favor that would tempt the Czar himself.

"Hey you, Wladek!"

The driver turned around. "Yes, sir?"

"What's going on between you and Magda?"

Wladek scratched his head. "She's a decent girl. My enemies make trouble between us."

"They envy you, eh? It won't do them any good. You'll get her."

Wladek halted the sleigh. "Her stepmother is mean. She hates me and I don't know why."

"An old dog in the manger," Sasha said. "Can't eat the hay herself and won't let others have it."

"Well said."

"I'll have a talk with her."

"Oh, sir, I'd be so grateful. The master is so kind!"

"Well, we're both men."

Yes, Sasha knew how to exploit everyone to his advantage; nevertheless he had his own troubles. First of all, Celina, his grandfather's widow, and her brood, his little aunts and uncles, had become his responsibility. From the day that Sasha took over his grandfather's contracts, he had paid them a weekly stipend. Celina went about disheveled; the children had runny noses, and Celina's old mother was living with them. Sasha wondered how long he could endure them. But his grandfather had left a will. Colonel Shachowsky was, in a sense, the protector of Celina. It wasn't easy to rid oneself of her. His mother's plan to travel to America also irritated Sasha. Observing the impropriety of strangers was not the same as seeing it in one's own mother. Since childhood, Sasha had borne grudges against this woman who had always vilified his father and run around with dandies. It was she who was the reason for his hostility toward the female sex. The affair with Zipkin, the bastard child she had borne him, the trip abroad with her lover, had humiliated Sasha.

III

After his grandfather's death, Sasha had divided the house. Celina and her brood lived in one part and he in the other. He had taken the divans, and all the best furniture. In Celina's part of the house the mess accumulated. It always stank of smoke, onions, and the lavatory. A Gentile maid, Hanka, took care of Sasha's rooms. She dusted, washed, scrubbed all day long. The master seldom ate lunch at home. He was always invited somewhere, or else ate in the restaurant of the officers' club. Hanka cooked small meals for herself and sang the day through like a bird. The master occasionally came to her bed at night, but he managed it so she shouldn't become pregnant. He brought other women to the house as well, but Hanka knew it was best to keep quiet about it. She swore by the cross that hung around her neck that she would keep her mouth shut. Hanka had one wish: that Sasha should not marry. She had already made up her mind that as soon as he brought a wife to the house she would curtsy politely, congratulate him, and be off. Now his mother had arrived, not a wife, but she also disrupted the household. Clara sent Hanka on errands, gave her advice on how to run things, and ordered her around: "Don't go there, don't stand here." Hanka was at odds with Celina and her children, but Clara invited these brats with their dirty noses, and their shirttails hanging out, into the apartment. She gave them cookies and wine and ordered Hanka to serve them milk or cocoa. It was an insult to Hanka, but she consoled herself that the fine lady would soon be leaving for America. Hanka eavesdropped when the master spoke to his mother. She demanded money from him. She cried, complained that she hadn't had a real life with his father. Hanka heard Sasha say to her: "You won't last long in America either!"

And Clara had replied: "If that's so, I'll throw myself into the ocean!"

The mistress was in a better mood today. She was sitting on the sofa, one leg crossed over the other, and knitting a jacket for her daughter, Felusia, who had remained in Warsaw with her governess. Hanka kept stealing looks at Clara. She wasn't a stranger, she was the master's mother. She had his eyes, his mouth, the same expression, the same shrewd smile. But how could a woman her age carry on love affairs with someone in America? Apparently Clara sensed Hanka's unspoken disapproval, for she suddenly exclaimed: "Hanka, come here!"

"Yes, mistress."

"Sit down. I want to talk to you about something."

"Oh, thank you, I can stand."

"Sit down on the footstool."

"Thank you."

Clara made a few more stitches, then placing the yarn on

her lap, said: "Hanka, you appear to be a clever girl. Tell me, what do you think of my Sasha?"

Hanka turned red. "Who am I to think anything? I am nothing but a servant here."

"What is a servant? Men are all the same. Give them an ugly queen and a pretty gypsy and you know which one they will pick. Hanka, I am his mother and I have the right to know. How does he conduct himself?"

"Oh, so-so."

"Do women come to him?"

"Sometimes."

"And they stay the night?"

"No."

"Does he sleep with them?"

"Oh, mistress, how would I know? I don't peek through the keyhole."

"When does he go to sleep?"

"Depends."

"Late?"

"Not early."

"And when does he get up?"

"Sometimes he sleeps late. But sometimes he has to get up at sunrise."

"Hanka, you are loyal to him, aren't you?"

"Yes."

"Hanka, a young man his age must not live like this."

"What can I do? I am only a maid."

"Sometimes a maid can also be effective, if she thinks."

"Mistress, he does as he pleases. He takes no advice. Everything must be exactly as he commands, to the letter. I listen to everything he says. Like a trained dog."

"A person is not a dog."

"Yes, but—"

A key could be heard in the front door. Sasha had come home. Hanka leaped up from the footstool and ran back to the kitchen. Until then she had never discussed the master's secrets with anyone, and now she had uttered words that she should perhaps have best left unsaid. The mistress would fight with him, quoting her. Hanka remained in the kitchen, tense, with cocked ears. "Oh, she got everything out of me, the black-eyed beast. He will get angry and throw me out. What will I do then? I've become attached to him, attached to him. I love him, for all his wildness . . . " Hanka felt a strong hatred for this sly woman who was running off to her lover in America and was robbing Hanka of everything—her job, her happiness. What was she to do? Take a rope and hang herself? Hanka heard talking, but she could not make out the words. Mother and son were arguing. Sasha raised his voice. "He may come and beat me—" Hanka said to herself. Once, when she had forgotten something, he had slapped her and pulled her braids. He carried a gun, too. Hanka had a holy picture hanging in the kitchen. She threw herself down on her knees, put her palms together, and began to pray. Afterwards, she tiptoed to the door. She walked silently, her head taut as a hunter's. She heard Clara say: "At your age, one does not give all of one's power to the devil. The stallions that are used for racing are not allowed to go near a mare."

"Mama, I don't want to hear such talk!"

"It's better now than later when you will be left without strength."

"I am as strong as a lion."

"A lion can also grow weak. Remember, my son, this is no small thing. We had a relative who lived in Lomza. He was a Kaminer too. A giant of a man. I used to call him uncle, though he was a distant cousin of Father's. He carried on with all the Gentile girls in Lomza. Suddenly he became paralyzed. The man gives away the marrow from his bones, and the woman takes everything into herself. You know the saying: 'A fool gives, a wise man takes!' "

"Mother, enough!"

"It would be better if you were married. It's all the same to me. I wouldn't mind if you made me a grandmother . . . I won't be here anyway."

"I'll never marry!"

"Why not?"

Sasha was silent for a while. "Rather than have someone sleep with my wife, I prefer to sleep with someone else's."

"For shame, how you speak!"

"It's the truth."

Hanka's eyes filled with tears. He'll never marry! I'll be here forever . . . She began to back away like an animal, before she turned and went into the kitchen. She had already eaten twice that day, but the good news made her hungry. On the stove stood a pot of leftover noodles. She had intended to throw them into the garbage, but instead she began to gulp them down, finishing every last one of them. Then she began scouring the pot with straw and ashes. "I won't let them weaken him," Hanka mumbled to herself. "I'll bewitch him, make him part of my body . . . " Hanka had heard at home in her village of such a love potion: the woman washed her breasts and then used the water in preparing the food of the man she wanted. It was disgusting, but if it helped, it was worth it. Hanka stationed herself before a mirror. For a long while she looked at her own reflection: the straw-blond hair, which here and there had golden glints; the red cheeks, short nose, blue eyes: the full lips that revealed wide teeth, as strong as a dog's. Her throat was white and thick and around it hung a string of coral, a gift from Sasha. Her breasts were so firm they seemed as if about to burst her blouse. "Why did he need those old biddies?" Hanka wondered. "I am prettier than all of them. I am more devoted to him too . . . " Hanka showed herself the tip of her tongue. She laughed, saw that her dimples were still there, and then turned her gaze to the wall, on which hung the copper pans and basins. This very night she would wash her breasts in one of these basins and at the first opportunity would pour some of the water into his soup. . . .

Calman sat in his House of Prayer studying the Mishnah. The day was cold but sunny. A lacework of light and shadow fell across the broad, yellow volume. Calman was reading the *Treatise of Sotah:* "When Rabbi Meir died, there were no more diligent students left. When Ben Zoma died, there were no more expounders. When Rabbi Joshua died, goodness departed from the world. When Rabban Simeon ben Gamliel died, the locust came and troubles multiplied. When Rabbi Eliezer ben Azariah died, wealth departed from the Sages. When Rabbi Akiba died, the glory of the Law ceased—"

Suddenly Calman heard footsteps in the other room. It was not the scuffling of Beila, the maid who came once a week. This was another footstep, long-forgotten yet familiar. At the door stood a noblewoman in a long fur coat, a wide-brimmed velvet hat trimmed with ostrich plumes. He was overcome by the odor of perfume. Calman paled. It was Clara, his divorced wife. For a moment he was unable to speak.

"Yes, it's me. Calmanke!"

Calman trembled. "What do you want?" he asked, choking. He could not catch his breath.

"What is the matter? Don't you recognize me?"

"I recognize you. You mustn't come in! We mustn't be under the same roof!" Calman warned her angrily, observing at the same time that she had aged.

Clara took a step forward. "Why are you shouting? I want to speak to you."

"We must not be under one roof!"

"What shall I do, tear the roof down?"

"We must not be alone together."

"Why not?"

"It isn't allowed! This is a holy place."

"Well, come outside then. Yes, still a fanatic."

"You go first!"

Clara shrugged her shoulders but did not move. He had grown entirely white and once again wore long sidelocks.

Clara could hardly believe that she had once been the wife of this ancient Jew. She felt ashamed, wanted to laugh. After a while Calman opened the door, so as not to be closeted in the room with her. He remained standing at a distance.

"What do you want?"

"I must speak to you."

"Speak."

"I can't do it like this. I can't shout at you. Here is a bench. Sit down and listen. May I sit down too?"

"What do you want? Why did you come?"

"I have an aunt here, and half sisters and brothers. I haven't, God forbid, returned to you, but I must talk to you. Or are you a savage?"

Calman looked around, fearing God and observers. Someone might come in. Mayer Joel, the maid, or even a peasant who remembered Clara. Jampol would have a good topic for gossip. Calman felt himself grow hot.

"You sit there, on the bench."

Clara wiped the bench with her glove and sat down on the part she had cleaned off.

Calman leaned against the oven. "I am sorry, but there is a law."

"Yes, a law. That's the kind of law that causes pogroms," Clara said. "We are still Asiatics. The civilized world laughs at us. But I didn't come to talk about that. I won't try to reform you. Have you become a rabbi? Your beard has doubled in length . . . Calmanke, listen to me carefully! I must go abroad and I am planning to leave Felusia with Celina and my aunt. With God's help, I'll send for her later. It's a question of six months, or at most a year. During that time she must be taken care of. Whatever you say, Felusia is officially your child and you have to pay for her upkeep. I am left without money. You're a pious Jew, to be sure, but you took everything away from me."

"I took everything away? You got twelve thousand rubles as a divorce settlement. You've cost me a fortune. You put thousands of rubles into the manor house and into all those other whims of yours."

"We won't settle accounts now. I could have had everything you see here. I didn't have to let myself be bought off for twelve thousand filthy rubles. But I've done so many foolish things. That was one more. You must take care of Felusia."

Calman grew pale. "Of that bastard?"

He glanced toward the door as if afraid that someone might be listening. A cry seemed to tear itself from his throat. For a second he wanted to run to her and hit her. But he restrained himself. He did not want a scene with this contemptible creature, nor did he want to touch her. She was filth.

"Have you stooped so low?" he rasped.

"Yes, I have."

"To whom are you going? To your lover?"

"Yes."

Calman shivered. His eyes bulged as he looked at her. There was something different about her, a blend of insolence and coarseness in her expression that hadn't been there when she had been his wife. She stared back at him with the viciousness and curiosity with which beasts sometimes examine a human being. This was not a woman but a devil. In *The Righteous Measure* Calman had once read of demons who disguised themselves as human females, lived with men, and even married them. The children they produced were half devil, half man. Could Clara be one of these creatures of the netherworld? Calman began to back away, his legs shaky, his face as white as his beard.

"Get out!" Calman shouted in a voice so loud and harsh that he himself was frightened by it.

Clara burst out laughing. "Calmanke, you really are a fool."

"Get out!"

"Calmanke, I don't need your money. I just came to say goodbye. I'm taking Felusia with me. I wouldn't leave her here for any treasure in the world. She has a rich brother and he loves her. He will provide us with everything we need."

"Why did you come here? To mock me?"

"No. Just to take a last look at you. After all, we're not strangers. We have a son. No power in the world can take that away. I'm not completely well and such a long trip is always connected with some danger. I wanted to see you once again. If you can forgive, please forgive me."

"What use is my forgiveness? You deliberately intend to do an evil thing. Don't you believe there is a Creator who can punish you?"

"Yes, Calmanke, I believe, but my love is stronger even than my faith and my fear of hell. A millionaire asked me to marry him. He was ten times as rich as you've ever been, but I could not stand him. He was too much like me."

Calman shook his head. "Is Felusia Zipkin's daughter?"

"Yes, Calmanke, she is Zipkin's daughter and I am taking her to her father. I have a feeling that I will not live too long and I want the girl at least to have a father. Why don't you get married? What kind of life is this, living here in the wilderness? Have you become a hermit?"

Calman stared at her. His eyes filled with tears. "Clara, it's not too late to repent. I pity you. I pity your Jewish soul. The Proverbs say of the sinner: 'Who confesses and forsakes shall obtain mercy.' "

"What good is mercy? I cannot live without him. I yearn for him day and night. Calman, there is one favor I want to ask of you."

"What is it?"

"If I die in America or on the trip there, see to it that Sasha says Kaddish after me. If he refuses, you say the Kaddish. After all, you loved me once. I loved you too in my own way."

"We could have been happy. But it wasn't destined. I have not deserved happiness."

"Will you do what I ask of you?"

"You will outlive me. But if you don't, I will do it."

Calman covered his face with both hands.

8

I

When Clara was a child, an older female relative had told her a story about a girl who had jeered at a zaddik. The saintly man had pronounced a curse on the girl: she was to remain young forever. All the women of her generation grew old, wrinkled, bent, but she retained her black hair and rosy cheeks. When her husband, too, grew old, she refused to live with him any longer. Her grandchildren were ashamed of her. The young women made fun of her and called her "grandma." Finally her life became unbearable and she drowned herself in a well.

Clara in a way found herself in a similar situation. She was too well along in her forties (how well along, she would not even admit to herself) to have such a young child and to be going off to America to join her lover. Although Calman Jacoby had been too old for her, Zipkin was too young! He wrote her such passionate letters! Clara was somewhat uneasy about the journey in general and about this distant land where it was night when it was day in Poland. Ships did sink. Passengers did become ill, die at sea, and their corpses were thrown overboard. The newspapers were full of such stories. America might be her undoing! Though Clara knew that her fears were all due to nerves, she could not prevent them from dominating her waking hours and even her dreams. To make matters worse, she began to have the early symptoms of menopause.

She felt hot and cold in turn, had flashes and headaches, and tired for no apparent reason. Her corset became oppressively constricting. Although the doctors assured her that these were all normal symptoms of change of life, she began to fear that there might be a cancerous growth in her stomach. In the past Clara had concerned herself little with the possibility of death, but now she was full of worries concerning her health. Women of her age died. They had heart attacks, neurological disorders, gall-bladder trouble. Her own mother had died young. Who knew whether there were good doctors in America? Alexander was virtually a pauper. She would not have a decent place to live. She might even have to work.

Clara had been having her hair dyed for several years, but now, no matter how frequently she had it done, the gray came through almost overnight. What would it be like aboard ship? An ocean voyage took two or three weeks, sometimes longer. Would there be a hairdresser available to do her hair? She would arrive in New York with a head of white hair! She would look more like Felusia's grandmother than her mother!

Luckily, Sasha did not need anything from her. He was, if anything, too independent. She knew he was involved with some of the wives of the officers and officials and that he owned a revolver. God, all the things that came into one's mind during a long, sleepless winter night. One's whole life flashed by, all one's mistakes, all one's foolishness.

Grisha, her first husband, had been dead for so many years, but she still remembered his insults, the names he had called her. She carried on old quarrels in her mind, easily finding the clever retorts she couldn't think of at the time. She settled accounts with her dead father. He had almost literally driven her into the arms of the Russians, from whom he got his contracts. Smirnoff had actually raped her. And then Calman! What had it all meant—fate? Both her grandfathers had been pious Jews. Her father, on the other hand, had been a *maskil*, an enlightened Jew. He had eaten on Yom Kippur and then smoked his cigar. He had used language a man does not use in front of his daughter. Well, let him rest in paradise. But she could not shake off the confusion of thoughts that crowded in on her night after night. Had she had the right to break up Alexander's home? Had it been right to keep him in ignorance of her affairs with the Russians? But such twinges of conscience were more than counterbalanced by the intensity of her desire. Fantasies tortured her brain. Sleep came in fits and starts, filled with spasmodic dreams: a hospital, a funeral, a morgue; or suddenly she would be lying with Alexander, or even with a total stranger who fondled her and spoke to her with words of madness.

One afternoon, on Clara's return from her lawyer's office, where she had filled out passport applications for herself and Felusia (Louisa was a French citizen), Louisa had met her in the entrance hall to tell her that a Monsieur Mirquin was waiting in the drawing room.

"Monsieur who?"

"Mir*quin.*"

Clara burst out laughing at Louisa's pronunciation of the name, with the accent on the last syllable. But when she spoke, she sounded irritated. "Why did you ask him to wait? If I am not at home, then I am simply not at home."

"Oh, madame, he nearly forced his way in. Such a wild Russian!"

"Well, he'll have a long wait."

Clara swept into her boudoir. The ardent wooer! She had developed an aversion to this wealthy man who had courted her in Europe, and was responsible for the break with Alexander. For a time she had heaped deadly curses on him. Still, when he had disappeared with no word at all, it had irked her, and after her return to Warsaw she had been lonely. Often weeks had gone by and the front doorbell hadn't rung. After all this time—Mirkin! What was the saying—sour cabbage doesn't spoil. It had been frosty outdoors. She had had coffee at Lurse's and had done some shopping at Jablokowski Brothers, bringing home a hatbox and a package. Now she stood before the mirror, touching up her hair. Her face was red with cold, and her eyes were shining. She applied a powder puff to her nose and sprayed herself with eau de cologne. Then she took a quick sip from a liqueur flask. What does he want, she wondered. On the way to the drawing room, she noticed the heavy fur coat, plush hat, and silver-knobbed umbrella hanging in the entrance hall.

As she opened the door, Mirkin stood up, a short, thickset man with a tanned face, milky-white hair, and a gray mustache tapering off at the corners. He was wearing a suit tailored in England, a broad cravat embroidered in gold thread, and a high collar. He reeked of wealth, travel, the Riviera. Removing the cigar in its ivory holder from his fleshy lips, he bowed, spread out his arms as if to embrace her, but Clara's look discouraged him. Deftly depositing his cigar on an ashtray, he lifted her hand to his lips. His fat fingers were covered with signet rings. He would have looked distinguished were it not for a grayish film, a cataract, covering his left eye.

"When one waits," he sang out in Russian, "one's patience is rewarded."

"I certainly did not expect you, Gospodin Mirkin."

"Forgotten me already, have you?" he cried hoarsely. "But Mirkin does not forget. If Mirkin likes someone, it's for good!"

"You never even wrote."

"What am I, a writer? I've just arrived on the Berlin Express. Clara Danielovna, you get younger and prettier all the time! Little dove, it's like tasting a delicacy just to look at you." He used the Yiddish word *maachel*, as he smacked his lips and vigorously clapped his hands together. Two links set with large rubies glistened in his cuffs. Clara smiled.

"Compliments so soon."

"Compliments? *Krasavitza!* I speak the truth. Boris Davidovich is no flatterer. With me, everything comes from here." And he thumped his broad chest.

II

Clara decided not to tell Mirkin she was on the point of leaving to join Alexander. He had not stopped talking, and mainly about himself. Yes, he'd been to Carlsbad during the summer: he'd had no choice. You can't fool the liver. If it goes without mineral water even for one season, it lets you know about it. As long as he had been in Carlsbad, why not go to Italy? Nice? Oh, yes. He had only just come from Nice. He was staying at the Hotel Europeiski. His secretary, Yasha? Why, yes, he always traveled with him. Monte Carlo? He had managed to squeeze Monte Carlo in, too. And luck had been with him; he'd won. He chortled noisily. Clara regarded him in open amazement. He spoke like a man who had no idea whatever that there were such things as poverty, sickness, failure, death. "Can he be pretending?" Clara asked herself. He was in his late sixties. Didn't he read newspapers? Didn't he see the obituary columns? He chattered on about an exposition, horse races, some baron or other, a lottery. After a time he began to question Clara. How was her father? Dead? Ah! And that fellow, her friend—what was his name? Oh, yes, Zipkin! Clara was about to invent some story, but instead she blurted out the truth. Alexander, she said, was in New York. She was preparing to go to him. He had been divorced from Sabina. What was he doing? He hadn't as yet fully established himself. He'd been thinking of going into farming. In the meantime he had a modest position and was studying as well. His sister Sonya was with him. She had learned a trade and was working. Mirkin gave a short cough and began to drum on the arm of his chair with his white-bearded fingers. When he spoke again, his voice had the self-confident tone of one who had quickly grasped and assessed a given situation.

"A farm, of all things! Why a farm?"

"His father had been commissar on the Radziwill estates. The farm was part of a collective run by a group that called themselves Am Olam."

"Socialists? Anarchists? I've heard of them. They founded a colony, but nobody wanted to work. They traded wives and went hungry. They ran like mice."

"Really? He's also mentioned private farming. The government offers land to settlers."

"Fantasies!"

"Actually, I'm hoping he will complete his medical studies. He already has five semesters of credit."

"Start now? Well, I suppose it's possible. But it will take an iron will, and money, too."

"I'm afraid he doesn't have much of either."

"Not if I remember him correctly."

Louisa came in and served tea and cookies. Early-evening darkness was filling the room. Clara suggested that she light a lamp, but Mirkin said he loved the winter twilight. It was one of the things that drew him back to Russia. The Riviera was superb, but one tired of it. Nowhere on the Continent was there such snow, such blueness, such stillness as here. True, Warsaw was not Moscow or St. Petersburg, but it was better than Paris. There it just rained and the cold was damp and miserable. One never saw a sleigh. London was simply as dark as Egypt. Mirkin had been to New York too, on business. A cold city, full of drafts. Clusters of houses, without charm, without intimacy. As it grew darker, Mirkin's face was lost in shadow. Clara could no longer distinguish his bad eye from the good one. His voice took on an intimate tone.

"I don't understand you, Clara Danielovna. Truly, *nie poniemayu!*"

"Have you never heard of something called love?"

"Yes, yes, but it must make sense! Let's not deceive each other. You're a mature woman, not a miss of eighteen. A woman of your age and in your circumstances needs comforts."

"True."

"Clara Danielovna, we could both be happy!"

"Are you starting that again?"

"I could not forget you. Zipkin is not for you. Absolutely not. A grown man, but with—what do you call it?—the psychology of a—a *maltshishek*, a boy, nothing more. To start studying at his age! He'll come to nothing. He'll ruin himself and, God forbid, he'll ruin you, too. He should never have left his wife."

"I didn't force him into anything, Boris Davidovich. I left a husband too."

"Is he really the father of the girl I saw in the hallway? She's a beauty."

"She is."

"I realize it's not a simple matter; but still—America? Who goes to America? The American rich spend more time in Europe than at home in the United States. Their children are educated in England. What is there to do in New York? Sew aprons?"

"As a matter of fact, he wants to settle in California."

"California. Well, everything is possible. Clara Danielovna, let's have supper together. Let's go for a sleigh ride."

"We can eat here."

"But we cannot go for a sleigh ride here."

"You haven't changed in the least. I must have a look at my Felusia. And get some light in here. It's snowing again."

Clara rose from her chair and in the same instant Mirkin jumped up from his, caught her in a quick embrace, and kissed her squarely on the lips.

"Boris Davidovich!"

"There'll be enough left for him. We could enjoy ourselves, Clara Danielovna, we could burn up the world! Money has no importance for me. All of Europe is open to us, the whole world!"

"You have a wife."

"A wife? A Xanthippe! There was never any genuine relationship between us. It's all a matter of spite with her, pure spite. She lets herself be led by a band of grasping lawyers. She wants only one thing—money. From the first time I saw you,

Clara Danielovna, that night on the Berlin Express, I have always thought: 'This is she. This is my angel.' "

"That's how you talk about all women."

"Don't insult me. I am no longer young, but my heart is full. One gets lonely, Clara Danielovna. One yearns for youth, the old times. We can go abroad, anywhere—everywhere, alone. A woman like you, my dear, deserves luxury. I'm not happy with my triumphs, that's the truth. I'm not understood. I need someone close, to whom I can open my soul. Most of the little ladies are simply—ducks."

Suddenly he gasped as though his breath had failed him. He lurched forward, pulling Clara to him. He held her pressed against his protruding stomach as in a vise. She tried to struggle free, but it was impossible.

"Please, Boris Davidovich!"

"Excuse me, excuse me. I did not realize—meant no harm. I tried to forget, but it's not easy to forget. I always saw you in my mind's eye—on the train, everywhere. I would still like a few good years—seven good years, as they say."

"And what happens then?"

"You will be provided for. Well provided for."

"I was provided for once before."

"I'm a rich man. I won't take my money with me when I go. My children have not behaved well toward me. They have always sided with their mother. They have made absolutely no effort to see my side. I'm a lonely man despite my possessions."

Mirkin's voice cracked. He was seized by a fit of coughing and pulled out a handkerchief. Outdoors, the street lights went on suddenly and filled the room with bright, snow-reflected light. Mirkin's blind eye blinked rapidly, as though it had seen something frightening.

"Well, well—I'm sorry. Please forgive me."

III

Clara seldom really talked with Louisa, Felusia's governess. For one thing, they had no language in common. Clara's French was inadequate and Louisa's Polish consisted mainly of mispronounced words and broken phrases. For another, Clara found it difficult to understand this French old maid living out her years in solitude, attaching herself to the children of strangers. Louisa could sit for hours at the window just staring at nothing, like a cat. Didn't she need a man? Had she no thought for her old age? She had brought with her from France a cookbook and a "dream interpreter." These two books comprised her entire reading. Nevertheless, now and then she let fall a word or phrase indicating that some process of thinking was taking place in her mind, that somewhere she had retained a vestige of French esprit. On a sudden impulse, Clara decided to take Louisa into her confidence. Louisa knew, did she not, that Clara loved Alexander. But now Mirkin had come back into the picture, desperate, offering to lavish his wealth on her, take her abroad in the most luxurious style. In fact, he wanted Felusia and her governess to join them. What should she do? She implored Louisa to be completely candid. What would Louisa have done in a similar situation? Louisa's dark eyes sparkled.

"I, madame, would go with Monsieur Mir*quin*."

"Even though you were in love with another man?"

"The other need not know. Monsieur Sipkin is in America. The trip can remain a secret. Monsieur Mirquin is rich. Monsieur Sipkin is *très charmant*, but poor as a churchmouse. Madame can arrange things so that Sasha can forward Monsieur Sipkin's correspondence to Warsaw. Madame could send her replies to Sasha, who could put Russian postage stamps on her letters and send them to America. Monsieur Sipkin need never know the truth."

Clara had to laugh. She had never expected such cunning from docile Louisa. Her face, normally placid—if not dull—

had become animated. Her words, accompanied by quick gestures, had spilled out so quickly and idiomatically that Clara had difficulty in following her. There had been a time when Clara could seek advice from her aunt, but the old lady was paralyzed. And suddenly Louisa, without hesitating, had offered a feasible plan. That very day Clara had received a letter from Zipkin: its tone was depressed and depressing. He missed Clara, to be sure, but she had better prepare herself for hardships. He was no longer working at the "shop" where he had been employed, because of a row with the foreman. He hoped to find another job, but there was a Depression—rents were comparatively high, and maids were downright prohibitive. There was no real middle class in America. People were either rich or poor. On his part there was not one bit of good news, but something wonderful had happened to Sonya. Yackiewicz, her friend from Kuniev, had come to New York. Sonya had no idea at all that he was there. Then, quite by chance, they had met at the Yiddish Theater and a few days later had been married. Yackiewicz had a whole circle of friends from Russia, and one of them had given the couple a party. There had been many toasts, plenty of drinking, and much lively discussion. Three days later they were back at work—Sonya making dresses and he in a shirt factory. Yes, things were rather prosaic in New York. The news from the farm in Oregon was not encouraging. There was, it seemed, a wide disparity between theory and practice. As Clara read on, she felt a growing emptiness in her heart. She had not quite finished when the doorbell rang.

Louisa came in and in a conspiratorial tone announced: "Monsier Mir*quin.*"

Mirkin came right in and began talking at once. He had tickets to the opera. First loge. *Rigoletto.* Would Clara come? He wanted to spend the day with her. He had a sleigh waiting outside. His voice was hoarse but strong. He hadn't even removed his fur coat. Eager for her consent, he stood on the threshold in a state of ill-concealed impatience, his fur hat in one hand, a cigar in the other. His face was flushed from the cold. His cataract-filmed eye blinked madly.

Clara raised her eyebrows. "May I change my clothes at least?"

"Every minute is valuable."

"To you—not to me. And if you don't mind, Boris Davidovich, hand your coat to Louisa. You're not a muzhik."

Mirkin was already taking her too much for granted. Still, Alexander's letter had weakened her position—there was no use denying it. She knew she was making a mistake once again to sell herself to an old man. But nevertheless she went off to dress. After all, who was she to be so proud? He could find younger, more attractive women than she. Alexander was totally impractical. She opened her clothes closet and stood there with her hands covering her face. What game was fate playing with her now? Why should this have to happen to her? She summoned Louisa to help lace up her corset. She stood with bared breasts in front of the Frenchwoman while, with deft fingers, she helped her dress, chattering all the while. But only one word registered with Clara: madame, madame, madame. Had the old fox bribed her? First her father had sold her, now she was selling herself. Yes, to be a "madam"—that would be better. Something inside her ached and laughed at the same time. She was aware of her own cheapness. Yes, both Grisha and Calman had been right. She was what Grisha had called her, vulgar. She sprayed herself with perfume and put a chocolate into her mouth. She felt better. What was the saying? If you can't go across, go around.

In front of the house stood a sleigh and two gray horses—not one of the little sleighs one rented for a few guilders to trot around the park, but a baronial equippage, elegantly fitted, with a handsome harness for the horses, brass lanterns on either side, and a bearskin rug to cover the feet. The coachman, too, was grandly uniformed. He cracked the whip, the horses bounded forward, and Clara fell on top of Mirkin. The sleigh went so fast that Clara had trouble orienting herself. The snow had transformed the city. The whiteness was almost blinding. The sky raced past. The houses glided backward. Clods of snow flew from the horses' hoofs. After a while Clara realized that they were on Marshalkovsky Boulevard.

"Where are you taking me?"

"To Wilanow."

"We'll never get back in time for the opera. And I have to change."

"There will be time for everything."

Mirkin was not Zipkin. Zipkin used to pull her into the first half-decent coffeehouse, order a cup of coffee, light a cigarette, and spin out his dreams. Mirkin arranged for everything in advance: the tickets, the sleigh, presumably the restaurant where they were to lunch. He did not need to agonize over every kopeck. Clara laughed to herself. How tightly he held her! And how loud his breathing was! She wondered if he had asthma. It might be better if she turned Louisa over to him. They had left Marshalkovsky Boulevard and were driving along the Mokotow fields—broad and white as far as the horizon's edge. The spirals of blue smoke curling up from the chimneys of the low houses suggested the burning altars of underground temples where idolatrous rites were being performed. The whip cracked, crows cawed, the snow alternately glistened white in the dazzling sunshine and blue in shaded areas that sparkled like closely set diamonds. The entire scene, the snow shapes—dunes, hillocks—awakened in Clara a youthful, half-forgotten lust for adventure. Well, Clara said to herself, I must live. Mirkin held her around the bosom, but she no longer fought him off. He pressed close to her, moved his heavy hand into her muff, breathing like a bellows. Well, he was paying for it. If you eat pork, let the gravy run! She would speak with him openly, have a clear understanding. Alexander? Men demanded chastity from women, but they themselves felt free to do anything they wished.

They did not go as far as Wilanow. A building emerged from the white landscape. It was a restaurant, with a snow-covered emblem over the door. The sleigh glided to a halt, and the coachman helped them out. A heavy door opened, creating a cloud of vapor. The walls inside were decorated with mounted heads of deer, stuffed birds, and a wild boar with long twisting tusks around his snout. It smelled of beer, wine, roasting meats. From another room came a burst of male singing. Clara hesitated on the threshold. It was altogether too Gentile. It was like falling into a robber's den. But the frock-coated headwaiter advanced toward her with an ingratiating smile. Everything was ready—it had all been reserved in advance—the table, luncheon, the wines, the liqueurs. There was a steady flow of plates, platters, glasses, bottles. The caviar was the best. There was lobster. The main course was venison. The rolls were hot from the oven. Mirkin chewed, drank, dabbed at his mouth with his napkin, and held forth about the various dishes. He bent low over his plate, fell on the food like a glutton, and kept refilling Clara's glass. Greed shone out of his good eye—the hunger of those who can never be sated. He perspired, panted, sighed. Clara turned away. She saw herself in him as in a mirror. He wanted to cram everything into the years that remained to him, to savor all he could before it was too late, just as she did.

"Clara Danielovna, I've rented a room upstairs, to rest in after lunch," he said in Russian.

Clara laughed, replying in Yiddish. "Boris Davidovich, you've made your decision without consulting the boss."

Mirkin was about to answer when Yasha Vinaver, his secretary, emerged from somewhere: a small man in a fur coat, a fur hat, a woolen muffler, and ear muffs. His face was round and red like an apple. He smiled joyfully and stretched out his arms and fur-gloved hands as if to embrace Clara. The waiter tried to take his hat and coat from him, but Yasha Vinaver seemed not to notice him.

"What is he, a spy?" Clara said to Mirkin.

"Not a spy, Clara Danielovna, my gracious lady, but your most devoted friend and admirer," Yasha Vinaver said. "You have become younger, madame, and even more beautiful, a splendid picture of feminine charm! Unbelievably beautiful! It makes my heart jump just to look at you!"

"You'd better check your coat and hat," Mirkin said.

"What? Of course! When I saw you, Clara Danielovna, I forgot about everything. I became, as they say, dazzled by your radiance . . ."

And he went to the checkroom.

He's Mirkin's spy. He will tell Alexander, Clara thought to herself. She suddenly knew that the pair had conceived some plot against her. Mirkin's visit and Yasha Vinaver's appearance had been arranged for some evil purpose. She had been trapped. She became both angry and frightened. She looked at Mirkin reproachfully and asked: "What is this comedy all about?"

Mirkin's healthy eye, behind its white brow, became round and gay. The eye of a pig, Clara thought.

"There's no comedy, Clara Danielovna," he said protestingly. "I love you and want you. It's as simple as that."

9

I

Years back, after Lucian had been caught by the police and the Warsaw press was regaling its readers with the details of the murder he had committed, how he had tried to rob Chodzinski, taken Kasia to the home of the Bobrowska woman, and abandoned his wife and child in the middle of Christmas dinner, it seemed to Felicia as if the world was ending. Articles about the crime by reporters and feature writers were spread over entire pages. They improvised and wrote deliberate lies. A noble Polish name was being disgraced and there was no one to prevent it. Could this be the behavior of a Christian country, Felicia kept asking herself. It was clear to her that everyone was enjoying her anguish—the police, the judge, the prosecutor, even her own maids, whom she had fed and clothed. Her husband, Marian, had begun to lose his aristocratic patients. Helena wrote from Zamosc that her children were ashamed to go to the gymnasium, because their Uncle Lucian was a murderer. Felicia locked herself in her boudoir, refused to come out, and wept. When she did come out, it was only to go to a church where no one knew her. She sank down in front of the statue of the Holy Mother, where she knelt praying for hours.

She stopped eating and couldn't sleep at night. She began to look drawn and anemic. Marian dosed her with all kinds of medicines, but she grew worse. She felt sorry for her husband. He, too, began to look thin. He had had to advance huge sums to the attorneys, pay for the victim's burial, support his widow and her orphans. Marian's earnings had fallen off and his savings were being depleted. Felicia became convinced that her death would free Marian from an intolerable burden, that she was only an obstacle to him, and she prayed to God to take her without delay. She could no longer satisfy Marian's masculine needs, and she was prepared to step aside for a younger, more attractive woman.

There were days when it seemed to Felicia that the end was imminent. She lay in bed hardly able to move a limb, dozed off, awoke, dozed again, only to awake once more with a start. She had nightmares in which she saw devils and angels. She saw in turn her dead father and mother. She saw colors of such luminescence that they could only be of heavenly origin. She smiled inwardly. How foolish man was to fear that which would deliver him forever. The soul only began to live after the body died. She begged Marian to buy a plot for her in the cemetery, order a coffin, and select a tombstone. Every time she suffered a spell of nausea and her head began to whirl, she would send for the priest to hear her final confession.

"A bit premature, my dear," Marian would remark. "You're getting better every day."

It developed that Marian was right; God was not quite ready to accept her. She began to sleep a lot to make up for all the wakeful nights of the past, and was assailed by hunger so ravenous that it was enough to cancel out all the days she had not eaten. But what had she to live for? What was there still for her to accomplish on this earth? Suddenly she saw her mission—she would be a mother both to Lucian's children and to the murdered janitor's orphans. What would become of them if she were to die? Marian would not for the rest of his life pay for the sins of his miscreant brother-in-law.

The answer was so simple that Felicia could not understand how she had not thought of it during all her months of illness.

Now that she had a purpose, she stifled her shame and visited Wojciech Chodzinski's widow in her cramped hovel. At first the woman drove her away. Wojciechowa's sons threatened to beat Felicia up.

"Get the hell out of here!" they screamed. "You lousy murderer's sister!"

They set the dog on her and threw sawdust and stinking rags at her. The girls insulted her, and her gifts were thrown back in her face. There was a moment when Felicia decided to leave the miserable household to its fate; instead, she mustered every ounce of strength she had. How would the good Lord Jesus have acted in such a case, she asked herself. What would the holy St. Francis have done? Would they have let themselves be driven off by taunts? She fell to her knees before the orphans, showered them with money and clothes. She even tried to help Wojciechowa with her washing, and it was the mother who was the first to be won over. Gradually, one by one, the children made peace with her. Who would have believed that after such rebuffs Felicia would meet with success? Even the dog ended by nuzzling her shoes and wagging its tail.

It took eighteen months for the case to come to trial. During this time Felicia clothed Wojciechowa's children, packed the little ones off to school, got the older boys apprenticed so they could learn trades, and sent the girls to work in decent homes. At first Marian laughed at her, called her a fool and a hypocrite. Like many liberals and radicals, Marian did not believe in philanthropy. Reform was what was needed! It was the government that must be forced to set up democratic institutions and thus bring about equality for the masses. What good was charity? But in time Felicia's goodness had its effect on him. He offered to help. Felicia did not stop at the janitor's family. She was prepared to take on Bolek, Lucian's illegitimate son, and Kasia as well. But Bobrowska had taken Kasia and her little boy under her protection. They moved in with her, and Bobrowska would have nothing to do with Lucian's sister.

As it turned out, Felicia's actions helped not only the murderer's victims but the murderer himself. The ladies of Warsaw began to talk about the Christian mercy Felicia had shown. Word of her deeds reached the prosecutor, the judge himself—a Russified Pole. Priests read sermons about the unhappy Lucian and his ordeal. Articles appeared in the press. Aristocratic ladies who had stopped using Zawacki's services returned to the doctor. And when Felicia was called to testify at the trial, the same reporters who had originally maligned her now described her as a martyr. She began to receive invitations from charitable groups that counted ladies of the highest society among their patrons. Lucian had faced twenty years at hard labor, or even life imprisonment. The judge, however, imposed the minimum sentence under the charge. Privately, he confided that he had been swayed not by the arguments of the counsel for the defense but by the sister of the accused—her words, her manner, her tears.

II

At the time of the Polish uprising against the Russians, Lucian had devised for himself a foolproof method of withstanding suffering—he would tell himself that he was dead. Each time that he was faced with an unendurable situation, he would imagine that he was no longer among the living, he was a ghost, a corpse, free of all hope, all need. He had heard about the living dead, those tormented souls who wander about in limbo unable to find refuge in their graves. He imagined himself to be one of them. He had read about fakirs who, in a state of self-induced catalepsy, let themselves be buried alive. Had not all his life been a futile struggle against the forces of darkness? Had not malevolent fate hung over him right from the start? Could the strange events of his life be explained in any way other than that he had been born under an evil star? Lucian had felt the hand of destiny while still a boy, the spoiled young panicz of the manor. He had been given everything:

clothes, weapons, food; the love of his parents, his sisters, his brother. The servants idolized him; the peasants fondled him; even the animals—dogs, cats, horses—were especially affectionate toward him. Nevertheless, the object of all this adoration suffered so miserably that even as a boy he had thought of shooting himself. He contracted every childhood disease and as an adolescent developed all kinds of phobias. He blasphemed against God and ran to the priest to confess. He stole, spat on sacred pictures, throttled chickens like a polecat, tortured rabbits. He had no inclination whatever for study but was adept at devising stratagems for avoiding it. Lust for women seized him early. He was afraid of contagious diseases, scandals in the family. Having read in an encyclopedia about consumption of the intestines, he promptly convinced himself that he had it. His mother mentioned an instance of insanity in the family, and he was seized by panic, certain that he was becoming mad. As far back as he could remember, he had always had a foreboding of some approaching catastrophe.

Catastrophe came soon enough with the uprising against the Russians. He roamed the forests, suffered hunger, cold, dug graves for friends. His father was exiled to Siberia and he himself was sentenced to death *in absentia.* Then the hiding in Warsaw, working in the furniture factory, moving in with Stachowa. Later his elopement with Miriam Lieba and starvation in Paris, his disillusionment with the Polish colony in France, his subsequent return to Poland, the entanglements with Kasia, Bobrowska, and the rest. The years had run by like a bad dream. But what had been the point of it all? And why had it all ended in the stupid murder of a poor janitor, the father of ten children?

In the long months in prison awaiting his trial, Lucian had groped for some answer, but this riddle had no solution. His life had been a crazy amalgam of bad luck, vicious circumstance, poor nerves, weak character, and lack of will power—one dreary waste. But then, weren't the lives of others—of the entire human species for that matter—just as chaotic? Felicia had sent him a Bible in prison, but, bored as he was, he had not been able to read it. The Jehovah of the Old Testament played cat-and-mouse with the Israelites. They were always being insubordinate and He was always punishing them. The New Testament promised bliss in the Kingdom of Heaven, but what guarantee was there that such a kingdom existed? Had not the Popes themselves carried on murderous wars? Had not the Russians, Prussians, and Austrians—three Christian nations—torn Poland to pieces, hanged men, whipped women, committed countless crimes? Would they have done these things if they truly believed in God and the teachings of Jesus?

Life was so senseless that death, by comparison, made a great deal of sense. Lucian entered into his death fantasy so wholeheartedly that it almost became true. He reached a state very like the Nirvana he had read about many years ago in his father's library. The examining attorney had had no difficulties with him. He had confessed everything, signed every paper placed in front of him. He had even told them about his plans to organize a Polish crime syndicate to rob Wallenberg. The lawyers retained by Felicia later pleaded with him to retract his admissions, but he would not hear of it. The other prisoners in his cell jeered at him and he took their mockery in silence. He was prepared to accept his fate, whatever it might be—to die on the gallows, to rot in Siberia. He lay in his bunk, ate the pasty bread and watery grits, patiently suffered the cold, the heat, the stench of the urinal, the filth all around him. The thieves and murderers who were his fellow prisoners played cards, smoked cheap tobacco, sang maudlin tunes about love and the women who betrayed it, about the convict's sad fate and his hopes for freedom. But Lucian felt no such sentiments. He had lost interest in the world, with its illusory joys and pretensions.

The trial was almost a *cause célèbre*. The newspapers published long accounts of it. Artists came to court to sketch Lucian's portrait. Ladies fought for tickets of admission. But none of it had an effect on Lucian. He barely heard the witnesses' testimony, the arguments of the prosecution, or even those of the defense counsel. Nor would he exercise his prerogative to make a final statement. When asked by the judge if he had anything to say in his own defense, Lucian had replied, "No, thank you. Nothing."

At the trial's end, however, something began to stir in him. The prisoners congratulated him and the guards squeezed his hand. For the first time that he could remember since his childhood, he was enjoying some prestige. A Jewish book dealer on Swiętokrzyska Street had published what purported to be Lucian's life story in a series of weekly brochures that sold for one kopeck an issue. The prison warden had summoned Lucian to his office to show him the brochures, and the warden's wife had come to see the hero of this odyssey in the flesh. The naïve woman had taken for truth the fabrications concocted by the author. When Lucian had tried to tell her he was neither as heroic nor as despicable as the brochure depicted him, the good woman begged him not to destroy her illusions.

Gradually life in prison came more and more to resemble life outside: it was trivial, monotonous, filled with futile hopes and senseless wranglings. Lucian took up cards, smoked Majorca tobacco, and waited for packages. Felicia came to see him and they conversed through the bars. Bobrowska sent him notes that a bribed guard wedged into Lucian's bread ration. From these he learned that Kasia had left Chodzinski and together with Bolek had moved in with Bobrowska. Bobrowska was teaching her to sew. After a time the letters stopped coming. Lucian learned through the grapevine that Bobrowska was again seeing her former lover. He was directing plays in a summer theater called Pod Lipkom. Lucian surmised how Bobrowska had gotten the old rake to come back to her; she had probably offered him Kasia.

III

The convict in the next bunk, Wojciech Kulak, was chewing on the heel of a loaf of bread and from time to time he spat. He was short, broad-boned, snub-nosed, with a long upper lip and the slanted eyes of a Mongol, an impression strengthened by his shaved head and yellow complexion. His nicknames were "Tatar" and "Chink." He was doing time for murder, and he had four more years to serve. He was also a *przydupnik*, or pimp, and still retained a partnership in two houses, one in Szylce, the other in Tamki. The madams brought him packages. Wojciech never lacked tobacco or the numerous other amenities that money could buy. He was paying monthly retainers to the guards and to the warden himself. He was regularly supplied with vodka, sausages, roast duckling. He received a steady flow of mail but couldn't read, so Lucian became his "interpreter," as Wojciech called him. For this he received Kulak's protection against the toughs and bullies who extorted weekly tribute from the more docile inmates. Everyone knew that Kulak kept a curved Tatar knife in his cell, and he had been heard to boast about a loaded revolver hidden away somewhere. In a fight, Wojciech seldom used his hands. He butted with his head, like a bull, or kicked with his heavy wooden shoes. He was afraid to hit with his fist, he said, because it was like delivering a death blow.

"Hey, you crapulous count!"

Lucian was silent.

"Hey! Lousy squire!"

It was early afternoon of a summer day, but the cell was dark. The bars were covered with wire meshing that cut off most of the light. Only on the cracked plaster of one wall was there a feeble play of sunlight. The ceiling was crisscrossed with massive beams. The outer walls were so thick that the tiny window was little more than a niche. Both Lucian and Kulak wore the regulation gray cotton pants and short jackets. Kulak had taken off his shoes and his enormous toes were as long as a man's fingers. He was reputed to be able to cut bread with them, and even roll a cigarette.

"Hey, you three-groschen aristocrat!"

Lucian had learned that in prison you don't answer the first or second time, not even when addressed by Kulak. The ones who jump at the first peep are the greenhorns, and usually all they get for their pains is an insult or a crude witticism. A seasoned convict pretends not to hear when spoken to, at least not until he feels like talking. Kulak, it appeared, had something to say.

"What is it?" Lucian finally asked.

"What are you thinking about?"

"Nothing. Nothing at all."

"Women, eh?"

Lucian smiled. "Can we help ourselves?"

"Don't get too deep into that mire; you can lose your mind, and then what? A little won't do you any harm, but too much and a screw goes loose or you burst a blood vessel."

"Let it burst."

"What are you gonna do when you get out? Thought about that?"

"No, haven't decided yet."

"What are you gonna do with that bitchy grandma Bobrowska? Let her live?"

"I don't want to end up back here."

"Afraid, eh? Wetting your pants, aren't you? Not me. I'll have somebody's guts. I'm gonna use that knife."

"They'll have you back here in no time."

"Not me. I was too damn hotheaded the last time. I let somebody have it in front of witnesses. This time it'll be a nice quiet job, I'll take him into the Praga woods. We'll eat, drink, chat, real chummy. Then I'll say to him: 'All right, my friend, you sang your little song. Cross yourself, you're going back to God.' Then, right in the guts."

"They'll nab you sooner or later."

"Crap. They don't nab so easily. Even when the cops suspect you, what can they do? I deny the whole thing. You, my noble sir, are afraid of a little persuasion. They slap your rear and you tattle on your own father. I can take a blow. If I keep my mouth shut they can't pry it open with hot pincers."

"In the meantime you're back rotting behind bars."

"How long? They can't just hold you, they gotta let you go. That's the law. We know the goddamned code better than the lawyers. A trial is a trial. And we know what to do when some bastard starts blabbing. We pack him off to the other side, and to make sure he gets there we put him in a trunk. Understand?"

"It doesn't pay. For that moment of revenge the price is too high."

"A preacher, huh? Then what the devil did you go chasing Chodzinski for? Why did you hang around with all that scummy bunch? You're gonna be one of us, all right."

"No, Kulak. I'm not going to spit out my lungs behind bars."

"What are you gonna do?"

"Go away somewhere."

"Where? What are you gonna live on?"

"Find something, some kind of job."

"Like what? What are you good for? You have delicate little hands. Nobody would trust you with a broken shilling. Where would you go, to the caves of Lucifer?"

"To Corsica. Maybe Sicily. Maybe California."

"And do what?"

"Buy a piece of land. A little house."

"And do what with the land? Cultivate it with your snout?"

"Oranges grow by themselves. You don't do any cultivating. You have a few hundred trees and all you do is pick the oranges when they ripen. You sell them and have your livelihood."

"Sure, sure, it's so simple a kid can do it. You're fooling yourself, my friend. They're waiting for you just like that?

There were three hundred Polacks on a boat headed for America—and thirty-one croaked on the way. It was in the papers. The food was all maggoty. They weren't even sent off like Christians, just thrown to the fish."

"Well, once you're dead it doesn't matter too much whether you're fodder for worms or fish."

"Once they get there—the ones that get there—they're sent down to the coal mines. The mine caves in and they're choked by gas. Sure, I'm no scholar, but I know what's going on. They got a Depression there, that's what they got."

"Still better than to rot here."

Kulak thought for a while. "You think I like it here? Every day is like a year. The goddamned honorable judge says: six years, six nice little years. To talk is easy, little father, but to sit in this pen is another thing, especially in this hot weather. You want to get out in the country, find a nice little pond and dive in—I can swim like a fish. You want to go to bed with someone. And what's wrong with dropping into a tavern and siphoning off a few mugs of beer? This is a dog's life. I lie in my hole and get all kinds of crazy thoughts. Hey, you. Nobleman! I want to ask you something."

"What now?"

"You believe in God?"

"Absolutely not."

"Then who made this swinish world?"

10

I

Lucian was released from prison in mid-May. Felicia, in her husband's carriage, waited for him at the prison's back gate. Although the weather was warm, Lucian appeared in a heavy overcoat, a pair of cracked shoes, and a faded derby. At first, sister and brother did not recognize each other. To Lucian, Felicia looked like his mother. Dressed in black with a veiled hat, Felicia was still mourning for Miriam Lieba. Her blond hair was shot with gray. Lucian had grown thin, jaundice-yellow, and there were threads of gray hair at his temples. Brother and sister embraced. A small crowd of curiosity-seekers had assembled at the prison gate. The coachman brandished his whip and the coach trundled into Iron Street and from there down Grzybowska Street—to Kreditowa Street. Lucian had recognized neither Warsaw nor Felicia's house. On Krolewska Street and Marshalkovsky Boulevard he had noticed horse-drawn trolley cars. He got out of the carriage and walked quickly through the gate of the building where Felicia lived. The maid had already opened the door to the apartment. No one saw the ex-convict as he dismounted and climbed the front stairs. Dr. Zawacki happened to be away from home that day. Wladzio and Marisia, Lucian's children, were at school. Janina, the daughter of the janitor whom Lucian had shot and whom Felicia had adopted without Lucian's knowledge, was also out. Felicia had prepared a room and clothes for Lucian. He went into the bathroom, where the fire already burned in the stove for heating water. On a bench lay underwear, a bathrobe, and a pair of new slippers. The tiled bathroom had a white marble bathtub. Lucian smiled to himself as he scrubbed his body with a sponge and scented soap: "If only Wojciech Kulak could see me now . . ." He dried himself with a Turkish towel and put on the bathrobe and slippers. In his room he found a summer suit, a straw hat, a linen shirt, a stiff collar, a silk tie, and a pair of shiny new shoes. One could apparently get everything ready-made in Warsaw now as in Paris. Felicia had even remembered to supply suspenders, cuff-links, garters. He stood at the window facing the courtyard. The servant girl who had let him in came up with a sack to remove his old clothing. She took it directly to the trash bin.

Everything took place quietly. He dressed and his appearance was completely changed. It was not more than two hours since he had left the prison, yet it seemed as distant as if it had happened years ago, or as if he had read about it in a book. Standing before the mirror, he hardly recognized himself. He felt the cleanliness of his shirt, the fresh underwear and socks. The shoes were so light that he seemed to be barefoot. The straw hat fit.

Felicia opened the door and cried, "My dear!" in a whimpering tone.

Taking his arm, she led him to the dining room. Lunch was usually eaten at four o'clock, but a second breakfast had been prepared for Lucian. A cook in a short apron, with a white cap over her blond hair, came in, and the maid, too, fussed about him. The table was covered with a white cloth. There were fresh rolls in a straw basket, milk, sour milk, white cheese, Swiss cheese, and a vase full of flowers. Was it like this every day or was it a holiday? In the years of his imprisonment he had forgotten that such things as saltcellars and flowers existed. He had almost forgotten how to cope with a napkin and the silver. He smiled at the servants, winked, but they looked embarrassed and did not smile back. Felicia asked if he wanted tea or coffee. When he had indicated his preference, she turned to the cook and said: "The Count will have coffee."

Lucian nearly burst out laughing. "The Count, of all things!" He ate and tried to remember his manners. One must not grab. One must not chew noisily. It was not proper to finish every last bit on one's plate. But he was hungry. The rolls were insubstantial, melted in his mouth. The fried eggs only increased his appetite. "Well, I'll not perish from hunger!" He drank the coffee and his head spun as if from liquor. He became sleepy and began to yawn, covering his mouth as he had been taught as a boy. Felicia nodded her head at him with motherly devotion. At first he had thought she reminded him of his mother; now she seemed to resemble their grandmother, whose picture had once hung in one of the manor living rooms.

"You're tired?"

"Yes, tired."

"Go to your room and lie down."

"Yes, I'll take a nap—" He spoke in the same plebeian, good-natured tone as Wojciech Kulak.

Felicia escorted him back to the room where he had previously changed. Only then did he notice the bed: two spotless pillows, a red satin blanket in a lace coverlet. A portrait of Lucian as a mischievous boy, painted by a French artist, hung over the bed. It was all too good to last.

"Shall I undress or lie down in my clothes?"

"If you're sleepy, undress. You still have three hours before dinner, and Marian may be late. He has a lecture—"

"Well, thanks."

Felicia threw him something like a kiss. Lucian began to undress. He was no longer accustomed to suspenders, a collar, cuff-links. The collar buckled. A cuff-link fell out of a cuff. When he finally lay down on the bed, he felt an odd sensation: he seemed to be sinking into a downy bottomlessness. He felt as if he were floating. Everything was too clean, too light. He was sleepy, but he could not sleep. "Is it still the same day? How can one day be so long? Am I really free?" In prison when Lucian had dreamed of the day he would be free, he had always imagined a tavern, noise, prostitutes, music. But Felicia had brought him home like a student from a boarding school. Acacia trees faced the window. Across the way, someone tinkled on a pianoforte, the notes blending with the song of a solitary bird. It was quieter here than in prison. "Is this happiness?" Lucian asked himself. "Did it pay to have dreamed of this?" No answer came to him. He closed his eyes and slowly fell asleep.

II

Lucian dreamed he was back in prison. There was a fight between Wojciech Kulak and another inmate. Someone drew a knife. Lucian awoke, frightened and lustful. He had long ago observed that dreams of murder provoked his lust. Was everyone like this? Or only he? Sitting up, he wiped the sweat from his brow. He had spent years in prison, had had innumerable thoughts, but had come to no decision. He had had many plans: to emigrate to America or Corsica, to become a monk, to settle on a couple of acres in Poland, to go to Siberia. But what he really wanted to do still escaped him. There had been fantasies too—to rob Wallenberg, to take revenge on Bobrowska's lover, to join the rebels who wanted to overthrow the Czar and abolish wealth. He had also dreamed of joining the underworld, Wojciech Kulak's gang. . . . What hadn't run through this mind that for years had had eighteen hours out of every twenty-four to brood in. . . . Sitting in bed now, Lucian yawned, stretched. All his emotions became entangled within him: fatigue, lust, embarrassment at the thought of meeting his brother-in-law, his own children. And Felicia had mentioned that she had adopted a girl. What girl? "Why would she adopt a girl if she already had Wladzio and

Marisia?" He had bathed, was clean, but he itched and had to scratch himself. He had an ache in one ear, felt a drawing sensation in a back tooth, a nostril was stuffed as if he had a cold. His hair, cut short across his skull, prickled. "Ah, the devil! This swinish life!" he muttered. "I must go to a brothel this evening!" Suddenly he burst out laughing. He recalled the day a new convict, a boy of seventeen who had slain his own mother, had come into the cell. Wojciech Kulak, the beast, had raped him that very night. . . . "Swine, real swine!" Lucian said to himself, "Life was raw there without hypocritical masks!" A shiver moved down his spine: an icy thread, zigzagging from nape to pelvis.

Someone knocked. Lucian had forgotten what to reply. "Well!" he called out.

Felicia opened the door. "You aren't sleeping? Dinner is ready."

"All right."

"Lucian, dear, I must tell you something." Felicia became grave.

"What is it?"

"I've told you that I adopted a girl. Her name is Janina. I want you to know who she is. I don't want any misunderstanding to arise."

"Who is she?"

"The victim's daughter. I had to do it. She's a fine child."

"What victim?—Never mind, I understand."

"The others I placed in jobs, but Janina is an able, noble girl. She is a good student. Outstanding. It would have been painful for me to place her in domestic service. She has forgiven you. She's a true Christian soul and has become so fond of your children that she's like a blood sister to them. More than once it was she who brought you packages where you were. I wanted to write to you about it, but then I thought it would be better not to."

"Oh?"

"Well, say something. I hope it doesn't bother you."

"Why should it bother me? People like me are used to everything."

"I had to expiate the sin. Perhaps that is why God heeded my prayers. . . ."

"It's all right."

"Don't remind her of anything. Above all, don't indicate that you know who she is. Certain things must not be said here."

"Yes, certainly."

"What's wrong with you? Are you still sleepy?"

"No, I'm not used to white bed linen."

"My poor brother! You've suffered enough! You've paid for your mistakes. May God fill your heart with good thoughts!"

Felicia's face grew blotched. Tears ran down her cheeks. Not having a handkerchief with her, she closed the door and went off to cry in another room. Lucian got out of bed. The soft mattress had made his bones ache. He clenched his fists and breathed deeply. He had an urge to spit but dared not stain the floor here. He wanted to use obscene language, to argue with someone, to curse. It was too refined here, too quiet. "It's not for me!"

He had learned stunts from Wojciech Kulak. He lifted his sock with his toes and brought it to his hand. Once more he had to put on the stiff collar, the tie, fuss with the collar pin, the cuff-links. "Filthy business! Worse than leg irons!" Lucian growled. "I have a scar on my Adam's apple already!" He began to yawn all over again and at the same time poked his finger against his chest. He had accustomed himself to the prison chamber pot, but this convenience under his bed looked too elegant. Was it porcelain? There they would have wanted to eat from out of such a fancy vessel! . . . Lowering his head, he meditated. Miriam Lieba was dead. He hadn't seen the children in years. Felicia had sent him photographs, but it wasn't the same thing. What did she say? The victim's daughter. "Well, who cares?" Lucian went in search of the drawing room or dining room (he had forgotten the arrangement of the apartment). He opened a door and saw everybody. Marian Zawacki did not seem old, but the two ruffs of hair on either side of his bald head were gray. Wladzio had grown half a head taller than Lucian. He resembled his mother, but everything that had appeared delicate, sad, sickly in Miriam Lieba looked masculine, strong, and youthfully brutal in him. He had flaxen hair cut in a brush, steel-gray eyes, and an upturned nose. He wore a school uniform with a high collar. He was to graduate from gymnasium in the summer. He stood up and walked over to his father. There were dimples in his rosy cheeks when he smiled. He kissed Lucian without saying a word. Beside his son, Lucian felt small and old.

"So, this is the way you are!" he said. "All grown up."

"Why not? Time doesn't stand still." The boy laughed.

"Do you remember him?" Marian Zawacki asked the boy.

"Of course. He once took me to the Lazienki Park and we ate at a table outside. He bought me a hoop. Do you remember?" he said, turning to Lucian.

"No, I don't remember. But I have a poor memory. Children always remember."

"I even remember Paris."

"That's impossible. You were three years old when we returned from Poland."

"I remember. The train and everything else. Father doesn't believe me. . . ."

Wladzio grew red. He had become accustomed to calling Marian Zawacki "Father." But now that their real father had returned, Felicia had instructed the children to call Zawacki "Uncle" and her "Auntie."

Marian Zawacki, after kissing Lucian on both cheeks, took hold of his arm and said: "Well, you're looking fine."

Marisia was four years younger than Wladzio and resembled Lucian. She was small, somewhat dark, with brown eyes. Her brunette hair was plaited in two braids. Not yet fourteen, she was already as reserved as an adult. She grew cinder-red, facing her father, smiled timidly and made a sort of curtsy. Lucian was immediately taken with his daughter. He kissed her on the temple, took her by the hand, and did not know what to say. Finally he said, "You're a pretty girl."

"Not so pretty."

"You look like your late grandmother, my mother."

"Yes, so Mother says. I mean Auntie . . . " And Marisia grew even more confused.

Janina, the daughter of the janitor, had also risen from her seat. Although she was dressed genteelly, Lucian recognized the peasant in her. She was a girl of seventeen, broad-boned, with a red face, protruding cheekbones, a round nose. There was a rustic amiability in her watery eyes. She reminded Lucian of the country girls who herded geese or goats. It was hard to believe that she was as adept at her studies as Felicia boasted. Her hair, put up in braids on each side, was straw-colored. Marisia had narrow hands with long fingers (Felicia had mentioned that she excelled on the pianoforte), but Janina had the wide hands of a servant, her arms covered with freckles. Around her throat, above the high bosom, was a string of coral. Felicia introduced her, "This is our Panna Janina."

Lucian extended his hand. The girl blushed furiously.

I am going to sleep with her, Lucian immediately decided.

III

That final morning Wojciech Kulak had reversed himself and given Lucian a lesson in self-control. "Don't go to that Bobrowska woman or to the other one. You'll kill one of them, and then what? You're too hot-blooded. If you've hidden a gun somewhere, forget about it. Men like you can't stop going 'bang, bang!' " He then gave Lucian the address of a friend of his on Marienstat Street, where there was a coffee shop and a brothel. He gave him the password and even recommended a one-time sweetheart of his own. "I'd rather it were you than others—" But Lucian did not go there. Instead, he went to Marshalkovsky Boulevard and from there to Iron Street. He stopped at a train crossing where for a long time he stared at the passing cars, the locomotives, the rails, the switches. Freight trains went by loaded with lumber, coal, naphtha. Whistles blew, grubby workers signaled with flags and lanterns. Chimneys belched smoke, steam. Lucian longed to be on a train going somewhere. But he had neither passport nor money. He turned back toward the city. Bobrowska's house was located between Lucka and Grzybowska Streets. The building had the same fence, older now, sagging, and broken down. It had been snowing the night he had left there. Now through the open gate he saw a pair of barefoot children, playing in the dusk. Suddenly a familiar figure approached. It was her walk, not her face, that he recognized. Kasia. She was dressed city style—without a shawl, in a calico dress, high-heeled shoes, and carried a basket. She had grown taller, broader, and wore a chignon like an older woman. How was this possible? How old was she? He stationed himself at the gate. Still she did not recognize him, but said, "Excuse me," as she was about to pass him.

"You're excused," he replied, not moving.

Kasia looked up at him and froze. "Lucian!"

"Yes."

"God in heaven!"

She could not speak, moved her hand as if to cross herself, but managed only half the gesture before dropping her hand again.

"Yes, it's me," Lucian said at last. After some hesitation he added: "I'm not exactly dead yet."

"When did you get out? You had another year or more."

"There was an amnesty because of the Czar's birthday."

"Oh, yes."

"Well, how are you? How is Bolek?"

"Bolek is a big boy. A real student. Goes to school. Every day but Sunday."

"Every day? What else? You've become a seamstress, have you?"

"Yes."

"Don't tremble. I won't kill you. I'm not even armed," Lucian said, astonished at his own words. Kasia was standing before him, pale, open-mouthed. She kept shaking her head.

"Oh, how you scared me!"

"You must have a bad conscience if you're so nervous."

Kasia didn't seem to understand. "You look so nice. Elegant!" she said.

"But not as elegant as that old goat Cybulski," Lucian blurted out, again surprising himself.

Kasia retreated a step, looking grim. "I must go in."

"Is he waiting for you?"

"I bought something for the house."

"What did you buy?"

"Thread."

"Thread? I won't do anything to you, you needn't be so afraid. I only want the truth."

"Yes, the truth." And Kasia looked as if she had swallowed something.

"Who drove you to all this?" Lucian whispered. "The old fool or you yourself?"

Kasia looked behind her. "We can't talk in the street," she murmured.

"Sure we can. Speak frankly."

"It just happened. You went away and we were left like orphans."

"Who is this 'we'? That slut, Bobrowska?"

"All of us. He was so friendly . . . He is such a good old man . . . He brought presents: sausage, whisky, this, that. We thought you'd never get out of that place alive."

"Oh."

"And there he was, so jolly. Joking about everyone. He promised to help the child and all of us."

"What else?"

"That's all."

"How do you manage this? All three of you in one bed?"

"What? God forbid!"

"How then?"

"Nothing."

"I want the truth!"

"He is so old. Perhaps seventy. He only wants to pat and kiss. Sometimes he pinches or tickles. Bares his soul. His life often is so bitter—"

"What's so bitter about it?"

"All sorts of things. He was driven out of the theater. The big one with the pillars. He started to drink. And he is Bobrowska's old friend. From way back, and—"

"And what?"

"Nothing."

"You love him?"

Kasia was silent.

"Speak! I'm asking you something."

"No. Yes. He's like a good grandfather. To the child and to everyone. Comes in and shakes his cane. Not to hurt anyone. Just like that. For fun. Then he starts looking through his pockets. For you a gift, and one for you. An anniversary or a birthday. Spends money. Sits down and makes himself comfortable. Speaks like a common person—one forgets he's a nobleman."

"A nobleman? Well, what else?"

"Nothing."

"And all this with both of you?"

Kasia did not answer.

"Have you lost all shame?"

"No. What are you talking about? I don't know what you mean."

"You know. I could kill you even though I don't have a weapon. I could throttle you right here and now. But I won't. All I want is the truth."

"I've told you the truth."

"You're pregnant by him?"

"Pregnant? No."

"You've completely forgotten me, haven't you?"

"I didn't forget. May God strike me! I thought of you every day. I lit a candle for you to Saint Michael. We knew you still had a year to serve and we've had bad times. People talk too, point at us. Someone put it in the paper. The women don't order new dresses but turn their old jackets inside out. Bobrowska got a needle through her nail and the nail had to be removed. She was afraid it was infected and the finger would have to be cut off. And then he came, a good person, and took her to the doctor. The doctor prescribed a salve and it healed. He took Bolek to school, bought him books, pens, a penholder, a briefcase, spoke to the teacher. This and that. Here are three rubles—to your good health. He isn't earning money now, but he saved it from the good years. A devoted person, even though he's old."

"And what else?"

"That's all."

"Is he there now, upstairs?"

"Upstairs? Yes, I guess so. He was supposed to come."

"I want to see him."

"Don't start a fight."

"A fight? If I wanted to, I'd squash him like a bedbug. All of you. But I don't intend to. I always hated that bitch Bobrowska, and you're a stupid peasant, worse than a cow."

"Don't say such things. God will punish you."

"Well, let's go!"

IV

Lucian opened the door and took in everything at once. Bobrowska, Cybulski, all the new things in the house. The windows were hung with embroidered curtains, the walls freshly painted. There was a cheap rug on the floor. Several prints hung on the wall: King Batory, King Sobjeski, a hunting scene with dogs. Cybulski sat on a new upholstered chair. Lucian recognized him. He had occasionally given Lucian a walk-on part. But in the years of Lucian's imprisonment, Cybulski had grown old, stout, potbellied. The hair on his big head was long. Dressed in an alpaca jacket, a soft collar with a wide, black silk tie, a golden chain across his silver-embroidered velvet vest, beardless and without a mustache, he looked at first like an old woman. He had a loose double chin with barely any neck. Large pouches, and beneath them smaller, wrinkled ones, hung beneath his olive-brown eyes. His pipe lay on a tray. Cybulski had apparently just finished telling a joke, for he was laughing, and all his pouches, folds, and wrinkles were shaking, and his silver-speckled vest was heaving. Bobrowska seemed both younger and older. She reminded Lucian of a warmed-over loaf of bread. Her hair was grayish, but her round face was less drawn than previously and it was heavily rouged. She was wearing a pink robe and mixing some batter in an earthenware dish. The first to speak at Lucian's entrance was the parrot. Emitting a shrill scream, the bird seemed to have recognized him. A frightened smile spread over Bobrowska's face. Kasia came in behind Lucian. Cybulski stopped chortling, wiped away his tears, and became grave and sad.

"Jesus Maria! Lucian!" Bobrowska cried out. She lifted the spoon out of the bowl and a chunk of the soft yellow mixture fell to the floor.

"Yes."

"How did you get here? Adam, look! Kasia! . . . Oh, children!"

"Don't spill the batter. . . . Yes, here I am. You didn't expect me, did you?"

"Oh my, whom do I see! Kasia, where did you find him? When were you freed? I can't believe it! As if fallen from the sky. Just today I was thinking about you. Kasia, you are a witness. I opened my eyes and said: 'Such a hot day and the poor fellow can't even cool off there. . . .' Adam, you remember him? You gave him a walk-on part. What was the play called? It's slipped my mind. Oh, what a surprise. When did you get out? We thought you still had another year in that hell."

"I was included in the amnesty."

"What amnesty? A miracle! How well you look! Magnificent! Kasia, why stand there like a dummy? Take this mess away from me. I was going to fry some pancakes. You remember Pan Cybulski, of course?"

"Yes, certainly, I remember. I've had the honor."

"Well, why stand at the door? A guest in the house, God in the house. And such a guest! If I'd known, I would have had flowers. Made a parade for you . . . as they say. Oh, what am I talking about? I'm completely confused. You look young, like a young prince! . . . Kasia, why don't you move? At least get a chair so he can sit down. Take this spoon from me. Poor me, I've lost my head. . . ."

Only now did Bobrowska approach Lucian. She moved mincingly, with half-outstretched arms, her glance one of sluggish doubt, as if she did not know whether to embrace him or not. Lucian backed away, saying: "Don't go to any trouble . . ."

"How else should we greet each other? I stand here with my head full of worries. I haven't been well, lately . . . arthritis. . . . The doctors have told me to go to Czechocinek to take the salt baths. . . . Suddenly he drops in like an angel. . . . Well, where is the chair? Wipe it off, Kasia, he'll soil his suit. How nicely you're dressed and how well everything fits you! When you went away it was wintertime and God's world was all snow and ice. Like my own heart. . . . You look good, but a little sallow. Don't tell me you've already eaten. I really want to fry these pancakes and I seem to remember that they are your favorite dish."

"I've eaten supper. I'm not hungry."

"Not hungry? Well, sit down, anyhow. My hands are a little soiled with eggs and flour. That's why I can't embrace you. Kasia, why don't you wipe off the chair?"

"With what? The rag is wet."

"Oh, you're such a child. Wipe it with whatever is handy. With your skirt. . . . Come closer. Don't try to tell yourself we've forgotten you. We talk about you, we two women and your little son as well. He's sleeping. He's already a grown boy. We've a new room, chopped through the wall of your alcove. That's where he sleeps and does his homework. Draws, writes—everything as it should be. I could kiss every one of his fingers. He's asleep already, the mischiefmaker. He's your son, your son! You men know each other, shake hands for me too."

"I remember the Count. He acted with us," Cybulski said in a rasping voice. He laughed as if he had made a joke. What began as a giggle ended in an asthmatic rattle with a falsetto echo as if he had two voices.

Lucian bowed. "Yes, I've had the honor."

"Certainly, you acted. Not any big parts, but you showed talent. What was the play called? An adaptation from the French, I think. In those days the theater still had a normal aim—to entertain the public, to educate and amuse at the same time. In our new era of empty positivism and so-called constructive work, they want to turn the theater into a university, a university of pedantic pomposity and false didactic with all the disadvantages of a university but minus its advantages. But what it tries to teach, no one knows, because it is all empty gestures and hollow phrases. One cannot, I say, teach merchants to keep their books in order and save capital if it isn't as natural to them as it is to the practical British or the money-minded Prussians. We Poles were always epigenous in every sphere, and as soon as we hear of a wedding somewhere, we try to dance at it. Our critics always burn their lips sampling foreign dishes."

Cybulski laughed. For a moment his face was radiant with a kind of joyful vindictiveness. He had, in the past years, suffered much from the critics. He had been forced out of the regular theater, and even the plays he had produced in the summer theaters were torn apart by the reviewers.

Lucian looked at him in surprise. "You are mistaken. Obviously you think I am someone else. I didn't have any roles. I was only a walk-on several times. . . ."

"Yes, you played. A walk-on? Elzbieta, this is a misunderstanding. You yourself recommended him. I remember as if it were yesterday. What was the part? An *amant!*"

And Cybulski again burst into laughter. His eyes filled with tears.

V

"You babble about art, you old dog," Lucian said to himself, "but your only comfort in life is an old bitch and a young peasant. . . . Someone shamed your swinish honor. . . . I remember when you yourself stepped on others. You came to rehearsals eating oranges and shouting: 'Begin again!' 'That's not the way to kiss!' 'A man betrayed doesn't speak that way!' 'That's not the way to walk!' 'That's not the way to stand!' Now the critics have knocked out your teeth and you've become softhearted." Lucian felt no anger toward him. This evening he had attained, he felt, an objectivity he had never known before. He was suddenly overcome by tedium. "Well, so he's sleeping with Kasia. Who cares? It's all a bore. Even more so than prison. . . . What is he, after all? A pompous windbag. One squeeze from me and he'd be done for. I could kill him simply by yelling."

He heard Cybulski say: "This cult that has formed around Modrzejewska is simply barbaric. She has talent, yes. But she isn't the only actress in Poland. Kochanska has more talent, and there are others equally gifted. This, my dear Count, is idolatry. They are engaged in a contest to see who can flatter best. May the ladies and gentleman excuse it. The expression is 'kissing the behind.' But why kiss a behind even if it belongs to a genius? Aren't all behinds alike? The mob must always have heroes, idols, and when none exists, one must be created. They take a dummy and put a laurel wreath on him—"

"It's all very clear," Bobrowska interrupted him, at the same time fussing with a pot. "The men begrudge each other, terribly! And whatever bit of praise they have must be lavished on a woman."

"There's a system in this," Cybulski continued. "Wickedness, that's what it is. They raise one to the skies, the better to flatten the others. From the Christian standpoint this is simple idolatry."

"Who takes Christianity seriously?" Lucian asked. "Isn't the Pope himself a sort of idol?"

"Well, my dear Count, let's not go too far. Without the Church it would be worse, much worse. I'm an old man already with one foot in the grave, as they say, but somewhere within me there's still a desire to devote my last few years to our faith. The Church must have a leader; otherwise it becomes a headless institution like Protestantism. Even the Jews have a miracle rabbi, a sort of elder priest of the Sanhedrin, or whatever they call it these days. In religion, one law is supreme: if you sin, you've sold your soul to the devil. When you repent, God will forgive you. But in the theater there's no law. That's the horror of it. You produce a play, put work into it, knowledge, your best efforts, and an ignorant puppy makes a joke of it. With one smear of his pen, you're finished. These people have no code in their death dealings. They are like those ancient Chinese rulers, boys of five, who would pick names out at random, and have the bearers beheaded. In Poland, my dear Count, the anarchy of primitive man rules."

"You, my dear Adam, take opinions too seriously," Bobrowska interjected again.

"Too seriously? What do theater people have besides opinions? What's left of my life but reviews? I have pasted everything in a scrapbook and that is, so to say, my estate. A writer leaves behind books, a painter—pictures. What remains of us? Time devours us like a wolf."

"And what remains of all other people?" Lucian asked, just to say something. "I have but one ambition: to live in the present. After I die, they can throw me to the dogs."

"And how can one live in the present, surrounded as one is by evildoers? I don't sleep well, my dear Count, and I have time to think. What separates these people from the underworld? They have the same morals, perhaps even worse. What the others do with a knife, they do with a pen. Throw me to the dogs after death? They throw me to the dogs while I am still alive. Not only me. Today one man devours another. It's a system. You lie down to sleep and I'll bite off your ear. . . . It hurts? Don't scream, because it's not manly. Where does it all come from? From man's abandonment of religion. I myself was an atheist in my younger days. We toyed with so-called progress. But one may shudder at the results. Your sister, my dear Count, has reached heights. I envy someone like her more than all the Modrzejewskas and Kochanskas or whatever they call themselves. Your son, Bolek, is a decent boy, pleasant, good-hearted, and with a mind of his own. Well, how did all this come about, if I may ask? One survives everything."

"Yes, one survives. In prison we say: 'Sooner or later you get out: either on two feet or in a coffin!' "

"Well, we should celebrate this occasion. Unfortunately I'm not permitted to drink. Health reasons. But we must have a taste of something nevertheless. Elzbieta—"

"Yes, I'll get it. There's still some vodka left from last time. Well, I'm not prepared at all. Where did Kasia go? Probably to get Bolek. She shouldn't wake him. It's not healthy for a child. Why don't you say something, Lucian dear? How was your day?"

"Oh, just a day. In the morning I was there and now I'm here."

"May I ask if you've already seen your sister?" Cybulski said after a while.

"Yes, she was waiting for me at the gate."

"Indeed! A marvelous person. Elzbieta and I are, so to say, old friends. Maybe even before the Count was born. Oh, what have I said? Women are, after all, always young. They never grow old, ha, ha. . . . There were all sorts of disagreements between us, but we never broke off completely. I mean—our friendship. What she did for Kasia is virtually noble. Pure altruism."

"Please, Cybulski, don't praise me."

"I'm not praising. There's good in all of us. I've always dreamed of rising above all the filth in my old age, of saving a few thousand rubles and settling on a small estate. As soon as one is surrounded by trees and sky and hears God's birds, the city, with its false ambitions and imagined accomplishments, disappears. But some accursed souls must suffer this stench to the bitter end. Everything, as they say, slipped through my fingers. I spent all my money. I didn't understand that thrift can be a great virtue, not for philistines, but especially for people like me. Well, these days I direct plays for the summer theaters and I'm not even sure it will continue. They want to take everything away, down to the last drop."

Bobrowska clasped her hands together. "Oh, Adam, what's happened to you today? You're usually so gay."

"Occasionally these things must come out. You, Count, must excuse me. It's time I left."

"What's wrong with you, Cybulski? I'm about to make pancakes."

"No, I just don't feel right. My stomach. Give the guest your pancakes."

Kasia came in from the alcove.

"I'm going, Kasia, my love."

"Why? It's not late yet."

"I didn't sleep much last night. That happens sometimes. My dear Count, don't take offense. I'm an old man, and the foolish things I've done and do are a result of loneliness."

"Yes, I understand."

"God meant man to be miserable, particularly in old age." Cybulski rose.

"Well, where's my cane?"

"Why run away? Kasia, hand him his cane. Take a droshky, absolutely!"

"Yes, I'll take a droshky. Well, we'll be seeing each other. Would you like to come to the theater, Count? It's actually in a garden, but a theater is a theater. There's one trouble with the open sky—no gallery, except perhaps for the angels. . . ."

And Cybulski again began laughing and raised his cane as if to poke someone.

"Good night!"

VI

"What happened? Why did he run away?" Bobrowska asked when Cybulski's footsteps had died away. "He's so sensitive! Old age has suddenly hit him. It's not time so much as the insults he's received. He worked for so many years and suddenly they spit in his face. Well, the spitters themselves won't rule forever . . ."

"If he went off on account of me, I'm sorry," Lucian said, knowing that he wasn't sorry and was speaking without conviction.

"On your account? Why? No, he suffers. He's an abandoned old man. At least he has a little money. . . . He's not entirely a pauper. Usually he's gay. He even jokes too much. Well, tonight is your night, Lucian. Kasia, why hide in a corner? Go to him, sit next to him. Don't be embarrassed. After all, you're the mother of his child. . . ."

"Bolek's sleeping. Shall I wake him?" Kasia asked.

Lucian placed his chair so that he faced Kasia. "No, don't wake him."

"Do you know what? I'll go off somewhere," Bobrowska offered after a pause. "I can let this batter go. Unless you want pancakes, Lucian?"

"Me? No."

"It won't spoil. I'm due at a customer's. I'll be back in a couple of hours and meanwhile you can talk things over."

"Where are you going?" Kasia asked distrustfully. "Who is the customer?"

"Oh, what's the difference? You don't know all my customers. Don't think I've told you all my secrets. I have a little pile somewhere, ha, ha. . . . One thing, children, don't argue. Lucian, she hasn't done anything to offend you. I say this sincerely."

"Nothing?" Lucian said. "What more could she have done other than enter a brothel?"

"What are you saying? He's an old man. Tell him, Kasia, tell him. Why should he think God-knows-what?"

"I've told him."

"What did you tell him? Well. . . . People like you, Kasia, spoil things for themselves. I want nothing. I'm not young any more. A little cheerfulness and a good word—that's all I care about. Cybulski is an old friend, even from the time that Bobrowski, may he rest in peace, was living. He loves Kasia like a daughter. He once kissed her on the forehead, but that's as far as it went."

"She herself says he slept with her."

Bobrowska stared with crooked, tearful eyes. "She said that?"

"Yes."

"Why did you tell lies?"

"I didn't say that."

"You did say it!" Lucian said. "Don't take back your words!"

"I'm not taking them back."

Bobrowska made a gesture as if to roll up her sleeves. "What did you tell him?"

Kasia was silent.

"Did he sleep with you or not?" Lucian asked without anger and with an expression of disgust.

Kasia's face became downcast. "In the beginning."

Bobrowska glared at her. "If that's true, then the two of them have fooled me."

"I didn't fool you. You knew about it. You talked me into it yourself."

"*I* talked you into it? Well, that's the gratitude one gets from people like you. He became sick and couldn't go home. He had to sleep here. That night he was more dead than alive. When did all this happen? Unless when I went out of the house. Of course, you're no minor. You already had a child by then. I talked you into nothing, and I don't want you to spread slander about me. A peasant remains a peasant. If you want to confess, go to the priest. I tell you what! Both of you go, and take your child. I haven't the strength any more for such mixups. If this is the reward for kindness, I'd rather be left alone with four walls."

Lucian stood up. "I'm going."

"You can take her along. I rescued her from the dregs. You went to prison and she was left with the boy at God's mercy. Her father, Antek, drank. He helped out with an occasional ruble, but as time went on, he gave less and less. His own woman deserted him. Everything fell on my head. She learned to sew a little from me, but she's no seamstress, can barely thread a needle. For what she's cost me, I could have hired a skilled seamstress. Isn't that true, girl?"

"It's not true. You sent me on all sorts of errands and I never saw a penny. Papa, Antek, paid. The Countess, Lucian's sister, sent money and you used it to buy a machine."

Bobrowska flared up. "Is that so? You filth, you ungrateful wretch! You lousy bitch! I owe you something, do I? Lucian, you did me a great favor. You went off to kill a man, and you left this bitch with me. Well, I've had enough. If you feel, you pig, that I've used you, go away and never come back. I'll be frank about what concerns you, Lucian! With people like you, one never knows. I don't want any problems or complaints. You're both young, but my spirit wants peace. Cybulski is good to me, a friend, as they say, from my youth. He also can't take troubles. He changed when you came in. His heart is weak—"

"If he has a weak heart, let him go to a doctor and rest under an eiderdown instead of chasing after women. And don't be afraid. I won't come again."

"You'd better take Kasia and your son with you. With things as they are, she'll only be a burden to me."

"Where can I take her? I don't have a home."

"Take her. You need a woman. At worst, she can be your maid. There isn't any work now anyhow. I hardly have enough for myself. After all, you made her unhappy. It's your child, your flesh and blood. This, I hope, you won't deny. I'll tell you the truth: Cybulski is clumsy. He's like a cripple. He lives with people, but they exploit him. He was about to move in, but now he'll be afraid to, poor thing. When you came in, he grew white as chalk. He began to talk as if it were a funeral."

"What was he afraid of, the old son-of-a-dog? I wouldn't kill someone like him."

"See, you're starting already. Kasia, why do you stand there like an idiot with your mouth open? I'm not throwing you out, but you'll have to go. Understand, it doesn't have to be this very night. I'll go out and you talk it over."

"What have we to talk over? Perhaps he has nowhere to go himself," Kasia said, and seemed frightened at her own words. "If you don't want me, I'll get a job."

"Who'll give you a job with a boy? They investigate you."

"I'll find something. At worst, I'll go to my papa's. He won't drive away his grandchild."

"A fine home for a child! Well, you're the parents and I'm a stranger. I love him, he calls me Grandma, but everything has changed. What do you say, Lucian dear? Or maybe I shouldn't address you informally any more?"

"Speak as you please. I'll take Bolek away from this house. You needn't worry. But I must have a few days."

"A few days won't make a difference."

"Well, I'd better go," Lucian said.

"Already? If you want to spend the night here, you can. It's all up to you. I can go away somewhere, or make myself a bed in the workroom."

Kasia suddenly took a step forward. "No, it isn't necessary."

"Are you ashamed?" Bobrowska asked.

"No, I don't want to!"

"Well, I won't force you."

"She is in love with the old man," Lucian said, feeling both disgust and amusement. He went to the door, raised the latch, and spoke. He seemed to spit the words out between his teeth: "I'll take the child, but I never want to hear from either one of you again. If you should run into me on the street, cross over to the other side. You're worse than dead to me!"

He slowly closed the door behind him and descended the rotting steps. On the other side of the gate, Lucian paused for a moment. His eyes narrowed and he muttered: "Well, I've survived this too." The taverns were already closed. Across the way, near a gate, a whore in a red shawl loitered. Lucian took his watch (the same one that he had worn that Christmas night) out of his vest pocket and looked at it under the street light. He could go home to Felicia, Zawacki, the children, or to the address given him by Wojciech Kulak. But he had no desire to go to either of these places.

TWO

II

I

Clara lay in bed, propped up by three pillows. Her hair was white, her face jaundice-yellow. Louisa too had turned gray, and Felusia had already begun to attend a gymnasium. For the thousandth time Clara scanned a bundle of letters that had also turned yellow. She read bits here and there. Louisa brought in some medicine and a glass of water. Clara took the medicine, grimaced, and drank the water. For two years she had been suffering from gallstones. She had been to several doctors, but her condition had worsened. Three specialists, in a consultation, had decided that an operation was necessary. But it was a dangerous one. Who would take care of Felusia if Clara should die? The girl had a rich brother, but what a pity it would be if she had to spend her adolescence in Sasha's wanton house. Perhaps Alexander would take her to live with him in New York, but he now had another wife and a child. He had finally succeeded in becoming a doctor. Although he did not write to Clara, he kept in touch with Felusia and sent her an occasional present. His name and address were printed on his stationery. He lived on a street called East Broadway. After her second adventure with Mirkin, Clara had received what in effect had been a final letter from him. In substance, he had written: "I want to forget. I beg of you—don't open old wounds."

Well, Clara had failed. Twice she had been on the point of marrying Alexander, and each time it had been Mirkin who had interfered. Mirkin was dead and he had not even mentioned her name in his will. Nor had his fortune been as great as had been supposed. It was thought that his secretary, Yasha, had robbed him. Clara had long since decided to blame no one. All her mistakes had been of her own doing. Besides the men whom she might have accused of having wronged her—her father; her first husband, Grisha; and Boris Mirkin—were all dead. Calman was an old man. Running into him in the street one day, she had barely recognized him. He seemed shriveled up. He had shuffled along, supporting himself with a cane, and looked like a beggar. As for Alexander, it had been *she* who had treated *him* unfairly.

When one lies ill in bed and no one comes to visit, one must think about something. When there is no future, the mind turns to the past. Occasionally Clara would ask Louisa to bring her the albums which she had kept since her girlhood. But indulging in nostalgia brought her little joy. Only now could she see how much mockery there had been in the notes and compliments of her fellow students and the Russian officers who had done business with her father. But Zipkin's letters still rang true. Even his reproaches were genuine. How he had struggled on his arrival in New York! What resentment he had had against the city! He had tried to settle in Oregon, in California, and had planned to return to Europe! At one point he had even been close to suicide. "What use is my life now that I no longer have any ideals, no hope of improving the human condition. I long for you, Clara. I know that it would be bad for me to be with you, but without you I am as if dead." "My only consolation is reading. There is a large library here where one can read free. I read so much, I'm afraid of ruining my eyesight." "Oh, Clara, if you were only here and we could walk together in Central Park on Sundays, or go to the country for a weekend." "Here, Clara, one can travel from the Atlantic to the Pacific, from parts of Canada that lie close to the North Pole, to Argentina, which is not far from the South Pole!" His letters were full of impossible propositions—that they live in a cabin in the woods, or settle somewhere in British Columbia, that he become a hunter in Mexico or Brazil. These dreams ended when he became involved with a schoolteacher; she and Sonya helped him through medical school. And finally he became what he had planned to be from the beginning—a doctor.

Clara tried to visualize America, New York, East Broadway. How did things look there? Were the houses like those in Warsaw or Paris? And the trains that "ran above the rooftops"? What were they like? Was Central Park similar to the Saxony Gardens? Clara imagined Alexander living in a house twelve stories high, overlooking Central Park. An express train ran above the level of the roofs, and Americans, Negroes, Chinese, Spaniards, and Jews milled about in the street below. Everyone was shouting. New York was a masquerade ball, an eternal carnival. Alexander wore a top hat and spoke English. He stepped out on his balcony and looked at the Atlantic Ocean. Ships from different countries floated by—from India, China, Japan, Europe. On the docks, tea, coffee, sugar cane, and furs imported from Siberia by Mirkin's children were being unloaded. Ladies rode by in carriages. Gentlemen tipped their top hats. Sailors went in and out of a small house with red lanterns. The sound of music, laughter, dancing, shouting, came from within. There were the great Broadway theaters, the circuses, the cabarets, the restaurants, and the Metropolitan Opera, where the most famous singers of Europe performed.

Yes, if she had not been foolish she might be there now in that glittering part of the world, in that house on East Broadway. She saw herself sitting with Felusia and Alexander in the balcony and through binoculars inspecting Central Park, the Atlantic Ocean, and various islands. After dinner, Felusia would do her homework and Alexander would take Clara to the opera. Then they would return home to bed. How did a

New York bedroom look? In New York, she would not be suffering from gallstones. Zipkin would have diagnosed her illness at an early stage. It wouldn't have happened at all; heartbreak had made her sick. She had read in the newspapers that women remained young in America. Sixty-four-year-old women carried on with young men while receiving alimony from their millionaire husbands; four hundred dollars a week. . . . Even Sonya, a naïve Sonya, had become rich in Columbus's country. Her husband, Yackiewicz, the former socialist, had opened a ladies' clothing factory. A childish thought occurred to Clara: did such factories have tall chimneys?

What was the use of dreaming? She was in Warsaw. Whatever Sasha did not give her, she did not have. Felusia was growing up without a father. Clara was ill. Dying? She didn't fear death. But what about afterwards? What happened when the soul left the body? Did heaven and hell actually exist? Would devils place her on a bed of nails or hang her by her breasts? Would she fly through wastelands pursued by snakes and lizards? Clara had more than once considered doing penance. But how did one repent? She wished she had asked Calman. Sasha had promised to say Kaddish for her. But could he be relied on?

Clara closed her eyes. She placed Zipkin's letters beneath her pillow. The doctor had spoken to her frankly. He wanted to operate but was uncertain of the outcome. She had developed a weak heart.

II

When Clara was well and mingled with people, she seldom dreamed. Now that she had been bedridden for weeks, dreams attacked her like locusts. Even before her eyes closed, they began. Again she was with Grisha, her father, Alexander. At times she imagined herself living in a palace with Calman, but instead of being her husband, he was her father-in-law. The palace became confused with Alexander's house in New York.

Jampol and New York became one. Russian officers marched under the elevated trains. There was a ball. Clara danced more gracefully than anyone. Her feet were light, without substance. Suddenly she rose from the floor. All the dancers stopped, stared, pointed. Clara floated in the air, slowly, at an angle like a bat. The music played on. Through the open windows the Atlantic Ocean could be seen, its waves roaring and splashing. They rose so high it was hard to see why they didn't inundate the shore and flood Alexander's drawing room. "God in heaven, I'm flying!" Clara said to herself. "One can fly without wings. . . ." Clara opened her eyes and saw by the clock that she had been asleep five minutes.

Louisa came in—short, gray.

"Your medicine, madame!"

"*Merci beaucoup.*"

"Would madame like a glass of tea?"

"Not now. In the bookcase there is a thick book with a lock. Would you please get it for me?"

"With the gold-tooled back? The prayer book?"

"Yes, how do you know what it is? It's in Hebrew."

"Oh, madame, I know everything."

Louisa brought the siddur that Calman had given Clara as a wedding present. It had been gathering dust for years. Clara had often wanted to throw it away or give it to a synagogue but somehow hadn't done so. The prayers were translated into Yiddish. She had studied Hebrew as a child and so she knew the Hebrew characters. She began to read a prayer: "God Almighty, I, Thy servant, stand before Thee with a broken heart and on shaking knees to pour out my prayer to Thee. Who am I to open my lips to Thee? I am only flesh and blood, steeped in sin, befouled by countless transgressions. But Thou, Father in heaven, are full of forgiveness and mercy, and Thou dost not disdain the supplications of a pauper—listen to my cry, Father, collect my tears in Thy gourd and remember that we are only dust, a dream that vanishes, a shadow that dissolves and a flower that withers. It was Thou, Father, who breathed a soul into our nostrils and gave life to our limbs. We are truly the instrument of Thy hands. . . ."

There had been times when Clara had laughed at such words. She even used to mimic women making the benediction over the Sabbath candles. God forgive her, but she had even done so in front of Gentiles. But now Clara could no longer mock the holy words. True, the language was old-fashioned, but the content was true. Isn't man sinful? And doesn't he truly resemble a shadow that vanishes or a flower that withers? How much Clara would have given to know that there was indeed a God in heaven. But according to her father, heaven was empty. A balloon had risen high above the clouds and its passenger had seen nothing but space. Alexander had told her the same thing. The earth, he had claimed, had existed for millions of years and no one had created it; it had torn itself away from the sun and had gradually cooled. After death man was no different from a cat or dog: the worms ate him and he vanished. If that were so, then what was the point of life? Wouldn't it be better not to have been born? . . .

Clara put the book away and turned her face to the wall. How long would this continue? How long would she have to endure this pain? Would anyone accompany her hearse to the grave? Sasha traveled frequently. When she died, he might be somewhere in Russia. Would someone notify Alexander? She would be buried near the cemetery fence and no one would know she had ever existed. And what if they *did* know? What good would it do her if she were buried in the first row and had a marble monument with her name engraved on it? If man was no better than a dog, let him be forgotten.

III

But Clara improved, recovered almost completely. The doctors warned her to maintain a strict diet: eat on time, chew well, and avoid fat. Thank God the pains and pressure had stopped. Louisa no longer had to heat a brick and place it against Clara's stomach. Clara got up, dressed, and immediately began to eat whatever she pleased. Why should a fat piece of meat be worse than a lean one? How could the stomach tell whether something was boiled, broiled, or fried?

During her illness, Clara had come to a decision. When she thought she was dying, she had worried continuously about Felusia. What would become of the girl without either father or mother? Clara had determined, should she get better, to take Felusia to Alexander. In New York, Felusia would have a home, perhaps even go to a university for women. In addition to wanting to provide for her daughter, Clara had for a long time yearned to see that fabulous country. She had no intention, God forbid, of taking Alexander away from his wife. She would buy a round-trip ticket for herself and leave her daughter behind in New York. The question was what to do with Louisa on her return. Clara had discussed everything with the Frenchwoman and she had agreed to remain in New York with Felusia for a few years. If Zipkin did not want to take the girl into his home, Louisa would find a job and visit the child on her days off wherever Clara settled her.

Clara burst into tears at Louisa's devotion. The American climate might be advantageous for gallstones. Perhaps Clara herself would remain a year or two. She no longer had any ties in Warsaw. Sasha was a grown man. He had neither the time nor the patience for Clara. Months passed without his coming to see her. Why should she remain on Berg Street and pay nearly thirty rubles a month rent?

She wrote a long letter to Sasha. He immediately came to pay his mother a visit. Sasha was of medium height, broad, and wore sideburns and a mustache. He had left his grandfather's house to Celina and had had one built for himself not far from the manor. The estate was now leased to him for the next ten years. He had even forced his brother-in-law out of the mill. Mayer Joel had moved to Warsaw and opened a flour store. Sasha rang the bell. Louisa, having opened the door, tried to kiss him but was pushed aside. She stank of garlic. Besides, how long could one go on kissing Nanny? The floorboards creaked beneath him as he walked. He glanced into a mirror, saw that a lock of his black hair lay across his forehead, and pushed it back. He wore an English suit and shoes made by the best shoemaker in Warsaw. He had a diamond stickpin in his tie, and diamond links in his cuffs. A two-thousand-ruble ring sparkled on his left hand. He opened the door to his mother's bedroom.

"Sashenka! . . . Dearest! . . ."

Sasha could hardly endure his mother's kisses either. He placed his foot on a chair and said: "When do you go? How much do you want?"

"Heavens, just look at him! Look at how quickly he wants to get rid of me! Sit down. Eat something."

"I've eaten like a hog. I must go soon."

"Where? I thought you came to see me."

"Yes, but . . . I have a hundred errands. Do your doctors permit you to go?"

"I haven't asked them."

"Well, you're a mature woman."

"You look splendid, but a little fat."

"I'm always hungry. I'll give you two thousand rubles. Will that be enough?"

Clara's eyes grew moist. "What a question! I don't need that much."

"I don't want my mother to want for anything. If it isn't enough, send me a cable."

"God keep you well."

"Stop blessing me. You're not a grandmother yet. What are you trying to do—take Zipkin from his wife?"

"Are you crazy? With this head of white hair? I want Felusia to have a father. I wrote you about everything."

"Well, so be it. With a sister in America, I'll have an excuse to go there. One needs someone to visit. Travel first class. Do you get seasick?"

"How do I know? I've never traveled on the ocean."

"Well, in a good cabin one suffers less."

"If only I could live to see you married," Clara blurted out. Sasha was silent a moment. "You want to be a mother-in-law, do you?"

"I want you to live like an adult, not run around like a boy."

"What difference does it make? Whether I sleep with one woman or ten, my health is good."

"Please, my child, don't talk like that."

"Mother, the world is meaningless. Everyone is false, greedy. Why be tied down when it's possible to be free? If I told you how I live, you'd laugh."

"What's there to laugh about? I understand love, but promiscuity is no good."

"Why not? It's insane to live with one woman, stagnation. Actually, the more there are, the better it is. Women are arrogant, but when they know they can be changed like a pair of gloves, they behave like lambs. I'd rather have one suit and fifty women than one woman and fifty suits."

"Where did you learn to talk like that? You're really a good person. You just don't know what love is. When you fall in love with the right girl, and she with you, you'll know what you've been missing. Where are you off to?"

"To the daughter of a general."

"A widow?"

"No, she has a husband."

"That's terrible. Does it pay to risk your life?"

"I don't risk my life. I carry a revolver. Life must be exciting. If not, it isn't worth a cartridge of powder. . . ."

IV

Clara wasted no time. She applied for a passport and gave her apartment to Sasha. He visited Warsaw frequently. Why should he pay for hotel rooms when four rooms with all conveniences were available? She took Felusia out of school and hired an English tutor to prepare her for the visit to her father in New York. Clara intended to surprise Zipkin and so she did not let him know she was coming. Everything moved smoothly and quickly. As soon as the passports arrived, Clara and Louisa began to pack. There was actually no one to whom she had to say goodbye. Her aunt, Celina's mother, had died. Clara was not friendly with her neighbors. She kissed Sasha and wept. "If I should die on the way," she said to him, "hire a Jew to say Kaddish for me."

"Don't worry, Mama. You'll live."

Sasha was leaving for Russia and could not accompany his mother to the station.

Clara, Louisa, and Felusia rode in one droshky, their luggage followed in another. Clara had bought round-trip boat tickets at an agency on Nowa Senatorska Street. The travel agent had telegraphed ahead to reserve hotel accommodations in Berlin, where they were scheduled to spend a night. Clara was astonished. It seemed only yesterday that she had been lying in bed making plans, and now she sat in a second-class compartment of the Berlin Express. Since the train was en route to a foreign country, even the Russian conductor was courteous. At every large station, newspapers, magazines, chocolate, and cookies were brought to the passengers by vendors. Felusia sat glued to the window. It was a mild autumn. The sun shone, birds that migrate at the beginning of September had gathered in the fields, preparing to leave for a warmer climate. At the border, customs officials scarcely searched the luggage. Felusia spoke to everyone in French. In recent years Clara had begun to worry about every little thing. She had consulted fortune tellers, had had gypsies read her future in cards. But now she took everything lightly. She no longer suffered pain after eating. Her gallstones seemed to have evaporated. She was not even disturbed at the fact that they were arriving in Berlin on the eve of Rosh Hashana.

They spent the night in Berlin and early the following morning left for Hamburg. Russian and Polish newspapers had recently been waging a propaganda campaign against Prussia. Russia and Prussia were engaged in a tariff war. The papers were filled with the savagery of the German police, the Junkers, the students. Clara observed only the civility of the Germans. They bowed, addressed her as "Gracious lady," concerned themselves with her comfort, and she tipped everyone lavishly. Felusia was showered with compliments. They were sailing on the *Blücher*, and the ship's boarding was equally pleasant. Clara occupied one of the most spacious cabins. It contained two beds and a sofa, and there was even a toilet. A mirror hung over the sink. The desk was supplied with stationery.

Clara went out on deck. The hold of the ship was open, and cranes loaded barrels, crates, trunks, enormous sacks wrapped in mats and banded with hoops. It was hard for Clara to imagine a ship taking so much cargo into its hold. She could see the passengers on the decks below and they looked nervous and unkempt. There was kissing, crying, embracing. Clara heard Yiddish spoken. In first class, however, decorum prevailed. Ladies promenaded in expensive dresses and jewelry, fanning themselves as if at a ball. Men walked about in top hats, smoking cigars. A general had come aboard to say goodbye to his daughter. Three huge Englishmen strolled by with a thin, freckle-nosed girl. A long-haired, stout man in a cape kissed the hand of a woman he called Countess. Clara had thought that the ship would set sail as soon as the passengers were aboard. But it remained docked for hours. The sun sank in the west. Flames ignited the muddy waves. Fire and water blended miraculously. The ships in the harbor belched smoke, blew their stacks. Waste poured from portholes. Sailors climbed ladders, pulled heavy ropes, shouted. Seagulls cried and circled the ships. The harbor smelled of coal and rotting fish. It seemed strange to Clara that this ship would carry her directly to New York, to the city that only a little while before had seemed like a dream.

The anchor was raised, hawsers loosened. At the sound of a

hoarse whistle, Clara clapped her hands over her ears. The houses, churches, spires, and chimneys of Hamburg began to recede. Windows reflected a purple sunset. The first stars appeared. They seemed to rock together with the ship. The horizon opened up. Lighthouses came into view and ships anchored in the sea, as if forgotten by God and man. A young man approached Clara, offering her binoculars. The ocean grew vaster, wider, and ships swayed on the waves like ducklings. Louisa came to get Clara. An official behind a counter was distributing numbered tickets for the dining tables.

Clara had read about ocean voyages in books. In them the ocean had raged, pirates had attacked ships, sea monsters had swallowed people. But the *Blücher* was like a hotel. Clara combed Felusia's hair and tied her braids with ribbons. In the magnificent dining salon they were served dishes rare in Poland: lettuce, salt-water fish, oysters. At an adjacent table, a magnum of champagne was being opened. Louisa, who was seated opposite a Frenchman, had begun a conversation with him. *Mon Dieu,* he came from the same section as she! She had known his uncle! There was still a France in this world! People still spoke French! Clara, whose school French was limited, conversed with two Hungarian sisters who were going to visit their uncle in Chicago. They spoke German and Clara managed to make herself understood in Germanized Yiddish. They assured Clara that her German was perfect. . . .

Clara had taken along lemons and sour drops to prevent seasickness, but the night passed calmly. The following day was sunny. It was not until lunchtime that the sky grew overcast and the sun rays like axes severed the clouds. A cold wind began to blow. The waves, all gold, silver, and green gall, grew higher. They rose like hillocks, spread like pitch, seethed, and churned. The ship began swaying. Felusia's complexion had turned green. Clara dragged herself out on deck in a fur jacket and muff. The wind whipped her skirt, drove her backwards and forwards. Salty spray filled the air. Clara had read somewhere that one must not permit oneself to succumb to seasickness. But her stomach turned and an unsavory taste filled her mouth. She stood at the rail for so long, gazing at the turbulent foam, that she vomited, recognizing the taste of yesterday's salad. . . .

V

Clara and Felusia were both sick. The storm raged on. Waves like tremendous hammers pounded the sides of the ship. Felusia lay in one bed, sleeping endlessly. Clara, in the other, was unable to close her eyes. From her bed she could look out directly on the sea. The sky was scaly with clouds, some of which were suspended like watery curtains over the desolate scene. The waves mounted so high that Clara thought the ship must be inundated. Watery mountains charged forward, black and angular, melted boulders, lava from a cosmic volcano. They came in multitudes, white, green, and black, veined and foamy, row upon row, like supernatural armies, ready to destroy and swallow. The *Blücher* rose, the sky began to unwind, and Clara's bed seemed momentarily suspended in space. Soon everything descended and the waves retreated: devils driven off by an incantation, ready to begin their wicked game again. The sea raged all day and night. Whirling shapes rose from the water, skipped across as if of their own free will, and disappeared again in the cauldron. The engines pounded, making the cabin tremble and vibrate. The ship's whistle kept blowing, long and drawn-out warnings of peril. Fortunately, Louisa did not become seasick. She brought Clara and Felusia food and made lemon juice for them. She also kept Clara abreast of all the scuttlebutt: what the captain had said, what the ladies wore at each meal. Most of the passengers were ill. The two Hungarian sisters no longer appeared in the dining room. She and the Frenchman were the only ones left at their table.

During the day it was bad enough, but at night Clara's anxiety became unbearable. Felusia sighed in her sleep. In the dark, Clara prayed to God. If only Felusia would come out of it safely! Clara's seasickness brought on a gall-bladder attack. The pain moved from her stomach to her right shoulder. She became feverish. The ship's doctor gave her ineffectual medicines. In Warsaw, Louisa had heated bricks and applied them to Clara's stomach, but here it was difficult to do anything. Clara groaned, sometimes crying out like a woman in labor. When the cramps ceased, she listened silently to the tempest. Drown? Be eaten by fish? A wet grave—would this be her fate?

Clara dozed and awoke. The wind howled. The bed swayed. Clara held on to the bedposts to keep from falling out. They squeaked, as if about to break loose. Running footsteps were heard in the corridors. There was a slamming of doors. The steamer moved with unusual slowness, as if in final effort. Despite her fear, something in Clara yearned for the catastrophic end. She would be spared the agonies of dying slowly. If there were a God, let Him find her in the depths of the ocean and cast her into the Gehenna she deserved.

After four days the storm abated. Felusia had recovered, but Clara still remained in bed. It was only the day before the ship docked in New York that she was able to dress and go to the dining salon again. The room seemed to have grown larger and less populated. The passengers appeared strange to her, as if they had boarded the ship in mid-ocean. Clara noticed with amazement that Felusia had matured in these few days. She behaved with more poise and already made efforts to adapt herself to foreign ways. Clara had grown unaccustomed to walking and the floor seemed to recede as she stepped forward. She was compelled to hold on to Louisa to keep from falling. Clara saw that Louisa and the Frenchman, a large-boned individual with a shock of gray hair and a dark mustache, had become more intimate during the voyage. They conversed and laughed. He poured wine for her, even helped her cut her steak. When later Clara questioned her, Louisa confessed after some hesitation that she and Monsieur Dujacques, a widower, planned to get married when they reached New York. She insisted that she would continue to feel like a mother toward Felusia. . . . Louisa swore that on the night before they left Warsaw she had dreamed she was being married, had seen herself being led to the altar, and that her bridegroom had looked exactly like Monsieur Dujacques. . . .

The sea was now as calm as it had been wild before. The crests of the barely rising waves bore bunches of seaweed. Men and women who had been confined to their cabins now came out on deck thinner, paler, wearing clothes that had been saved for the last part of the voyage: plaid shirts, shawls, capes. Interrupted friendships were renewed. Each told the other of the miseries he had endured. The air grew warmer. Flying fish rose from the water. Dolphins, like great mice, leaped out of the waves. A steward brought out deck chairs and blankets. Older women allowed themselves to be tucked in and took up their interrupted knitting, discussing migraine headaches, rheumatism, and cough remedies. Sitting among them, Clara found herself unable to enter into their conversation. It was not only that they were speaking German rather than Yiddish, but that something within her separated her from the rest. These were settled people. They had husbands, sons-in-law, daughters-in-law, grandchildren. They knew precisely where they were going and how long they would stay. Clara's life was planless. She was, however, too old to join the younger group. She observed with astonishment how freely the young men acted with the women, and how boldly the young women behaved toward the men. They laughed and giggled, already on an informal and even intimate basis. "What was so funny? Why did they laugh so hard?" Clara asked herself. Were they actually so happy? Did they think they would remain young forever? Several young Englishmen in caps and checked suits began to play shuffleboard. The women joined them. An elderly man with a monocle excelled at the game and several people applauded him. Felusia played with them and spoke to them in French.

Clara tried to rid herself of her bitterness but was unable to do so. She saw herself as a sinner but could not stand loose behavior in others. Her thoughts kept turning from the vanity of life to the unknown entity called God. Even Felusia detected a change in her.

"You've grown so old," she said to her mother. "No one believes you're my mother. They think you're my grandmother."

VI

It was raining when they docked in New York. Clara, Louisa, and Felusia went through customs—a huge shed full of baggage and officials—and came out into a street paved with broad stones. Now it was covered with puddles and horse manure. Everything was wet: the brick-red houses with their fire escapes, the storage buildings, the horse-drawn trolleys, the crowds of pedestrians jostling about. In the distance Clara saw the train that seemed to be traveling over rooftops. Actually it moved over an iron bridge supported by thick pillars cemented into the pavement. Everything here seemed strangely old and worn, as if it had been in existence for hundreds of years. The rain fell at an angle, in sheets of spray, and through the watery net the city rose gray, straggling, all metal and stone, flat-roofed, small-windowed, full of chimneys, smoke, and dreariness. The first-class passengers, who had been allowed to disembark before the others, got into hansom cabs, whose drivers wore oilcloth raincoats and wet top hats. A relative had come in a carriage to meet Monsieur Dujacques and he asked him to drive Clara, Felusia, and Louisa to their hotel.

They rode through streets lined with brownstone buildings that had narrow entrances instead of gates. Looking through the carriage windows, Clara marveled. Was this New York?

Compared with Berlin and Paris, it seemed like a small town. In the puddles of the gutter floated bits of paper, cardboard, and rags. Clara had never seen so many broken umbrellas. Drenched pedestrians jumped over ditches, bending under the rain. Huge express wagons stood beside a watering trough. Everything seemed strange. They passed a barbershop. Through the shop window could be seen men lying on chairs, wrapped in sheets like patients prepared for an operation. A sign indicated facilities for baths as well as haircuts. Restaurant patrons sat in a row on high stools next to a counter. The carriage passed by factories where workrooms could be glimpsed in which both men and women were busy at machines, handling pieces of material. There was a brightly lit confusion and bustle within, a kind of chaos Clara had never witnessed. Even the noise differed from that of Berlin or Paris. It was hard to know where the hammering and crashing came from. Iron bars jutted from unfinished houses. Sodden posters and half-torn placards hung on fences. A Negro walked along, protected from the rain by a sack thrown over his shoulders. In a meat market a butcher in a bloody apron sawed at a bone. Other markets and stores came into view. In their windows hung bundles of dried mushrooms, strings of garlic, cheeses bound in cloth. Everything was jumbled together: onions and oranges, radishes and apples, sea fish, lobsters, mussels. In the midst of it all, the sun came out, turning the day summery and humid. The carriage pulled up to a hotel. A porter quickly picked up Clara's bags. The desk clerk smoked a meerschaum pipe and spoke in German. The three ladies climbed a narrow, red-carpeted stairway. Their rooms smelled of dry wood, bedbugs, and insecticide. Their luggage was brought up. They were in New York. . . .

God in heaven, from her earliest childhood Clara had heard about the wonders of America. But it was a city like all cities. The sky was above, not below. Clara sat at the window looking out. Lifting the lorgnette that hung around her neck, she looked through it at this once-distant country. Clara thought that if there was a life after death it would be like this—different and yet the same. Who was that giant carrying a sign? Oh, he was walking on stilts. He wore a red-and-white striped top hat. A clown from a circus? A peddler hawked his wares in a loud singsong. A crowd gathered around him. Was he giving things away? People grabbed up something, laughing. They were all so quick, so active, dressed garishly in bright colors or checks. Across the street, the entire window of a clothing store was filled with mannequins, dressed in silk, velvet, fur coats and stoles somehow different from the ones one saw in Warsaw. The crowds of women in front of the windows wore dresses and hats that looked new. Good God! There was a girl riding a bicycle! Why was everybody carrying so many boxes and packages? Yes, it was different. Louisa and Felusia were looking out the other window. Felusia kept shouting: "Louisa, Mama, look!" A street photographer was leading an animal along that was neither a horse nor a donkey, nor even a colt, although it resembled all three. There was a small saddle on its back. A man with yellow trousers and a feathered hat carried a parrot on one shoulder. A young man was selling cardboard marionettes that moved their arms and legs when he pulled a string. Adults as well as children seemed to play games here. Newsboys shouted. On a roof opposite, someone with a long pole was chasing pigeons.

"Well, Felusia, how do you like America?" Clara asked.

"Oh, Mama, it's funny!" she said and made a gesture that was completely like Alexander's.

Felusia was hungry and went with Louisa to a restaurant across the way. Meanwhile, Clara examined their rooms. She felt the mattresses, pulled out bureau drawers. In the hall there was a separate toilet as well as a bathroom with a long bathtub. Clara opened the taps and to her astonishment there was hot water even though she had not ordered any to be heated. From habit, she nevertheless rang for a maid and in a mixture of Yiddish and gestures indicated that she would like to have a bath. Replying in English, the maid smiled and ran the water in the tub. Part of an American newspaper lay on a chair. Clara could not read English, but she could tell from the pictures that they were advertisements for cosmetics, corsets, brassières, ways of removing unwanted hair, poison for cockroaches. One advertisement showed two pictures of the same woman: in one she was elderly, wrinkled, disheveled; in the other she appeared young, elegant, poised. Underneath were the words "before" and "after." Clara guessed their meaning. The thought that she too might become young again in this country ran through her mind. A new desire for life awakened in her.

VII

Everything took place more smoothly than Clara had anticipated. Louisa was invited to visit the family of Monsieur Dujacques and took Felusia with her. The weather turned cooler and Clara's fall clothes were more comfortable. She had already spent half a day in a beauty salon. She had been massaged, had had her hair dyed and set, her face made up. She had shopped for various trifles. In Warsaw Clara had bought a book of English phrases for travelers. She immediately began to pick up words, expressions. What was so difficult about being in America? For money, one could get anything. There were hansom cabs and coaches in front of the hotel and Clara got into one and asked the driver to take her to East Broadway. It turned out that the coachman spoke Yiddish. Clara burst out laughing when she heard his flat Polish accent. He was actually from Warsaw, where he had driven a droshky. As they rode along, he carried on a conversation over his shoulder. Did he know Warsaw? He had cut his teeth there. Berg Street? That was where the aristocrats lived! The very rich. Why had he left? He had been involved in a lawsuit. Why should he sit and wait until the anti-Semites threw him into jail? They wouldn't live to see that, the Russkies. May their flesh rot . . . their bones crumble! . . . He kept turning for a better view of Clara and almost ran down several pedestrians. "Whoever stays with those hooligans is crazy! America is a wonderful country. If one has a few dollars, it's paradise." English? One could learn it. Whom had the lady come to see? Relatives? She planned to go back? How foolish. It was good to be in Columbus's country. Everyone ate white bread, even the beggars. He was able to send his old mother a few dollars out of his small earnings. . . . "Whoa. Steady! Hey there, uncle, where do you think you're going? Are you blind? These pushcarts block up the streets and you can't get through. They're all Jews! In Warsaw they peddled in Goscinny Dwor, and now they peddle in New York. They make a living, don't have to have a license. Everybody works hard, but if one has a few cents, one is free as a bird. There are Jew-haters here too. They call Jews sheeny, kike. But you give it back to them. When two people fight, others don't interfere. There is a saying: 'Mind your own business! . . .' Hey! . . ."

The cab came to a stop. Fire wagons had appeared. The men did not wear brass helmets as in Warsaw. Here they wore black hats. They reminded Clara of executioners. Bells rang, the wagons flashed by, the horses in their brass harnesses straining from their reins. The driver turned to Clara. "They start fires, a curse on them. They carry out the merchandise at night and put a match to the building. If they're caught, there's trouble, but what won't they do for a few thousand dollars? When I came here, fire insurance was dirt cheap. Now it's sky high. If I ever caught such a fellow, I'd rip off his foot. The companies get rich but people's lives are endangered. Once a whole family was burned! The culprit himself was injured and that's how he was caught. He'll rot in prison, the lousy bum. He'll have to pray to God to come out in this lifetime. . . . Hey! . . ."

The traffic had become entangled: dray wagons, cabs, express wagons, even bicycles. Windows opened and heads were thrust out. Children played on the sidewalk. A small boy, stout as a barrel, with a stocking cap on his head, kept waving a short stick that reminded Clara of a rolling pin. Children screamed. The houses here had neither gates nor courtyards. Everything took place in the street. Laundry was hung on the rooftops. Garbage cans full of ashes were placed before the entrances. A heavy woman with painted cheeks, mascaraed eyes, and red stockings on her massive legs screamed at someone in a mixture of English and Yiddish. The driver leaned back toward Clara confidentially and said, "She's one of those, a streetwalker, a whore, may her mother's mother go to the devil. Don't want to work in America. Those loafers only live for sin. They're syphilitic themselves and make others sick. They have worms in their blood. A boy lands in their hands and his nose rots away. I have a wife and children, God give them health. The eldest is already in high school. At home we call it gymnasium. Who in Warsaw could afford to send a child to gymnasium? Here, Uncle Sam pays, each person gets the same as the next one. Each one is a citizen! . . . Here's East Broadway. What number do you want? There's a synagogue. There are plenty of religious Jews here. My own boy went to study at the Talmud Torah . . . I made a bar mizvah for him."

This street seemed more prosperous than the surrounding ones. The men wore top hats and the women were better dressed. A tall, gray-haired man in a cape and top hat exchanged greetings with someone. He raised a white-gloved hand and waved a cane with a silver head. He looked like a musician or an actor. Clara had seen a poster advertising Yiddish theater in New York. The cab stopped at a two-story red-brick house. There were three windows on each story and a stoop at the entrance. Yes, this was it. The number was painted in gold on the windowpane of the door, and a plaque announced: *Alexander Zipkin, M.D.* The coachman waved his whip and drove off. Here it was! And she had visualized a palace. Nevertheless, her throat contracted.

"God in heaven, if only I don't have an attack right here! If I only live to see him. . . ."

Breathing deeply, she calmed herself. Lifting the folds of her heavily ribboned dress, she climbed the stairs. "What is there to fear?" she said to herself. "He won't eat me. . . ."

She rang the bell. A girl came to the door. She looked like a maid and spoke English, but Clara replied in Russian. The girl showed Clara into a waiting room. Two other women were sitting there. One looked like a market vendor; the other, who wore glasses on her crooked nose and a bonnet, was probably a rabbi's wife, Clara thought. There was an aquarium with goldfish in the room. A landscape hung on the wall. A tiny garden with two naked trees was visible through the window. There was an odor of cabbage cooking which penetrated from the kitchen. Shakily Clara selected a magazine. She tried to look at the pictures, but her eyes refused to focus on them. The page turned green, gold, and the lines of print lifted as if drawn taut by a string. . . . The rabbi's wife coughed. The market vendor sighed. Clara hid her face in the magazine. From the other side of the door she recognized Alexander's voice, which had grown somewhat deeper and hoarser.

VIII

When the market vendor entered the office, she stayed for a long time. Clara heard the voices of both doctor and patient. Zipkin spoke in Yiddish. It was the first time that Clara had heard him speak Yiddish, and she was surprised at his Lithuanian accent. For a moment it made her want to laugh. She raised the magazine higher to make sure her face was covered. Leaning against the arm rest of the chair, she threw back her head and tried to relax. "Nothing good or evil can happen to me any more," ran through her mind. The door opened; the market vendor left and the rabbi's wife went in. From the threshold Zipkin said something about a teaspoonful after breakfast, lunch, and dinner. "What shall I say to him?" Clara thought suddenly. "I must not humiliate myself. I'll tell him that Felusia is here, nothing more." Through the magazine, Clara sensed Zipkin looking at her. She turned her hand to make it appear smaller. . . . The rabbi's wife stayed even longer than the market vendor. What was he doing? Why was it so quiet in there? Was he performing an abortion? Clara smiled at this ridiculous thought. The woman was undoubtedly a grandmother. . . . For a while, Clara stopped thinking. A child's wailing could be heard from another part of the house. Clara imagined that she heard the angry hushing of a woman. The room was too warm and stuffy, too full of dust and charcoal fumes. Clara began to fan herself. Perhaps the door would never open again. He would remain with that woman—two petrified mummies. At that moment the patient came out. Behind her, Zipkin gave instructions on how to use an inhalator. He imitated the sound: "Ah-ha. . . ." Clara shifted the magazine a little so that with the corner of her eye she could examine the lower part of Zipkin's body: a white smock, checked trousers. His shoes seemed unusually large. Did he have such large feet? She put down the magazine and saw everything as through a haze. The doctor's voice said: "Please come in."

Clara stood up, her feet numb. She looked at him. It was Zipkin, but older, his hair no longer thick. At the top of his closely cropped head there was a bald spot sprouting fuzz like swamp grass. His brows had grown together and he squinted myopically. Two wrinkles bordered his mouth, indicating the impatient bitterness of one who does things against his will. He had not recognized her! She wanted to cry. Perhaps she should not allow herself to be recognized at all. The office was furnished as simply as the waiting room. A desk, two chairs, a lamp. A stethoscope lay among the papers. There was an eye chart on the wall. Zipkin again said something in English and

Clara coughed to dispel the dryness in her throat. She addressed him in Polish. "Please excuse me, Doctor, I speak no English. . . ."

There was silence. They both sat down. Though he said nothing, Clara knew he had recognized her voice.

"Am I mistaken?" he asked tremulously.

"Yes, it's me."

He did not get up. He lifted his brows, in an expression both dumfounded and indifferent, as if he no longer wanted anything to happen. A strange thought ran through Clara's mind: He is disappointed that I'm not a patient . . .

"Really, this is a surprise," he said in Polish that already had a foreign tinge.

"Yes, isn't it?"

Again they were silent. Searching blindly in her pocketbook for a handkerchief, Clara inadvertently brought out a mirror, which fell into her lap.

"What has happened? Why didn't you let me know you were coming? God!"

"I don't know. Your daughter is here too."

"Felusia? Where is she?"

Clara named the hotel at which they were staying. "Louisa is here too."

Zipkin could not speak. Standing up, he glanced toward the door. For a while his tall figure towered over Clara. After some hesitation he sat down again. He looked at her—and she at him. Shoving aside a stethoscope, he said: "Quite a surprise."

"I hope I'm not inconveniencing you."

"What are you saying? I thought I'd never see you again." And his mouth twitched.

They began speaking, haltingly, incoherently, about the ship, the journey, where had she embarked, when had she landed, and as they made small talk a connection began to form mysteriously between the past and the present. The changes that time had brought to their faces, voices, and figures seemed to disappear. A hidden pencil retouched wrinkles, filled in crevices, smoothed everything. Zipkin grew younger and assumed his former boyishness and the Don Juan arrogance that had so appealed to Clara. In Clara's eyes the old flame again became ignited. Her face again grew impudent, passionate, vulgar, and at the same time Semitically gentle and maternal. It all happened within several seconds. "It's the same Alexander—why did he look so strange to me at first?" Clara wondered.

"Yes, it's the same Clara!" Zipkin decided. He rose and opened the door to the waiting room as if to convince himself that no new patients were waiting for him. He also glanced at another door that was covered with green drapery and that obviously led to his private quarters.

IX

"What made you come to America?" he asked, realizing at once that his question was rude, but unable to withdraw it. Clara thought it over for a moment.

"It's quite simple. Felusia is your daughter and she needs a father. One greeting card a year doesn't satisfy her. She goes to school and all her friends have fathers. It's different when a girl, God forbid, is an orphan—" Clara stopped, the last sentence had come out clumsily. Zipkin lowered his head.

"Just lately I've been thinking of you. Constantly."

"Constantly?"

"Yes."

"I thought you'd completely forgotten me."

"No, Clara, I have forgotten nothing. I tried to make myself forget. What else could I do? After what happened between you and Mirkin, I decided everything was lost."

"Mirkin is no longer alive."

"When did he die? I don't hold any grudges. That is the way you were and you couldn't change. You do know I'm married."

"Yes. I heard a child crying. Was it your son?"

"Yes, my son. He's a nice child. My wife is from Hungary. She helped me complete my studies."

"How is Sonya?"

"Sonya is wealthy. Her husband owns a factory, and she has three children."

"Do you see her?"

"Not very often. She's a devoted mother. Her husband, Yackiewicz is his name, has forgotten all his former dreams. I myself am not in the movement, but I still sympathize with it. There are many socialists and anarchists here. Their headquarters is in this neighborhood."

"I imagined New York would be entirely different."

"What did you imagine? It's the same world and the same people. They keep coming from Russia in shiploads. It never occurred to me that you might come too."

"I've only come for a visit."

"For a visit? For how long?"

"I don't know yet. It depends."

Zipkin covered an unfinished prescription with a blotter. "Well, at any rate you're here now."

"Yes, Alexander, I'm here. Although it seems to me that I'll wake up at any moment and find myself back home. I've been very ill. I almost died. But I'm better now. I had a severe gall-bladder attack and as I lay in bed, I decided not to leave Felusia an orphan. How was she guilty? Each person must be punished for his own sins, not for those of others."

"Yes, that's true."

"After recovering I determined to make this trip. When one accepts death, there's nothing more to fear. It all happened so quickly. You remember Sasha, of course. He was your pupil, after all. He took over his grandfather's, my father's, contracts and is even more successful than he was. He's well loved and received by the most important people. The generals ask his advice about matters that have nothing to do with provisions. He has an unusual intellect and is almost too smart. I'd be happy if he accepted life without philosophizing. But apparently he takes after me. Anyhow, I told Sasha everything and he helped me. I can't tell you how kind and generous he is. A real tycoon!"

"Is he married?"

"No, if only he would get married!"

"Why? As you see, I'm a doctor here on East Broadway. Fate worked out this way."

"Are you satisfied?"

"Satisfied? Yes, I bear no grudges against anyone. My goal was Western Europe, not America. But it's a free country here. One can say what one wants to and write what one wishes. The President is criticized more than the bath attendant at home. But when it's legal, it doesn't matter. Why push against an open door? I received Felusia's photograph. When was it taken? She looks splendid."

"Yes, when you see her, you'll realize that she makes up for both of us."

"Why do you run yourself down? I'm not, as you can see, wealthy, but the house I live in is mine and I have my practice. Also, I'm resigned," Zipkin said, astounded at his own words. It had never occurred to him to think of himself in this way before.

"Why do you say you're resigned? You have your profession and your family."

"Yes, but—I had aspirations once. What satisfaction is there in treating these women? My wife is a decent person, but she's Hungarian and somehow that puts her in another world. They seem to think the way we do, but they're different. They're so neutral. Everything is so clear to them, so simple. They have none of our doubts. The Russian and Polish cultures are combined in me—a crazy mixture. You didn't marry again?"

"Marry? You know I didn't."

"How should I know? It's been years since I heard from you."

"You didn't want to hear from me. You didn't even want to know the other side of the story."

"The facts spoke for themselves."

"The facts? There are some things, Alexander, that one cannot judge unless one knows all the details. In France a woman committed a murder and a jury unanimously freed her. They even showered her with flowers. When they learned how much she had suffered, they saw she was a saint. Thus far, I haven't killed anyone. If I destroyed anyone, it was myself. If I had stayed with you, you might have become a tailor instead of a doctor."

"Am I to assume that you did it for my sake?"

"No, I'm not saying that. What's the difference? The past can't return. If only it could! If only I'd been as wise at eighteen. You wrote letters that seemed to drench me with ice water. Felusia was a child, and Mirkin came along and turned my head with his tales of wealth. I mustn't speak ill of the dead, but I've never met a greater liar. He fooled himself, that was the worst part of it. I don't say I acted cleverly; when I thought of it later, it seemed as if he had cast me under a spell. Only God knows how many tears I shed. I became dangerously ill. You asked if I married again. You married, not I. Perhaps while you were accusing me so bitterly you already had your Hungarian fiancée."

Zipkin lowered his head. "In that case, the blame is on me."

"No, I don't blame anyone. I paid dearly for my mistake—the highest price!"

X

"Kubuś is still in Warsaw, isn't he?" Clara inquired.

"Yes."

"Do you hear from him?"

"Seldom."

"Did she marry again?"

"Sabina? Yes, she did."

"Well, why not? People take care of themselves. No one wants to remain alone in the world. Alexander, I don't want you to think I came to ask you for favors, or to saddle you with Felusia. I can see that this is not the home for her. I had imagined something altogether different. Louisa is getting married. Imagine, she met him aboard ship. She has already promised to take Felusia into her home until my plans are clearer. She herself is too old to have a child. One doesn't realize how attached one's employees can become. I can ask you for support for our daughter, but I haven't fallen so low. I only want one favor of you: that Felusia gets to know her father. I don't want her to feel like a neglected orphan. Come and see her. She's yours. I have made peace with my fate."

"Where are you staying?"

Clara again told him the name of the hotel.

"Why there of all places? Well, it's all one and the same. My wife is very jealous," Zipkin said, lowering his voice, "although she has no grounds for suspicion. She's religious too, keeps a kosher kitchen and so forth. But I've remained an atheist. She has all sorts of idiosyncrasies and I don't want a scandal. She's capable of eavesdropping on a patient. If you want to continue our conversation, I had better come with you to your hotel."

"Why not? Felusia isn't at home. She went along with Louisa. I thought it would be better if we talked things over first."

"Yes, we'll take a carriage. Some doctors have their own and drive themselves. But I didn't want to become a coachman, and to hire one is too expensive here. Everything is different in this country. Everybody is democratic, or that's what they call it. All traditions have been upset here. If I'm called to a patient, I walk or I take the El—that's the city train. You must have seen it. Wait, I'll tell my wife you came to take me to a patient."

"If you wish. Perhaps if you're so afraid it might be better if you didn't come?"

"I'm not afraid. You don't wear the mark of Cain. Don't think I'm such a henpecked husband, but I simply want to avoid arguments, and I don't want to hurt her either. You can't imagine how people like her suffer."

"I know, I'm not made of wood, even though you may think I'm a slut. I'd like to ask you one thing: who wrote that letter?"

"Which letter?"

"The letter about my being with Mirkin."

Zipkin grew pale. "I don't know. It was anonymous."

"You once wrote that it came from Warsaw."

"No, from Paris."

"Do you still have it?"

"Perhaps. But I'd have to look for it."

"And I, idiot that I am, suspected my poor child, my Sasha. In what language was it written? In Russian?"

"Yes."

"Well, it must have been Mirkin himself, or his secretary, that charlatan. You must certainly remember him: Yasha Vinaver."

"Yes, I do."

"I don't know what he had against me. I never did him any harm."

"Then you're only troubled by the fact that he informed against you. Your own conduct doesn't bother you."

"My own conduct concerns only God and me, no matter how close you and I may have been. I can't even describe to you what happened. Even if I were to tell you, you wouldn't believe me. I once thought that no one can be fooled, and especially that I couldn't be, but Mirkin deceived me from the beginning. Perhaps I should not tell you this. I don't need to defend myself before you. He was impotent, and I knew this. Not from him—he played the role of a great lover—from a doctor who treated him. Yes, there are doctors who reveal their patients' secrets, especially after a glass of wine. That's why I agreed to go with him. He promised to buy shares for me that would make money. He promised me the sky, but it was all nothing but lies. Sick as he was, he associated with whores. Yasha Vinaver swindled him. He was a disgusting creature, but Mirkin continued to employ him. Believe me, Alexander, from the day that we first became intimate, I never stopped loving you and longing for you. I am prepared to say this before God when I'm called to my judgment. You may be a freethinker, but some power must have placed obstacles in our way. Some perverse spirit has trailed me since my childhood. You may think I'm crazy, but what I saw with my own eyes cannot be denied."

Zipkin frowned. "What did you see?"

"I can't tell you now. We'll talk again. When you know the whole truth, you'll agree with me."

"I want you to know one thing, Clara: I'll never take you seriously again."

"Take me as you like. . . ."

"Wait, I'll be back in a moment."

Zipkin rose. Suddenly he placed his hand on Clara's cheek. Clara caught hold of his wrist and kissed his hand. It happened quickly and unexpectedly. He opened the door behind the green drapery and left the room. Clara sat with her head lowered. Though Zipkin's hand smelled slightly of perspiration, it had awakened her desire. All the feelings she had tried to extinguish in the course of the years had returned with his touch. "I love him! I must have him even if it kills me," she said to herself.

12

I

The rain dashed hail-like against the roof. It had been pouring for three days. Fortunately the house stood on a hill. Below, in the valley, the puddles looked like small lakes, and on the naked branches reflected in them an occasional withered leaf clung obstinately. The birds that had twittered the first afternoon were now silent. From time to time a crow cawed. As the rain drummed on, a smoky mist rose over the puddles, so that the surrounding tangle of brush and plants looked as if it was smoldering. When a window was opened, there was a smell of skunk and rot. Cold pervaded the rooms. Alexander kept feeding the parlor stove chunks of wood and thin logs. Sitting before the fire, one felt one's face burning while one's back remained chilled. During the day, a murky light came through the dripping windows. There was a road a short distance from the house. The whistling and puffing of locomotives could be heard coming from tracks some distance away. But nothing could be seen except crooked tree trunks and the dripping sky. The man from whom Zipkin had rented the cottage for a week had told him that there were wild animals in the adjacent woods. In case of emergency, they were provided with two hunting rifles. Moldy books were stacked on the shelves. There were portraits of Civil War officers on the walls, hooked rugs on the floors, and the patchwork quilts covering the beds were mosaics of bright materials that Miss Clark, a spinster and the former owner, had sewn together during the long winter nights. Miss Clark had been dead for eight years and the property now belonged to her brother's son, a railroad official who lived in Croton-on-Hudson. The family used it only in the summer.

To go there in mid-autumn had certainly been an act of folly, but Clara had accepted the fact that everything she did must meet with failure. Zipkin had once spent a summer in this area. He had lied clumsily to his wife, telling her that a former patient of his was dangerously ill and Zipkin was the only doctor he would trust. Zipkin had sent a telegram to himself and made his wife send the reply. Felusia was staying with Louisa. Alexander had withdrawn some money from the bank, and he and Clara had come out for a week to pay off old debts of love and say things long unsaid. There was nothing to do in this retreat but lie in the broad bed under double covers. There wasn't even much of anything to eat. The nearest store was some distance away. Zipkin had stocked up on bread, cheese, sausage, butter, and eggs, thinking that they would be able to augment their supplies. There was wood and kerosene in the cupboard, and a bushel of apples picked in a nearby orchard. Zipkin and Clara had arrived on a mild October afternoon. It was an Indian summer day, balmy, the air filled with gossamer. But overnight the weather had changed. Zipkin was afraid that the rain might turn to snow and leave them stranded. All sorts of difficulties could ensue. His wife might become anxious and try to communicate with him. The local police would discover that they were not man and wife. The neighboring farmers were God-fearing Yankees. Yet Zipkin had taken the risk. Life with his wife was too monotonous. He had not been able to forget Clara.

At night in the dark, Clara's hair seemed black again. She told him everything, withholding nothing about Grisha, Calman, Smirnoff, Mirkin. She confessed and begged his forgiveness, enumerated her sins, and clung to Zipkin with renewed passion. How odd human nature is! That which hurts in the light, pleases in the dark. Jealousy becomes a source of pleasure. Clara's stories of unfaithfulness increased their passion. He questioned her, anxious to know, probing every detail. She even invented depravities to satisfy him. She in turn asked to hear about his experiences and he described them to her. She insisted on knowing everything about Sabina, about his present wife, and all his other women, the peasant girls on the Radziwill estate and the whores to whom he had gone with his fellow students at the university in Kiev. Alexander and Clara embraced, talked. Would they be able to live separately again? Clara argued that if he had been able to leave Sabina, why not this Hungarian frump? And if Sabina had been able to find another husband, why couldn't Lisa? He could give her his house and go away with Clara. She had a little money, some jewelry. Sasha would help her out. Alexander could practice elsewhere, in California, in Argentina, in South Africa, even in France or Italy. They had their daughter, that would be their treasure. Instead of hiding in some freezing hole, they could live together and be happy. "How much longer, dearest, do we have to live, after all?" she insisted. "As long as we remain alive, let's be together. Why spend our nights yearning for each other? Do those who languish for love gain paradise? . . ." Clara spoke and pressed her face to Alexander's breast. She had only articulated what he had been thinking. He had again made a mistake. Lisa was frigid. Sleeping with her gave no satisfaction. She only worried about their child, fretted about her own health. Her thoughts revolved around her housekeeping, her washing, her economies. In their first year together he had barely managed to communicate with her in broken German. Later they had switched to a stilted English, for both of them a language without flavor, without associations.

Clara, ill as she was, still seethed with passion. Her obscenities were blended with mysticism, her solemn amorousness was tinged with irony. She could act as silly as a fifteen-year-old or speak like a person with one foot in the grave. She jabbered in a mixture of Russian, Polish, and Yiddish, described all manner of experiences, related her girlish fantasies. Even while discussing death, she managed to inject lust. When she died, she would leave him her pearls and he was to present them to the woman who replaced her. She forced him to promise not to mourn her when she died, but to go to bed with another woman right after her funeral. Strange how this type of nonsense could arouse him! This treacherous witch with her gray hair and gallstones brought back his youth. But could he, for the second time in his life, desert a home and family? Could he trust her? The fervent promises he had made to her were just part of a game. The vows he had sworn to her had to be broken. Behind the intoxication of kisses and the endearments lurked a sober mistrust.

During the night there was lightning and thunder. Wind shook the panes. The chimney whistled. Branches broke from trees. Zipkin imagined himself a Robinson Crusoe who had been shipwrecked with Scheherazade. But the storm would not last forever, and Scheherazade would run out of stories. He was not prepared to abandon his house, which was almost paid for, his faithful wife, his son, who bore his father's name (Berish had become Bernard), and start life all over again with an aging adventuress. He still remembered those months in Paris when Clara had returned to Warsaw and he had haunted the boulevards and eaten watery soup at the free kitchens of the Alliance Israelite. . . .

II

"If you don't want to marry me," Clara argued, "let me be your mistress. I'm worth that much. I am, after all, the mother of your child. I'll rent an apartment in New York and whenever you can you'll come, and when you can't I can always imagine that I'm still in Warsaw. That apparently is my fate."

"You mean you want to settle here?"

"I don't know what I want. What did I do in Warsaw? I ate my heart out. I was a lost soul. Here, at least I know I exist. If you can't come every day, you'll come twice a week, or whenever you can."

"I have so little time."

"What do you mean by little time? One needn't be the prisoner of one's wife. You always came to me from someone else. It used to be Sabina. Why not Lisa? If there were no Lisa, someone else would come along. This is what I've made of my life!"

Clara began to weep. Zipkin kissed and consoled her. The rains had stopped, but the sky remained overcast. A dense, milky fog enveloped tree trunks and bushes, floated in huge seal-like shapes over the horizon. If one wandered only a few steps from the house, one might lose one's way. The sleepless nights had left Zipkin exhausted. At home he never lay down during the daytime, but here he napped. Yes, it was good to be with Clara. But she too was worn out. She looked withered. There were double rings, blue and bluish-green beneath her eyes. In the mornings, when she arose, her face was wrinkled. She tried to cook something, but the stove smoked. She walked around in a bathrobe, slippers, and Zipkin's overcoat draped across her shoulders. For the first few days Zipkin had not even looked at the books. Now he began to read. The novels in the library were all trash. Because there was nothing else of interest, Zipkin chose a book on occultism. At first the subject bored him, but gradually he became absorbed in the case histories. Was it possible? Could there be a grain of truth in them? The corroborations of many witnesses were presented. They all began the same way: as skeptics, who had to be won over. Zipkin read of one medium, a Mrs. B., who when in trance spoke in the voice and accent of a male Susquehanna Indian. This dead one-time chief could read minds and foretell the future. He was so omniscient that he could rap out on a round table the answers to anything asked of him. During Mrs. B.'s séances little flames lit up the darkness. Faces appeared, there were cold breezes, trumpets blew by themselves, mysterious hands composed of unfamiliar matter moved chairs about, lifted dishes, even playfully slapped someone's face or pulled an ear. Zipkin grimaced. He recalled that he had heard of similar black magic from the peasants on the Radziwill estate, as well as from his own parents. A dibbuk had entered the body of a girl, the daughter of a chandler. She chanted the Torah, recited the Talmud, uttered chapters of the Scriptures perversely, divulged the sins of influential citizens, defamed their wives. They had tried to exorcise the phantom by blowing the ram's horn, by excommunication. They used a fire pan, amulets, but the evil spirit continued to mock and blaspheme. The weak hands of the maiden lifted a rock so heavy that three men together could not have lifted it, and rolled and juggled it up and down as if it were a pebble. . . . "Why should people all over the world concoct such lies?" Zipkin asked himself. And why were these stories all so similar?

He discussed it with Clara and she insisted that these stories were true. She swore that she herself had witnessed how a table had indicated the number of coins each person present had in his wallet. And while she was still living with Calman, a fortune teller had predicted that a dark man would come into her life and that she would bear him a child. During her illness in Warsaw, a gypsy who read her fortune in cards had told her that she would take an ocean voyage. Clara nodded her head.

"Why do you think, dearest, we are here now? Because for years I called to you and you answered me. I heard your voice distinctly. You were calling: 'Clara, Clara . . .' "

"It's all illusion. We simply missed each other."

"It's not that simple. One has a soul, and souls yearn for each other. You won't believe me, but Grisha still comes to me in my dreams."

"Why shouldn't I believe you? I still dream about old Count Radziwill."

"Sometimes, Grisha is angry with me. He's beaten me too. I

used to wake up with a dead man's bruises on my arms and breasts. Lately he's been kind to me. Perhaps because the time of my departure is growing closer. . . ."

"Nonsense!"

"Dearest, it was predetermined that we meet. When I saw you in Mirale's room on Zielna Street, I knew you were the one . . . Everything within me glowed. . . ."

The first part of the week passed swiftly. Now the days grew longer. Zipkin and Clara had petty squabbles. They dressed and, braving the foul weather, crept along the muddy road until they came to a country store where they bought provisions. On the way back, it began to pour, and they were soaked through. Night fell and there was nothing else to do but go to bed. They covered themselves with every blanket they could find. Their bodies were warm, but their feet remained cold. Their talk about love, passion, and longing had become repetitious. Clara fell asleep murmuring. She awoke with a backache and stomach cramps. Zipkin heated a brick for her in the stove. She had taken the medicines brought along from Warsaw, but they hadn't helped her. The lovers slept fitfully. The night split into many parts. The mattress sagged, the pillows were hard, the bed linen coarse. Zipkin smoked. Clara kept puffing on his cigarette. She made him keep his hand on her belly because it soothed her.

"Now you can see what a wreck I am," she said.

"No, darling, I love you."

"What sort of love is this? No, I'd better keep quiet."

"Clara. You know it's all your fault."

III

Clara awakened him with a kiss. He opened his eyes and she called out: "*Mazel tov,* it's snowing!"

He sat up and saw that, outside, the gray of yesterday had changed overnight to a bright whiteness. The winter birds chirped. The frost glistened in the sunlight. The surrounding landscape that had disappeared behind the fog during the rainy days could again be seen. In the distance a roof with a smoking chimney indicated that they had been closer to their neighbors than they had imagined. Zipkin felt a boyish delight in the first snow of the year. Hurrah! It was winter! He embraced Clara. He thought of the winters on the Radziwill estate, and the later ones in Kiev: the skating, the sleigh rides, the fur coats, the supper parties. Who in America could understand how gay it had been back there? The students and the young ladies would pile into a sleigh, and the driver in his bearskin coat, felt boots, and cowl-like fur hat would urge the horses on. They sped up and down the hills. The young people giggled and snuggled together. Even though they belonged to the middle class, they shared many of the pleasures of the highest aristocracy. Later they drank tea from samovars, ate preserves, smoked innumerable cigarettes, and held discussions until three in the morning. Both boys and girls worried about the fate of the world. The fathers, though they visited the rabbis of Hushatin and Turisk on the holidays, were tolerant of the times and sought educated husbands for their daughters. The mothers, who still wore wigs themselves, helped their modern daughters arrange rendezvous. Each new poem that appeared in a magazine was a matter of importance. Each article merited a debate. Every idea or social movement brought to mind Siberia, the Shlisselburg Fortress, flight to Europe, and fantasies that hummed in the wind, droned in the telegraph wires, and formed on the windowpanes along with the frost patterns. But what did all these dreams matter now? The "honeymoon" week was over and, since Zipkin had not yet decided to leave his wife, it was time to return to the city. Zipkin and Clara ate their last meal together. Zipkin brought in cold water from the well, washed, and dried himself. Nine days before, he had been anxious to come here, but now he was eager to return. He clowned like a boy. He went half naked into the snow, which was full of bird tracks, tried playfully to pour a pail of water over a flock of crows, who fluttered their wings and cawed. He threw a snowball at the window.

They had to walk to the railroad station, because there was no one from whom they could rent a sleigh. It hadn't even been necessary to lock up the house; merely closing the door was sufficient. This was not an area for thieves. Zipkin carried both their suitcases. They passed snowed-in farms, crooked shanties, houses with smoking chimneys. If it were not for the smoke and the barking dogs in the dog houses, one might think no one lived here. The depot was empty. The train to New York had just left. As in Russia and Poland, there was an odor of tobacco and smoke. A fire burned in an iron stove. Various notices were pasted on the plastered wall. A kerosene lamp hung from the ceiling. A single fly that had survived the autumn flew about, buzzing. Zipkin seated himself on a bench, smoking one cigarette after another. Clara tucked her hands into her muff. Through the dirty windowpanes could be seen freight trains carrying coal, logs, planks. They moved slowly, their sides and doors inscribed with indecipherable names.

Men came in, knocked tobacco from their pipes, addressed Zipkin just to make conversation, saying it was cold, that it had come early and wouldn't end quickly. (Later Zipkin translated for Clara what they had said.) The Americans looked neither like squires nor like peasants. They were a type of individual not seen in Russia: a blend of landowner and intellectual. There was a boyish good nature in their eyes, a readiness to shake the hand of any stranger, a willingness to laugh, a desire to do a favor. They weren't swathed in furs like the Russians, nor were they as broad of bone, or as heavy. Long legs extended from beneath their sheepskin jackets. To Clara, they were another race. Even the dogs they led seemed more civilized than the Russian hounds. A telegraph key could be heard clacking. The depotmaster looked like an ordinary man. No policeman asked for papers.

Afterwards, Zipkin and Clara sat with the other passengers in a car and rode through snowy spaces along a river. The conductors walked back and forth. It began to snow again. Sheets of snow rose in the wind, whirled about, flew over half-frozen waters. The sky blended with the river. Mists drifted by. The forests were white. It could as easily have been part of Russia or Poland. Zipkin stared out the window. He seemed unable to satiate himself with the sight of snow. Clara shut her eyes. Well, if that was how it was going to be, so be it. Each day she lived now was a gift from God. He wanted to remain with his wife? Let him do as he wished. Clara had become resigned. She would rent an apartment somewhere and take care of Felusia. If he came, he came. If not, too bad. Clara surrendered herself to melancholy. Men did not know what love was. Clara opened her eyes. It had been light a moment ago; now night was falling. The snow had taken on a bluish cast. Alexander sketched in a notebook. They stopped in a village, and the train remained there for some time. Someone carried a bundle of straw brooms into the train. A stout woman in a fur coat and a velvet hat got off. Someone carried her basket and a small valise. Her plump, red face wore an expression of self-assurance that one never saw in European women. The train started again, the snow became thinner, falling at an angle, beating sharply against the windows. As they rode along, the frost drew all sorts of trails, sprays, needles, and blossoms on the panes. The locomotive whistled, its stack belched smoke. Huge areas fell away without village or house —a white desert. "Where are the peasants, the fields?" Clara wondered. "Where does the food come from? One doesn't see any farms." Clara remembered stories of Indians. Perhaps they lay ambushed in caves and forests, prepared to attack the train. And what happened to the souls of the dead here? Was there an American heaven and hell or did they return to the Old World? What strange thoughts came to her.

Zipkin took her arm fondly. "Aren't you sleeping? I thought you were. In fifteen minutes we'll be in New York."

13

I

Mirale's son, Karl Frederick, had died of an inflammation of the lungs. Ezriel and a handful of young people from the "Proletariat" circles walked behind the hearse. There had been a row about the burial. The Jewish cemetery would not accept the child for burial because he had not been circumcised. The Catholics did not want him in their cemetery because he had not been converted. After much difficulty, permission was received from the Evangelical cemetery to bury him there. One of the group tried to give a eulogy during the funeral, but his words could not be heard amidst the thunder and rain. Among the mourners were Esther Eisner, a woman they called Carola, and a stout man called Bleiweiss. Ezriel learned that one of the young men who used to visit Mirale on Zielna Street had committed suicide—no one knew why—and that Stefan Lamanski had become an outright agent of the government abroad and was spying on socialists in Switzerland and France.

After the funeral, Ezriel gave much thought to all this. What had become of his parents' progeny? Their daughter was an exile in Siberia. One grandson lay in an Evangelical cemetery. Another was a settler somewhere in Palestine. Ezriel himself lived with a convert. And what about that young man who had put a bullet in his brain? Couldn't he wait for the inevitable revolution? Or had he lost faith in it? Had he feared arrest? Suicides occurred often in revolutionary circles.

And how could Stefan Lamanski have become a Czarist spy? Was this his revenge on the comrades who had been suspicious of him? Or was he still being falsely accused? It seemed that, among the rationalists, one found the most irrational people. They could not explain why they did things, involved themselves in tragic love affairs, risked unnecessary torments. It occurred to Ezriel that the new literature had also become puzzling and undisciplined. From time to time he read a current novel or poetry in a literary magazine. The authors preached, wrangled, criticized, constantly wrote about suffering, darkness, fate, but Ezriel couldn't see what they were getting at. Like the suicide, they implied a great deal but were never explicit. Well, and what about himself?

One evening as Ezriel walked along Marshalkovsky Boulevard (he had decided to walk a verst each evening) someone called his name. It was Esther Eisner. She still looked attractive, though she was beginning to show signs of middle age. She had grown stouter and there were lines on her round face. She was elegantly dressed. Ezriel would have liked to avoid this meeting. Who could tell? Someone might be following her: Warsaw was full of spies; every janitor was an agent. Ezriel was not entirely without guilt. The government files contained a record of his association with a self-education group. They also knew about his sister. However, it was not natural for him to run away from someone who had greeted him. It was already late spring—Esther's hat was decorated with many flowers—but the weather was cold and rainy.

"Are you too famous to recognize people?" Esther Eisner asked coquettishly. "It's true that I've grown old, but that's not my fault."

Ezriel gave her the compliment she had asked for, expressing the reverse of what he observed: the years had had no effect upon her, she had remained eternally youthful. . . . Esther laughed, thanked him, took his arm. After a while, she released it. She began to ask if he had heard from Mirale, and interrupting herself, she said: "Oh, I forgot to tell you the most important thing."

"What is it?"

"They've killed Stefan Lamanski."

Ezriel felt himself grow pale.

"Who did it?"

"Someone."

"How?"

"With a bullet."

Ezriel's throat tightened. "You know my views."

"No matter how you look at it, he deserved it. It's a shame he was spared for so long. He informed on your sister. You can be sure of that."

"Yes, that's what they say."

"He did enough harm in his lifetime."

"Perhaps."

"What's wrong? You seem to feel sorry for him."

"No, but—it's painful nevertheless."

"Spies must be exterminated," Esther said. "I bless the hands that killed him."

"Would you have done it?"

"If I had had the chance? Surely. A *provocateur* is worse than a dog."

After a long silence, Ezriel asked: "Is there still anyone left of your family?"

"My parents are dead."

"What was your father? You told me once, but I've forgotten."

"Why do you ask?"

"No reason."

"He was a fine man. At first he had a store; later the poor man became a Hebrew teacher."

"A Hebrew teacher?"

"Yes, a Talmud teacher. He was a Hassid of the Kozhenitz rabbi."

"How many spies did *he* shoot?"

Esther laughed.

"You ask such strange questions. You're in a bad mood today. If I've upset you, I'm sorry."

"No, you haven't upset me, but what has become of us Jews in the span of one generation? At least we used to avoid bloodshed."

"Are you turning pious? It's a life-and-death struggle. What has all this to do with Judaism?"

II

At first Olga tried to persuade Ezriel to get a divorce. There was no difficulty in obtaining one's freedom from an insane person. But she finally wearied of his procrastinations. Apparently he did not want to divorce Shaindel, nor did he want to become converted. Olga and Ezriel began to live together. Neighbors and acquaintances were unaware of the fact that they were not married, or at least pretended to be. To everyone, Olga was Mme Babad, but on her documents she remained Bielikov. He remained a Jew, while Olga and the children—Natasha and Kolia—belonged to the Greek Orthodox faith. Each time she and Ezriel considered taking a trip, there were complications because of the different surnames on their passports. They could not stay together at a hotel. But Olga realized that anger would solve nothing. Eventually she hoped to rescue Ezriel from his environment. When their affair started, he had been a poverty-stricken doctor on Nowolipki Street, with a practice consisting of market women and peddlers. In the hospital and clinic he had worked for groschen. There hadn't been a decent piece of furniture in his house, not even a rug. Shaindel had left everything in a state of confusion when she had entered the asylum. Olga had arranged for Ezriel to move to Marshalkovsky Boulevard, furnish an elegant office and apartment. Misha had been so neglected by his disturbed mother that he had been near a breakdown. He wept, raged, and suffered cramps. Olga had restored the boy to health. She had urged Ezriel to interest himself in hypnotism. Although Ezriel was misanthropic and isolated himself, Olga had convinced him that it was important to cultivate the friendship of the better families by inviting them to social functions. She had made him understand that windows needed curtains, floors rugs, walls pictures. Ezriel had retained the Jewish feeling of abnegation for worldly needs. He knew nothing about plans, budgets, lived for the moment, practiced no economies, paid interest to usurious moneylenders. In the end he had had to admit that it was Olga who had brought him a wealthy practice, secured him from need, and helped him gain a reputation.

But, as the saying goes, the more things change, the more they remain the same. Basically, Ezriel was no different. Seized with despair in the midst of a party, he would go and lock himself in a room. He said the wrong things, told patients how little he knew and how unadvanced medicine was. Women patients complained that Dr. Babad did not greet them when they met in the street, and walked by without tipping his hat. The neighbors had similar comments. He now owned a coach and employed a coachman, but whenever he went somewhere on foot, he lost his way, even on his own street. Instead of going in the direction of Krolewska Street, he would head toward the Vienna Station. No matter how many umbrellas and rubbers Olga bought for him, he managed to leave them behind somewhere. He hypnotized those who suffered from insomnia, constipation, stomach pressure, but neglected his own illnesses. No matter how often Olga spoke to him, she always had the feeling that he was concealing something from her. But what was it that tormented him? Was he secretly ill? Was he longing for Shaindel? Was he a victim of the so-called *Weltschmerz* that was being discussed in the literary magazines?

At least Olga was sure he loved her as a wife. In moments of excitement, he kissed her, embraced her, made up funny and endearing pet names. He could become childlike, optimistic, openhearted, and perform all kinds of foolish tricks. He himself admitted that he was like those lunatics who went from depression to exaltation. He switched from moods of penny-pinching to extravagance; he would isolate himself, and then suddenly he would join her and the children, and share in their games. No matter what happened between Ezriel and Olga during the day, there was always a truce at night. There had developed between them a harmony, a ritual of symbols, a private language. Ezriel more than once remarked to Olga that sexual inspiration had within it all the symptoms of insanity. Their nightly caprices had laws of their own, an irrational "logic." During the day they avoided any talk of the fact that they were living together illicitly. But at night it was a favorite topic of conversation. In the dark Andrey was resurrected, Olga was again a Jewish girl from Lithuania. She spoke Yiddish, using idioms and expressions that she thought she had forgotten. Everything became jumbled together: life and death, Lublin and Vilna, Jewishness and apostasy, chastity and wantonness, tenderness and evil. At moments of orgasm Olga saw strange images, monsters. No matter how often Ezriel asked her about them, she could never explain the meaning of these visions. They became accustomed to this nightly intimacy and daytime remoteness. Essentially, Ezriel remained for Olga, odd, secretive, treacherously alien, just as Andrey had once been. The bit of happiness he gave her barely balanced the scale of pleasure and pain. The slightest conflict was enough to upset it.

His daughter, Zina, hated Olga and did not conceal her feelings. This twenty-year-old girl, just out of the gymnasium, treated Olga as if she were not the lady of the house. Zina came and went, slammed doors and gave orders to the maids. She had planned to study abroad after obtaining her diploma, but instead remained in Warsaw. She resembled her father, was tall, golden-haired, with a skin like porcelain. She was considered a beauty, but Olga did not find her attractive. Zina's life was empty. Not only was she at odds with Olga, but she seldom exchanged a word with her father. She dressed shabbily, kept her distance from young men, had no friends, read cheap books, and was not interested in anything worthwhile. She had studied English and Italian, but what good were languages to a person who did not speak for days on end? Ezriel more than once chastised her, but she had placed a seemingly insurmountable barrier between them. She avoided him, made impudent replies, and talked of moving out. When at home, she would lock herself in her room, and ate alone. Above all, she had no fixed schedule for anything, whether it was eating, sleeping, reading, or studying. Ezriel was able to understand others, but his daugher remained a riddle to him. Was she a melancholic? Was she possessed by some *idée fixe?* Did she silently suffer for her mother? Olga had her own opinion of her stepdaughter: Zina was simply a spoiled brat, egoistic, sullen, indifferent, heartless—an enemy in the house. . . .

III

Sunday mornings Olga took Natasha and Kolia to church. She did not want her children to grow up atheists. Her churchgoing also served to emphasize the fact that although she lived out of wedlock and with a Jew, she was nevertheless a devout member of Greek Orthodoxy. The governess took care of Ezriel's son, Misha. On the fourth Sunday of each month, Ezriel would visit Shaindel.

Between Blonya and Prushkov, not far from where he and Olga had once spent a few rainy summer days, Professor Przeborski's sanatorium for the mentally ill was located. At first Professor Przeborski did not want to accept Shaindel: she showed signs of religious mania, made scenes about the impurity of the food, and prayed in Hebrew. Even in an insane asylum there is a "dominant culture." Some of the emotionally disturbed were, in their own fashion, anti-Semites. But because she was the wife of a psychiatrist and because Ezriel had engaged a private attendant for her, Professor Przeborski had allowed himself to be persuaded. With the passage of time, Shaindel had improved. Her suicidal tendencies seemed to be in check and she no longer talked to herself or paced endlessly back and forth with folded hands. She was now in the state that psychiatrists call chronic melancholia, where there is a measure of improvement and an adjustment to circumstances. The prognosis was not a hopeful one, because the patient was not young enough and because she knew that her husband lived with another woman, but Shaindel's condition had become stabilized.

She now had her own room in a small house in the section reserved for the less critically ill. She was treated with opium, chloral, Turkish baths, massages. Twice daily her attendant took her for a walk in the garden, or she went out alone. People at the institution had become accustomed to the sorrowing woman with black, sad eyes, and a sparse beard sprouting from her chin, wearing a sagging gray dress, and a kerchief over her head. The attendants, male and female, called her Mama. Her private attendant cooked for her in kosher pots, and food was sent to her from Blonya. On Passover, she ate matzos. On Rosh Hashana and Yom Kippur, she was taken to worship at the women's synagogue in Blonya. She was often seen seated on a bench outside her cottage, knitting a sweater she never finished. On Fridays, this disturbed woman lit five candles in a brass holder: for herself, Ezriel, Joziek, Zina, and her youngest, Misha. In Blonya, in Prushkov, in all the surrounding area, everyone knew about her. Jews said that she was sane and that her husband, a charlatan, had committed her to the sanatorium so that he could carry on with others. . . .

The coach arrived, Ezriel stepped out, and Shaindel came to the door. Her attendant, Mrs. Shumkin, a lame woman who came from Lithuania and was the widow of a surgeon-barber, greeted Ezriel, said a few quiet words to him, and limped away, leaving husband and wife together. Ezriel approached Shaindel.

"Good morning, Shaindel."

"Good year."

"How are you?"

"As you see."

"May I come in?"

"Why not?"

The room contained a bed for Shaindel and a bench-bed for Mrs. Shumkin, a dresser and a commode. It resembled a room in Jampol. Even the smells were those of Jampol: a blend of onions, chicory, mold. A cat sat on a footstool. Shaindel sat down on the edge of the bed and Ezriel on the bench. He placed two packages on the table—gifts for Shaindel and for Mrs. Shumkin. Shaindel sat, bent over, tense and shy. Old age had come to her early. Her face was wrinkled and warty. The patches of hair that strayed from beneath her head-kerchief were streaked with white.

"You are better, yes?"

"So-so."

"Misha is a fine boy."

"Eh? Yes."

"He sends you his love."

"I thank him kindly," Shaindel said, as if quoting from a primer.

"Zina sends her love too."

Shaindel thought a while, "Already engaged?"

"No."

"What is she waiting for? She's already eighteen."

"You're making a mistake, Shaindel, she's twenty."

"How is that possible? Well—"

For a long time they were both silent. Then Ezriel said: "Mrs. Shumkin tells me that you aren't eating enough."

"I eat. How much can one eat? I'm not hungry."

"If you eat, you'll become stronger."

"What do I need strength for? My life is finished."

"Is Mrs. Shumkin a good cook?"

"Too much salt."

"You can tell her to use less salt."

"I tell her. Does anyone listen to me then? Do I count for anything? I am less than this filth." And Shaindel indicated the dirt under her nails.

"I'll tell her."

"Don't tell her. She'll torture me even more. She's made a pact with the Gentiles. She winks at them and sleeps with them. A wanton woman."

"You just imagine that, Shaindel. She's no longer young. She's crippled too."

Shaindel laughed. Her eyes became mad. "She's pretending, she's pretending. When no one looks, she walks straight. If someone winks at her, she runs like a girl. She was pregnant and miscarried. She buried the infant with a spoon."

"What are you saying? She's a woman in her fifties."

"Well, what of it? When is the Pentecost?"

"In three weeks. I gave you a calendar."

"They stole it from me."

"Who?"

"They steal everything. It's a pity—your money. She steals all my things. She tears out pages from my prayer book, to keep me from saying a Jewish prayer."

Ezriel stood up. "Show me. Let me see."

The prayer book was on the table. Ezriel began to leaf through it. All the pages were there from beginning to end. He said: "Not one page is missing."

"They're missing."

"Which pages are missing?"

Shaindel did not reply. It was hard to know if she hadn't heard or had pretended not to hear. She closed her eyes, placed her wrinkled hands in her lap, and sat in secret agony. For a moment she smiled mockingly as if to say, "How easy it is to deceive a man!"

Ezriel asked: "How do you sleep?"

Shaindel seemed to shrink. "I sleep if they let me."

"Who doesn't?"

"They don't let me."

"Who, Shaindel, who?"

She looked at him painfully. "Leave me alone!"

"Shaindel, I'm your husband. I want to help you. I'm a doctor, too. Who doesn't let you sleep?"

"They don't let me—go, go away. I will be dead soon."

THREE

14

I

In the homes of the Marshinov Hassidim, the young men whispered among themselves. Reb Shimmon's Hassidim, the deserters, had won a victory over Marshinov. The rabbi's son, Zadok, had put on the short coat of the heathen—had become depraved. His father, Rabbi Jochanan, was growing more and more feeble. The rabbi was seldom strong enough now to go to the study house to pray. Warsaw doctors insisted that the rabbi should move to Otwock, or go away to the mountains. They ordered him to eat fatty foods, but the rabbi could not even tolerate lean food. He could take nothing more than a glass of milk and an egg cookie. On the Sabbath, he tasted a sip of wine, a crumb of Sabbath loaf, a bit of fish, a sliver of meat. Reb Jochanan had become emaciated, skin and bones. His face was white. His beard and sidelocks had turned gray early. Only his eyes remained shining. The rabbi was studying the Cabala: the Zohar, the Tree of Life, the Covenant of Rest, the Book of Piety, the Book of Creation. He sat all day in his prayer shawl and phylacteries like an Ancient. He had separated himself from Tsipele, no longer even slept in her room on Friday nights, which were the nights of union. Mendel the beadle related strange tales about Jochanan. He had almost ceased going to the place where even the Czar goes on foot. When he prayed, or studied, a heat emanated from his body that was not of this world. Once it happened that Mendel picked up the cushion of a chair in which the rabbi had been sitting as he recited the Song of Songs. The cushion was so hot that Mendel had almost burned himself. Mendel swore by his beard and sidelocks that in the dark a pale light shone forth from the rabbi's face. He slept no more than two hours out of the twenty-four and in his sleep his lips continued to murmur. Mendel had listened and had heard the rabbi whisper holy names in Aramaic. Honest Jews who were known not to exaggerate bore witness that they had seen the rabbi perform miracles. He would reach for a pen (the rabbi wrote with a goose quill) and it would be drawn to his hand like a magnet. The pages of the books he read turned by themselves. Everyone who visited the rabbi's study agreed on one thing: his body smelled of myrtle and clove—the aromas of the Garden of Eden. Hassidim who had given the rabbi their lists of requests would emerge from his study pale with astonishment. On one occasion the rabbi had read out the name of a child, and although the father had requested that the rabbi pray for the boy so that he would be diligent in his studies, the rabbi instead prayed for his complete recovery from a current illness. The Hassid had not even heard from home that his child was sick. Later the father received a telegram saying that the child had been ill. He had recovered at the exact hour of the father's audience with the rabbi. Another time, a father came to the rabbi complaining that his son was rotting away in the Czar's barracks because he refused to eat the non-kosher food. The rabbi lifted his shoulders in surprise. Barracks? His son was not in the barracks, he told the astounded Hassid. How was that possible? The father had just received a letter from him. Several days later the father learned that his son had deserted his regiment and had stolen across the border. Once, the parents of a schoolboy who had suddenly lost his sight came to Marshinov. All the specialists had given the boy up. The rabbi listened to the parent's story and ordered that the boy's eyes be bathed with tea. Within a week his sight was restored.

Oddly enough, the rabbi himself was not aware of his powers. He asked Mendel the reason for the large crowds that came to him, not only for the holidays, but on weekdays as well. When Mendel replied that it was because of the miracles, the rabbi looked puzzled. For the first time since he had become rabbi, he grew angry at Mendel: "What miracles? Which miracles? Don't talk foolishness! The Almighty," the rabbi said, "needs no miracles. He carries out His will through the laws of nature." Tsipele related to Calman examples of the rabbi's powers. A letter had arrived from her daughter, Zelda, who was living with her father-in-law in Wysoky, to say that she was pregnant, blessed be the Lord. When Tsipele went to the rabbi to give him the good news, he already knew it and wished her *mazel tov*. Tsipele's hands and feet had grown numb. There had been no visitor from Wysoky in the past weeks, and Zeldele had kept the matter secret because of her fear of the Evil Eye. How then had the rabbi known? Another time, when Tsipele had brought him a letter, he had begun to read its contents while it was still in the envelope. He had suddenly realized what he was doing, grown shy, and stopped. Tsipele told her father about these incidents and wept: it was too much for her to live with such a saint. She was afraid of his holiness.

"Father, he has completely estranged himself from me!"

And a muffled cry came from her, as she concealed her face in a batiste handkerchief.

Calman grew sad. "God willing, in a hundred years you will sit with him in Paradise."

"Papa, I want him here!" Tsipele cried.

Over the years, much had happened. Calman had moved away from the estate. He had not even gone to live in Jampol but had settled in Warsaw. His in-law, Reb Menachem Mendel, Ezriel's father, had died a few weeks after having been operated on for cataracts. Tirza Perl, his widow, had gone to the Holy Land. She wrote that she prayed at the Wailing Wall, at the shrine of Rabbi Yehuda the Hassid, and at Rachel's grave. She had seen Uri Joseph, Ezriel's son, who lived on the land, had become a colonist. Tirza Perl sent Calman a present of a bag of Palestinian earth as a token of gratitude for having paid her fare to the Holy Land. Calman had taken over Reb Menachem Mendel's flat on Krochmalna Street. Here everything had remained the same: the table on which Reb Menachem Mendel had studied the Torah, the bench, the Holy Ark, the books in the bookcases. Many matches had been proposed to Calman, but he had not remarried. His white beard had grown sparse and he wore long sidelocks. His teeth had gradually fallen out, but what were teeth? Enemies that caused pain. He wore spectacles and needed a cane, but his powers had, thank God, not yet entirely left him. He cooked his own oat grits. He shredded a chunk of bread and ate it with borscht. On Fridays he carried his own Sabbath pot to the baker, and invited a guest for the Sabbath meal as well. The Society for the Care of the Sick still prayed on the Sabbath at Reb Menachem Mendel's house, and Calman became their beadle. A few days a week he slept at sick people's homes to help out. His children, his grandchildren, his business got along without him. But the sick needed him, and Calman had read in one of the holy books that a person belonged to those who needed him, not to those whom he needed. It certainly wasn't easy for Calman to stay up nights, to sit in stuffy rooms, carry bedpans, or listen to the sighs and complaints of the sick—nevertheless, he daily praised God for having been sent the blessing of doing charitable deeds.

But since his son-in-law, the Marshinov rabbi, was not well, and his daughter had begged him to come to her, he had left everything and gone to Marshinov. If it counted as a good deed to visit an ordinary patient, surely it meant infinitely more to be with a patient who was a saint. On the other hand, one could grow angry at an ordinary sick person who did not heed the doctor's orders. One could even administer medicine to him forcibly. What, however, could one do with a saint, who didn't care about his health? Calman had countless times determined to reprove his son-in-law, to caution him to follow the doctor's advice. Yet whenever he found himself in the rabbi's presence, looking into his face, he became as if paralyzed. This was not Tsipele's husband, but an ancient sage. Outside, the rabbi's door it was the mundane middle of the week, but in Jochanan's room it was Yom Kippur at all times. Candles burned. It was as if the sun shone there with a festive light. The warmth was like the inside of a Holy Ark. The glory of God reigned over Reb Jochanan's countenance, over the braid of his prayer shawl, over each fringe of the ritual garment. One actually sensed the awe of angels, the fire of the seraphim, the flapping of wings, the secrets of heaven, the presence of God's host. Even a fly on the wall did not seem common. How was one such as Calman to open his lips there? Jochanan conducted himself simply. He stood up before Calman and said fondly: "Peace on to you, Father-in-law! How is Father-in-law?" and presented a hand that burned like a living coal.

II

The Hassidim told wondrous tales of Reb Jochanan—the enlightened Jews could not stop relating the wonders of Zadok. Those close to him swore that this was no young man but lightning itself. One could not believe half the things reported of him if one hadn't witnessed them. When Zadok decided he wanted to learn French, he read a Polish-French dictionary three times over from A to Z. After the third reading, he remembered each word. Once through the grammar and he knew every rule, every exception. In this fashion he studied Greek, Latin, even English and Italian. He enrolled in the Warsaw University's faculty of mathematics, but it was little more than a formality. The other students were like kindergarten children compared to him. The professors invited him to their homes, discussed mathematical problems with him as with an equal. Zadok became a frequent visitor at the home of Professor Dickstein, an assimilated Jew. He hadn't up to that time tasted non-kosher food, although he already went about with his head uncovered and drank tea and coffee in the homes of the assimilated Jews. In addition to mathematics, Zadok studied physics, chemistry, biology, philosophy, and just about everything else that was offered. When Zadok visited his uncle, Dr. Babad, Ezriel was astounded. The young man knew anatomy and physiology. His professors warned Zadok not to spread himself so thin, but Zadok only laughed. One had to be aware of everything. There was room in the brain for the knowledge of all the ages. On the contrary, the more one knew, the easier it was to remember.

Zadok's assimilation was the talk of Hassidic Poland. He had been married at sixteen when he had still been pious. Reb Joshua Walden, his father-in-law, demanded that his daughter, Hannah, divorce her heretic husband, but Hannah wouldn't hear of it. Zadok now dressed in modern fashion and Hannah no longer wore a wig. Zadok still had five years of board due at his father-in-law's, but he and Hannah moved into a flat in the Old City. The assimilated elders of the Warsaw community voted Zadok a subsidy. He also did some tutoring in a wealthy home. Hannah, the pampered child, secretly accepted money from her mother, but what was money to Zadok? He went to bed with books and arose with books. In the hundreds of years that the Jews had studied nothing but the Talmud, the Gentiles had produced an Archimedes, a Euclid, a Copernicus, a Galileo, a Newton, a Pascal, and a Darwin. The Jews had stuck to ancient Talmudic precepts and the Gentiles had built railroads and steamships, had invented the telegraph and the telephone, designed microscopes and spectroscopes. They had harnessed the forces of nature. Each day Zadok discovered new wonders: Mendeleyev's table of atoms, Lobachevsky's non-Euclidean geometry, the findings of Faraday and Maxwell, Helmholtz and Hertz. Because the Jews had remained voluntary prisoners of their ancient legends, they had forfeited an ocean of knowledge that could not be drained. In Poland there were few scientific publications, but from Gebetner and Wolf, dealers in foreign publications, Zadok had obtained the most recent German books and periodicals that dealt with the very latest achievements and experiments. He did not read but scanned. He leafed through a book or magazine so rapidly that those who witnessed it hardly believed that he could have managed to read a line. Later, when they discussed it with him, it was clear that he had absorbed everything, and missed nothing. . . .

But where did all this secular learning lead? Evenings, Zadok liked to go over to his Uncle Ezriel's house on Marshalkovsky Boulevard and talk. With his Uncle Ezriel, Zadok could speak rapidly, cut his sentences short. They discussed Spinoza, Kant, Hegel in the same way as the Mishnah and the Gemara. Zadok had not lost the Hassidic gestures, the clutching at the beard, which he had already shaved, the wrinkling of the brow, the nail-biting. When he became excited over Fichte's *Ego and Non-Ego*, or about Schopenhauer's "blind will," he was capable of overturning a glass of tea on Olga's best tablecloth. Olga made no secret of the fact that she could not stand him. This genius brought into her splendid home the cackling sound of Yiddish, the manners of Grzybow Place, the chant of the synagogue. Even when he kissed her hand in the manner of a gallant, his nose interfered. Olga remarked sarcastically that he kissed ladies' hands as if they were his ritual garment. She had an even more serious complaint: each time Zadok came, he left Ezriel disturbed and melancholy. Despite Olga's grumbling, Ezriel continued to encourage Zadok's visits. Zadok intrigued the male guests who came to the Babads'. They asked him complicated questions, to which he replied in the wink of an eye. Within half a minute he multiplied two rows of six figures, and calculated square and cube roots with ease. He was always asked how he did it. How could a brain work so swiftly? Did he actually calculate with such speed or did the answer come to him automatically? It was something to talk about and argue over. Zadok made the evenings interesting. In addition to Zadok's lightning mathematics, there were always the discussions about hypnotism.

Ezriel had, at first, as good as rejected hypnotism. The sessions that he had witnessed at the hospital had not convinced him. He could not see where hypnotism could be effective as a cure. He had tried hypnosis on Shaindel, during the time when she was still at home, but the results had been negative. The entire concept of forcing one's will upon another's seemed to Ezriel irrational, a sort of modern abracadabra. For if staring into someone's eyes and repeating words could work, why couldn't Reb Jochanan's good wishes, or the Evil Eye of a witch? Mesmerism was bound up in Ezriel's mind with spiritualism, mind reading, clairvoyance, and other such occult matters that had nothing to do with science and were more likely to awaken old superstitions than to heal. Deep within him, Ezriel felt that all spiritual diseases, even the so-called functional ones, were organic and had to do with the structure of the brain or its chemical processes. Could words and glances alter cells and tissues? The more Ezriel doubted, the more he studied these matters. Investigations into this subject were being conducted all over Europe, although France—Nancy and Paris—remained the center. Slowly Ezriel began to believe that this was indeed a factual force, not some sort of fancy. Bernheim, Charcot, Janet were not charlatans. Feldman's demonstrations in Warsaw were not hocus-pocus, not hallucinations. He himself had witnessed cases of hypnotic catalepsy, lethargy, somnambulism. He had seen hypnotized patients shiver from alleged cold, perspire from nonexistent heat, react to suggested hallucinations, carry out post-hypnotic orders. There could be no thought of chicanery or make-believe here.

It wasn't long before Ezriel himself began to use hypnosis on his patients. He practiced on Olga. He reached a stage where he could rid her of a headache over the telephone. Olga had for years suffered from insomnia and Ezriel had hypnotized her so that she could sleep. He would seat his subject in an armchair, request her to make her mind as empty of thought as possible, to think about nothing. Then he would instruct her to stare at the lid of a silver watch which hung on the opposite wall, and he would begin to speak: "Your lids, dear lady, are growing heavy; they will soon close. Your gaze is tired, misted over. Your arms and legs are sinking; a weariness is coming over your limbs; you barely hear my voice; you're growing sleepy; you can't keep your eyes open any longer . . ." At times he would place his hand on the patient's abdomen. . . . His patients actually fell asleep, carried out his suggestions. Despite the fact that he had achieved hypnosis so often that there could no longer be any question of his ability, his own doubts of his performance persisted. Each time he hypnotized a patient, he could not help being suspicious that he or she might be playing along with him.

III

It was odd that Zadok not only allied himself with the extreme assimilationists but went even further than they. On a visit to Ezriel, he clutched at his chin and argued with his uncle in a Talmudic-like chant: "If you believe that everything the rabbis scribble in their commentaries was given to Moses on Mount Sinai, then conduct yourself according to *The Beginning of Wisdom*. On the other hand, if you are a freethinker—what does 'Jew' mean? In nature there is no such specie as Jew. All these labels—Jew, Gentile—aren't worth a fig."

"The fact that Moses did not speak to God is no indication that He does not exist," Ezriel interrupted.

"And supposing He does exist, what of it? Since we do not know what He wants, why compound nonsense with more nonsense? Where is your logic, Uncle Ezriel?"

"My logic is that the spiritual development of man is as much nature as physics or embryology. Since Judaism does exist, that means the powers that be want it to continue existing."

"One can say that about every religion."

"That's true."

"What about the religions that have disappeared?"

"They were intended to disappear."

"Then perhaps our time has come?" Zadok asked.

"Even an incurable patient calls a doctor. No one dies willingly."

"What about those who commit suicide? Their desire too is rooted in nature."

"They are the exception rather than the rule."

"What is an exception in nature?" Zadok pinched the spot where a sidelock once grew. "The universe is not a grammar book. In nature as in mathematics, there are no exceptions."

"Who says that nature is mathematics."

"It's certainly closer to mathematics than to grammar."

"Let the suicides kill themselves, I want to live, both as an individual and as a nationality."

"In that case, you should do what Joziek did, emigrate to Palestine."

"You're right about that."

"But if you don't believe, what tie do you have with the Jews of Yemen or India? Nationalism is nothing but inertia. The Jew has built his entire existence on a legend four thousand years old."

"This legend you refer to gives me sleepless nights. What about the pogroms we suffer? They are something concrete."

"The reason for pogroms is that we have remained as Haman described us: 'There is a certain people scattered abroad and dispersed among the people in all the provinces of thy kingdom; and their laws are adverse from all people; neither keep they the king's laws,' " Zadok began to chant in the tune of the Book of Esther. "We want to be everything at once: Russians, Jews, Frenchmen, Turks. We want to be an amalgamation of all the nations. If one lives in Poland, one should be a Pole, not stand with one foot in Warsaw and the other in Jerusalem."

"What is your solution? Conversion?" Ezriel asked.

"Wallenberg is right: you cannot live in someone else's country and consider his daughter taboo, his meat impure, his God an idol. So long as men separate into groups, there cannot be a group within a group."

"You talk like the anti-Semites!" Ezriel said.

"Maybe they are right?"

"And what if the socialists were to take over thirty years from now?"

"Then humanity would become a single entity and there would be no place for either Jews or Gentiles."

"That means that I must now become a Gentile, so that in thirty years I will become an internationalist."

"History is dynamic. Have you read Hegel's *Phenomenology?* The spirit is dialectic. I, myself, Uncle Ezriel, am a hedonist. When man does that which brings him pleasure, he is following the right path. Jews suffer, an indication that theirs is the wrong path."

"Poles suffer too. It would be better to become a German or an Englishman."

"If I could, I would surely do so."

"As an Englishman, you'd be drafted to fight the Boers."

"If I had no choice, then I would fight."

"The English demand that you fight with zeal."

"Who would care what they wanted."

"Is that your philosophy?"

"It's Spinoza's."

"What about the Jew who enjoys his Judaism?" Ezriel said.

"Only the pious enjoy it. What can your Judaism mean to you, Uncle?"

Olga knocked on the door. "Tea is ready."

Ezriel and Zadok went into the dining room. The samovar

stood on the table around which Natasha, Kolia, and Misha were already seated. Natasha, now a girl of fourteen, was a fourth-form student in the gymnasium. She was tall, slim, with a turned-up nose, black hair, and dark eyes. Her mouth was too large for her face, and the boys called her "frog." Kolia was eleven. He was the image of his mother: black eyes, straight nose, and long chin. His hair was cut short in military style. He wore a student's jacket with brass buttons and a high collar. Misha, too, was going to school. He resembled Shaindel. In the short time since Olga had left the room to summon the men, Misha and Kolia had located a piece of string and were playing a string game, "Etel Betel." They were taking turns removing the string from each other's hands, each time forming a prescribed pattern called "water," "cymbal," a "broom," and so on.

Olga put her hands to her head. "Again they've got hold of that dirty string! Go wash your hands."

"Ma, it's not dirty."

"Go wash your hands, I say!—Wait!"

Olga went into the kitchen and returned with a wet sponge and towel. Natasha smiled wisely like an older sister as the boys' hands were being washed. Kolia stuck his tongue out at her, and Misha began to laugh. Ezriel poured tea for Zadok and himself. The children added granulated sugar, but Ezriel and Zadok bit into pieces of lump sugar. The cook came in and out of the room as she served cookies and cake. She wore a white apron and a cap over her blond hair. Olga glanced at Zadok: "Well, Pan Zdzislaw, how are things going?"

Zadok started. She had interrupted his private thoughts.

He replied in flowery Polish with a Jewish accent. "Thank you, honored lady. How can things be going? One stumbles along. We have discussions, but what comes of our words? At times I envy the animals who carry out their functions silently. Animals, like nature itself, know only deeds, therefore an animal can no more make a mistake than a rock. A pebble showed that Aristotle was wrong. I'm referring to the experiment on the leaning tower of Pisa."

"Are not words deeds too?" Ezriel asked. "Isn't our intellect a part of nature? Why should a stone be infallible and our brains continue to make mistakes?"

"What is Uncle trying to say? From the pantheistic point of view, there are no false ideas, only crippled ones. All errors are subjective."

Olga rapped on the table. "They're starting again! Talk about something the children can understand."

Natasha suddenly spoke up. "Papa, animals can make mistakes too. If one puts duck eggs under a chicken and she hatches them, she thinks the ducklings are hers—is that not a mistake?"

"I want to say something, too." Kolia raised his hand like a pupil in class.

"See how talkative they are all of a sudden," Olga said, half reproachful, half smiling.

"What do you want to say, Kolia?"

"When we were in Wilanow, at Madame Malewska's, the boys dug a trench and put a kerchief over it. The cat did not know that there was a hole beneath it and fell in."

Misha burst out laughing. "Oh, how funny!"

"How about their arguments?" Ezriel asked.

Zadok had apparently already been thinking about something else. He raised the lids over his large, black eyes, made a grimace, and began to scratch his left temple. "The cat? Ducklings? I don't know if one can rightly call these happenings errors. Properly speaking, an error occurs only when one has made a mistake about a definite fact. The hen and the cat do everything by instinct. It only means that instinct is not perfect either, and that is known. The hunter places a wooden decoy in the water or simulates bird calls to fool his prey. But let us imagine that animals are capable of thinking and making mistakes—what does that have to do with our discussion?"

"If error is possible, then sin exists. If sin is possible, there is no determinism and there is room for absolute ethics and religion. Maybe man has to discover God in the same way that he discovered America or gravity?"

"Well, there they go again! Children, drink your tea. Misha, don't puff your cheeks out," Olga ordered. She turned to Ezriel.

"Pan Zdzislaw is right. If one does not know, one should not speak. It's better to believe without philosophies. One cannot find God through reasoning."

"Certain truths have already been found, eternal truths, that are forever valid."

"What truths?"

"The Ten Commandments."

Zadok jerked his head as if to dislodge a fly. "What sort of discovery is that? The struggle for existence is a biological law. According to Malthus, wars are necessary. The entire history of man is filled with wars. The very Bible that says 'Thou shalt not kill,' orders the killing of men, women, and children."

" 'Thou shalt not kill' means within one's own group."

"In what way is one's own group better than other groups? These are all social laws. It's the same to nature who kills whom. For thousands of years bulls have been slaughtered and nature has kept quiet. Can it be possible that mankind will have to account for all the bulls, calves, and chickens it has slaughtered? Why should a human life be so dear to nature?"

"Because man suffers more. He can foresee suffering. He does not live exclusively in the present."

"And if he suffers, does that make him privileged? Nature would not care if man had remained a cannibal."

"According to you, Zadok, one is permitted to make pogroms . . ."

Olga shivered.

"I beg you, stop this babbling!" Olga said sternly. She had countless times asked these yeshiva scholars not to conduct their futile discussions. But no sooner did they get together than the wrangling would begin in a Yiddish-spiced Polish. They argued like the impractical idlers in a House of Study. Zadok, for all his bad manners, at least had a modern outlook, but Ezriel still clung to the glorification of the moldy Judaism of his origin. He had somehow remained entangled in its fanaticism. Above all, Olga wanted to avoid talk about religion, since the household was mixed. In the school which Misha attended, he had to leave the room when the priest came to give his lesson. The children absorbed all sorts of nonsense. Each time Kolia and Misha quarreled, Olga was afraid lest Kolia call Misha Jewboy. She considered Ezriel's reference to pogroms at the table tactless. Whose fault was it if stupid peasants allowed themselves to be agitated into savagery? Why expose the children to such horrors?

It suddenly became so still in the dining room that Misha could be heard sipping his tea and tapping his spoon against the glass. Kolia grew serious. Natasha turned her head away. Ezriel drank and drew his brows together. He realized the logical weakness of his arguments. His father had applied the same type of reasoning. "If what you say is so, then this is an unbridled world!" he would insist. Well, maybe the world was unbridled? Perhaps one was permitted to stage pogroms? . . . It seemed strange that Zadok, who had so recently abandoned piety, had been able to make peace with life, while Ezriel still became indignant at every evil deed. Each time he read a newspaper, he was dumfounded. It only contained reports of beatings, slaughter, attacks on innocent people. The Russian Jews were chased from the cities, driven from the villages. They fled to Poland, and the Polish press ranted against the "Litvaks." All of Russia was one skein of injustice. The police were corrupt, the courts were crooked. Criminals occupied seats in the most exalted Synod. The Poles, victims themselves, nevertheless behaved most severely toward the Jews. The Jews, on the other hand, did not live honorably. Competition was ugly and each grabbed only for himself. Palestine?

They couldn't all emigrate to Palestine. The Turks had already forbidden Jews to purchase land there and the Arabs resented them. Assimilation? No one wanted this raggedy crew outside of a few paid missionaries. Socialism? How would it come about? Who would bring it about? It would again be a case of violence, murder, evil. And what assurance was there that the socialists would be saints? They were already divided into factions and fighting among themselves.

No, this slaughterhouse could not be cleansed with more blood. This was clear to Ezriel. But with what, then? And what was his role in this mire? To be a swine at the trough? To grab for himself as long as it was possible? To send Kolia and Misha to the university and raise two more lawyers? To get Natasha an officer for a bridegroom? . . . In all the years that Ezriel had studied, had wrangled with himself, he had believed that he was destined for something higher. He had been dazzled by such words as culture, humanity, progress, civilization. Now the awakening had come. He had been left without a belief, without an ideal, without hope. His youth had passed. The work grew ever more difficult, the expenses higher. He did not speak of it to anyone, but he spent sleepless nights pondering these "eternal questions." "Why am I living? What am I doing here? What is my mission? What is my duty?" he asked himself again and again. "Or does man not have any duty? Is he simply a cow that needs to graze until he dies or is killed?" Yes, Zadok was right: according to logic, and according to science, might was right . . .

"Why are you letting your tea get cold?" Olga asked.

15

I

Olga had a stroke of luck. Wallenberg had kept his promise, and left her seven thousand rubles in his will. For a long time Olga had wanted to build or buy a villa. It was a residue of nostalgia for the time when she had lived with Andrey in Druskenik near the Niemen River. All respectable Warsaw doctors had their own summer homes. More than thirty years had passed since the Uprising, but Poland was still full of bankrupt nobles, whose dilapidated manor houses could be purchased at a low price. Olga consulted brokers and began to look for a country house. Ezriel himself yearned for some property outside the city. He wanted to get away from the noise. What better escape was there than fields, lakes, and forests?

The agents soon became active and every Sunday Olga insisted that Ezriel accompany her to look at some property or other.

The trips themselves stimulated Ezriel. Warsaw was crowded, dusty, noisy. The houses kept growing taller and the sky narrower. But as soon as one left the city, one saw God's world: a broad sky, distant fields. Storks circled in the blue as they had in Jampol or Turbin. Time seemed to have stopped. Creatures quacked, chirped, twittered, whistled, each had its own tune. Ezriel again heard the sound of the cuckoo as on that day in Otwock, on his last visit to Miriam Lieba. Looking at the properties disturbed Ezriel as much as it pleased him and he would have signed any contract. Olga, more knowledgeable, haggled over prices, found fault with the plumbing, the building, even the grounds, and asked all sorts of questions about taxes and mortgages.

It seemed to Ezriel that nothing would ever appeal to her. But, finally, she found what she wanted. Not far from Warsaw, between Zakroczym and Nowydwor, near the Vistula, there was a small estate, of some hundred acres, mainly pasture land for cattle. At the river's edge the soil was entirely sandy, but the property included a large orchard of apple, pear, and plum trees, as well as gooseberry and currant bushes. There were forty cows (with meager udders), several horses, a pair of goats, even some hogs; and, in a half-muddy pond, carp and wild ducks. The squire, a drunkard, had neglected everything, but the old villa had a foundation of stone and was as solid as a fortress. Poplars that dated from Napoleon's time shaded the windows. The estate included stables, barns, sheds, storage huts, and an ancient structure for drying cheese. The price was modest, but there were mortgages and some renovations would be needed. The old peasants working there had once been serfs. Olga didn't hesitate for long. She left a down payment and settled with the debtors. Ezriel put in everything he owned and even borrowed money from a bank. He had high hopes. If worst came to worst, he could move out there, isolate himself from the world, and live off the land. The estate was bought in both their names.

Ezriel suggested that they postpone the renovating, but Olga was impatient. She engaged a crew of workmen. The roof needed repairs, stoves had to be replaced, a road paved, a second well dug. They needed new furniture. Olga had promised Ezriel that she would not borrow any more money, but once the work of renovating the house had begun, she couldn't stop in the middle. They were soon forced to take out another loan. One day Ezriel had money saved up for a rainy day, and the next he was in debt and paying interest to banks and usurers. He maintained two households, one in Warsaw and the estate in Topolka. Overnight he had become burdened with maids, male servants, and old Gentiles who were crippled with rheumatism and whom he had to provide with a sort of pension. As if to spite him, he had fewer patients, since most of the rich women whom he treated were vacationing.

Ezriel sat in his office and spent every free moment adding up figures. The first few weeks showed that there would be no revenue from the estate. The farmhands demanded higher wages. The grass became sun-scorched and the cows gave little milk. The fruit was stolen from the trees or they were picked clean by the birds. The peasants had all sorts of privileges: they had the right to fish in the pond and chop wood in the forest. It was probably necessary to hire a steward, but all stewards drank and stole. The peasants' dogs were wild and Ezriel was constantly being attacked by them. Even bathing in the Vistula wasn't easy, because of the river's stony bed, and the peasants had warned him that not far from shore was a whirlpool that could engulf the best swimmer. Some of the neighbors told Olga that it was advisable to keep rifles on hand because of bandits. There were other neighbors who turned out to be anti-Semites.

The illusion that one could find peace and serenity in the country did not last long. As a rule, Olga gained weight during the summer, but this year she became as emaciated as a consumptive. She had made a mistake but refused to admit it. Her children and Misha were in Topolka for the summer, but Zina had stayed in Warsaw. Olga wrote to Ezriel daily. Sometimes she sent him telegrams. She needed all sorts of supplies. The workmen procrastinated, did their jobs badly. The plumber's estimates had been inaccurate. The government demanded overdue taxes. Everyone seemed to realize that Olga and Ezriel were amateurs. Olga, who until now had been sympathetic toward Poland, began to be resentful. One Sunday night Ezriel and Olga were awakened by the sound of shots fired close to their bedroom window. Who had done the shooting and why, no one knew.

II

Before calling in his first patient, Ezriel paced nervously back and forth for a few minutes in an effort at self-hypnosis to bolster his confidence. These people came to him for courage, and like a false prophet he soothed them. "Peace, peace," he said. A loved one had died? Well, one must keep on living. One feared death oneself? How unhealthy. The main thing was to enjoy life as long as one could. One had been betrayed by one's husband or wife? One's children were selfish? One was going broke? Or approaching old age? Life was tedious? It was all a matter of nerves. All one had to do was get a grip on oneself. Other doctors prescribed remedies, but Ezriel tried to cure with false encouragement. That morning when he opened the door to the waiting room he saw Esther Eisner sitting there.

Ezriel called her into his office. "Well, who has been shot now?"

Esther looked at him gravely. "Your sister is in Warsaw," she said quietly.

"Mirale?"

Esther's voice grew even softer. "She has escaped from Siberia."

"I see."

"She must leave the country at once."

"Where is she?"

Esther gave him the address. Then she shook his hand and left. There was only one other patient, whom Ezriel quickly dispensed with. He was due at the Jewish Hospital that afternoon, but he telephoned that he could not come. Standing at the window, he looked out. He had an odd feeling—as if Mirale had returned from beyond the grave. How old was she? . . . How long was it since she had opened the door in the Hassidic House of Study in Jampol and said: "Come home. Your future father-in-law is waiting!"

He would need money. Mirale was probably penniless. He stood beside the bookcase, took out a book, looked into it, and replaced it. Then he picked up a pen and wrote some figures on a sheet of paper. "How have I accumulated such expenses?" he wondered. He glanced at his mail, which consisted almost entirely of bills. The Jewish community demanded their taxes. Joziek, in Palestine, had married. He wanted to become his own master and asked his father's help. Topolka was a real burden. Olga had written that she was in trouble. And so it went. As soon as Ezriel deluded himself that there was a slight respite, some new complication arose. Some force was toying with him, placing difficulties in his path, as if to thwart all his earthly hopes. He walked along the hall and heard Zina murmur something in her room. The girl should have been in Topolka in the fresh air, taking care of Misha, but she chose to spend the hot days in the city, atoning for what sin? Could she too not make peace with the world? What was bothering her? She had no religion. She had been raised in a secular atmosphere. He felt like going to her and asking the familiar paternal question: "What will become of you?" But instead he waved his hand, walked down the stairs and into the street. A new house was being built nearby. Municipal workers were repairing the pavement and the tracks of the old horse trolley were exposed. There was a smell of lime, fresh dung, big-city heat. The visit to Mirale had its dangers. One could not know. Perhaps she had been allowed to escape to see whom she would contact. Ezriel was hot and sweaty. Rather than take a droshky, he walked, now and then looking back to see if anyone was following him. For some reason the police were out in force. Had some dignitary been assassinated? Was a funeral for some revolutionary scheduled? It would be both foolish and tragic to end up in prison for no reason at all. He suddenly realized that he was praying to

God, promising a donation to charity in return for his safekeeping. "God Almighty," he thought, "save me from falling into their trap. And help Mirale, too. She has suffered enough. . . ." He stopped, wiped his forehead, and said to himself: "I do believe in God and in the power of prayer."

Ezriel had not been to Dzika Street for a long time. Ragged young men stood about, talking and smoking cigarette stubs. Dray wagons carrying loads of iron pipes rolled across the so-called cat's-head cobblestones of the street. The noise was deafening. At the gates to the courtyards, vendors sold rolls, bagels, baked apples, peas, beans, licorice, and halvah. Porters carried overstuffed baskets or pushed carts. Ezriel remembered when this had been a quiet section. Now there was a sign on every window, behind which machines wove, spun, cut, rolled. On Gęsia Street, clerks stood in front of stores, inviting the passers-by in. Little hotels and restaurants had sprung up everywhere. A man with long hair, a broad-brimmed hat, a black ribbon tie, obviously an intellectual, walked by. A Hebrew teacher? A revolutionary? It was in this neighborhood, somewhere in Krasinski Park, that the young radicals had their meeting place. At the gate to the house he was looking for, Ezriel glanced back for the last time to see if he was being followed.

Slowly he walked across the courtyard. He had been foolish. He should have brought along his instrument bag. In case anything happened, he could explain that he had been called to attend a patient. But where was the patient? . . . Below, to the right, there was a Hassidic study house. Through an open window half-covered by curtains, Ezriel heard the singsong recital of the Talmud. He glimpsed a white face, a skullcap, the cornice of a Holy Ark, the flame of a memorial candle. "Perhaps I should go in and remain there. I have two hundred rubles with me. I'd have enough for a year and a half. I once lived in Warsaw on two rubles a week. I could sell my watch, too. . . ." The fantasies began to multiply. Olga would search for him for a while and finally give up. Mirale would go abroad even without his help. Olga would remain in Topolka. Zina would have to find herself a job. But it would be a pity for Shaindel. Shaindel would undoubtedly be transferred to the Jewish Hospital. Misha would remain with Olga, without a father. She had grown fond of him. Or perhaps Mayer Joel would take him in, or Rabbi Jochanan. . . . And what would he do? Sit and study. If he had to run away, it would not be to Topolka. If religion was opium, as they say—it was the opiate most suited to the Jewish soul. Jews had been dreaming over the pages of the Torah for two thousand years. These were noble dreams at least, not bloody nightmares. . . .

He saw the number he was looking for and knocked on the door. Soon he heard footsteps and someone asked: "Who is it?" "The sewing-machine salesman," Ezriel said, repeating the password Esther Eisner had given him.

III

The door was unbolted. A dark woman with upswept hair held at the back with a comb confronted him. "Please, come in!"

He walked through a dark corridor redolent of kitchen odors and dirty laundry. Ezriel heard a voice singing a lullaby: "Ah-a-Ah-a-Ah-a-Ah—" The little one at least, Ezriel thought, needn't fear the police. He was led through a dining room where a young man sat at a table, his sleeves rolled up, fussing with some sort of mechanism. "Is he making a bomb?" No, it was only a wall clock. They came to a door, the woman knocked and then pushed it open. Ezriel saw a small woman, middle-aged, almost old, wearing a black skirt and a gray blouse. Her hair, a mixture of black and gray, was combed up into a tight knot. For a moment he did not recognize her. Suddenly he realized that it was Mirale. Yes, it was Mirale, but completely changed. Her face was wrinkled, red as a frozen apple. "It's you," he said.

"Ezriel!"

They embraced. Beneath the sleeves of her blouse her arms were thin and bony. She said in Russian: "Your sister has grown old."

"Mirale, why do you speak to me in Russian?"

"I've forgotten Yiddish. . . ."

Nevertheless, she began to speak in Yiddish. Seating herself, she indicated a chair for him. "Has she grown smaller?" Ezriel asked himself.

He continued to look at her. This was Mirale, his younger sister. Her fingers were bent. One of her nails had grown horny. A bone jutted from her wrist. Her throat was as wrinkled as tissue paper. They had made sand pies together, had played house. Ezriel's eyes dimmed. When had her R's grown so hard, he wondered. At first her words made little sense. She stammered, spoke of their parents, asked whether the anniversary of their father's death was being observed. She mixed broken Yiddish with Russian. Her speech sounded like a Litvak's, Ezriel thought. Mirale related how long it had taken her to make the trip to Warsaw, how many weeks she had been dragged along in carts and sleighs. She mentioned the names of Russian cities, villages, and spoke of how the peasants had helped her. "You won't believe it, but once they hid me in a wagon, under a sack of oats, in a chest like a coffin. I breathed through a hole. It was so frightening. But it's difficult when one must urinate. Well, I'm stronger than I thought. I survived everything. . . . They believe I can do more for our cause abroad, but I doubt it. . . . I'm neither a speaker nor a writer, just an ordinary woman. . . ."

"How did you manage to stay alive?"

"I managed. You almost never answered my long letters, but you did send money. Thanks for that."

There was a pause while they looked at each other hesitantly, estranged by time. Ezriel felt as if Mirale by some miracle had become the elder. He even felt a kind of jealousy of this weak woman who had chosen her path and followed it unwaveringly. He detected a bit of sisterly sarcasm in her tone when she said, "Well, you're a real doctor."

"Yes."

"What happened to what's-his-name?"

"Zipkin?"

"That's right."

"He's a doctor in America."

"Another doctor? Well, and what about—what was her name?"

"Vera Charlap? She died."

"I was still around then. No, I was in prison."

"Rose Berkowicz committed suicide."

"Why? Well, such things happen. In Siberia suicide is quite common. Especially among the men. She was a fool, that Rose Berkowicz."

"I thought her intelligent."

"No, a chatterbox. Couldn't forget either her gymnasium or her father's tannery."

"Do you still believe in the revolution?"

Mirale looked serious. "I believe."

"Here in Poland everything has come to a halt."

"Oh, I don't know about that. How can an ideal be stopped? The worker is still enslaved. The peasant is still hungry. The bourgeoisie persecutes everyone. You should see whom they're sending to Siberia! Civil servants, teachers, and petty officials. There aren't enough soldiers, and women or peasants with sticks are sent to guard the prisoners. Ah, what this degradation has led to!"

"It's always been the same."

"No! The masses are losing patience. The peasant is embittered. The boil is ready to burst."

"Where will you go?"

Mirale thought for a moment. "As yet I don't know. Wherever the Central Committee sends me. I'll be in touch with someone today. I'll probably get my orders tomorrow."

"How's your health?"

"So-so. I have rheumatism, but that's not fatal. The important thing for me is to get across the border."

"How much money do you need?"

"I don't know. You're always willing to help."

"You're my sister."

"Yes, but you've become an aristocrat. What happened to your wife?"

"She went out of her mind."

"Why? She was such a happy person. Naïve, but lively. Esther Eisner told me about it. Esther's remained a child—still uses the same phrases. Who's the woman with whom you're living?"

"A doctor's widow."

"Well, she exchanged one doctor for another. We really didn't live in Siberia. Time stopped for us. But the railroad strikes show that the people have awakened."

The woman who had opened the door for Ezriel knocked and brought in two glasses of tea with cookies. She looked as if she were performing some holy rite during which one must not speak a word. Pious Jewish girls once served yeshiva students in the same way. Ezriel thanked her. Mirale looked at her somewhat mockingly. "Thank you for the trouble. . . ."

Like an old woman, Mirale took a piece of sugar, dunked it in the tea, then bit off a piece. "Is it chalk or something?" she asked.

Ezriel also bit off a piece. "Why chalk? It's sugar."

"There's no sweetness in it."

"What are you saying?"

Brother and sister exchanged glances. "I seem to have lost my sense of taste. It's from all the traveling. There was a little too much of it. Well, I'm resting now. I still don't know how I'll get to the border. How far is it from here to Mlava? I'll have to ride in a cart. In Germany, I'll be able to take the train."

"You seem tired."

"Yes, I am tired. When I look at you, I see that you resemble Father. You're different, but still—you also have something of our Grandfather Abraham Hamburg about you."

"Yes, Mother used to say that too. It always struck me as ludicrous. You look like Mother."

"Yes, sometimes I frighten myself. I say something and I feel as if it were Mother's voice, even though I speak Russian, not Yiddish. I only had occasion to speak Yiddish a few times. This insane government exiled a completely innocent Litvak from Slutzk, a worker, and he had a hard time with Russian. He was so funny. Really, rather common. He had brought along his phylacteries and prayed every morning. He knew nothing about the movement and only wanted to know when Hanukkah and Purim and Passover fell. There was no Jewish calendar. It was known that I was a rabbi's daughter and so people came to me with questions about religious matters."

"What happened to him?"

"He grew sick and went out like a candle."

"How many victims has the revolution already swallowed up?"

Mirale paused for a moment. "I don't want to argue with you; no matter what you may think, people must have food and clothing. A regime that can't take care of its people must be overthrown."

IV

Only the next day did it occur to Ezriel that the piece of sugar's tasting like chalk to Mirale was a symptom of illness. She must have typhus. It was impossible for him to take her to a hospital, because the police were searching for her, so she remained in the same small room in an iron bed. Ezriel was her doctor. Soon in delirium, she chattered in Russian, Polish, and Yiddish. She raved about having been sentenced to hang. Another woman who was being hanged with her had kept the noose from being tightened. Mirale leaped from her bed, determined to flee to the border. The Central Committee was expecting her. The success of a railroad strike in England was at stake. There was a spy in their midst who must be silenced. "I'll shoot him down like a dog!" Mirale screamed.

Comrades soon came to inquire after her illness. Though leeches had already gone out of style, doctors still relied upon bleeding. When the leeches were applied, Mirale suddenly asked: "What are they, capitalists?"

Ezriel told Olga nothing of what had happened. She arrived in Warsaw sunburned and angry. Why hadn't he come to Topolka on his days off? What had he been doing all alone in hot, dusty Warsaw? The way she spoke of her burdens, one might have thought she was working like an ox. Yet she intended to give a ball and had already set the date. She had invited all the landowners and officials in the district and had included Wallenberg's children. The ball would be expensive but would further Ezriel's career. She had all sorts of plans. A squire owned a forest not far from Topolka. They would obtain permission from him for their guests to hunt in his woods on the day before the ball. For the women, she would arrange an excursion on the Vistula. Natasha must meet young men. As for Olga, she was not going to spend her entire life behind a stove. Having settled in Topolka, they should make the most of it. She was full of enthusiasm and was furious because Ezriel reacted with indifference.

"I can't lead your sort of life," she announced. "I want to be a cosmopolitan, not a rabbi's wife."

Ezriel explained to her that the ball would cost hundreds of rubles and increase his debts, but Olga answered, "If you weren't so impractical, everything would be all right." She used the Yiddish word *batlan*, and enumerated half a dozen doctors who were rich, owned villas, bought their wives expensive pearls, and charged twenty-five rubles a visit.

"You may give ten balls if you like, but I'll neither pay for them nor attend them!"

"Is that your final word?"

"You can count on it."

"Well, no is no. But I have no intention of living in a convent."

She announced that she would sell her last piece of jewelry if necessary to pay for the ball. It suddenly occurred to Ezriel that she had chosen the eve of the Ninth Day of Ab for her party. It was a leap year and so the Ninth Day of Ab came late.

Ezriel had no choice. He had to tell Olga that Mirale was in Warsaw.

"Do you want to be arrested?" Olga cried out in anger.

"Shall I let my sister die?"

"There are other doctors in Warsaw. What do you know about typhus? You might do her harm."

Since Mirale's illness was approaching its crisis, Ezriel spent the night at her bedside. It was hot, but the window had to remain closed, covered by a curtain so that no light could be seen in the courtyard. The janitors were all informers and reported every trifle to the police. Mirale, covered by a feather quilt, lay weak and flushed, her eyes closed. Her hair had grown dry. She tossed, trembled, breathed laboriously. Ezriel wiped away her sweat. How helpless medicine was in such cases! How ironic it was to survive Siberia and later to perish because of some bacteria! Mirale, warring against the autocrats, was now battling inner forces that wanted to destroy her. War everywhere, war in the forests, in the city, in the field, in man's body. She wanted to free the peasants and the proletariat. Like their father, she campaigned against the company of Satan. But what would come after victory? Not redemption, not saints who benefited from the splendor of the Divine Glory, but lots of newspapers, magazines, theaters, cabarets. More railroads, more machines. . . . Did it pay to die for newspapers, theaters, machines? And would anyone remember what the Mirales had done? . . .

V

After her illness, Mirale was so weak she could not stand on her feet, and had to learn to walk all over again. It was not safe for her to remain in the room on Dzika Street. One of the Committee members of the second "Proletariat"—the authorities had liquidated the first—had a house near Falenica. Mirale was taken there and planned to stay through the holidays. The house belonged to a comrade, Jan Popielek, a machinist in a steammill in the Praga suburb.

Ezriel bought some especially nourishing food for Mirale and decided to bring it out himself. In the horse-drawn omnibus to Praga, he sat beside the window, looking out. Warsaw was full of dirt. A stench arose from the gutters. The farther one went from the center of the city, the more old-fashioned the buildings became. The houses in Praga were ancient. Even the people seemed to belong to another generation. Their clothes dated from the time of King Poniatowski. On benches, outdoors, cobblers worked on boots, wrinkled old women with white hair wandered about in torn shawls and wide aprons reaching to the tips of their shoes. Their paws extended, dogs crouched and yawned. Cats sat on low, mossy roofs. A paralytic, wearing thick socks instead of shoes, lounged on a bench near a fence. A church bell rang. A catafalque arrived from somewhere. A number of old women grouped themselves around it, made the sign of the cross, and whispered to one another.

Then Ezriel saw something so unusual that he could not believe his eyes. Not far from a factory, near a wooden lamppost, stood his daughter Zina speaking to a man in high boots and a cap. "I'm imagining it!" Ezriel said to himself. His bus came to a stop. Yes, it was Zina. Ezriel barely restrained himself from calling to her. Had she become a streetwalker? He felt himself grow red. He arose as if about to get off. Suddenly Ezriel understood: Zina was a member of the "Proletariat" group. He sat down again, dumfounded. He would have expected any nonsense from her, but not this. She was such an egotist. Why should the workers and peasants concern her? He asked himself how it could have happened that he had never even suspected her of joining the organization. To be so completely fooled! He felt ashamed for himself, for her, for Olga. Who knew what she might be keeping at home? She might have placed the whole family in danger!

He rode to his destination and left the package for Jan Popielek. Then he took a droshky home. Zina probably was no longer a virgin either. The comrades believed in free love. . . . He sat there dazed. She read Alfred de Musset and Baudelaire, admired Byron and Leopardi! Had all that been a pose? She had been in a dark mood the last few months, had attacked the suffragettes and educated women. But she had taken the courses she had planned to take, and spoken of becoming a nurse. She had found a pupil to tutor. One thing should have made him suspicious: she showed no interest in clothes and was content to wear Olga's discarded jackets and coats. What else should he have expected? His daughter barely knew the Hebrew alphabet. He had taught her everything, except Judaism. He himself had shown her how to escape one's heritage. At the gymnasium she had attended she had not liked the few Jewish pupils and had been proud of looking like a Gentile. . . . She had actually expressed hostility toward Jews on several occasions. And this was his daughter, the granddaughter of the Rabbi of Jampol. How had it happened? Ezriel had to laugh. Every week he read articles on education in the Hebrew magazines, and he had raised an ignoramus. The writers of the articles themselves did not give their children a Jewish education. They were all the same—the Hebrewists, the lovers of Zion, the radicals. Ezriel reminded himself of a saying in *The Best of Pearls:* "The children are the secrets in the hearts of their parents." The children testified to the hypocrisy of their fathers. . . .

Arriving home, he immediately went to Zina's room, but found it locked. He got the key, opened the door, and began to look through the bookcase. There was no trace of illegal literature. He searched in the drawers of the dresser and desk, even lifted the pillow on the bed. Suddenly her mattress seemed overstuffed. He lifted the sheet, found papers inside, hard objects. He felt like a policeman searching someone's house. He got a knife, tore the mattress open, and found it filled with pamphlets and handbills. Suddenly Ezriel spied a bundle wrapped in paper. It was so heavy he could barely lift it. Inside he found a gun and cartridges. It was the first time in Ezriel's life that he had touched such an instrument of destruction, and its weight astounded him. He didn't know how to handle it and was afraid it might go off. Sweat appeared on his forehead. What did one do with such a weapon? Where could one hide it? If he were caught with it, he would rot in jail or die on the gallows.

16

I

On the eve of the Ninth Day of Ab, the huge, blazing sun was beginning to sink behind banks of clouds that looked like glowing coal. In Nowydwor and Zakroczym, the benches in the Houses of Prayer had already been placed on their sides as a symbol of mourning. In the menorah, only a single candle burned. The last meal before the fast, bread with ashes and a hard-boiled egg, was being prepared in Jewish homes. The men and women would soon remove their boots and shoes and remain in their stocking feet before reading the Book of Lamentations. But at Olga's, preparations were being made for a ball. Many of the guests had arrived early that morning to hunt in Squire Sadowski's forest. The women had gone rowing on the Vistula, which was as smooth as a mirror. In the kitchen, food was being cooked in huge pots and kettles. Outdoors on a spit a whole pig was roasting. It had been slaughtered the day before, by Antony, one of the servants. Ducks and geese were browning in the ovens. The cooks were preparing appetizers and desserts. There were odors of meat and fish, chicken-fat dumplings and noodles, parsley and paprika, cinnamon and saffron, pepper and cloves. Olga came in and tasted each dish: one lacked salt, another spice, a third herbs. The dining-room tables were already set with linen cloths and napkins, silver, porcelain dishes, and crystal glasses. Decanters and carafes, filled with wines and liqueurs, reflected the colors of the sunset. In the drawing room, everything had been readied for dancing. The musicians had tuned their instruments. The piano stood open. Ezriel had not come.

Olga did not dare to calculate the cost of her party, but at least the important guests were there—Wallenberg's daughters: Pani Malewska with her husband, and her younger sister, Pola, with her; a retired general dozed in a chair under a tree; a colonel in the artillery, the county natchalnik, the military natchalnik, the natchalnik of the post office, some officers, and nobles from the surrounding neighborhood, were out hunting in the woods; even a priest had come. In front of the house were britskas, phaetons, and several carriages. Coachmen and lackeys lounged about, talking and eyeing the peasant girls who were helping out in the kitchen. An old cow with a shrunken udder had been slaughtered. But other cows grazed in the pasture, twitching their tails. The poultry population of Topolka, however, had suffered almost complete decimation. The garbage trench behind the kitchen was full of the bloody heads, feet, wings, and innards of fowl and attracted hordes of flies. Although the sun had barely set on the horizon, a three-quarter moon accompanied by a bright star had appeared in the sky. As it grew dark, Olga began to worry about the hunters, who had not yet returned. However, they soon arrived with their booty: several rabbits, a pheasant, a few wild ducks. The dogs ran along wearily with lowered muzzles, several of them limping. The hunters carried their double-barreled shotguns like canes. Some stopped at the well to wash. Others went to their rooms to change. Natasha, who had made friends with a young lieutenant, sat with him on the balcony. They were poring over her autograph album, reading the verses that her girl friends and even boys had written in it. Although he had used the verse for all his girl acquaintances, the lieutenant pretended to think a moment, then wetting the tip of his pencil on his tongue, wrote:

"Deep within me
I feel your gaze.
Your charm
disturbs my soul—
Graceful as a young doe,
you move away—
But what will I do
now you are gone?"

Suddenly there was the sound of screaming. A boat had overturned in the Vistula. The women were drowning. There was a tumult among the men. The hunters threw down their guns and hurried to the shore. At the river, the men shed their uniforms and swam quickly to the boat. Luckily the water was not deep and everyone was rescued. Servants brought cognac and dry clothes to the shore. Some of the women laughed—others cried. There were guests who felt that the ball should be postponed, but the orchestra began to play and the fireworks were set off. Several officers shot their guns into the air. A kind of Bacchanalia ensued. Everyone got drunk. The dinner turned into bedlam, with some of the guests sitting, others standing. The orderlies, who had helped in the rescue, mingled with their superiors. One officer who had lost a boot danced about in his socks. The same women who earlier had filled the air with their screams now laughed hilariously. Ivanov, a military doctor, begged the guests to seat themselves at the table. Olga could barely control her tears. At last there was a semblance of order. Dr. Ivanov drank a toast to the hostess and everyone shouted "Hurrah" and "Vivat." After dinner there was more dancing in the salon.

Dr. Fyodor Petrovitch Ivanov danced with Olga. He was in his fifties, a giant, straight as a board, his hair gray at the temples, his face square. He had a snub nose and blue eyes that were set a bit too far apart. He wore a decoration seldom awarded to any but professional soldiers, for he had taken part in several expeditions to Middle Asia. He was born in the Urals and had been exiled to Poland because he had been involved in a duel with a high-ranking officer. Dr. Ivanov, a bachelor, had brought with him from Russia a woman companion. It was known in the area that, although he did not take bribes, Dr. Ivanov was lenient with the Jewish draftees, especially the young Hassidim with their sunken chests and curved spines. They were sure to receive the blue or white certificates of rejection from him.

In the years of Olga's mourning for Andrey, and later while she was living with Ezriel, who could not endure the sight of a strange man's arm around her waist, she had avoided dancing and had practically forgotten how. Besides, new dances had come into fashion. Nevertheless, she danced with Dr. Ivanov. He led her like a dancing master, guiding her attentively. He exuded strength and military discipline. Ezriel always transmitted his unrest to her, his complexities, his guilt feelings. Because of him, she had become nervous about everything. He had tried to restore her spiritually to a world to which she did not wish to return. After all the preparations and mishaps, it was relaxing to dance again, to allow herself to be led by someone who knew exactly how to conduct himself. A short distance away, Natasha was dancing with the lieutenant who had written in her album. How many times had she danced with him?

II

Despite its ill-fated beginning, the ball was a success and the guests danced until dawn. Olga had renewed relationships with old friends, received invitations, obtained innumerable compliments, from men and women alike. The Polish nobles, who usually became sullen in the company of Russians, had for the moment forgotten the old grudges. Olga had danced three times with Dr. Ivanov, more than was fitting, and he had suggested calling on her in Warsaw. The sun was already shining in the east when the last guest departed. Olga went up to her bedroom, fell upon the bed, and still in her ball gown, slept until eleven. As a small girl, she had fallen asleep in the same way on Passover nights after asking the four questions and drinking the traditional four goblets of wine.

The following day there was a great deal of packing and commotion in Topolka. Natasha and Kolia had to return to their respective gymnasiums, Misha to grammar school. It was necessary to clean up after the guests and to prepare for the trip home. Olga had various errands in Zakroczym. Only when she reached town did she realize that it was the Ninth Day of Ab. Having discarded their shoes as a symbol of mourning, Jews walked around in worn slippers and shabby capotes; boys aimed thorns at their elders' beards. The women went about unwashed and with saddened faces, dirty kerchiefs covering their heads. Through the open doors of the houses, Olga saw old Jewesses sitting on stools nodding over threnodies. Disheveled girls bustled about in the kitchens. Though the world had moved forward, in Zakroczym they were mourning a temple that had been destroyed two thousand years before. Many of the stores were closed; others did business but were half shuttered. Olga made her purchases and found that, despite the fact that it was a fast day, she still had to bargain so as not to be overcharged. From the back rooms there emerged little boys in feather-covered gaberdines. They had pale faces, untidy sidelocks, and soiled fringed garments. They stooped as if with age, and persecution already showed in their eyes. Through the open doors, unmade beds with their soiled linen were visible. There was a stench of rotting objects and chamber pots. Multitudes of flies buzzed over every dish of food. Dust covered everything. So this is the Judaism for which Ezriel yearns. He came from this and wishes to return to it! "But it's not for me!" Olga said to herself. "Not for me or my children!"

On the way back, Olga rode past a cemetery. She had forgotten the Jewish customs. Wailing women lay stretched out on the graves. Olga ordered her coachman to stop for a moment. Apparently there was a funeral in progress. A crowd of Jews, their heads bowed, were gathered around a grave. Someone was reciting Kaddish. She told the coachman to drive on. Flowers decorated the graves in Christian cemeteries; here everything was naked, sandy, desolately Asiatic. "I hate it, I hate it like death itself!" Olga murmured to herself. "I would rather die than return to this filth!"

Leaving Topolka was not a simple matter. It did not pay to hire a steward. There was an old peasant caretaker, but one could not depend upon him. Olga was afraid that the cows would not survive the winter, or that they would simply be slaughtered. The peasants were digging potatoes, but there could be no thought of selling them. The money Olga had invested brought her nothing. She was puzzled that she could have been so mistaken and blamed Ezriel. A man who does not know the right way himself confuses others. Topolka would not be a loss in other hands. If it were lived in year round, it might even be made to yield a profit. But when one had to worry about every ruble in Warsaw, one could not maintain such a property. Landowning was not for Jews. That was it. If someone like Dr. Ivanov owned Topolka, he would turn it into a paradise.

On the following day Olga, the children, and a maid seated themselves in a carriage. Behind them was a wagon containing their luggage. Once more they passed through Zakroczym. Jewesses sat on the porches of the houses darning socks. From the House of Worship the words of the Torah could be heard. A boy with long sidelocks, carrying a prayer book, walked by. Kolia pointed to him and said, "That's a Jew."

"Papa said I'm a Jew too," Misha said.

"That's right, you are."

"Why don't I have sidelocks like him?"

Natasha laughed. "Give yourself time."

"What is a Jew?"

"Judaism is a religion."

"Is it true that Jews are devils?"

Natasha and Kolia both laughed. Olga looked at them sternly. "It isn't true, Misha dear. Jews are people like everyone else."

"Why do the Jewish boys leave class when religion is taught?"

"Because the Jewish religion is different."

"What is the Jewish religion?"

"Oh, the same, only a little different."

"The Jews don't believe in God's son," Kolia interjected. "The Jews killed God."

"Can God be killed?"

"Stop this nonsense," Olga said, growing angry. "Children shouldn't speak about religion."

"Why not?"

Natasha smiled, but Olga saw that her mind was full of other things. The girl had fallen in love with the lieutenant who had written in her album.

"Well, it can't be helped. It happens to every woman." Olga had an odd sensation, as if in the last few weeks the ground beneath her had collapsed. The night before, she had suddenly awakened and had been unable to fall asleep again. A childish thought had occurred to her: a bed was only a pair of boards and how easy it would be to fall out! Olga knew she was being foolish, but in the dark the idea assumed an uncanny importance. She had climbed out of bed and placed chairs on either side of it. . . .

17

I

In mid-October, Shaindel died. A telegram had arrived stating that she had been taken ill. Ezriel went to see her at once. She had pneumonia in both lungs. Ezriel and the doctors at the institution did what they could, but it was impossible to save her. She died on the ninth day of her illness, and for the final five days of her life Ezriel sat by her bedside. Calman was unable to come to her funeral. He had been operated on for a rupture and was in the Jewish Hospital. Tsipele and Jochebed came to the town of Blonya, where Shaindel was buried. Jochebed looked like an old woman. Her daughter and two daughters-in-law had come with her. Kaile, the maid, accompanied Tsipele. During her illness, Shaindel had shown no signs of insanity. She had spoken rationally and groaned like a sane person. Her staring eyes reflected a fear of impending death. She made Ezriel promise to have Misha say Kaddish after her, but she never once mentioned Joziek or Zina. The day before she died, Shaindel asked Ezriel to recite the prayer of confession with her. He had no prayer book, but remembered the words of the daily prayer, "We have trespassed." He quoted the words to Shaindel and she repeated them after him, attempting to smite her breast with an emaciated hand. Shaindel knew by rote the prayer said before going to sleep and the one used for candle lighting. She lay in bed, mumbling the sacred words, dozing off, waking, and muttering them again. On the last day, a surgeon operated on her. He cut away a piece of her rib to draw the pus from her lungs. But it was too late. Shaindel opened her eyes and with her last breath said to Ezriel: "Did you have something to eat?"

The Burial Society in Blonya wanted three hundred rubles for a cemetery plot. Ezriel did not have that much money, but Tsipele, the rabbi's wife, pawned her earrings to help him. In Blonya, there were no followers of the Marshinov rabbi, and the society exacted a high price. Until the funeral, Shaindel's corpse, covered with a black cloth, was kept in a poorhouse. She was laid out on the floor, with her feet toward the door. At her head, which rested on a sparse bundle of straw, burned two candles in clay candleholders. The women from the Burial Society sat on a bench and sewed a shroud. The sheet out of which it was made was not cut with scissors but torn and basted with large stitches. The women quickly fashioned a pair of long drawers and a cowl. On the very stove where they heated the water with which to purify the corpse, the poorhouse women cooked groats for their children. The ceiling was as black as in a bathhouse. There were pallets of straw on the floor, and some cripples rested on them. After the cleansing, Shaindel was placed on a stretcher, and four men carried her to the cemetery, which was a long distance away. It had begun to snow. Jochebed was led by a daughter and a daughter-in-law. Tsipele supported herself on Kaile. Ezriel had wanted to bring Misha along, but the youngster happened to have a cold. The snow became heavier. From time to time the carriers halted, switched shoulders. At the cemetery, the gravedigger promptly began to dig the grave. Ezriel stood numbed. How long ago was it that he had become her bridegroom. He relived everything—the Simhath Torah when Shaindel had worn a gourd with candles and had pulled him by the sidelock and called: "I am the Queen of Jampol"; the writing of the articles of engagement at Calman's estate; the invitation to the in-laws, during which he and Mayer Joel had had a debate about a dibbuk; the wedding. It seemed only yesterday that it had all happened. But in this time Shaindel had managed to bear children, to become insane, to spend years in an asylum, and to die. Tsipele's sniffling was replaced by a choked weeping. Jochebed made old-womanish utterances in a wailing singsong: "Already, all finished!" she cried. "Cut down in her prime, woe unto us! She was the most beautiful in the family! She shone like the sun. Why did it happen? She was a pious woman, a sainted soul! Mother, you know that she is coming to you. Holy angels, guide her! She should not know punishment! She has already had hers. . . ." From time to time, Jochebed cast a murderous glance at Ezriel. She had remained angry with him, convinced that it was he, the heretic husband, who was responsible for Shaindel's death.

The gravedigger sighed and dug. The earth had already begun to freeze. A worm wriggled in the mud. Two planks were laid on the floor of the grave. Shaindel was lifted and placed between them. Then she was covered with earth. The gravedigger recited the passages from the Scriptures. Ezriel said the Kaddish. An earthen mound remained and snowflakes fell upon it. Several strange women had followed the funeral. Ezriel only now noticed them. They stood there, stooped, mumbling, wrapped in thick shawls, with clods of mud clinging to their shoes. Some wrung their hands, others thrust them out for alms. A crow, on the tip of a birch, looked out over the graves, over the tombstones, over the fence, into the white distance. Mrs. Shumkin, Shaindel's companion, was also there. She had limped the entire distance, leaning on a cane. She said to Ezriel: "You should know no more sorrow! . . ." and burst into tears. She had, apparently, become accustomed to Shaindel, to the asylum, to its personnel.

Customarily the seven days of mourning are observed at the locale of death. But neither Tsipele nor Jochebed were able to stay. The rabbi was ill and Tsipele did not want to leave him alone. The two sisters hired a sleigh and left for Marshinov. Ezriel returned to Warsaw. There were moments when he was inclined to believe in the immortality of the soul, but that ditch, those chunks of clay mixed with roots and earthworms, had severed the flimsy membrane of his faith. Where would Shaindel's soul go? Into the atmosphere? The worm was well off, born right in the grave. Ezriel's sorrow did not diminish after the funeral. A part of his life was in Shaindel's grave. He remembered her complaints that he was driving her to madness, when she first began to be ill. Perhaps if he had remained a proper Jew, she would still be alive and healthy. "Well, I'm full of sin and don't even have the will to save myself. . . ." Ezriel was debilitated through lack of sleep, and numb with grief, yet within him an imp argued: now he would no longer be burdened with the expenses of maintaining Shaindel and her companion. He would be able to repay the debts that had accumulated because of Topolka. His own thoughts disgusted him. He spat and said to himself: "Ghoul! . . ."

At home he was met with another tragedy. Olga, weeping, threw herself on his chest. For a moment he was surprised, thinking she was overcome by sympathy. Yet he knew that Shaindel's death could not have affected her so. He soon learned that her sorrow had nothing to do with Shaindel. Natasha, who was barely sixteen, had run away with the sublieutenant she had met at the ball. She had left a letter for her mother. Olga handed it to Ezriel. Natasha wrote that she loved Fyodor more than her own life and was going with him to the city where his regiment was stationed. She loved her mother, Ezriel, Kolia, Misha, even Malvina, the maid, but without Fyodor she could not take another breath. A moment without him was worse than death. . . . She asked her mother not to search for her and not to advise the police. She would marry Fyodor when they arrived at their destination. She was actually his wife already.

Natasha concluded her letter with a whole row of dots and dashes.

11

Through Dr. Ivanov, Olga learned that Fyodor had been assigned to a regiment somewhere in Tashkent. Olga could have had the young officer brought up on charges before a military court and gotten her underage daughter back by force. But she did nothing. The girl had disgraced her and was not the same Natasha as before. Olga wept. Natasha in her letter to her mother had promised to write, but many weeks had now passed without a word. Had she married her seducer? Was she dead or alive? Ezriel consoled Olga as best he could, but she would not be comforted. She had sacrificed herself for the girl. Was this her gratitude? It wasn't easy to hide the facts. Natasha's classmates came to inquire about her. Kolia cried because he missed his sister. Misha wanted to know where she had gone. Olga was compelled to find new excuses for the neighbors. Natasha had gone to a foreign school to finish her education. But what school? What was her address? The girls concocted a story that Natasha had been kidnapped and sold into white slavery in Buenos Aires. Olga telegraphed the garrison in Tashkent. There was no reply. She began to talk about going after Natasha. But supposing she found her? She could no longer live at home. She might even be pregnant, or infected with venereal disease. Nor could Olga leave Kolia and Misha alone. There was no one to take care of them. Olga had been prepared for the fact that Natasha would eventually marry, but the girl's elopement was a blow from which Olga was unable to recover. She considered her life finished; there was nothing left to hope for.

During the daytime, Ezriel was busy. His practice was not large, but he still worked both in the Bonifraten and in the Jewish Hospital. After Shaindel's death, his expenses had grown smaller, but he was still in debt. He owed several thousand rubles for Topolka. Olga began to practice economies in her housekeeping. Now that Zina had moved to a furnished room after quarreling with her father, and Natasha had eloped, the apartment seemed as if emptied by a plague. If anyone spoke, there was an echo. Olga compared herself to the father in Slowacki's poem, "The Father of the Plague Victims." Kolia was too old to play with Misha and wandered around like a lost soul. Olga trembled over him more than ever. Who could tell? Perhaps some dark force would snatch him away too? She became too attached to him and could no longer conceal her concern. Ezriel warned her that she would only cause damage to the child by such an attitude. Ezriel and Olga sat together over lunch like mourners. The maid brought the food in silently. Olga had lost her appetite. The large pots no longer seemed suitable for their small family.

At night, both Ezriel and Olga slept badly. They dozed off and awoke. The clock in the dining room seemed to tick more loudly than usual, chiming out the hours and half hours. Sounds that had previously gone unnoticed now bothered them: the trembling of the windowpanes in the wind, the squeaking of furniture, the footsteps of the tenants in the apartment above, the ringing of gate bells by late homecomers. Somewhere in a closet, under the floor, they heard a rustling. At first they suspected a mouse, but it wasn't a mouse, and no matter how much Ezriel and Olga racked their brains they could not figure out exactly where the sound came from. One could imagine it to be a time bomb that might explode at any moment, or some mysterious creature that had stolen in and was undermining the foundation of the house. Olga talked and talked. How could she go on living? She had lost all faith in the world. What use was Topolka now? With whom would she go there in the summertime? It seemed to her that behind her back everyone was laughing maliciously, talking about her, enjoying her disgrace. But was she guilty? Had she not raised Natasha properly? Topolka had brought her nothing but misfortune. If not for Topolka, Natasha would now be sleeping in the next room. Perhaps all this was a punishment from God? Or else Andrey had punished her because she had replaced him with another.

Olga also blamed Ezriel. His worrying and doubts were contagious and had disrupted the family.

For the hundredth time, Ezriel observed that misfortune drew people to religion and mysticism. Olga lay awake through the nights, seeking an answer. Were these afflictions her punishment for being converted? Although she had never been very devout, neither had she been a heretic. Only a year before meeting Andrey, she had still fasted on Yom Kippur. But when Andrey had been forced to become a Christian because of his position, how could she have remained Jewish? And did God care whether one worshipped Him in Russian or Hebrew? Was it possible that God actually sat in heaven and judged everyone? Even if it were so, she had suffered enough. Perhaps she should go to a fortune teller? She knew of a medium who foretold the future and helped find lost objects.

Although Olga in the past paid little attention to Ezriel's arguments, she was now eager for his opinion. Did he truly believe God wanted people to pray in Hebrew and wear earlocks? Who had heard God say this? Didn't all religions speak of God? Was it possible that God demanded something different from each race, each era? In the name of God people had hanged, slaughtered, burned others. How did Ezriel account for that? And what about animal sacrifices?

Ezriel explained that he neither believed in revelation nor had faith in religious traditions or dogma. Man must continuously seek God. The entire history of man was one great search for God. But in addition man must also serve God. When he ceased to serve God, he served tyrants. Undoubtedly Judaism had come closest in the search for God. Christianity and Islam were both products of Judaism. Jewish suffering had produced a spiritually superior type. For two thousand years the Jew had not been in power and had not carried a sword. Even the current endeavor of the Jews to return to the land of Israel was unique. In the passage of two thousand years, hundreds of nations had become assimilated into other cultures. But the Jews still struggled to return to the land of their ancestors. This fact alone proved that the Old Testament contained divine truths.

III

Natasha wrote from somewhere in Samarkand that she had broken with Fyodor. He had gone back on all his promises and refused to marry her. She would have perished long ago if a wealthy merchant, a widower, had not taken her in. He was not young, had married daughters himself, but Natasha intended to become his wife so that her child would have a father. Olga wept. So this was what had become of her little girl! The merchant wasn't even a Russian, and had an Asiatic name. Her little Natasha was pregnant with a bastard. At seventeen, she would become the stepmother of two women older than herself.

Ezriel did not even attempt to console her. He had his own troubles. Mirale was now ill with consumption. She had succeeded in getting out of the country to a sanatorium in Switzerland. Zina had disappeared; months had passed without a word from her. The number of his patients decreased and they refused to pay his former fees, as if sensing that his spirit had weakened. The banks demanded payments and interest on loans. At night, when he could not sleep, it seemed to him that he could almost feel the hands of destiny upon him. What was being demanded of him? Was he about to die? He felt that some further blow awaited him. At the Bonifraten Hospital, the chief doctor started an argument with him. It concerned a trifle, but they exchanged angry words out of all proportion to the incident. It became clear to Ezriel that the hospital authorities wanted to get rid of him and were only looking for an excuse to do so. But why? Was it the recent rise in anti-Semitism? There were only two Jewish doctors on the staff. In astonishment Ezriel saw his former friends becoming his enemies. Even the nurses grew insolent. What was happening? Had someone made a false accusation against him? He couldn't even defend himself or tell Olga about it. There was nothing to tell.

Ezriel waited. Perhaps he was imagining things. Had he developed a persecution complex? Intrigues had also started at the Jewish Hospital. Incidents occurred that could not reasonably be explained. Occasionally an insane patient would attack a doctor, but this now began to happen to Ezriel too frequently. The patients taunted him, threatened him. It seemed that the wishes of the sane were being turned into action by the insane. But what could be the explanation for such a turn of events? Was it chance? Was he himself unwittingly the cause? Did others see something in him that he did not see? Olga experienced similar torments. She complained that the storekeepers were becoming impudent to her. They let her wait while they served customers who had arrived later. They packed her purchases carelessly and overcharged her for the merchandise. Neighbors who had always exchanged salutations with her pretended not to see her. Even good-natured Kolia suffered. His fellow students beat him and called him insulting nicknames. The teachers gave him poor marks unfairly. To top it all, Misha became melancholic. Ezriel could not fit these facts into any sensible theory. He was still a believer in causality.

Olga began to indulge in all sorts of irrational conjectures: perhaps there was a curse on Topolka; perhaps Zina had cast a spell on her. Ezriel grew angry. Since when had she become so superstitious? But Olga did not cease talking, partly to him, partly to herself. How could Natasha have committed such an outrage? It was not in her character. And where had Olga's eyes been? Why had she permitted this Fyodor to seduce Natasha behind her back? No, the thing wasn't that simple. An Evil Eye had been cast upon her. The Jewesses of Zakroczym looked like witches. The old peasant women at Topolka had eyes like hawks. Had they sneaked some magical herbs into her food? Devils existed. She herself had seen a house haunted by an evil spirit. She had known a girl who had been cursed by her stepmother and had grown a mouth as crooked as a frog's. Olga thought of her own mother; perhaps her mother's spirit was offended with her. She had never lit a candle on the day of her death. Her mother had died in a leap year, and they had never known exactly when the anniversary fell. Suddenly Olga conceived a new idea. She accused Ezriel of denouncing her to the Rabbi of Marshinov and because of that the rabbi had cursed her. These saints were filled with hate and revenge.

Ezriel made fun of all this nonsense, but something of what she said remained with him. He observed, as he had many times before, that latent madness in the human brain always showed up in a crisis. Primeval fears had not vanished. There existed in everyone a hidden desire to worship idols, to perform black magic. The Book of Deuteronomy constantly warned against such dark propensities. Whoever its author was, he apparently knew that fatalism was the most profound malady of the soul.

Ezriel felt that he was on the brink of disaster. Perhaps it would be best to leave the city temporarily, or even forever—to go off somewhere. As the Talmud says: "To change one's place is to change one's luck." Ezriel thought of Palestine. Joziek was not religious but he had remained a Jew. Now he even wrote in Hebrew and signed his letters Uri Joseph. He had married a Jewish girl. His children would be educated in Hebrew schools. On the spur of the moment, Ezriel decided to visit Joziek. He would see his son and witness at first hand what was being done in Palestine. Suddenly Ezriel understood the reason for all the recent incidents. Providence expressed itself in events. The forces that moved the most distant stars and the tiniest microbes had ordered his departure. Like the patriarch Abraham, he had received the commandment: "Get thee out of thy country." He knew it would be impossible to make anyone, even Olga, understand his reasoning. Nevertheless, he did not doubt that he had found the only solution.

18

I

Herr Nelke was the proprietor of a combined beer hall and restaurant on Fourteenth Street. A widower, he lived in the downstairs apartment of a house he owned on Tenth Street and Avenue B. He rented his upstairs apartment to Clara. She occupied three thickly carpeted rooms hung with tapestries on which were embroidered such German proverbs as: Rise early, Work diligently, Save money. There were also portraits of Herr Nelke's parents, both stout, he in a top hat and wearing side whiskers, she in a high coiffure with bangs. Herr Nelke himself had side whiskers and smoked an amber-stemmed pipe with a porcelain bowl. On Sunday mornings, he attended the Lutheran church. When he returned home, he played a few old German songs on a zither. Later his guests arrived. They drank beer, ate the sauerbraten and dumplings prepared by the old servant, Frau Hanse, and conversed in thunderous voices. Each Sunday Clara feared a fight would break out among them. But it never did. They left early. In a corduroy jacket and gold-embroidered vest, Herr Nelke would stand in front of his house calling after them: "*Auf Wiedersehen, grüss Gott, danke schön.*" Herr Nelke was both a devout Christian and a socialist. The disputes among his guests concerned articles in the German socialist newspaper. It was through an advertisement in this paper that Zipkin had found the apartment for Clara.

There wasn't a single Jew living in the neighborhood. The horse-drawn streetcar would bring Zipkin directly there. Felusia began to go to school. Herr Nelke's "dear departed wife" had left a spinet and Clara was permitted to use it. She also had kitchen privileges and for a small compensation received lunch from Frau Hanse. A milkman left milk at the door. Food was delivered from the grocery. A nearby butcher provided not only meat but also German veal sausages, ham, and knackwurst.

In the beginning, Alexander kept his promise and visited Clara twice weekly. In the interim Clara studied English at the public school, knit a jacket for Felusia, read Russian and Polish library books, and looked for bargains at the stores. Once in a while, just to pass the time, she took the El uptown, passing factories, billiard parlors, various shops, offices, restaurants, and dance halls. There were empty lots and unfinished buildings on some streets. In this scattered city that seemed to be growing in all directions, Clara thought everything unusual. Her fellow passengers wore outlandish clothes. The locomotive shrieked, the wheels screeched. It seemed to Clara that at any moment the train would plummet down onto the stores, stables, express wagons, the masses of people wandering through the cold, the snow, mud, and horse droppings. Here and there, she could see a Negro, a Chinese. Clara felt that everyone here had been exiled to a sort of American Siberia. Everybody hurried: the working men and women at their machines; screaming newsboys; pedestrians. Clara closed her eyes, letting herself be carried along. It was miraculous that she always returned in one piece from these trips.

Later that winter there was snow such as Clara had never seen before. It fell heavy as sand. The tracks of the streetcar that led to Zipkin's house were buried. As soon as the snow was shoveled away, another storm came, to be measured in inches by the newspapers. The days grew as dark as during an eclipse, the nights dense and black. The city was disease-ridden. Zipkin's wife and child became ill. He suddenly found himself with more patients than he could handle. Clara's disenchantment with America increased. There were no cafés where ladies could sit down and read. The theaters were far from where she lived. Clara had nothing in common with the neighboring German women. In the evenings, no light could brighten the city's murkiness. Clara's only consolation was an occasional letter from Sasha. But even these were delayed by storms. Alexander's visits brought her more anguish than pleasure. As soon as he entered he would announce that he couldn't stay long, nor could he eat the meal she had prepared. Despite his gifts to Felusia, he seemed to have little affection for her. After she retired to her room, he would drum with his fingers on the table and peer at his watch. Even his kisses and endearments were full of impatience.

No, this wasn't what Clara had dreamed of. This bustling New York wearied her more than Jampol. Numerous divertisements were available, exhibitions, balls, and dances, but a lady could go nowhere unescorted, especially when she knew little English. It might have been easier for her had she lived in a Jewish neighborhood. The Jewish immigrants amused themselves by attending the Yiddish theater, lectures, discussions, celebrations. Even in wintertime, the Jewish quarter was congested. People converged in groups outdoors, talking as if it were summer. There were employment offices, tea parlors, and cellar restaurants where home cooking was served while musicians played. Fraternal societies held meetings. The stores remained open late. Barrels of herring, sour pickles, sauerkraut stood in front of stores. Home-baked bread, buns, challah, bagels, poppy-seed rolls, and cakes were sold from pushcarts. In the delicatessen stores, people ate hot frankfurters and mustard. On East Broadway, the crowds streamed down the street in groups. They all seemed part of one family. Each ship from Europe brought socialists, bearded and long-haired revolutionaries who made speeches about the struggle for freedom. New "greenhorns" arrived daily from abroad. Every home had a room or two rented out. Every third housewife prepared homemade meals for boarders. Yeshivas and cabarets, kosher restaurants and travel agencies, wedding halls and matrimonial bureaus abounded. Prostitutes hailed men to their rooms—sextons called them to a quorum in the synagogue. In the shops, the workers sang both liturgical and socialist songs. In the evenings, boys and girls danced in the narrow, gaslit rooms. Everyday was a holiday. But Clara was not a part of it. She wandered about the snowy sidewalks alone. Not once did she pass Zipkin's house on East Broadway at night to see if the lights were on behind the curtains.

II

The cold hung on. Felusia had gone to visit a school friend. She was learning English rapidly and becoming Americanized. She was making every effort to rid herself of her Polish accent and even went so far as to mock her mother's halting English. Clara had gone out to shop one afternoon. She needed wool for a cap for Felusia and a Christmas present for Frau Hanse. In his last letter Sasha had asked his mother to send him a photograph. Clara needed other small items as well: a darning needle, underwear, garters, a feather for a hat. Clara put on her fox fur, warm overstockings under her galoshes, and thrust her hands inside a giant muff. She spent about half an hour in a large store on Grand Street, then she walked to a restaurant on Delancey Street, where she ordered a meal of tripe, consommé with groats, boiled beef, a piece of honeycake, and tea. She had found everything she wanted except the right kind of feather. She rummaged through hat stores and remnant stalls. Then she visited a photographer, who posed her in a carriage to which a wooden horse was harnessed. Usually Clara knew which streetcar to take home, but she was in an unfamiliar neighborhood. It was evening and it had grown colder. People walked rapidly, emitting vapor from their mouths and nostrils. Horses slipped on the ice and the teamsters shouted. Fire wagons went by in a blasting uproar. Clara stopped various people and asked for directions, but they all contradicted each other. She had come out on the Bowery and was advised to take the El. She climbed the stairs and waited for the train. The wind lifted her hat and she had to hold it by the brim with both hands. The cold penetrated her heavy clothing. Her forehead smarted, her nose felt wooden, and her eyes teared. There must have been an accident. She waited fifteen minutes and when no train arrived went down to the street again. She had to warm herself somewhere. Her hands were stiff. Her eyebrows prickled. The snowflakes on them made everything rainbow-colored. Suddenly Clara caught sight of a jewelry store. It was still open. She decided to go in and get warm. She might even purchase a trifle. A dense fog formed before her eyes. Men were standing behind counters under bright lights. One man was fussing with a jewelry box. Another was looking through a magnifying glass. Clara wanted to say something in English, but she seemed to have forgotten the little she had learned.

Suddenly she heard a familiar voice, speaking in Russian. "Do my eyes deceive me? Can it really be Clara Danielovna?"

Clara trembled. In the glare she saw a man with a black mustache, in an unbuttoned fur coat, a light suit, and a *papacha*, a Russian fur hat. Clara wiped her face with a handkerchief and said: "Yes, I am Clara Danielovna."

"Clara Danielovna!" the man cried. "If this is possible, then anything is! I recognized you! . . . What a coincidence! Can it be, madame, that you don't recognize me?" He clapped his hands together.

"My eyes are tearing from the cold. Who are you?"

"Sit down, Clara Danielovna, give me your packages. Oh, this is unbelievable! Mr. Schwartz, we will postpone our matter until tomorrow. But you look frozen. To see you here, of all places! I don't know whether you remember me: I'm Yasha Vinaver," he said suddenly in a lower tone.

Clara's heart leaped. Yes, she had recognized him. It was Yasha Vinaver, Mirkin's secretary. The man who had written that calumnious letter about her to Alexander. She glanced toward the door, ready to flee, but he had already taken her packages. He was much stouter, but it was the same man, the same square face, the same Mongolian eyes. His nose was as square as a wooden peg. He was, apparently, well off. He wore a gold watch chain on his vest and a ring on his finger. Clara seated herself on a chair. A young man brought her a glass of water. She drank it and thanked him. The cold began to recede from her hands and feet; her fingertips tingled. She placed her muff on the counter. The proprietor too spoke to her in Russian, and she explained that she had lost her way. He smiled sympathetically. "We are people, not animals. It could happen to anyone. Besides, you are a friend of Gospodin Vinaver."

"Clara Danielovna, God must have directed you here!" Yasha Vinaver said, bending over her. "Who could imagine that you were in New York? Suddenly a door opens and in you come. Like a vision. As I love God—a miracle! One of those things that cannot be foreseen. . . . Why were you wandering about in this blizzard? I beg you, Clara Danielovna, come with me to have some tea so that you can warm up. Then I will see you home. On a night like this, it's a tragedy to get lost."

Only now did Clara find her voice. "I'd like to go home. That's all."

"Well, where do you live? I'll get a cab for you. Ah, what a strange meeting. Such a coincidence!"

They went out into the street, but there wasn't a cab or sleigh in sight. Just then a streetcar appeared, headed east. Yasha Vinaver helped Clara in. He paid their fare, threw the tickets into the glass receptacle, and obtained two transfers.

Later they would have to take a streetcar going uptown. Clara sat down. Vinaver was still carrying her bundles.

"I believe you married that physician—what is his name?"

"No, I didn't marry him," Clara replied dryly.

"No? Then what are you doing in New York, if I may ask?—Ah, a foolish question. I'm really so surprised to see you that I talk nonsense. This is my fourth trip here on business. I deal in jewelry and fur. The jeweler in whose store we met is one of my customers. You know undoubtedly that Mirkin died?"

"Yes, I know."

"Lived, as they say, like a fool, and died like a fool. He was a decent man, but without sense. His wife is scum, she's still alive, I believe, and the children take after her. I used to argue with him: 'Boris Davidovich, come to your senses!' This business of chasing after women in his old age was not good for him. What did he need them for? And a man his age should have written a will, not left everything to his enemies and a fig to his friends . . . but man is foolish . . . well, may he rest in peace. He had his good side. And what about you, Clara Danielovna? You won't believe it, but I've been thinking of you lately. Where is she, I thought. What became of her? There was a terrible storm at sea when I was coming over. I was sure it was the end and then one thinks all kinds of things. Such an unexpected encounter! We will be getting off soon to change streetcars."

III

The other streetcar came promptly, and they got in. Clara wanted to return the money Vinaver had spent on her fare, but her purse lay buried somewhere in her muff and she couldn't get it out. What a strange situation: for years she had imagined revenging herself on this man who had ruined her life, and now he was escorting her, sitting beside her like a cavalier.

"Clara Danielovna, what became of your doctor? Did he get married?"

Clara felt a stabbing in her side. "Gospodin Vinaver, I am grateful to you for getting me home, but I am not the fool you imagine me to be."

Yasha Vinaver's face grew grave. "What do you mean? What are you talking about, Clara Danielovna?"

"Doctor Zipkin showed me the letter you wrote to him. I know your handwriting very well."

"What letter? What handwriting? I don't understand, Clara Danielovna."

"You understand very well. The letter you wrote from Paris to Alexander Zipkin. You maligned me, although you gained nothing by it."

"Really, Clara Danielovna, I don't know what you mean. There must be some misunderstanding. I never wrote any letter to Zipkin about you. You're confusing me with someone else."

"I'm not confusing you with anyone. There were times when I could have shot you or thrown acid in your face. But my anger is spent. When one grows older, one realizes that it doesn't pay to make too much of a fuss about anything. But you slandered me, Gospodin Vinaver, made an accusation just for the satisfaction of hurting me. Why?"

"Did what? When? Honestly, Clara Danielovna, I don't have the faintest idea—"

"Don't pretend to be a simpleton. You sent a letter to Alexander Zipkin telling him I was with Mirkin. I have the letter at home and it's in your handwriting. If you like, I'll show it to you. You even used indecent expressions. To me that piece of paper is an example of human baseness."

"No, no, no, I'm a victim of a false accusation. How can you be so sure that it is my handwriting? I'll tell you what we'll do. We'll go to the most reputed handwriting expert in New York and let him decide. If he says it's my handwriting, I'll pay a penalty of five thousand rubles. No, I'll do better, I'll jump off the Brooklyn Bridge. If you like, I'll make these statements before a notary. I won't leave the country until this matter is cleared up!"

"But, God in heaven, it's definitely your handwriting!"

"Let the professionals decide. I've committed sins, but I've never denounced anyone, particularly a woman. And where would I have gotten Zipkin's address? It all reminds me of the blood accusation of Damascus. I don't want to speak ill of the dead, but couldn't it have been Mirkin?"

"I know his handwriting."

"Well, the truth will out, as they say, like oil on the water. I'll stay here until I clear myself even if it takes months. Meanwhile, I swear to you by everything holy that I never wrote anything about you to anyone. I would have had to be not only a scoundrel but insane to have written such a letter."

"I don't understand."

"You don't understand, but you blame me. Is the letter signed by me?"

"No, it's anonymous."

"Anonymous? Then why pick on me—why not someone who would have been directly interested? After all, your business was with Boris Davidovich, not with me. It's true that sometimes your conduct did not seem correct to me, but I'm not God, nor am I, as the saying goes, God's Cossack. If I hadn't been discreet, who knows how many families would have been broken up. I am, as you know, a bachelor, and no one hears more about what goes on in family life. Partly because we know how to keep quiet. God, if I were to tell all the things I know! Believe me, Clara Danielovna, if you accused me of killing someone, I wouldn't feel as hurt. It is, pardon me, like spitting in my face!"

Clara sat without speaking for a while. "I don't know what to say," she finally stammered.

"I must see the letter tonight!"

"Very well. It's late, but come to my apartment. I have no intention of using the letter in any way."

"What do you mean, using? It's a question of honor. Duels are fought over things like this. There are wrongs a person can commit and still remain at peace with himself, and there are other deeds that make one's life worthless. Every person must retain his self-respect. I believe that Mirkin, with all due respect to him, forged my handwriting."

"Why should he have done that? I didn't try to deceive him. I told him quite frankly that everything was over between us and that I was going to Alexander. He even said that if I left he would follow me."

"Why didn't he? I knew that you were making a mistake, because Boris Davidovich had a big mouth. But it isn't in me to meddle in someone else's business. He seemed very confused in his last years. But why he should write such a libel is beyond me. Anyhow, I'm innocent. None of us will live forever. We'll all stand before God, and I don't want to, as the saying goes, carry someone else's sin in my satchel."

"If you're innocent, I apologize."

"No, that isn't enough! Near what street are we? Ah, we're only at Fourth Street. It's true that you were always nasty to me, but what can one do when one is looked down upon? I, too, have my pride. But I would never deliberately harm anyone."

Clara lowered her head. "I'm afraid I've made a terrible mistake!"

"Well, we'll soon see."

For a time they were both silent. Then Yasha Vinaver took out a cigar, placed it between his lips, held it there awhile, and withdrew it. "What actually happened, Clara Danielovna?"

"I lost everything."

"You had a daughter?"

"I still have her, thank God, she's here with me."

"And the doctor married?"

"Of course. What else should he have done after a letter like that?"

"Well, I'm not guilty. God is my witness. I have no wife or

children to swear on. But I did have a mother once and I swear by her bones that I am innocent!"

"I believe you."

Clara covered her face with her muff.

IV

It disturbed Clara to take a strange man to her apartment at this late hour. It was enough that Zipkin came to see her. Herr Nelke and Frau Hanse knew that Dr. Zipkin was Felusia's father. Vinaver's visit might arouse their suspicions. They might even tell her to move out. Fortunately, Frau Hanse did not open the kitchen door, as she customarily did when she heard footsteps. Felusia was already asleep. Clara tiptoed into the bedroom. The letter was in a dresser near the girl's bed. Clara opened drawers in the dark, felt around for papers..

"God, the things that happen to me!" Clara thought. "For years I've borne a grudge against someone without reason. If he only knew what I had wished upon him! . . ." If not Vinaver, it had to be Mirkin who had tried to destroy her. But why? Why were people always so hateful to her? Clara went into the living room. Vinaver's fur coat and hat were lying on the sofa. He was sitting at the table. Only now did Clara notice the gray at his temples and in his mustache. He had lost half his hair. Yes, he too had aged. The light-colored English suit and the pearl stickpin were of little help. Clara put the letter down in front of him. He quickly took out a pair of pince-nez and placed them on his nose. She stood off to one side. He read, removed the glasses, held them awhile between his fingers, then put them back. He drew an envelope from his breast pocket and looked from it to the letter. Doesn't he recognize his own handwriting, Clara wondered. He stood up and seemed to weigh both papers. Then he began to read the letter again. An expression of astonished absorption spread over his face.

"Well, what do you think, Gospodin Vinaver?"

"I don't know. I don't know anything yet."

"What do you mean?"

"It looks like my handwriting."

Clara barely kept from bursting into tears. "How is it possible that you don't remember what you did?"

"I don't understand. Clara Danielovna, I am a lost man!"

"Perhaps you didn't write it. How could you possibly have forgotten?"

"Look here, compare the handwriting. I swear to God I remember nothing. Unless someone forged my handwriting."

"Perhaps someone did?"

"Who? Boris Davidovich wasn't capable of it. I'll take it to a handwriting expert anyhow. This is unnatural."

And Yasha Vinaver again snatched up the envelope and the letter, wrinkled his nose, and stared at them. He moved closer to the lamp. For a while, he contracted his brows as if about to detect an error. But instead his face again reflected confusion and astonishment. He said: "If it was copied, it was the work of a master."

Clara moved a step closer. "No matter what it is, I see you regret it, and that satisfies me."

"It may satisfy you, my dear, but not me. When a person does something, he should remember what he did. But I don't remember anything. I swore by my mother's bones, and I would never knowingly have lied on such an oath."

"You simply forgot. One does many crazy things when one is young," Clara said, trying to justify his action.

"I wasn't so young. And why would I have done such a thing? Perhaps Mirkin dictated it to me? But I remember nothing, absolutely nothing. No, it can't be!" Yasha Vinaver's tone changed. "It's some kind of misunderstanding, a terrible thing. Truly, it's a mystery. Clara Danielovna, I am completely confused!"

"What is your father's name, Vinaver? Unfortunately, I've forgotten it."

"Moisey."

"Jacob Moiseyevitch, I see that you are an honest man, and I forgive you. It happens that sometimes we do a bad thing and it flees from our memory. I've suffered enough as a result of this piece of paper, and I don't want anyone else to suffer because of it."

"Yes, but how did it happen? It's entirely out of character for me. It's as if someone were to come to me and say that I'd cheated a widow. Clara Danielovna, the light isn't very good. Would you be kind enough to light another lamp or a candle?"

"Yes, but I don't think you'll solve anything."

"Do me a favor and light another lamp. This is terribly important to me."

"Very well. I'll light one, but don't be so upset. It was all fated. It was destined that my life be bitter. You were only the messenger. . . ."

"Please light the lamp."

Clara went to light a kerosene lamp. Her heart seemed to twist as she fussed with the wick, the disk, the globe. The lamp shook in her hand, the flame rising in its chimney. With a final effort she placed the lamp on the table. Yasha Vinaver again busied himself with the letter, then turned up the lamp wick, panted, and mumbled to himself. He burrowed in his vest, took out a jeweler's lens, and skillfully tucked it beneath his eyebrow. He stared stubbornly at the yellowed piece of paper with the experienced eye of a professional. For a while he remained motionless. Then he smiled, but instantly he grew grave again. For a moment Clara thought that perhaps this was not Yasha Vinaver, who had had a lot of hair and as far as she knew had been a man without conscience. This man was half bald.

V

Yasha Vinaver removed the loupe from beneath his eyebrow. His eye seemed changed. Clara was sitting opposite him.

"Clara Danielovna, I know everything now!"

"Yes?"

"This is my handwriting, but it is not my style. Boris Davidovich, may he rest in peace, must have dictated this letter to me, that's why I had forgotten it. He dictated thousands of letters to me. Clara Danielovna, come closer and I'll show you what I mean. No, stay where you are. I'll come to you. Each phrase is typical of him. The very first words: 'Esteemed Doctor, be informed that—' is not an expression I use. I call people by their names, not titles, and as far as I can remember, he wasn't even a doctor then, only a student. Read further on: 'Your beloved is a slut, reveling in Paris with a lover.' That's not my style. Absolutely not. He was fond of that word, 'reveling.' I never used it, nor the word 'slut.' Never! The entire sentence structure is incorrect. I don't claim to be especially educated. I only went as far as the fourth grade, but, as the saying goes, I've developed a style. Even if I were writing to a peasant, I wouldn't be vulgar. The pen is, to me, a holy thing. But here the language is uncouth. He must have dictated it to me with many other letters, perhaps at night, following a hard day, and I simply forgot it. See what it says here: 'She's behaving wantonly with others as well.' That is disgusting, the language of scum! Clara Danielovna, I could deny having had anything to do with this. One doesn't go to jail for this sort of thing. But it is a question of truth. I am as much responsible for this letter as I am for all the other inanities he made me write for him. In this case I was nothing more than the lackey you once called me in a letter to Mirkin."

"I called you a lackey?"

"Have you forgotten?"

"Absolutely."

"You see? One forgets. I happen to remember: 'What the pen writes, the ax cannot chop off!' I too was angry and hurt for a long time afterwards."

"I really don't remember."

"Yes, time tends to wipe out the things we do that are alien to our nature. Clara Danielovna, I have not been lying, although technically I did write the letter. It's the intent that matters. Let us read on: 'She writes passionate letters to you, but considers you a simpleton.' "

"No, don't read any more! I can see that you're right! I should have seen it immediately. He used that expression often."

"I'm glad you understand. It's really scandalous."

"Scandalous! He broke all his promises to me and ruined my life as well. And all this on the threshold of the grave. The fool."

"Yes, as I mentioned to you, Clara Danielovna, despite his cleverness, he was without insight. He came, may he forgive me, from a low-class background. His father was a blacksmith. Clara Danielovna, he died owing me wages. Some of his tricks would make your ears ring, but it's too late to discuss them."

"How late is it? I'll go down to the kitchen and make some tea."

"No, Clara Danielovna, I beg of you, don't bother."

"At least have some cookies or fruit."

"No, thank you. Why did he do it? In a way it's a compliment. He was jealous of you. But even if he didn't want something, he'd always spoil it for others. Once we went fishing. There was no sense taking the fish home and I suggested giving them to the boatman or throwing them back while they were still alive, but no. Later, he just left them on the beach. That's how bullheaded he was."

"Why did you say, 'Even if he didn't want something'? He wanted me very much. Too much. You know that quite well."

"I know nothing of the kind. If he had wanted you, then he could have had you."

"You know very well, Jacob Moiseyevitch, that Mirkin was impotent."

"Is that so? No, I didn't know it. I thought it was quite the opposite."

"What do you mean?"

"Well, this isn't fit for a lady to hear, but he was a lecher to the very end. I was compelled to witness his behavior."

"What did you see? Well, I'd better not ask."

"Clara Danielovna, I don't get involved in the affairs of others—on principle. And I keep my opinions to myself. The doctors had warned him against sexual excesses and against overeating. His heart was surrounded by fat, but he called them idiots. He was made of iron; he might have lived another ten years. As a boy, he had helped his father at the anvil. That was Boris Davidovich."

"That doesn't mean you know everything about him."

"The less I know, the better. God is merciful. . . . Clara Danielovna, what about you, if I may ask? Do you live alone?"

"Only with my daughter."

"Why is that?"

"Oh, I am a fool too. Everyone is a fool in his own way. Alexander married a Hungarian spinster. She simply bought him by helping him through the university. But I, foolishly enough, longed for him. Jacob Moiseyevitch, one mustn't judge, one dare not. If years ago someone had described to me the kind of woman I've become, I would have called her an idiot. I was deathly sick and thought my time had come. I wanted my Felusia to get to know her father. She used to ask about him. My son, Sasha, is, thank God, wealthy and respectable, my only source of comfort, unbelievably good to me. I told him my troubles, kept no secrets from him, and he said, 'Mother, go to New York!' I left him my apartment. He has a house in Jampol that is virtually a palace, but he has business in Warsaw. To be brief, I came to America and Alexander fell at my feet. He was unhappy with his wife, she did not understand him, and all the rest of it. I decided to wait it out here, and we see each other when he can tear himself away from his patients, and right now there's an epidemic of grippe. That's how it is."

"A bad situation, Clara Danielovna. You're still attractive. You deserve a better fate."

"Thanks for the compliment. But one gets what one deserves. I have no resentment against anyone but myself. What do you do?"

"Well, my situation is, as they say, a good one, but—one grows older."

"Wouldn't it be fine for women if men grew younger!"

"Well, if you can still joke, matters could be worse. It's when one is satisfied that the worm begins to gnaw. I live in Kiev, but I'm on the road most of the time. I'm a merchant of the First Guild. I have a warehouse in Kiev and numerous employees. A relative keeps house for me. After Mirkin's death I decided it was time to stop serving others and strike out on my own. He didn't leave me a penny, although for years he spoke about making me rich after his death. Anyhow, I was lucky. I went into businesses I knew nothing about, but I had, as they say, a little common sense. I've been all over Europe and even traveled to China, and in America they know Vinaver too, at least in trade circles. I'm staying at the Astor House with the millionaires. But one gets depressed—especially on this last trip across the Atlantic. I nearly went out of my mind."

VI

"Why did you never marry?" Clara asked.

Yasha Vinaver smiled. "The old question. I happen to be distantly related to Boris Mirkin, may he rest in paradise. I began to work for him when I was still young and we had many adventures together. He would always say: 'Don't get married. Take me as an example of what happens.' His wife was a real witch. In those days he was still living with her, and I had a close view of family life. He was having an affair with a druggist's wife and it was really funny. 'Every woman has her price,' he assured me, and his words have stayed with me. He always insisted that it was best to have an affair with a married woman, and that's how it turned out for me. Often I doubted my success, but how does the saying go: 'Even a rabbi's wife will listen.' I remember one incident with the wife of a lumber merchant. She behaved very affectionately toward him. She used to drape her shawl across his shoulders and, when he coughed, bring him hot water to soak his feet. A handsome female. The merchant and I did business together and we were neighbors. When the merchant had to make one of his trips to Vilna, his wife packed for him, putting in all sorts of medicines and a jar of raspberries. I stood at the window and watched as he seated himself in the britska and she fondly kissed him goodbye. Suddenly my door opened. She came in without even knocking. 'Jacob Moiseyevitch,' she said, 'kiss me!' Those were her words! I could scarcely believe my ears. She burned like a flame—"

Clara raised her brows. "There are all kinds of people."

"Well, such experiences make one lose one's faith. Meanwhile, the years went by. I traveled with Mirkin and shared his life. You couldn't drag a lady through that kind of muck. Family life was impossible for me. Now I'm not young any more. A woman my own age doesn't attract me, and a young woman would deceive me as sure as that lamp stands on the table. And why not? As long as they don't believe in God, why should young blood deny itself? And what would I do while traveling? You should see how our traveling salesmen behave. Still, they demand faithfulness from their wives."

"Well, if that's how it is, you mustn't complain."

"Right. But at times loneliness overcomes me. I work, travel, run around, but for whom? I don't know why, but the sea makes me melancholy. The waves roll and rush, but where to? Usually I make friends, but on this voyage everyone was seasick, especially the women. Suddenly I had the most profound feeling of depression! I wanted to jump into the sea."

"Why?"

"Well, I don't know. Moods accumulate storms of their own."

"I understand. How long will you be here?"

"Several weeks."

"How do you spend your time?"

"Quite well. But I'm often unhappy. Clara Danielovna, what's the sense of your life here?"

"Who knows?"

"Why not let me take you to the theater or a concert? After all, your doctor isn't free every evening."

"No, he isn't. He has his family. I could go out sometimes, but I don't understand English."

"They have something here called vaudeville. There are also cabarets where ladies may go."

"Yes? Well, it's possible. I held an unreasonable grudge against you."

"When does your doctor come?"

"No definite time, that's the trouble. But we don't have a contract saying that I must sit here and wait. When he finds me, he finds me—if he doesn't, he doesn't. You said you wanted to jump into the ocean. You're a man and can go anywhere. I sit here as in a dungeon, and at times I feel like laughing. I've imprisoned myself just so that he can drop in for a couple of hours. But why am I telling you all this?"

"I'm your friend."

"Friendship. Love. They're words. Everyone is out for himself. First I hated you and now I'm baring my soul to you. I can't quarrel with Mirkin. He's dead."

"Do you believe in another world, Clara Danielovna?"

"I don't know, Jacob Moiseyevitch. Why?"

"One has thoughts. For example, what possibly could the soul of Boris Davidovich be doing in heaven?"

"Perhaps chasing women there too?"

"Most likely. Well, I'll be going."

"Thanks very much, Jacob Moiseyevitch, for bringing me home. You saved my life."

"Well, it wasn't that bad. Perhaps it was ordained in heaven that we should meet here and clear things up."

"Why do you keep talking about heaven? You're still a young man. You'll stay on earth for a long time."

"Who can tell? No one knows what tomorrow will bring. Both my parents died young. There was a time when a man my age was considered old. I always remember my grandfather with a white beard, but when he died he was barely sixty. At times I regret not having a child."

"Well, for a man it's never too late."

"Oh, yes, it is. Good night, Clara Danielovna, forgive me. I'll come to see you."

"Yes, do come. You'll be a welcome guest."

"I wouldn't want to meet your doctor, though."

"Why are you afraid of him? He's not a jealous type. Besides, if you come during the day, you'll never meet him."

"Good night. Thank you."

Yasha Vinaver left. Clara held a lamp at the head of the stairs to light his way down. Returning to the apartment, she paced back and forth across the living room, casting two shadows. A huge head wobbled on the ceiling. For a while Clara shrugged her shoulders as if arguing with someone. "Well, what shall I do now? I'm not even sleepy, I'll read this book." But she had no desire to read it. "Why the devil don't I get old?" She wished Zipkin would suddenly walk in. She would tease him about Yasha Vinaver. But Zipkin was at home yawning. Well, all was lost. Let old age come and put an end to everything! . . . Clara went to the window. The night outside was frozen desolate. Stars blinked in the sky. Clara began to pray: "Dear God, I've had enough. . . ."

19

I

At winter's end, Clara returned to Warsaw, taking Felusia with her. Zipkin had come less and less often. Clara had yearned for Sasha, for her apartment on Berg Street, for Warsaw itself. The idea of sitting on Tenth Street and straining her eyesight for Alexander had become ever more painful. Instead of being helped by the American climate, Clara had suffered from stomach trouble, from her gall bladder, from nerves. Neither Zipkin nor the other doctors in New York whom she had consulted had been able to help her. Why then should she stay and be sick in a strange country? In the few weeks that Clara and Yasha Vinaver had seen each other, a friendship had developed between them. Yasha Vinaver had taken her out among people, to theaters and restaurants. He had insisted that he loved her, even proposed marriage. Clara had made it clear that she loved only Alexander. But the contrast between Yasha Vinaver's and Alexander's behavior toward her made her realize how badly Zipkin had been treating her. He had never had a free evening for her, had never brought a friend to visit, had kept her isolated like some cheap mistress to whom one came when one needed her.

Yasha Vinaver, who had returned to Russia, assailed Clara with letters. He intended opening a Warsaw branch of his business and made numerous suggestions. Would she accept some light employment with him and agree to live with him? He was not Mirkin, did not need ten women at once, nor did he want a woman merely for her body, but for companionship.

While still in America, Clara had tried to play Yasha Vinaver against Alexander. She had shown him Vinaver's letters, but this had only estranged Alexander further. He had insulted her and for two weeks had not come to see her at all.

Once, when Clara had berated him for being so cold toward Felusia, Zipkin had replied: "I don't know whether she's my child or not."

"You should be ashamed."

"You lived with two men!"

There had been only one way out—to go away. When Alexander heard her decision, he tried to dissuade her, but Clara said: "You can always come to Warsaw."

No, this was no longer the same Alexander. He was older, stouter, more settled. He had grown fond of his wife and was apparently afraid of her. He always came to Clara in a state of fear, and actually they had not spent a night together all winter. He remained distant toward Felusia. Clara went to a travel agency and bought a ticket for Felusia. She had left Warsaw on the night before Rosh Hashana. Her ship was scheduled to sail from New York on the last day of Passover. She was accustomed to traveling now, had packed her things and was ready. She had written to Louisa, who had settled in a town near the Canadian border, but she had received no reply. She said goodbye to Herr Nelke and Frau Hanse, her only acquaintances in New York beside the milkman, the groceryman, and the Chinese laundryman. In the final days before her departure, Zipkin had tried to convince her that she was being foolish, that he would act better toward her. He had even promised to take a trip with her during the summer and take care of Felusia, but Clara replied: "If you love us, leave her and come with us."

"You know that's impossible," Zipkin had said.

At two o'clock in the afternoon, Clara had been driven to the ship. Alexander came later to see her off, carrying packages, one for her and one for Felusia. The ship wasn't due to leave for several hours and Alexander came to Clara's stateroom. Felusia, who had learned English, had made friends with an American girl of her age on the ship, and the girls had gone out on deck.

Alexander sat down and said to Clara: "We haven't really had a chance to talk things over."

"If you have anything to say, there's still time."

"Clara, I love you."

"*Mazel tov*. If this is love, then I'm the rebbetzin of Jampol."

"Clara, you don't understand me."

"What is there to understand? You had your chance."

"Clara, I'm in a dilemma."

"I've heard everything. You couldn't even manage to come to see me once a week."

"Clara, everything is too complicated."

"Why do you tremble so before her? The ship will be sailing soon. If you have anything to say—then say it. If not—"

"Clara, I'll miss you."

"Well, then, get to know the taste of it. I lived twelve blocks away from you. It was I who came to you, not the other way around. Now if you come to Warsaw, I'll know that I'm worth something."

"It may happen."

"Then come quickly or it may be too late . . ."

Zipkin lit a cigarette. "Clara, why did you take this trip with Mirkin?"

"That story has a white beard."

"I can't forget it. Each time I think of it, I feel sick."

"Well, feel sick then. What's happened can't be changed."

"You don't even regret it."

"No, I don't regret it. I regret nothing."

"Now you're going to that informer, Yasha Vinaver."

"What of it? You've earned it. I'll tell you something, Alexander: I don't love that man. He disgusts me physically. But if he is persistent, I'll live with him."

"In that case, you're a real whore."

"Yes, that's what I am. Keep well, Alexander, have a happy family life."

"I'm going."

"Enjoy your sleigh ride."

"You're the worst woman I've ever met."

"Thanks for the compliment!"

"I don't intend to desert an honorable woman for filth!"

"Stay with her! I don't envy you the pleasure."

"*Adieu*, slut!"

"*Adieu*, idiot!"

Zipkin, white-faced, turned to leave.

"Come here, give me a kiss," she said.

"No, you bitch. . . ."

Alexander ran out of the cabin. He left his cane behind and did not return for it. Clara took it to Europe . . .

II

The trip back was as calm as the first crossing had been stormy. The days were balmy. When the ship stopped in England, Clara went ashore for several hours. A Jewish woman, a Mrs. Bachrach, with whom she had become friendly and who was on her way back to Berlin, accompanied Clara. She showered Clara with attention and even proposed that Clara come to live in her house. She had two rich sons in America and told Clara that she was returning to Germany because she wanted to be buried alongside her late husband when she died. How peculiarly humans behaved! Clara told this elderly woman everything, all her secrets, all her sins. The woman consoled her. Yes, Clara had made mistakes, but Dr. Zipkin seemed a heartless man. He deserved losing her. He would come to Warsaw and fall at her feet. Clara was astonished at herself. It wasn't like her to place her trust in strangers. She had always been so proud. Suddenly she was possessed by a feeling of freedom. She smiled, and was smiled at. In all the years during which Clara had been involved with Grisha, Calman, Zipkin, and Mirkin, she had been filled with fury, with a bitterness that she had almost been able to taste. She had only been concerned that no one get the best of her. Now that was all gone. Her table companions grew friendly with her. How had it all come about—had a curse finally been lifted from her, Clara wondered.

Between meals, Clara sat in a deck chair. She was as usual knitting something for Felusia and would occasionally glance at the waves, the sky, the blue edge of the horizon. Who could tell? Perhaps she would not have suffered so much had she known how to be good from the beginning. She should never have dared to say all those terrible things to Calman, or to be unfaithful to him! And since she had been in love with Alexander—what had been the sense in becoming involved with Mirkin? In all her cleverness, she had disregarded life's most elementary rule: do not unto others what you would not have others do unto you. But would she be able to redeem herself? Should she return to America, throw herself at Alexander's feet, and tell him she could not live without him? Sasha had written that his father was ill. Perhaps she should find some charitable work to do: helping the sick or the poor? Clara's thoughts swayed in rhythm with the waves. Often Madame Bachrach sat with her, embroidering a tablecloth and relating stories of her relatives, of doctors, of spas. Once such family tales would have bored Clara. But now she was interested in Madame Bachrach's anecdotes and even asked for more details.

As far as Felusia was concerned, Clara both loved her and had begun to feel some resentment toward her. On the one hand, Felusia kissed and comforted Clara when her mother complained about her life. On the other hand, she often behaved as if she were ashamed of her. She had begun to criticize her mother's taste in clothes and tell her to lower her voice when she spoke. When Clara attempted to express herself in English, Felusia would make fun of both her Russian accent and her mistakes in grammar. Although it had not occurred to her to use the word, she indicated in many ways that she thought her mother was vulgar. It seemed heartless that Felusia cared little about her father, whom she might never see again. The only person she really missed was Louisa. She said quite openly that she would have liked to remain in America with her former governess and Monsieur Dujacques. She now disliked Russia and insisted that she would not go back to a Russian gymnasium. She would go only to an English school in Warsaw or, if that was not possible, to a French one. Young as she was, she had managed to make the acquaintance on shipboard of passengers who ignored Clara and who seemed to express an unspoken pity that so refined a young lady should be saddled with such a mother. Sometimes it seemed to Clara that the girl could hardly wait for the time when she would be old enough to free herself from her mother entirely and live her own life.

The days went by one way or another, but at night Clara was afraid. She had left Alexander. With every beat and turn of the engines, she was leaving him farther behind, and she already longed for him. He had been an infrequent visitor in New York, but he had come. What would she do in Warsaw? Yasha Vinaver? She no longer had the strength for a new affair. She couldn't love another man. Why had she fled? Why hadn't she bought a house in New York and tried to settle down? Alexander apparently was beaten too, or he would not have abused her so. It was possible that he had been telling the truth: he really was in a dilemma. . . . "Well, if worse comes to worse," she thought, "I'll go back. I'll spend some time in Warsaw, see Sasha, then leave again. . . ."

The ship docked in Hamburg. Clara stayed the night there and then took the train to Berlin, where she spent three days with Frau Bachrach before taking the express to Warsaw. She had grown accustomed to spending nights in trains. Felusia lay down in their compartment. Clara dozed sitting up. The clacking wheels helped her sleep. She heard the locomotive whistle through her dreams. At the border, the customs officials searched her baggage, turned everything upside down, but Clara wasn't troubled by it and did not argue when she had to pay duty. She hadn't spent much money in America. She still had a considerable part of the two thousand rubles Sasha had given her. In the morning, the train arrived at the Vienna depot in Warsaw. Clara thought she could detect the special odor of Warsaw air. Everywhere there were swarms of soldiers, officers, policemen. All Warsaw seemed to be one big barrack. She rode in a droshky to Berg Street. When she opened the door of her apartment, she realized with astonishment that her son had not used it during her six months' absence. The windows were closed, the shades lowered, the beds made. A thick coat of dust lay over everything. Before going away Clara had left everything in order, but in her last-minute hurry she had dropped some orange peel in a basket in the kitchen. She now recognized the peelings, which had become blackened and shriveled as if petrified. Clara began to laugh and cry at the same time. She had crossed oceans, been happy, had suffered, and here lay the orange peelings from a piece of fruit she had eaten just before leaving. Felusia began to sneeze from the dust. The janitress came up, complaining that Pan Jacoby had never come and that she had not had a key to let herself in to clean up. The woman went up to the sink, turned on the faucet, and after a snort, a thin stream of water black with rust began to trickle out.

III

Sasha came to see his mother, but his visit was short. On that very day, he was scheduled to leave on a trip. He told her that his father was sick, had a growth in his stomach. Sasha scarcely spoke a word to Felusia. He had never recognized her as his sister. She was the daughter of his one-time tutor, a disgrace to the family. Clara went to Krochmalna Street to see Calman, but he was away at his daughter's in Marshinov. The rabbi's days were numbered, Calman's cleaning woman told her. Warsaw became too warm and Clara would have liked to be in the country but could not decide on a place to go. Yasha Vinaver had unexpectedly gone to St. Petersburg, and she was annoyed with Sasha, who had become gross and sullen and had developed a brutal look about his mouth. His hair was as wildly wavy as that of a gypsy, and he told his mother depraved stories about his affairs with officers' wives, about a quarrel with a colonel, and about a Russian woman whom he had made pregnant. He talked like a libertine, boasting of his conquests and deceptions.

Clara tried to admonish him, but he laughed and replied: "You have no right to preach morality!"

"But I am devoted to you."

"The devil won't take me, and if he does, it'll be too bad."

"Remember that my life depends on you!"

"Each of us is responsible for himself. . . ."

Before leaving, Sasha again showed Clara his pistol and bragged what a skillful shot he was, always hitting the mark. She was in a state of anxiety when he left. "What has happened?" she asked herself. "Have I developed scruples or has he become baser?" His showing off revolted her. When he told her about cheating the officers who were commissioned to buy provisions for the soldiers, Clara had been disgusted. How casually he had related it! Didn't he understand that soldiers worked hard when training and needed to eat their fill? What else did a soldier have besides his bowl of groats and portion of meat? Clara reminded herself that her own father had sold inferior products. She recalled arguing with Calman when he had been her guest in Jampol: "Everyone cheats . . . if you want to be a saint, Reb Calmanke, donate a scroll to the synagogue as my Aunt Sprintza did. In business, one can't be softhearted . . ."

"How could I have been so callous?" Clara wondered. "Oh, it's all my fault—Sasha drank evil with my milk. . . ."

Several days passed. Clara had been in touch with an employment agency and they had promised to send her a maid, but so far no girl had appeared. In the evening, Clara prepared supper for Felusia and herself.

Clara paced back and forth across the parlor. Zipkin's cane hung on a hook in the corridor, and Clara suddenly felt like examining it. Perhaps there was some inscription on it that she had overlooked, or it might be hollow, containing a letter or a piece of jewelry. . . . She walked toward the corridor but froze after two steps. A strong pain shot through her left breast. Her heart, her arm, her shoulder ached. Her breath failed. She struggled back to the parlor, fell into a chair, and remained sitting there, stricken, unable even to cry out. Her head drooped to the left, her brow grew moist. She wanted to call Felusia but the girl would be frightened, and besides her voice seemed muffled. "Well, it's the end! God in heaven, take pity on me!" Clara prayed. She had pills for such an emergency, but they were in a drawer of her nighttable. The pains grew even more piercing. Suddenly the doorbell rang. It rang again and again. Someone began to knock on the door. Clara tried to rise, but her knees buckled. The slightest movement cut her like a knife. She heard voices. There seemed to be two people outside. The knocking and the ringing grew even stronger. Suddenly Clara saw Felusia. The girl had been awakened and stood there in her nightgown and barefoot.

"Mama!"

"Open the door," Clara groaned. "I'm sick."

"Mama! Mama!"

"Quickly! They will help me . . ."

Felusia went to the door. Clara saw the woman from the

employment agency and a stout Gentile woman with straw-like hair and red cheeks.

Felusia began to scream: "A doctor! A doctor!"

"A miracle!" Clara thought. Clara mumbled to the agency woman, asking for the pills from her nighttable. The maid brought a glass of water and the agency woman ran to fetch a doctor. The maid suggested an ambulance, but Clara managed a protest: "I don't want to die in a hospital," she said.

A doctor, who happened to live nearby, gave Clara a sedative, and she was carried to bed. The pains were no longer so sharp, but she was left with an unusual fatigue, a feeling of heaviness, as if her body had already become a dead weight. "At least I will die in bed, not in a chair," Clara thought. She no longer feared death. If only her suffering would end! . . .

A few days passed. Once, when Clara opened her eyes, Sasha stood beside her. An old man with a dirty white beard, a sallow face, long sidelocks, thick brows, entered. "Did they bring me a rabbi?" Clara wondered. Then she recognized him. It was Calman! She was overcome with joy. "He has forgiven me! . . ."

She whispered to Sasha that he would be left without a mother. . . . Then she grew silent. God above, she had already experienced all this. She remembered everything: Calman's serge capote, the fringes of his sash, Sasha's summer suit, the medicine bottles, and the half orange on the chair. She had witnessed this whole scene in her dream that night, years ago, when she had returned to her aunt's apartment after her first night with Zipkin. . . . A mystical sadness overcame Clara. Her final days had been revealed to her years before. The half orange glistened in the afternoon sun, red as wine, and the seeds and veins could be seen exactly as in her vision.

Calman leaned over her, and his braided sidelocks hung down in a straight line. "How are you?"

Clara replied: "Well, as you see. . . ."

IV

That evening, Clara thought the end had come. But days went by and she lived. Sasha arranged a consultation of specialists. Besides the maid, Clara was attended by a nurse, who had worked at the Jewish Hospital. Once again Clara began to feel better, regained her appetite, even wanted to get up, but the doctors forbade it. With the fountain pen she had obtained in America, Clara wrote a letter to Sabina, Alexander's first wife, and sent it off with the maid. For a long time Clara had wanted to see her. After all, her son, Kubuś, was Felusia's brother. Perhaps, since Clara was on her deathbed, Sabina might relent and come to visit her. Sabina had married a wealthy merchant, a Pan Max Mandelberg, and probably no longer felt so embittered. Clara begged Sabina to come, to forget past wrongs, and if possible bring Kubuś along. Felusia was his sister, and a sister is a sister whether the rabbi has spoken the marriage vows or not. Clara signed her letter: "The dying one." The maid returned with the reply that Sabina would come the following day.

Before writing to Sabina, Clara had sent a lengthy cablegram to Zipkin, informing him of her heart attack and asking him to take Felusia into his home and if possible to come for her. A telegram was also sent to Kiev to Yasha Vinaver's office, with a request that it be forwarded to him wherever he was. Within twenty-four hours she received Vinaver's wired reply that he was on his way to Warsaw. Somehow or other, Esther Eisner, Zipkin's old friend, had learned of Clara's illness. Although her hair was almost all gray now, Esther was still associated with the radicals. The second "Proletariat" had been all but liquidated. The two new socialist parties were at war with each other. Innumerable groups and programs had emerged, but it was difficult to tell what exactly each one represented. One heard the names Mendelsohn, Rosa Luxemburg, Dashinski. Jewish labor circles wanted to form a separate party. In Russia, the social democrats had moved even further away from the Narodowolces, or Social Revolutionists, as they now called themselves. But Esther Eisner, still a seamstress, remained on good terms with all factions. She came with her friend Carola and a large bouquet of flowers. Clara would meet Esther on the street occasionally and had once ordered a dress from her. Tears came to Clara's eyes when Esther arrived with the flowers. She remembered their first meeting years before in Mirale's room, the same night she had met Zipkin.

"Now all good things come . . ." Clara said.

Calman recited prayers in her behalf in the House of Prayer. He had sent a note to the rabbi in Marshinov asking him to pray for Clara and came each day to inquire after her health. Zipkin sent a cablegram saying that he would take the first available ship. Yasha Vinaver had interrupted all his business transactions to come to her. He had brought not only flowers but a whole basket of delicacies that Clara was not permitted to eat: caviar, lox, pastry, liqueurs, and delicatessen. Now in midsummer, he wore a white suit, white shoes, and a panama hat he had bought in New York. His many-colored tie had a diamond stickpin in it.

Kneeling at Clara's bedside, he cried: "Clara Danielovna, you must get well, do you hear?"

"Well, if I must, I must," Clara replied sarcastically.

"Clara Danielovna, you're still young. You still have many years before you."

"God will be interested to learn that."

He seated himself beside Clara's bed and refused to stir. He told her about his travels, his business affairs, his acquaintances; he spoke of his longing for her. Sasha came, and Clara introduced Jacob Moiseyevitch to him.

Vinaver said: "You do not know, Sergei Calmanovitch, what a mother you have!"

"I know, I know. But tell me."

"A remarkable woman. Still beautiful. Clever as the day is long."

"Do you hear, Mother?"

"Yes, I hear. Where were all these words before?"

The doctor forbade Clara to talk too much, and Yasha Vinaver finally left her and seated himself in the living room. He had tipped the maid and the nurse, and they served him tea. He tried to be on fatherly terms with Felusia, but the girl stayed in her room most of the time. She seemed to regard her mother's illness as sham, another of her self-indulgent whims. Vinaver smoked a fat cigar and conversed with Esther Eisner and Carola. They said that the current regime could not last very long, that the people would revolt.

Yasha Vinaver remarked: "One company of Cossacks will scatter them like mice."

"Louis XVI had an army too."

"Cossacks are not Frenchmen. When they charge on horseback with bared sabers, heads roll . . ."

"Why is that idea so pleasing to you, Gospodin Vinaver?"

"Who says it pleases me? But we must have order. The Bible says that when a slave gets to be king the earth trembles."

"Let it tremble, then," Esther Eisner interrupted, "and let all the tyrants tremble too . . . Their end is coming . . ."

"As far as I'm concerned, let it come. I'm no tyrant. But have you ever traveled on a train whose staff was about to strike?"

"It wasn't very comfortable, was it? It will get even less comfortable, Gospodin Vinaver. This is only the beginning . . ."

The front doorbell rang. Sabina had kept her word and had come to see Clara, although a day later than she had promised, and without Kubuś.

V

Each day Clara grew stronger. She wanted to get up, but the doctor said the danger was not over. Yasha Vinaver had put aside all his business affairs. He spent entire days with Clara, and even nights, sleeping on a sofa. He read the newspapers to her, discussed politics, the theater, opera, the stock exchange, advised her to buy certain shares that would bring big dividends and that he had bought for himself. Frequently he suggested that she come to live with him as soon as she recovered. He would marry her, adopt Felusia. Clara kept saying it was too late, but, deep within her, hope stirred. Who could tell? People did get better. She was not yet old. Wasn't it a miracle that even in her present state a man was in love with her? A man like him could get a young woman. Yasha Vinaver chattered away and Clara closed her eyes. This endless babbling was his greatest defect. She was not accustomed to a man who said whatever came into his head. He was like a gossipy woman. But, in her condition, could she be fussy? She began to regret having summoned Zipkin, who would only upset her. But she did want to see him, and it was good to know that he was willing to come.

Sabina turned out to be sour as vinegar, exactly as Zipkin had described her years before. Dried out and wrinkled, she wore expensive clothes, but they looked as if they had come from a trash heap. Sabina asked all kinds of questions about Alexander but said things to Clara that almost caused her another attack. How could she be sure that Felusia was Alexander's daughter and not that other man's, what was his name? And even if she was Alexander's, Kubuś was a legitimate child, who could not be brought face-to-face with a bastard sister. Besides, he also had a brother in America. As far as Sabina was concerned, that chapter of her life was closed, and she did not want to reopen it. Sabina would not even sit down. She stood there in her hat and gloves, poured out her quota of bitterness, and left, without even a good wish for Clara's recovery. It seemed to Clara that the woman had left a bad odor behind her. She told the maid to scent the air with perfumed paper.

Visitors continued to come. Celina, her aunt's daughter and her father's widow, came from Jampol with two of her girls, Clara's half sisters. Celina had not remarried after Daniel Kaminer's death. She and her numerous children were supported by Sasha and partly by the rent she obtained from Daniel Kaminer's house. The time when Celina spent half her days lolling in bed had passed. She had lost her looks. She had become a sloppy matron, with sad, weary eyes, and legs swollen from difficult childbirths. The girls were pretty but starved-looking and unmannerly. Clara was afraid they would soil her apartment. They sat in the kitchen, eating. The maid complained that they snatched food from the pots. Although Celina had come to ask about Clara's health, she did nothing but complain about herself and her family. She opened Clara's pantry, her dresser, handled each dress, petticoat, and pair of drawers. She rummaged about, asking Clara whether she still needed this or that article of clothing. Clara presented her with everything. Celina took the delicacies Yasha Vinaver had brought, storing several small items in her bosom, the rest in a basket. Clara said jokingly that perhaps Celina should leave quickly, because sometimes the one who comes for an inheritance ends up paying for the funeral.

Celina took offense. "But it's all for your little brothers and sisters."

"Yes, I know."

Celina and the two girls left with armfuls of packages. Even though she reproached herself, Clara felt that these children of her father's old age were strangers to her. In her will, Clara had left everything to Felusia. The maid, this time, needed no orders to use scented paper. She washed and scrubbed after the Jampol visitors, and even complained that the girls had left fleas behind.

Sasha had to return to Jampol on business. After several

days, Yasha Vinaver too began to attend to business transactions. He told Clara that he would have to go abroad but had postponed his departure until she was fully recovered.

"I don't know what you see in me, Jacob Moiseyevitch," Clara said, "a sick woman, no longer young."

"What am I, a stripling?"

"You could get a young girl."

"I've had young girls."

"Or are you so anxious to become a widower?"

One evening, when the twilight remained blue for a long time and Clara's face was bathed in shadows, Yasha Vinaver confessed that he had fallen in love with her when she had been with Mirkin. Mirkin had maligned her, had related that she had indulged in all kinds of perversions. It had made Yasha hostile, but these feelings had soon been transformed into a kind of love. During the nights she had been with Mirkin, Yasha had been unable to sleep. He had tried to convey his feelings to her, but she had answered disdainfully. She had constantly emphasized the fact that he was a mere valet. Once, when all three of them had been playing cards, Clara referred to the jacks as valets, lackeys, bootpolishers, and glanced slyly at him. It had made him so furious he had sworn he would have his revenge by making her fall in love with him and become his mistress.

"Was that why you sent the letter?"

"No, Boris Davidovich dictated it to me."

"No, Jacob Moiseyevitch, Mirkin did not dictate it to you. You wrote it yourself."

"No, really."

"Yes, you did."

"I swear before God I didn't."

"Well, all's fair in love and war," Clara quoted.

For a long while they were both silent. Then Clara said: "If I recover, I'll let you have your revenge."

VI

But Clara grew worse. She suffered a second attack, and the doctors said they could do nothing more. She sank into a lethargy. She lay there sleepy, spent, unaware of the passage of time. She dreamed incomprehensible dreams. She was, at the same time, in Warsaw and America; she was both on a train and on a ship. The train rode into the ship and Clara wondered: "How is it possible? Unless tracks had been laid across the water. It must be a dream. I must be close to death. . . ." It occurred to Clara that she must say confession, but she forgot about it immediately afterwards. She remembered that Alexander was coming to see her and imagined herself with him. It seemed that he had made a mistake. Instead of coming to Warsaw, he had gone to India, or China, among savage tribes who were ruled by a khan, a caliph, a maharaja. The sultan wanted to marry his daughter to Alexander, but Alexander refused. He was determined to come to Clara. He had bribed the eunuchs, but someone had informed on him—Yasha Vinaver! Now Clara would no longer believe anything he said. But how could Alexander be in India when he was sitting at her bedside talking to her? He still acted as though he were devoted to her. "Well, it is all in my head."

"My dear lady, let me apply this compress!"

The nurse placed a cold compress on Clara's breast and gave her some medicine. Clara could barely swallow it, she had lost all desire for food and drink. What she had just experienced was strange indeed. She had lifted her right hand, but it remained lying on the bedspread as if there were two of them. The hand she had raised was transparent; through it she could see the clock, the upholstery of the chair, the tiles of the oven. "Did I imagine it, or was it really so?" She looked down and could see through the blanket. "Has anyone noticed what is happening to me?" No. She had two heads now, and the second one tore itself free from the first. Was her body a shell for another body? Or was this her soul? "Am I dying? Or am I dead?" No, she was still alive. The maid lit a lamp. Jacob Moiseyevitch was reading a newspaper. "What was he reading with such absorption? Why was he so preoccupied?" Clara felt like laughing. She had often dreamed she was flying. But this was no dream. For a while she left her bed, the same Clara, but weightless and ethereal. She soared across the room. God above, she floated over the table, the chair, over Jacob Moiseyevitch. She glanced at the paper and read the headline. Someone had resigned. She hovered over Jacob Moiseyevitch and his newspaper, then over the headboard of her own bed. Great God, she was staring at herself. She looked down and saw another Clara, sick and pale. Was the other dead? No, she still breathed. But Clara had no pity for her. She was as indifferent to her as one is to cut-off hair or the trimmings of fingernails. The other person was not herself, but a garment. Could she fly farther? Clara moved and passed through the wall. She was outdoors and saw windows, balconies, trees. There was a moon in the sky. She wanted to go farther but something held her back. Pulled by an irresistible force, she penetrated the walls back into the room and was drawn into the other Clara, who was gasping for air.

"Clara! Dearest! Clarachke! . . . Mama! . . . "

Clara opened an eye. "What is it?"

Something was being poured into her mouth. Something damp was being rubbed across her brow. She smelled the odor of vinegar and valerian drops. Clara realized that she was dying but had been brought back to life. For a long while she lay quietly, feeling all the pains and pressures of the flesh: the bloated belly, the paralyzed intestines, the heavy heart that beat weakly as if it were hanging by a thread. She wanted to speak, but the words would not form. She gathered her strength and murmured: "What's in the paper?"

Everyone grew quiet, exchanged glances. Then Jacob Moiseyevitch replied: "The Minister of the Interior has resigned."

"Show me the paper."

Again those present looked at one another. Jacob Moiseyevitch brought the paper and held it for Clara to see. She recognized the huge letters and the name. She had not been dreaming. She had actually soared over Jacob Moiseyevitch's head and the *Courier Paranny*. She smiled, closed her eyes, and felt lighthearted. Suddenly she opened them again. Next to the stove, figures materialized. She recognized them all: her father, mother, aunt, grandparents. Their faces glowed, casting a light that dimmed the lamp on the table. A joy such as she had never seen before exuded from them. Who was that—Grisha? They looked as if they wanted to approach her, but could not. Clara wanted to speak to them, but her lips would not open. She shut her eyes, but they were still there. Her mother smiled. "How is it possible that I can be her child?" Clara asked herself. "She is still so young. I could be her mother . . . "

That night Clara died. She wasn't laid on the floor, as is customary among the pious, but was left in her bed. Her face was covered with a silken shawl, and two candles were lit. Felusia had been sent to stay with the wife of an officer, a friend of Sasha's. The whole night through, Jacob Moiseyevitch sat at the bedside of the dead woman. He found Clara's prayer book and after some hesitation began to recite Psalms in the melodic chant he had heard as a child from his father, mother, grandfather. He did not understand Hebrew, but somehow the words themselves had substance. From time to time he lifted the cover from Clara's face. Did she know he was sitting there? Did she hear his voice?

As hour after hour went by, the corpse became less and less Clara. The nose grew longer and acquired a Semitic curve, as if during her lifetime Clara had been able to keep it in check. The mouth fell open and Jacob Moiseyevitch was no longer able to close it. An eye opened and the pupil within looked out blindly. It was no longer Clara but a shape, a fragment of eternity.

20

I

Summer passed, and autumn, and winter settled on Warsaw. The city was progressing—it already had electricity. Soon, it was said, it would be possible to telephone from Warsaw to Lodz, or even all the way to St. Petersburg or Paris. News of technological discoveries appeared almost daily in the press. But, in spite of all the achievements, Warsaw was still knee-deep in mud, full of ragged, hungry people. Many additional houses had been built, entire streets rose from the ground, and the congestion grew worse. Families huddled in damp, dark basement rooms, and rents kept going up. The liberal Dr. Marian Zawacki had published a series of articles in a popular medical journal in which he cited statistics showing that, thanks to industry and new developments in medicine and hygiene, Poland's population had grown to a point where there were more mouths than bread. With the exception of the current year, in which the population growth had, uncharacteristically, fallen off slightly, if it should continue at the same rate there would be a permanent crisis—in short, hunger. Reminding his readers of the Malthusian law, Dr. Zawacki called on Russia, too, to throw off its medieval superstitions and give some serious thought to birth control, as England, France, and all the civilized countries had done. A Catholic journal promptly published an article attacking not only Dr. Zawacki but all liberals, suffragettes, socialists, and atheists. And for good measure, the writer included the rich Jews who took up every new cause and tried to foist Western European decadence on Poland.

Through one of the vagaries of fate, while Dr. Zawacki was occupying himself with this polemic, a tragedy was taking place in his own home that he would surely have called medieval. Felicia's brother, Lucian, who had been living with the Zawackis for several months, had suddenly disappeared. He left the house one afternoon in early October and never returned. Felicia had worried and wept for several days before she finally notified the police. Their search was futile. She advertised in the Warsaw newspapers, but nobody responded. In utter desperation, she finally visited a clairvoyant and medium, a woman called Pani Chmielska. Pani Chmielska attempted to call up Lucian's spirit and, when it would not come forth, came to the conclusion that he was not yet "on the other side." After consulting a crystal ball, she announced that Felicia's brother was alive. He was living either in Warsaw or in its vicinity and would return to her. To convince Felicia, she called forth the spirits of Count and Countess Jampolski, who assured their unhappy daughter that Lucian was indeed alive but was enmeshed in a love affair from which, with God's help, he would presently untangle himself. The medium had drawn all the curtains, then seated herself at a table with Felicia and gone into a trance. The voice that had come out of the darkness through some horn or tube was not Chmielska's but a man's. It was the voice of an old Polish general who had fallen at the Kosciusko uprising. During the séance, Felicia was aware of a cool wind passing over her. Something or someone touched her neck and patted her cheek. She had no doubt whatever that Chmielska had actually made contact with spirits. What troubled her was the propriety of consulting such a person. Should she have come? Wasn't the Chmielska woman a kind of witch? The church denounced spiritualists and their ilk in the strongest terms and called them agents of the devil. Marian, on the other hand, laughed at them, dismissed them as charlatans. Felicia decided to say nothing about the visit either to her husband or to her confessor. It was the first time she had ever withheld a sin from the priest, and she was tormented by pangs of conscience. She again began to suffer from insomnia.

Lucian's disappearance had its effect on the children as well. Wladzio, who was preparing to enter medical school the following semester, complained that the newspaper stories about his father were making things difficult for him and that he was being snubbed by the more aristocratic student groups. He now spoke of going away to study in Krakow, or even in France. It was widely known in Warsaw that his mother was Jewish and his father had served a prison term for murder. One student had even discovered the name of Wladzio's grandfather, Calman Jacoby, and had taunted him to the point where Wladzio challenged him to a duel. Only the last-minute intervention of other students had averted what would have been certain bloodshed. The boy was heard to say he would be relieved if his father never returned.

Lucian's daughter, Marisia, had grown fond of her Tatuś. He kissed her, fondled her, brought her presents. Now she had settled into a mood of despondency. She had grown silent, morose, and cried in her sleep. Oddly enough, Janina, too, had changed since Lucian's abrupt departure. She and Marisia had shared a bedroom, but now it was as if a black cat had run between them. Janina moved into a tiny back room, though it was unheated. The only one not too deeply concerned about Lucian's disappearance was Dr. Marian Zawacki. Lucian, he said flatly, was a psychopath, a maniac, a criminal, and it would be better for the entire family if he kept away. While living at the house he had never lifted a finger. All he had done was to jabber, boast, sleep, and stuff himself. Marian had given him a manuscript to copy, but Lucian had never got beyond the first page. The fact that his children had turned out decent and hard-working, Dr. Zawacki took as convincing refutation of the claims for heredity made by some scientists. In his own household, three children were being reared who belied the myth of heredity and offered solid support to the case for environment and education.

Dr. Zawacki had been taking on a steadily increasing burden of work. He kept regular office hours at home, was associated with two hospitals, and made outside calls in his carriage. He wrote medical papers, contributed to an encyclopedia, had written a book, and was active in numerous associations. The lamp in his study was seldom turned off before two in the morning. He had been considered for a professorship at Warsaw University but had ruined his chances because of his liberal opinions. Nevertheless, he was still held in high esteem. He had several times attended the Governor-General at his palace. He was personal physician to many members of the Polish aristocracy on the highest level. Marian Zawacki, the son of a shoemaker from the Old City, had come far. Felicia, his wife, was aging and had long since lost her feminine appeal, but Marian Zawacki was still in love with this wilted woman. She was as devoted to him as a mother. She was an excellent housekeeper. Their adopted children afforded him as much joy as if they had been his own—more, perhaps, because he did not worry about them so much.

One night when Dr. Zawacki was at work on an article on the pathology of the heart, he heard soft footsteps outside his study door and then a knock. It was Janina, wearing slippers and a robe over a long nightgown. Zawacki looked at her in surprise.

"Not asleep yet?"

"I'm sick, Father."

"What's the matter?"

"My heart."

"Your heart? How do you know it's your heart? Because you live in a doctor's house?"

"It's beating."

"It's supposed to beat. Come over here."

He held the stethoscope against her breast. "You're healthy as a cow," he growled. "Go to bed."

II

Janina was in her senior year at the gymnasium and was due to graduate the following summer. But suddenly she began to get low grades. She had begun her studies late. The other students called her "matka," mother, because she had once blurted out that she intended to have twelve children when she married. The teachers often joked with her too. To the teachers, she was Panna Janina, the oldest girl in the class, set apart from the younger girls by her high bosom and wide hips. A peasant's daughter, she had never taken readily to studying. Now she seemed to have lost all incentive to learn. Felicia talked about getting her a tutor. Zawacki called her into his office one evening to test her on trigonometry. The girl had no idea of the difference between a sine and a cosine. He took a sheet of paper and a pencil and had her bring her compass and slide rule. Quickly he drew angles, lines, and figures, all the while chiding Janina with mock ferocity. Soon he was denouncing the entire Russian educational system, and his anger became genuine. In Western Europe, educators were working ceaselessly to modernize teaching methods, to make learning more practical, more accessible, more inviting—whereas in Poland hardly anyone was even aware there had once lived a man named Pestalozzi. Zawacki showed Janina how simple these mathematical concepts were in essence. Sine, cosine, tangent, and cotangent were not some weird abracadabra but expressed values and relationships that a child of eight could understand.

As Zawacki warmed to his theme, his voice rose and Janina's face turned redder. She was uncertain how much of his criticism was directed at her personally, and she had to struggle to hold back her tears. He can help me, she thought. Should I tell him the truth? He was shorter than she, but this smallish man with the creases in his forehead and the two clumps of gray hair around his pate had money, power, knowledge, wisdom, while she had nothing but a thick head and was, in addition, sinful. She had lost her innocence. She had given herself to Lucian, her father's murderer. And this was the third month that she had missed her period. Oh, she had betrayed everyone: God the Merciful, her blessed father, the good, noble people who had taken her in, Marisia, Wladzio, everyone. There was only one way out for her—death. No, she would not tell him, Janina decided; better perish. She picked up the papers and instruments with trembling hands and returned to her room. Her feet felt like two blocks of wood, so heavy she could barely lift them. At the threshhold she stumbled, nearly fell. Had he noticed anything? Did he have an inkling? "Oh, God, let death come to me! Let it come now! Deliver me from this shame!" In her room she collapsed on the bed. "What has Lucian done to me?" she moaned. "What has he done? Far better if he had sent me where my father is! I deserve this punishment. Death is too good for me. I should be cut to pieces and have vinegar poured on the wounds. At least if I had enough courage to go to confession —but I can't. I can't. I contaminate my soul, the Church, Holy Communion." Janina had a small bottle of iodine she had bought at the chemist's. But was this enough to poison herself? Maybe she should hang herself? Or perhaps she should go up to the attic—where she had committed the sin—and throw herself out the window? But no—why sully the street with her bloody remains? And why put the Zawackis to the expense of buying her a coffin and paying for her burial? The best thing would be to throw herself into the Vistula. There the fish would eat her, and then her soul would go to hell.

She was sobbing silently and she put a towel over the pillow so as not to wet it. Yes, she must do it, before the Vistula froze over. Should she leave a letter? Should the Zawackis know who was responsible? And what of her own family? She had a mother, sisters, brothers, and they were all so proud of the education she was getting and of the fine house in which she was being reared. And—what of him? Where was Lucian? Did he ever think of her? Was he sorry? No. Men like him did not suffer from the pangs of conscience; they bragged about their conquests. Sleeping with her, he had said things about her father—she didn't remember the exact words—but he had seemed to be boasting! Could anyone imagine such monstrous behavior? And who would believe that a girl like Janina could stoop to such debauchery! Embracing her father's murderer, listening to his evil words as he defiled her body! Kissing the lips that blasphemed God, man, everything holy. Was there a more debased person in the whole world? Lucifer himself could not conjure up anything more heinous.

Her weeping became convulsive and she put her fist in her mouth to keep the noise from penetrating to the other rooms. Gradually it subsided and her tears dried. She lay in the dark, silent, tense. The details of the "courtship" came back to her in a rush: the way he had kissed her in the corridor, whispered compliments, bitten her earlobes; the alluring stories he had related, all calculated to inflame desire—about the uprising, the apaches of Paris, about Stachowa, Kasia, Bobrowska; about Miriam Lieba, his Jewish wife who had died in Otwock. Gradually, she had let herself be won over. Then he had promised he would take her to California, Corsica, on ocean voyages; they would start a new life, a new family. He had brought her to a state in which she could think only of stealing every possible minute to spend with him. She resorted to outrageous ruses as easily as if she had been born a cheat. She had taken risks that she now saw were insane, such as going to bed with him in an upstairs room, the door of which did not close properly, while Felicia was entertaining guests in the salon. She had been seized by a whore's lust. And what was she now? Was she any better? If anything, she was worse. And afterwards, when she had begun to reproach herself—and him—he had simply left without a word. He must surely be prowling around Tamki with Wojciech Kulak's fine friends, probably carrying on with ten other women. Or, who knows? He might have gone back to Bobrowska, especially since Kasia was there too.

All at once Janina remembered something. The day before Lucian left, he had been reading a newspaper in the attic—and she remembered him saying, "So the old dog finally croaked." He was referring to Cybulski, Bobrowska's lover. She was sure she remembered Lucian mentioning that the old director had been living with those two. In that case there might be an address in the paper. A hazy plan, born of desperation, was taking shape in Janina's mind, one of those straws a drowning person clutches at. It occurred to her that the newspaper must still be upstairs, because the little room had not been touched since then. She sat up, listening, holding her breath. Even though she was about to end her life, she wanted to see him just once more, to say to him the things she had been saying in her mind a hundred times a day.

III

Before leaving for gymnasium in the morning, Janina told Felicia she was going to visit her own family that evening. Felicia was somewhat surprised because Janina usually went to visit them on Saturdays, but she made no objection. Felicia was well aware that the girl was suffering, but attributed it to her poor grades. In school that day Janina did not hear a single lecture. The graduation certificate which once had seemed so important had lost all value. The wisdom, the knowledge the professors were attempting to impart seemed so remote! One of them with gray sideburns and a red face was lecturing on logic, explaining something called a syllogism. To help the class remember the rules, he recited a short Latin verse, one word of which remained in Janina's mind—Barbara. What had Barbara to do with it, she wondered. At recess Janina slipped into a toilet to avoid talking to the other girls. Two girls went into an adjoining compartment together and Janina could hear them tittering, saying dirty words, she imagined. Well, they could do that, they were still virgins. . . . She left right after her last lecture, not waiting for Marisia, who was in a lower class. The gymnasium was on Marshalkovsky, and Janina headed toward Swiętokrzyska. From there, by way of Bagno and Panska, she would come out on Iron Street.

Janina had found the newspaper, and Cybulski's obituary notice had the address she was looking for. In recent weeks, the item said, the deceased had been living at the home of a friend, Elzbieta Bobrowska, widow of the actor, Vicenty Bobrowski, who had appeared in a number of character roles under Cybulski's direction. Janina set out to find Lucian.

It was still daylight when Janina left school, but the winter twilight descended rapidly. It had rained in the morning, but in the afternoon it grew cold and the rain had turned into sharp snow, thin as needles. The sky, hanging low over the tin roofs, was a rusty yellow, and the snow came down in gusts as big as blankets. On Swiętokrzyska, a man busied himself with a small portable stove. He was selling baked potatoes, a sure harbinger of winter. A tiny trail of smoke was struggling to escape from the little chimney. Porters stopped to warm their hands. Their eyes had the fixed dullness of those with nothing left to hope for. An old washerwoman came into view, stumbling under an enormous bundle of wash. It was hard to see how she could keep from falling under such a load. "I'm not the only one," Janina thought. "Others are suffering too. Why hadn't that occurred to me before?" She looked around for someone to give alms to, but the beggars seemed to be avoiding the outdoors because of the weather. If only there were a church where one could kneel before a holy figure! Janina began speaking to God. Words, phrases she had heard from Felicia came to her lips: "Oh, Thou, who art full of compassion! Thou seest my sorrow, Thou knowest my weeping heart! True, I have sinned, but I was bewitched, blinded . . . Holy Mother, what am I to do?"

The snow grew drier. The snowlike needles landing on Janina's fur collar no longer dissolved but clung to it, forming a white ridge around her neck. The street had emptied out. Janina was now walking on crackling, salty whiteness. Around her, everything had turned white: the sidewalks, the balconies, the chimneys. A Jew with a snow-covered black beard passed by. Wearing a long caftan and broad boots, he was pushing his way through the driving snow. Where could he be going? To his church, she was sure—whatever they called it. He must pray too. In a small shop behind a counter sat an old Jewess with a bonnet on her head, knitting a sock, her fingers deftly working the four needles. Did she know her good fortune? She had a husband, and her children were legal, not bastards; she had no need of examinations or matriculation. A tall man appeared from nowhere carrying a pole with a flickering flame on top of it—the lamplighter? Or was he an angel bringing fire from heaven? The street sloped sharply at this point. Janina passed a cluster of little shops where shoemakers, tailors, and tinsmiths lived and worked. A man with unkempt, wiry hair, his face smeared like a chimney sweep's, was tugging at something with a pair of pliers. I mustn't look at him, Janina thought. The child may be born with a defect! And she smiled faintly at this first blossoming of her motherly instincts.

At last she was on Iron Street, but there were still difficulties. There were no lamps in front of the houses as in the better neighborhoods, and the numbers were obliterated by the snow. Her eyelashes were thick with snow and the light from the street lamps came to her in slanted rays, like fiery straws. Finally someone pointed out the right house and she turned in at the gate. A dog lunged at her, but she shooed him off with her schoolbag. A slovenly girl came out and emptied a bucket of slop water right at Janina's feet. In answer to Janina's question, the girl gestured toward the outside staircase and pointed up. The steps were rickety, and Janina made her way up cautiously. She knocked on the door, but there was no answer. She pushed it open and instantly someone screamed, "Shut it! It's not summer!"

A stout woman stood at a table, pressing a dress. The room was lighted by a naphtha lamp. A parrot began to screech. Janina saw everything in swirling spirals and circles.

"Stay where you are! I'll brush the snow off." The woman grabbed a broom and brusquely swept over Janina's shoes. "What brings the young panna here in such a blizzard?"

"Are you—are you Pani Bobrowska?"

"Sure, who else?"

"Excuse me, but—" She could not bring out another word.

"Well, talk. The iron's getting cold. What do you want? Do you want to have something made?"

"Excuse me, please, but would you know a—a Count Lucian Jampolski?"

"I knew it!" The woman stamped her foot triumphantly. "Just as if my heart could talk. What did he do, make you a belly?"

Janina felt a sharp pain and began to back away.

"No need to run away. I'm a plain woman, and I talk plain words. Take off your coat and sit down. Warm yourself. I have an experienced eye, that's all. Nobody has to put a finger into my mouth. Here's a stool, get up close to the oven. If I can help you, I will."

There was a lump in Janina's throat. Her fear was blending with a long-forgotten submissiveness, relief at being able to share her burden. She managed a barely audible "Thank you."

"Get them off, get them off. You'll go out and catch cold, on top of your other troubles. I'll be finished in a little while. That's it, put it down on that bench. This Count of yours is a brute, a criminal, the worst scoundrel in Warsaw. How did you ever fall into his claws? You look like a decent child."

"*Proszę, Pani—*"

"No, no. No crying. I'll just finish this jacket and we'll talk. Awful weather, isn't it? You should have worn galoshes, taken an umbrella. Put down your books. Nobody will bite them here."

Bobrowska took a mouthful of water from a mug on the table and sprayed it on the garment she was pressing.

IV

Janina talked and cried. She blew her nose and wiped the tears away with her handkerchief. She did not touch the tea Bobrowska placed before her. Bobrowska listened intently, now and then clapping her hands in a gesture of exclamation.

"Great God!" she finally burst out. "The victim's daughter! Put the father six feet under and ravished the daughter. Gave her a bastard. Is there anything more despicable in the whole world? This man has no heart but a stone! There's no God-given soul in this creature, but a devil. The devil incarnate. These good people took you in, together with his children, the children he had with that Jewish consumptive. Oh, my dear, I'm sick! It is not to be believed! No conscience! A mad dog, a ravenous wolf! And how could you go to him after what he did to your father? Yes, yes, of course. Those sweet words, that smooth tongue. Oh, he knows how to do it all right, he knows how. When he wants something, that Satan, he's soft as butter. I know him well. I wish I didn't. Runs around making bastards. He's blackened my face, too. He was a friend once, in and out all the time, eating my bread. I got him parts with Cybulski, may he rest in peace, and how did he thank me? Gave me a bad name, got dragged into court on account of him, smeared in all the papers. Went off and did a hellish murder—and left me with a sweetheart and her bastard. Her mother—I mean Kasia's mother—saved him from the gallows, and he violated her daughter. It's a habit with him, he ruins the whole family. I'm honest with you—I don't see how anybody could go to bed with her father's murderer, but it's done, and that's all there is to it. You can't get your virginity back— No, no. I'm not blaming you, I can't throw stones at anybody, God knows. But as long as you've come here, you have to open up, as if it was to your own mother."

Janina exploded into a new flood of tears. "Where—where is he?" she sobbed.

"Where is he?" Bobrowska laughed raucously. "That's a good question. He stopped by when he got out of jail, but I sent him to the devil. I sent that Kasia packing too. She's around here somewhere, in service, and the boy is with her father, an irresponsible drunk. I'm sorry for the child, but what could I do? I couldn't have her in the house any more, not with that fine lover of hers moving in as a permanent guest. If he's staying away from you, child, you'll never find him. Either he's out of the country somewhere—and good riddance—or he's moved in with some of those low-lives he got to know in jail. And even if you found him—then what? What would you do, pour salt on his tail?"

"Please, Pani. What should I do?"

"Well, enough crying. If you were a common girl, I would say, have the baby. With so many bastards running around, what's one more? But in your station you can't go around with a belly. Can't see much yet, but soon it'll show and then you'd be disgraced. How long since your last period?"

"The third month."

"Then there's still a chance. I know a woman who could do the job for you. A scraping—she scrapes it out and that's it. It's risky, and it's a sin—if that bothers you—but what can you do? They would drive you out of the house, and your own mother—the disgrace would kill her, or she'd put an end to herself. It's done quite a lot now. Used to be very seldom, but now all kinds of fancy ladies go to have it done. God cursed us women. It costs money, and there's some danger. But the one I'm telling you about is trained—what's it called—a trained accoucheuse, worked in a clinic at one time. It costs twenty-five rubles, but you won't get a bloodclot there. You go home, lie in bed a few days, and nobody's the wiser. She makes one condition: if something should happen—after all, you could break a leg just walking across the street—you have to keep your mouth shut. Why aren't you drinking your tea?"

"Thanks, thank you."

"Well, wipe away the tears. You fell into a garbage pile and you have to scramble out. You'll know better next time—maybe. Do you have the money?"

"Money? No."

"You have to pay twenty-five rubles. In advance. And you have to drive home in a droshky. Once you get home, you'll find some excuse: you're not feeling well, you fainted, something like that. It's not hard to pull the wool over people's eyes. If I had the money, I'd give it to you, or lend it to you; you'd pay me back, and if you didn't, it wouldn't matter either. But I have nothing myself. Do you have any jewelry or anything?"

Janina was feeling more at ease. She had stopped crying, removed her beret, and eaten the bowl of grits and the slab of bread Bobrowska had served her. She listened to the older woman and was surprised at her own readiness to confide in this total stranger. Yes, she did have a ring with one stone, and some earrings. Pawn them? Yes, she was willing to pawn them, but wouldn't the pawnbroker suspect her? He'd be sure to think she was a thief. Anyway, she had no idea where to find a pawnbroker— As she talked, her own words sounded strange to her. In this one evening she seemed to have grown more mature. She was naming things that a short time ago would have caused her revulsion. To her own ears she sounded like the wives who used to visit her mother for a heart-to-heart woman's talk. Even her voice sounded different. Was it possible? Could she have changed so much in so short a time?

"Why should he suspect you?" Bobrowska was saying. "You're grown, a young lady. Just don't wear that cap, or carry those books. The best thing is to go to a Jew. The Jew doesn't care who you are, or where it comes from, all he wants is his profit. He looks at what you bring under his glass to see if it's real, then you get your money and a receipt that says you have to pay him interest until you take your stuff back. If you don't pay him the interest, he has a right to sell your jewelry."

"Where can I find somebody like that?"

"Plenty of them around. There's one not far—right on Iron Street."

"Will I get twenty-five rubles?"

"If your stuff is worth five times as much."

"But when can I do it? I attend gymnasium."

"You can forget about the gymnasium!"

"How? I can't just go to them and say that—it costs plenty of money, too."

"Well, I can't help you there. God knows I don't have to get involved in these messes. You're a complete stranger to me. I could have told you to go tell your sad story somewhere else, but that's the way I am. If I see somebody in trouble, it catches me here—even if it's a total stranger, even a Jew."

"Could you possibly—would the pani find it possible to pawn the things for me? I'm so clumsy."

"When? How? Much more likely they'd suspect me. I have no jewelry. Used to have. Nothing left now but this little crucifix. When do you want to do it? The sooner the better. The longer you wait, the riskier it gets."

"Yes, I can see that."

"What in blazes do I have to get into these things for?" Bobrowska burst out in self-reproach. "Don't I have enough troubles of my own? Eh—go on, go on, finish your grits. At my age it's time a body had a little rest, that's all, as God is my witness, it's time."

Bobrowska rose, then sat down again. In her lap on one side she placed one hand, knotted into a fist; in the other she held Janina's empty teacup.

V

It was late Saturday night. Dr. Zawacki, Wladzio and Marisia had gone to the theater. Felicia refused to go. She disliked all those frothy French comedies that mocked God, the church, family life. How could people listen to the profanation of everything holy on Saturday night, then calmly go off to church on Sunday morning, Felicia wondered. How do they reconcile that loose, trivial talk with Holy Writ? Dr. Zawacki pointed out that, in the first place, everyone was attending the theater nowadays, even priests. Furthermore, all that lofty verbiage in the Scriptures simply had no relevance to daily life. The French comedies, frivolous though they were, were truer to reality than pious preachments. But Felicia was not to be swayed.

"I'd rather read a book," she said.

Zawacki had asked Janina to come too, but she'd had to go to visit her mother. She had left early, right after lunch, explaining that an uncle of hers, from Plock, was visiting her family and they were having a party for him. Felicia had never heard the girl mention an uncle in Plock, but she couldn't keep the child from visiting her mother. Janina was looking so pale, so preoccupied lately. The gymnasium was putting too much strain on girls these days, Felicia thought. They had to know the history of every Czar, every Ivan, from the very beginning. They were stuffed with figures and calculations that would be of no earthly use to them. They were taught everything, except how to be pious Christians, faithful wives, and capable housekeepers. This new pedagogy was ruining the young people, no doubt about it. The children were learning greed, egoism, godlessness, and indifference to their elders.

Felicia was in her boudoir, reading a history of Christian martyrs. It was an old edition, with gold-tipped pages and rare woodcuts—an heirloom handed down by her grandmother to her mother. But her mind kept straying from the text. Where was Lucian, she wondered. In what mire was he wallowing? How had such a son come to her parents? She had just received a letter from Helena, in Zamosc. Helena was the mother of five children. Felicia's eldest brother, Josef, who had gone to England after the uprising, already had a grandchild, a little girl with an English name—Catherine Joan. From his meticulously detailed letters—sent once a year, before Christmas—Felicia noted how much Polish he had forgotten. He included numerous Anglicisms and expressions that, although written in Polish, sounded foreign. Even his handwriting seemed different. Who knew if he was still a Catholic? He had married an English girl, and those Protestants knew precious little about true religion. Felicia's eyes drooped and she dozed off. Almost immediately she was dreaming—a brief but extraordinarily vivid dream. There were lighted candles all over the room. On the table lay a coffin. Nuns were reading from their missals in buzzing undertones. Girls came into the room—Felicia shuddered into wakefulness. She crossed herself. Oh, dear Jesus! Oh, Holy Mother, have mercy! Mercy! She wrung her hands in anguish. She had seen everything so sharply: every candle, every wick, the silver stripes on the coffin, the nuns' black habits; she had even smelled the sweet scent of wax and incense. What sign was this? What new ordeal? Had she previewed her own death? But no girls would be paying their respects to her. . . . She felt suddenly cold. If only there were a prie-dieu, like the one her parents had! In her prayers she invoked the martyred saints she had been reading about. She crossed herself over and over again. Lost in her devotions, she became dimly aware of an insistent ringing—the front doorbell! Could they be coming home from the theater already? The clock showed only a quarter past ten. An accident? Her hands shook so, she was barely able to stand up. She hiccuped, and acrid saliva filled her mouth. God in heaven, if it's a calamity, let it happen to me! I offer myself as the sacrifice! I gladly give the victim the years left to me! Felicia heard the maid go to the door. She wanted to run into the corridor herself but was stopped by fear. What was taking so long out there at the door? They were carrying a body! "Oh, Jesus, give me the strength to withstand this new trial. May your name be blessed unto all generations!" At that moment the door to the room was opened, and Janina was led in. The maid was holding her by one arm and a stranger, a coachman, by the other. She was white as chalk, but she was alive.

Felicia was both alarmed and relieved. "What happened?"

The coachman raised his head. "She got sick in the droshky."

"Quickly, put her down on the sofa," Felicia commanded, an angry edge to her voice. "What's wrong with you?" she cried. "You're going to live, do you hear! You're going to live! I have given you my own years. Run for a doctor, quickly. I'll telephone the first-aid station."

Dr. Zawacki had had a telephone installed in his office some time ago, but Felicia had never used it until now. She trembled every time it rang. She was convinced there was some diabolical power, or magic, in all these newfangled mechanisms. She rushed to it, but the study was dark. She hurried to the kitchen for matches and could find none. She picked up the naphtha lamp and carried it back to the study. It shook so much, she feared it would fall out of her hands and start a fire. The flame rose and the glass enclosure wobbled. She managed to set it on the table and went to the wall where the instrument hung. She lifted the receiver, as she had seen her husband do, and attempted to bring it to her ear. But it was the speaking end she was trying to listen to. She tried to reverse it but became entangled in the cord. She heard a squeaky murmuring.

"Quick!" she screamed. "Emergency! This is Madame Zawacki, the doctor's wife!"

The voice at the other end was shouting something, but Felicia was unable to understand a single word. The coachman! Maybe he will understand them. She ran back to her boudoir, struggling with each step to keep her balance. Janina was lying on the sofa with open eyes. Her coat had been removed and blood showed through her dress.

"Dear man! Can you use a telephone? Quick! Call the first-aid."

"My horse is freezing."

"Help me, please, please help me! I'll pay you. Magda, bring some water. Here, take this and cover your horse."

She tore a small plush tapestry from its position on the divan and held it out to him. He started to put his hand out, then withdrew it.

"In the name of heaven, will you go to the telephone! Magda, show him where!"

"I can't be talking on any telephone. She's bloodied up my carriage. I have three rubles coming."

"We'll pay you, we'll pay. Where's my purse? Jesus, help me! Child, what is it? What happened? Did you fall down? Were you run over—answer me! Oh, great heaven—"

The coachman pushed his cap back. "Nobody ran over her, ma'am. It's just that she's about to give birth. That, or a miscarriage. Better get a midwife, d'you see?"

21

I

It was an afternoon that same winter. Felicia sat in her boudoir as she so often did, browsing through her history of Christian martyrs. Zawacki was seeing patients in his office. Felicia scanned the pages, stopped to contemplate, and now and then forced her drooping eyelids to stay open. Thank God, Janina had not died (perhaps because Felicia had made her a gift of her early years). But Felicia would not keep her in the house, nor could the girl continue at the gymnasium. Zawacki had found her a post in a hospital where she was to enter a nurses' training course to earn her keep. The whole affair had been a blow to Felicia and a disaster for the children. Felicia's thoughts often reverted to her dream. Was it possible that a *fatum*, a predestined event, could be reversed? Suddenly she heard the soft sound of a key turning in the front door. Or was she imagining it? Then the sound of rapid footsteps approached and the door of her room opened. It was Lucian, dressed in a short jacket, high boots, and the peaked cap favored by laborers and underworld habitués. He was sporting a short beard. He removed his cap and said, "Well, here I am."

"Why didn't you ring? Did you pass by the patients?"

"I didn't care to talk to that garbage," he said, referring to the maid.

There was a time when Felicia would have greeted such an

unexpected visit with delighted surprise. But since the Janina incident, she had reached a point where nothing in this world could any longer surprise her. It would not startle her if Marisia were to do the same thing Janina had done, or if Wladzio were to follow in his father's footsteps, or if she discovered that the doctor had a mistress.

"Well, you're alive."

"Yes, I'm alive. Don't think I've come to stay. I wanted to say goodbye, that's all."

"You're leaving?"

"Yes. For America."

"You had better watch out for Marian. He might do something foolish."

"Something foolish? I'm armed. If anybody as much as musses my hair, he gets a bullet in his head."

Felicia shuddered. "Stay away from him!" she said. "He's a good-hearted man, but he has a temper. He doesn't mean any harm. He really loved you like a brother. He's older than you are, too."

"How much older? Nobody loves me and that's the truth. I hate everybody and they all hate me. I'm a hounded beast. I must get away from this accursed Poland. Everybody wants to ruin me here."

Felicia felt as if all her strength had ebbed away. "Who wants to ruin you? You are your own worst enemy."

"Enough of this grandmotherly twaddle! I didn't come to be preached at. I need money, that's why I've come."

"Thank you for being so honest."

"How much can you give me?"

"What I have, no more. I can't take anything from Marian. How much do you need?"

"Five hundred rubles."

"I'll give you my pearls. Pawn them. But they're worth much more."

"How much more?"

"Twenty times more."

"I'll bring you the ticket, or pawn them yourself, if you want to. Where's that Janina?"

"Not here any more."

"Where is she?"

"What do you want with her? Haven't you done enough harm?"

"Tell me where she is!"

"I don't know. In some hospital. Training to be a secular Sister of Mercy."

"What hospital?"

"I don't know. I don't know! What do you need her for? Leave her alone. You're leaving anyway! You've caused us enough trouble as it is."

"What trouble? You sit warm and cozy by the oven while I rot away. You lay under your counterpane while I was fighting that damned Ivan. I rotted in the woods, ate grass. I could have married well too, and driven around in a carriage. I could have knuckled under to the Russians like all the swinish traitors, all the lackeys of Ivan!"

"Little brother, what good are words? Poland is sunk in darkness. Only God can help us."

"What God? There isn't any God. We could have helped ourselves if we weren't a nation of mice, lice, and roaches. I don't want to be a Pole any more, you hear me? I want to go to America and forget this evil-smelling country. There one has a right to be a freethinker too. I'm sick of having to live with all these lies, all these fairy tales about the Redeemer, the Holy Mother, the rest of that foul cant. Mary was an adulteress, plain and simple. Jesus was the bastard of a Jewish carpenter, *that's* the true story!"

Felicia shook her head sadly. "What is it that ails you, little brother? What hurts you so?"

Lucian grimaced. "Everything, that's what! What kind of swinishness is all this life anyway? We're born in slime and blood, we suffer through a few years and are chewed up by the worms. The whole thing disgusts me! What good are these cursed children of mine? They'll croak too. Marisia will surely betray somebody. Wladzio is a young brute, but—I don't like anybody. Maybe you, a little, but you're an old woman already. You look seventy. Are you sick?"

"Does it make any difference to you?"

"No difference at all. I walked in and thought I was seeing Mother. How old are you?" Suddenly his tone changed. "Felicia, I must get away!"

"Well, I can't keep you back."

"You know what ails me? Everything. I'm hungry, poor, persecuted, sick."

Felicia became alarmed. "Are you sick?"

"It's not important."

"Is it serious?"

Something like a smile crossed Lucian's face, an illusion caused perhaps by the fact that one of his eyes was bigger than the other. He stood opposite her, pale as the snow outside, gray streaks in his beard, a high forehead, deep wrinkles, his hair half gone. There was a vague smirk on his lips, something like drunken mockery. Felicia scanned his face, seeing things that only an elder sister would notice: some of their father's characteristics, a suggestion—a faint intimation—of some feature of their mother's, and in his expression much of what he looked like as a child, when Felicia had played with him. He seemed on the verge of saying something funny but couldn't decide whether to utter it or not.

Finally he said, "It's not exactly the fashion to admit it, but I have what is politely termed a 'social disease.' "

"It can be cured."

"Yes."

Felicia covered her face with her hands. Lucian walked over to the window. She lowered her hands and regarded him. He hadn't looked so old from the front, but seen from behind he had more than one aspect of middle age. A shoulder drooped. The hair on his neck stood out like silvery bristles. The feet encased in the long boots seemed unevenly matched. All at once Felicia felt a resurgence of strength in her limbs. She stood up and walked over to him.

"Take that jacket off. You'll catch cold."

Lucian did not turn around.

"Lucian! It's still not too late."

He turned quickly. "Give me the pearls!"

"You'll get them. They're yours. You need a doctor."

"What kind of doctor? Your stinking husband? I must go."

"Why? Where to?"

"I have to, that's all. Leave me alone."

He thrust his hand into his trouser pocket. Felicia sensed there was a revolver there. He looked at her with a maniacal stare that was at the same time inexplicably childish, like a little boy with a new toy. "He's liable to shoot," Felicia thought. Strangely enough, she had no sensation of fear, but something like a spasm of inward laughter shook her. "Is this what they are, the murderers, the wicked, the sinners, the seducers? Is this how they look? A boy, a foolish boy! A child playing with a gun!" A verse from Luke flashed through her mind: "Forgive them, Father, for they know not what they do." She touched him on the arm. "Take your hand out of your pocket."

He recoiled from her touch. "I'll shoot her too," he thought suddenly. "She suffers too much. I'll let her have it right in the forehead." He stood staring at her with a kind of insane haughtiness, with the pride of one who has reached the very depths. "I'll soon find out if there is a God or not. . . ." As if he had articulated his thought for her to hear, she said, "Foolish boy. There is a God."

And she started for the door, to have a talk with Marian. All at once it became clear to her that, despite his anger with Lucian, Dr. Zawacki would help him.

II

Lucian spent that evening with Felicia and Marian. Venereal diseases were not Marian's specialty, but he examined Lucian and gave him some medication to alleviate the pain and arranged for him to see a specialist, one of Marian's colleagues, the following day. Lucian even saw Wladzio and Marisia for a while. All three adults sat in the dining room talking till late. Marian spoke of the recent achievements in medicine and reiterated his belief that man has no soul. What we call soul is nothing more than brain and nerves. Man is a machine, Zawacki insisted, a complicated machine, but a machine. All of nature, in fact, is a machine—the solar system, the cosmos, every leaf on a tree, every flower in the flowerpot. The textbooks distinguish between physics, chemistry, botany, zoology, cosmography, but in nature all these forces work in unison. Felicia protested, but Lucian sided with Marian.

"What's wrong with me?" he asked Marian. "Is it my physics or my chemistry?"

"Your illness is functional."

"What exactly do you mean?"

"The machine is sound, but there is a loose screw."

"Do you think it can be tightened?"

"All you need is a wife and a profession."

"What can I turn to now?"

"First, get well. If I were you, I'd study pharmacy."

"Study? At my age?"

"You're not that old. You might find a well-to-do wife."

"Well, brother-in-law, you're an optimist."

"No. Women have perverse natures. They like a charlatan." And Zawacki winked, to show he intended no offense.

Lucian had already bathed. He had tea with raspberry juice and kissed Felicia before going off to bed. He was seized by a deep tenderness for the sister to whom he had brought so much shame and suffering and who forgave him everything. If there could be one such person, then why not the whole human race? "Could her physics or chemistry be so different from mine?" Lucian thought. "We're brother and sister." He entered his room. He had a home again, at least for the time being. For a long while he sat on the bed, astonished at his own life, at all the traps he had been lured into, all the tribulations he had suffered. "How had it all happened? Why?" he asked himself. "Did some demon take possession of me?" There must be an end to the farce! He stared at the toes of his boots. "I'll simply stay here, that's what I'll do. I've had enough. Absolutely. Permanently. I'm cured—cured." He undressed and placed the revolver in the nighttable drawer. He drew up the covers and fell asleep at once. He slept deeply, without dreaming, for several hours. Suddenly he woke, opened his eyes wide, sated with sleep. He sat up, looking into the darkness. The burning pain of recent days had stopped. He began to think of Janina, who had come to this house as a result of his killing her father and who had been driven away because of an equally impulsive action on his part. "Has she forgiven me?" he asked himself. "Yes, she has. And she loves me. A pity she has no money," he thought suddenly. "She could have been the well-to-do woman Marian had suggested. I could become a pharmacist, and she the pharmacist's wife and assistant. We would measure out dosages together behind the counter." Lucian smiled to himself. "And I was all set to run off to America or put a bullet through my head. It's simply nerves. I no longer have the strength for this kind of life. The few years left to me I must spend in peace."

No sooner had this thought struck him than he was assailed by the extraordinary feeling that he had no time left at all, no years, no months, not even a few days. He had reached the farthest shore. He sat motionless, listening to his innermost being. He had no cares, no desires, no need for sleep, no wish to be awake. "What is the matter with me?" he asked himself. "Has there been a sudden change in my chemistry?" A sickening tedium enveloped him, a dreariness such as he had never known before. He opened his mouth to yawn, but what came out was a belch. A pharmacist, of all things? Study? He wanted to laugh. America? On a ship? To those Yankees? Insane. Insane. The aches, the ambitions, the concern with people fell away from him. He had gorged himself to satiety. Suddenly it came over him that living itself was a corruption —sleep again? Wake again? Eat again? Bah! Go to the doctor? Phew! Enough! Something in him was running down. Something in his mechanism was grinding to a stop, like a machine chugging spasmodically on the last drop of fuel. He seemed to be inhaling clouds of gas; he was full to the bursting point. He tried to visualize a future, but his imagination was paralyzed. He could only turn his thoughts backward, not ahead. But even the past had lost all color, all taste. There was nothing left but words, names: Marisia, Stachowa, Kasia, Bobrowska. He made an effort to visualize their faces but could no longer remember what they looked like. Soon the names, too, slipped away. A strange process was taking place in his brain cells. His memory was fading from minute to minute. Bobrowska became Chrobowska. He knew this was an error but was unable to correct it.

He opened the drawer and took out the revolver. "Yes, now is the time!" a voice said. "There's nothing left for you." He fumbled with the heavy thing in the dark, his hands weak, as if asleep. He could barely make out which end was the muzzle and which the handle. Well, it is the end! God forgive me! He comprehended something, not with his mind but with some nameless sense. He had completed some mission and was being called back to where he had come from. He coiled a finger around the trigger, then brought the muzzle up to his temple. For a time he sat nodding, almost dozing, with his eyes open. The muzzle slipped down to his cheek and rested against his chin. He was not really Lucian any more. He was involved in an action which he could neither comprehend nor describe in words. He was becoming one with something he had never previously known, not even in a dream. He listened to it as it whirled, loosened, and dissolved—a substanceless body, a thinking entity without meaning. The barrier between interior and exterior had dropped away. "Is this death?" he asked himself. "But I am still alive." His insides seemed to have stopped their motion. He was seized by an urge to vomit, to spit out his entrails. He could no longer endure the weight of his flesh. It was the end! In the final seconds, his mind was still engaged in some thought that he could not grasp. It was as though he were speaking a language he could not understand. "Now!" a voice commanded. It was an order that could not be ignored. He had a last act to perform. With the dregs of his strength, he raised the revolver and pulled the trigger. It was as if a blade had parted his skull: there was no pain at all.

The next morning Lucian was dressed in fresh clothes and placed in a coffin. Felicia collapsed, but Marisia and Wladzio stayed with the corpse. Zawacki was without religious belief, but Marisia started whimpering, demanding a proper Christian burial for her father. Candles were lit in all the sconces and candelabra. The coffin, uncovered, was placed on a table. Two nuns—one young and one old—came from Felicia's church and stood by the coffin reciting the Office for the Dead. At nightfall Felicia had regained her strength and was led into the salon. She recognized everything—the silver-striped coffin, the dripping candles, the nuns, the odor of wax and incense. Lucian's head was swathed in a bandage and rested on a silk cushion. It was no longer Lucian but a stranger with unfamiliar features—sunk in a silence that had an element of alarm in it. It seemed to Felicia that the silence was screaming. Nevertheless, a solemnity filled the room, as though it had been turned into a church. "Where are the girls?" Felicia asked herself. The door opened wide and Janina entered with two other girls. Janina's weeping sounded almost like laughter. She ran screaming to the coffin and sank down beside it.

"I love you! I love you! What have you done? What have you done?"

She threw herself on the coffin, covering it with kisses.

"Ei—ei," she wailed, "ei—eeei . . ." It was a dirge sprung from the village, from generations of peasants. It had in it something of the strangled whine of a wounded beast. The two girls with Janina were fellow students from the hospital.

Felicia stood in stony silence. "Is it all determined in advance? Is man nothing more than a toy? Had this end been predestined for Lucian?" Something in her emptied out. She folded her hands. She could not even cry. Dr. Zawacki came up to her.

"Why did he do it? Such a hothead," he said.

"Be still, Marian."

"You must go back to bed. You're pale as wax." He took her by the wrist, held it, and strained to listen for her pulse. It was irregular and slow, as though deliberating whether to go on or stop.

22

I

Ezriel had an unexpected visitor. Among the patients in the foyer there was a woman dressed in mourning. One of the first to arrive, she apparently wished to wait until everyone had gone. Each time Ezriel opened the door, she indicated with a black-gloved finger that he should take the others before her. Finally, she came into his office and raised the heavy veil from her face. Ezriel saw an elderly woman, wrinkled, with white hair and sad eyes. There were silver hairs on her chin and her mouth was sunken. Yet she conveyed an air of faded elegance.

"You do not recognize me, Doctor, but I recognize you," she said.

"I'm terribly sorry."

"I am the wife of Dr. Zawacki . . . Perhaps you'll recognize Countess Felicia."

"Yes, of course! Now I remember you!"

"I remember your wedding. I stood beside the wedding canopy."

"My first wife is dead."

"I know. Occasionally I read *The Israelite*. I saw the obituary."

"Yes."

For a while they were both silent.

"And how is Dr. Zawacki?" Ezriel asked then.

"Don't you know? Marian is gone."

"When?"

"Doesn't the doctor read the newspapers? He is gone. He got up one morning hale and hearty and suddenly passed away."

Again there was a pause. People perished like flies. He had grown afraid to inquire about anyone.

"I am sorry," Ezriel finally said. "Dr. Zawacki was a good physician, and what's more important, a decent human being."

Felicia nodded her white head. "Yes, a great man. In his own fashion, a saint."

"This world is nothing more than an inn—we are all guests."

"True."

Felicia took out a handkerchief and wiped her mouth. "Doctor, I'm not a patient. First of all, I'm not sick, and even if I were, I wouldn't visit a doctor. I have come on a private matter."

"I'm at your service, gladly. Please sit down."

"Dr. Babad, I know you will laugh at me, but I'm accustomed to that. The doctor knows, of course, that my brother, Lucian, left us of his own free will."

"Yes, I know everything."

"He came home from prison sick, beaten. We wanted to help him, but he was doomed. He put an end to himself. He left two lovely children, your late sister-in-law Miriam Lieba's children. I hear that the children's grandfather is still alive, but he doesn't want to know them, and they are not interested in him. Our society is filled with prejudices. Doctor, this is what I came to tell you. Since Lucian's death, I have more than ever become involved in occultism, or spiritualism. I feel it is a part of the Christian and even of the Jewish religion. How can a religion omit the immortality of the soul? After Lucian's death, I threw myself wholeheartedly into this belief. I know all the arguments of the skeptics, and I don't blame them.

There are doubts in all of us, but when we see the truth it becomes sinful to doubt. I'm neither insane nor untruthful. I've seen spirits, talked with them, touched them with these hands. It's as true as I'm standing here."

"Yes, please continue."

"Doctor, I have no desire to preach or to try to convince anyone, but I pity those who are at the spring and do not drink. It's better for some people never to be enlightened. Most of them are afraid. They prefer to believe in the devil. . . . I came to see you, Doctor, to bring you greetings."

Ezriel raised his head. "From whom?"

"From Miriam Lieba. At the last séance, she sent them. She also said she had met her sister, your wife."

Ezriel bit his lip.

"Doctor, I know what you think, but her voice was as clear as yours is now. The dead live absolutely."

"If only it were true."

"It is true, Doctor. A daughter knows the voices of her parents. I've spoken with them innumerable times. They've told me things no one but I could have known."

"Well, I'm listening."

"Doctor, I know how busy you are. But I'd like to suggest something. We're very exclusive and don't invite just anybody. Cynics would disturb our group. But I believe you're searching for truth. The late Miriam Lieba spoke about you often. She praised you immensely. It would be a great joy for her to contact you."

Ezriel smiled briefly. "She must know my address."

"Oh, Doctor, by all that is holy, don't be sarcastic. These matters are too serious."

"I'm sorry, madame, but I find it hard to believe that a woman who is dead and decomposed can speak and send greetings. How can she speak when her vocal cords are silenced? And if her spirit lives, why does it speak only during a séance? Even if one accepts the fact of spontaneous revelation, these mediums are known to be thieves and scoundrels."

"How can you be so sure? I admit that there are swindlers, but you find them in all professions. Pani Bielska, the leader of our group, is a woman of extraordinary powers."

"What powers? How did they come to her? I'm drawn to religion, but I can't stand fanaticism and lies, or those who take advantage of the lonely and disturbed. If a trace of Miriam Lieba exists, why reveal itself to some Pani Bielska? Why not to me, or to her sisters? Where is the logic?"

"Doctor, our terrestrial logic cannot explain everything."

"Well, I can't believe in all these phantoms. I can accept the fact that Miriam Lieba's soul is in paradise. Everything is possible with God. But that Miriam Lieba's soul should reveal itself and send me greetings from the other world only when a bunch of charlatans turn off the lights is too much."

"Well, Doctor, I'm sorry. My intentions were good."

"I don't doubt it and I thank you heartily. If your belief is helpful to you, I don't want to take it away."

"You can't—my eyes have seen and my ears have heard. After Lucian's death, I was a shard. About Marian's passing I cannot even speak. My poor head seems to be an anvil for God's hammer. The blows began when I was still a girl. One catastrophe followed another. That in itself was the hand of Providence. I would have gone out of my mind if not for this consolation. I won back everything: my parents, Lucian, Miriam Lieba, and my husband. They show their love for me, guide me, and teach me to stand all trials. I know I'll soon be with them and I look forward to that day. Wladzio and Marisia no longer need me. I once adopted a girl, but, thank God, she is studying to become a nurse. But my poor brother left another son, an illegitimate child, and he worries me the most. The doctor perhaps remembers—"

"Yes, I do. He had a boy with some servant girl."

"Kasia. That's the mother's name. His name is Bolek. The mother has remained a creature of the dark. She works as a maid. A certain Bobrowska tried to teach her how to be a seamstress, but the girl could not master the trade. I am still puzzled how my brother could have had dealings with such a common woman. Now a son has grown up who isn't of our class. I sent Bolek to gymnasium, but he ran away. He became a waiter and isn't even good at that. He keeps coming to me for money and is forever involved in unsavory affairs. He's my brother's child and a grandchild of the Jampolskis. His father and grandparents can't rest because of him—he doesn't let me die—"

"Then he has a function in this world."

"It's not a joke."

"I know. My dear madame, there is such a thing as heredity. Despite all denials, it is one of the strongest influences in our lives."

"Why didn't Wladzio take up these odious ways?"

"The law of heredity remains a mystery. More mysterious than all the mediums and their black magic."

"I believe that every drop of semen contains a spirit."

"Then every man carries within him millions of spirits."

"Yes."

"Perhaps. I myself, madame, am thinking of visiting Palestine, even settling there. Tell my sister-in-law about it. Perhaps she will come to say goodbye to me."

"Why Palestine, if I may ask?"

"I don't know why myself. I have a son there. Something is driving us Jews back to where we came from."

"Well, and at the same time you are a rationalist?"

"I am no rationalist."

"I read about the emigration of the Jews in *The Israelite*. They are fleeing the Czarist pogroms, but clearly it's all part of God's scheme. But I assumed that it involved only those interested in agriculture. Is it possible to practice medicine there?"

"I hope so. Why not? But Jewish culture cannot integrate with other cultures. We must either become complete Jews or perish."

"That's true."

"What is it like in the other world? Have the Jews assimilated there?"

"Oh, Doctor, if you didn't remind me of my husband I'd get angry. He had a similar sense of humor, but behind it all he was a mystic. He passed away like a saint. His ideas are changed now. He keeps telling me that the truth is to be found only in evangelism, and not in worldly knowledge."

"What do the Jews, the Mohammedans, the Buddhists, the Brahmins do in the other world? Can there be various religious truths?"

"I don't know, Doctor. I am only in contact with Christians. The spirits are not all the same, either."

"It seems that way. According to you, madame, the other world is just as confused as this one."

"God has many mansions."

II

A short time after Clara's funeral, Calman had to be rushed to a hospital. His urine was blocked. He was operated on, but days passed and he wasn't able to sit up. Jochebed came to see her father daily. The Society for the Care of the Sick, whose members prayed at Calman's house, and of whose congregation Calman was one of the beadles, sent men to sit at his bedside. Jochebed suggested that Calman have a room to himself, but he did not want to isolate himself from his fellow men. It was difficult to put up with the noise, the smell, the groans of the other patients, but was man born to indulge himself in pleasures? The nurse put up a screen, and Calman put on his prayer shawl and phylacteries. He had brought along a prayer book, a Pentateuch, and *The Beginning of Wisdom.* Calman asked for no dispensations from the Almighty. He had lived out his allotted span. Whenever he had a free moment, he said his prayers and read his books. Sasha visited his father and brought flowers and other gifts, but Calman ordered these trappings taken away. The cookies and chocolates were distributed among the patients. Sasha promised to say Kaddish after Calman, and Calman nodded his head. Calman knew well enough how Sasha was living. Calman looked back on his life. Wealth had come and gone. He had buried two of his four daughters. His son-in-law, the Marshinov rabbi, was at death's door. Ezriel was living with some converted woman. Calman had been charitable, but not sufficiently so. He could have provided for many men with his possessions, but instead he had yearned for new tracts of land, new leases. He could have married a respectable woman, but had become enamored of Clara. Well, soon he would have to give an accounting of himself! Behind him he left Gentiles, irreligious Jews, generations of base individuals. . . . He thought about Zelda. Would he be allowed to be with her? She had died pious. Who knew to what heights her soul had risen? He would be punished. There was one consolation: God was merciful. He knew the measure of man, that he is ashes and dust.

People all around Calman were dying. A patient asked for a glass of tea and, soon after, he was lying still and the orderlies took him to the morgue. All night long a young man had been screaming. In the morning he fell silent. Here, in the hospital, man could be seen in proper perspective—a pile of bones. But was man entirely responsible for his follies? He had to eat, have a place to live. As long as he breathed, passion filled him. The younger doctors eyed the nurses. Wandering among the dying, the nurses smiled, flirted, and giggled in the corridors. To the left of Calman lay a heretic Jew who told Calman he knew Ezriel. Todros was his name, Todros Bendiner. Ezriel had once lived in his house at 19 Krochmalna Street. But in recent years Todros had been living in a home for the aged. He was suffering from cancer of the spleen. His face was yellow as saffron, but he said to Calman: "Your psalter was not written by King David."

"By whom, then?"

"It's a collection of many writings. They were first assembled during the time of Ezra."

Calman wanted to remonstrate with him, but checked himself. Instead, he asked: "Do you believe in nothing?"

"Man is no more than an insect."

"An insect is also created by God."

"And who created God?"

"Well, enough of that!"

Todros also read, not holy books, but secular ones. Students came to visit him: young men in short coats, clean-shaven, bare-headed. They discussed politics and world affairs, used Hebrew expressions but looked like Gentiles. Calman wanted to ask the doctor to change his bed but was afraid that Todros would be offended. Well, he would soon see, soon know the truth. There was a God. The world was not mere chaos. From the hospital window, sky and clouds could be seen. Birds flew about. An orderly had opened an upper portion of the window. A yellow-specked butterfly had flown in. Such a tiny thing and able to fly! Where had it been all winter? It had certainly had a mother, and she in turn had had a mother, generation after generation of butterflies. . . . Could all this have happened without someone watching? Was he, Todros Bendiner, wiser than the Almighty? "Father in Heaven, forgive him!" Calman prayed. "The temptations are great." Tears came to Calman's eyes. He wept for this wise scholar who had wasted a life and spent his waning days with idle books, jokes, and foolish students.

Several more days went by, but Calman was unaware of their passing. One morning he opened his eyes and saw that Todros's bed was empty. Someone had removed the bedding. A small woman in a nurse's cap, with freckles across her face and a pointed nose, was spreading a fresh sheet over the mattress. Calman wanted to ask her about Todros but did not have the strength to speak. Besides, he knew the answer. Where did one go from here? The sun was shining. Some of the sick people conversed. Others groaned. A young man had been discharged, and his neighbors congratulated him. Calman wanted to sit up but could no longer do so. His body had become too heavy, his distended belly was filled with pain. Nauseating odors rose from his stomach to his mouth. He wanted to say the Prayer upon Arising but was too weak even for that. "Woe is me, I'm powerless," Calman thought, "but once I was a powerful man. . . ." He closed his eyes and no longer wanted to open them. He felt that he had ceased to be Calman and was becoming something else, a tangle of dreams, sayings, visions. He opened an eye, and the sun no longer shone. Ezriel was standing over him. "Father-in-law, how are you?"

Calman moved his lips, but no words came. Yet he remembered that Shaindel had died and that Ezriel was planning to visit the Holy Land.

III

A strike was brewing in Lodz and someone was needed to smuggle in revolvers and ammunition. Zina volunteered. The arms were packed in two valises. The cartridges were to be wrapped around her body. She stripped and an expert woman smuggler wrapped Zina from loins to knees with the "noodles." Zina could scarcely move. But what could be expected of a "pregnant" woman? Pretending to be in the final stages of pregnancy, she even painted some flecks on her face. Her stomach was padded with a pillow, in which another pair of pistols were placed. The woman, who was supposedly Zina's mother, took her by droshky to the Vienna depot. There, she placed her "daughter" in a second-class carriage. She carried a novel and some knitting for the "infant." An officer gallantly gave her a seat by the window. An elderly woman began to confide her own experiences, about how she had an urge to eat eggshells and the lime from the walls. Zina could barely keep from laughing. The child, whom the old woman discussed with such fondness, was now an officer somewhere in the Caucasus, probably one of those reactionaries and despots that the revolution would have to shoot. The conductor came in and

Zina gave him her ticket. A huge gendarme, with a chest full of medals, looked in, nodding at Zina. The bell rang three times and the train began moving. The "mother" shouted after her: "Remember, daughter, take care of yourself! . . . Be careful!"

"Don't worry, Mother, everything will be all right!"

Zina hid her face in her novel, but she was thinking of her father. How could he have been taken in by this new nationalism of the vicious Jewish capitalists? He had read and studied, had once belonged to a self-education group, and had kept in touch with her Aunt Mirale until she had been exiled to Siberia. How could he not see that the world was divided into exploiters and exploited? Wasn't he aware of Russian despotism? Didn't he know how imperialists achieve their aim? How could he ignore the condition of the Russian peasant, the Polish worker, and occupy himself with old wives' tales from the Bible? Should Jewish masses desert everything and go to Palestine, where the so-called philanthropists would exploit them in the name of a newfangled nationalism? And who would praise him for his sacrifice? An invisible God? But hadn't Dostoevsky been a Slavophile? Wasn't Tolstoy making a fool of himself? Weren't all universities filled with professors who knelt before every religious statue and kissed the priests' hands?

Zina sighed. She was hot. Her skin burned. The woman had bound the cartridges too tightly about her. They clung together like an armored plate, pressed against her loins, her belly. She was sheathed in a hot mass of metal. God in heaven, if they went off, she would go up like a human torch! And what then, eh? The masses would struggle, triumph, exult, and she would be a pile of ashes. . . . They would not even remember that there had been an individual called Zina. Well, but there was no other way. Someone had to make a stand. A struggle had to be launched against such injustice! . . . Zina had a piece of chocolate in her bag and a couple of cookies. She took out a piece of the candy and ate it. She kept mopping her brow with her handkerchief. She had never known that a person could sweat so much. Streams ran down her back, her sleeves. Her face and head grew even hotter. She began to suffer from thirst. How could she have forgotten to take along something to drink? Suddenly she had an urge to urinate. "Mother, my insides are turning over." She felt a piercing and burning in her stomach. Had she eaten some spoiled food? No, she would not go. She would sit there for the few hours the trip would take. In her torment Zina attempted to read, but the type danced before her eyes. The page became blank, spotted. Ethereal circles danced among the letters. "If only I don't faint. No, it mustn't happen. I must keep control of myself! Thousands of lives, hopes, ideals depend upon me! . . .

"Be strong, Zina! Be strong!" she mumbled to herself. "God in heaven, have mercy upon me!" some part of her cried. She caught herself praying and was astounded. "Oh, I don't know what's going on inside me! I must get up! . . ."

She attempted to rise, but her legs seemed to be paralyzed. She tried fanning herself with her book. Hammers seemed to be beating at her temples. Her heart pounded. Fiery sparks flashed before her eyes. Bells rang in her ears. Her mouth filled with a tasteless fluid. Did they know what was happening to her? Why was the old man staring? And the officer? "Oh, Mother dear, I am lost . . ."

Leaning forward as if to vomit, Zina fell on her face. The old woman cried out. The officer jumped up, trying to lift Zina by her shoulders. The cartridges tore loose and began to roll out from under her dress. There was pandemonium in the car. Other passengers came running, mostly military men. "What's that?" shouted a colonel with a red beard. The onlookers restrained their laughter. Cartridges kept falling out of Zina's clothing. Water was brought. The train was halted. Two gendarmes appeared from the next car.

IV

The one person who could probably have saved Zina was her Uncle Sasha. Sasha had taken over his mother's apartment after Clara's death. The maid and Felusia were still there. Since Zipkin in the end did not come, Yasha Vinaver had arranged to take Felusia to him. Ezriel rang the doorbell, and the maid answered. He asked for Sasha, but he was not in town. The maid told him that the master had not slept at home the past two nights. Without a mistress, the apartment was in disorder. The maid seemed to have visitors in the kitchen. They were laughing. On the way down, Ezriel ran into Esther Eisner. She had come to see Felusia, but Felusia was not at home either. Esther Eisner had already heard that Zina had been arrested. Her arrest had disrupted the organization, and further arrests were feared. A short distance from the house, Ezriel and Esther met Yasha Vinaver. Esther introduced Ezriel to Yasha, who immediately began to eulogize Clara.

"Doctor, to you she was, how shall we put it, a stepmother-in-law. But she was very close to me."

"Where did you meet her?"

"In Berlin, America, Monte Carlo, under various circumstances, but she was always a woman. You understand, Doctor? A woman! One hundred percent! . . ." And Yasha Vinaver snapped his fingers.

"Are you really taking Felusia to America?" Esther Eisner inquired.

"I wrote a long letter to Dr. Zipkin. If he consents, I'll adopt her. I haven't any children, and I'd like to have a daughter of my own. I'll place her in the finest boarding school. One can't live all alone. Impossible! . . ."

"A fool!" Esther Eisner exclaimed after Yasha had said goodbye and left them.

"There's room for people like him in the world too."

Esther Eisner recommended an attorney to Ezriel, but what

could an attorney do? The least Zina's sentence could be was three years in prison, and she could even be sentenced to hang. Someone influential was needed, someone who was friendly with the authorities and could have the matter quashed before it came to trial. Ezriel went to Jampol. Perhaps Sasha was there. Ezriel hadn't been there for years and found the town unrecognizable. Buildings had been put up, stores opened. There was even a depot. Young men walked about in short coats. There was a lumber warehouse where Calman's store had once stood. Ezriel passed Jews and Jewesses, but no one seemed familiar. Where was everybody? Probably dead. Finally he recognized a water-carrier. Ezriel hired a britska to take him to Sasha's house.

He passed what had been Calman Jacoby's estate. The sky, the cornfields, the cornflowers at the edge of the road, the birds—had all remained the same. The peasant women who kneeled beside the seedbeds, pulling out weeds, seemed the same as ever: the same calico dresses, the same blond braids. The storks flew in the same circles. Every cricket made the same sound it had made when Ezriel was a boy daydreaming about Shaindel. A bee suddenly landed on Ezriel's sleeve. Two butterflies, both the same color, with twin markings, fluttered next to each other. The air smelled of earth, manure, summer aromas. Cows grazed in a pasture. One cow lay down, weary of nibbling grass, dribbling saliva. The great eyes which were all pupil stared wonderingly about. To Ezriel they seemed to be asking, "Where have I come from? Why am I a cow? . . ."

The coachman, a youth in a leather-visored cap, turned to Ezriel: "Does the gentleman want to see the master?"

"Yes. Pan Jacoby."

"He can't be at home."

"Where is he?"

"Sometimes at the barracks. Mostly in Warsaw."

"I've just come from Warsaw."

"We never know where he is. Disappears and shows up again like magic. Gee-up! . . ."

"What about the lime quarries? Exhausted?"

"Altogether! . . . The older Jacoby died."

"Yes, I know."

"Whoa! . . ."

Sasha was not at home. A Gentile woman suggested that perhaps the master was at the barracks. Ezriel looked at her and knew—instinctively—that this was no maid but a mistress. Bluish circles ringed her eyes. Looking at Ezriel with the curiosity of a relative, she dragged out her words. "Yes, the master does come home, but I couldn't say when. He might come today or tomorrow or the day after tomorrow. One never knows. Who should I say has called?"

"Dr. Babad."

"Aha."

"I'll try the barracks."

"Yes, maybe the master is there, maybe somewhere else. Only God knows." And she sighed.

"I understand."

Sasha wasn't at the barracks either. Or, if he was, Ezriel couldn't find out where. There was no one to ask. In the large parade ground, a sergeant-major was drilling soldiers. Cavalry horses were being groomed, their sides curried with combs and brushes. Officers strolled back and forth. Two soldiers carried an empty kettle on a pole. Bayonets gleamed in the sun. The soldiers shouted coarsely, attacking a dummy, piercing it, turning the bayonets as if to gore its intestines. There was an odor of hay, sauerkraut, leather, and sweat. Everything was the same, even the putrid odors. But the young soldiers Ezriel had run after as a young boy were now old men or dead. Ezriel wondered sorrowfully about Zina. What were her thoughts in prison? The afternoon sun warmed him. Meanwhile, the coachman went to fetch water for his horses. Ezriel put his arm over the horse's neck. It stood there, this creature of God, silently, with bent head, drooping ears, hanging tail, its eyes full of humility. It seemed to Ezriel that the horse was saying: "One is born, and one must die. Everything else is unimportant. . . ."

V

Sasha was visiting not far from the barracks. Lydia Michalovna, an officer's wife, was sitting in a rocking chair, knitting a tiny sacque. She was of medium build, a trifle overweight, with a high bosom. Her hair would not lie flat but stood on end like the hair of Negresses in the illustrations in textbooks. She had a round forehead, a Russian nose, black eyes, and full lips. Lydia Michalovna was only twenty-seven but looked older. In the next room in a cane crib a child of four was sleeping. A maid sat at its bedside. In the courtyard an orderly was chopping wood. Lydia Michalovna's bedroom was filled with knickknacks. On the sofa, which was covered with cushions, lay a huge doll. On a side table were three gold-tooled leather albums, one on top of the other. Lydia Michalovna had just celebrated her birthday, and presents were heaped everywhere: little boxes with colored covers, bottles of perfume, bonbons, books, and vases filled with flowers. Everyone in the officers' club agreed that Lydia Michalovna was not pretty, but nearly all the men were attracted to her. The women gossiped about her, swore that she cuckolded her husband, who had gone into debt for her and paid exorbitant interest. A few days before, he had fallen from a horse and dislocated his shoulder. He was now in a military hospital in Warsaw, because the local company doctor was an alcoholic and considered incompetent. Lydia Michalovna was a favorite subject of discussion for the officers' wives. What did men see in her? A young officer had mentioned that Lydia Michalovna had an unusually white skin, a statement that caused both merriment and malicious gossip. Everyone knew that Sergei Calmanovitch Jacoby, the Jewish contractor, was a frequent visitor at her house, but since it did not disturb her husband—what business was it of theirs? The women had something to chatter about during the long summer days when their husbands were occupied with their duties, or at night—playing cards.

Lydia Michalovna rocked herself as she knitted, and from time to time raised her black eyes questioningly to Sasha, who walked to and fro in his high boots. His hands were restless, and as he moved about, he kept touching things. He went over to the clock, held the pendulum for a moment, then swung it to the left. His hair was unruly. He wore a blouse with a tassel like a student or a revolutionary. He stopped before a round mirror in an ornamental gilt frame and began making faces into it. He moved his lips, his brows, his nose, like an actor rehearsing a role.

Lydia Michalovna suddenly flared up: "Will you stop running around like a wolf in a cage?"

"Well, speak, I'm listening."

"Sit down. I can't shout. Today you are wilder than usual."

"I'm not wild. These summer days drive me crazy."

"Why blame it on the days? Darling, it can't go on like this!"

"Well, I've heard that before. You're repeating yourself. It's second nature with women. You've said it and I've heard it."

"I beg you, don't 'thou' me. Not now. I wasn't born for this sort of life. I don't care about people talking. I swear by everything sacred that gossip bothers me less than the barking of a dog. But I must feel right with myself. It doesn't concern me that others have no respect for me, but I cannot lose my self-respect."

"Empty phrases. All the ladies talk the same nonsense. Truly amusing. What is respect? Respect for what? We are all animals."

"I know, I know, but I cannot go on in this way. I can make peace with the fact that I have a lover, but he must conduct himself like a lover and not chase every petticoat in sight. I can share with a wife, but not with every peasant woman in the village. I haven't fallen that low yet."

"What's all this foolishness? With whom are you sharing me? Unless you're jealous of Hanka?"

"I can't stand the sight of her. She looks at me like a bleeding calf. If she is nothing to you, as you say, why don't you send her away? The longer she serves you, the worse it will become."

"I've sent her away a thousand times, but she won't go. She'll throw herself into the well, and I don't want any scandals. Girls like her are capable of anything."

"Maybe you're afraid that she'll throw acid at you?"

"I'm not afraid. I'm not afraid of anything. When I saw them put my mother into the grave, I decided that this world is nothing but a plague and we're all a bunch of worms. I'm ready to put a bullet through my skull. That's the truth."

"You're ready to shoot yourself, but you chase after every woman. Everyone is talking about you. It will end in disgrace, if not catastrophe."

"What are you? A gypsy? A seeress? I'm risking my skin, not yours. Besides, you know I don't beg anyone for anything. It's all the same to me: yes-yes, no-no."

"Why do you speak like that? You're still young. Truly, this sort of fatalism is bad. When you began—when we began, you were different. Then you spoke like an idealist."

"Idealist? I told you frankly I wanted you. I desired you. I still do. Everything else is garbage."

"It isn't garbage. We're getting older. What will you be like at forty, if you feel like this now?"

"At forty I'll be lying with my head down and my feet up."

"But why? Why? You're healthy and capable. I don't want to throw myself at anyone, as God is my witness, but we could be happy. What I have with Kostia is no life at all."

"What's wrong with him? No one could be better than he.

He's diligent, devoted, tolerant. I'm the third lover you've had, and—"

"What do you mean, the third? You know that's not true."

"I'm not lying."

"Well, I'm not going to bicker with you. I mention something and you make a mountain out of it. You may think what you will, but I'm not a cynic. I would have been a good wife if Kostia had been different."

"Well, I must go."

"Where are you going? What's the matter with you today?"

"You're making me nervous. You used to behave like a woman. Now you preach like a priest. I'm tired of your admonishments. If I live, I live, and if I croak, I'll be dead. If you think I'm too cynical, I can leave you alone. From today on—from this moment on. *Adieu!*"

"Where are you going? God in heaven, I didn't mean to insult you. Don't you believe that a person can love?"

"Love, not harass."

"Well, I pity you. Don't run away. You're liable to wake my child. Your mother did well to die. . . ."

Lydia Michalovna remained sitting in astonishment. She had turned pale. The last words had slipped out as if of their own accord. Sasha had an urge to slap her, but he thrust his hand into his trousers pocket. After a while he left without saying anything. He walked past the living room and went outside. For a while he lingered on the threshold.

"Well, let her go. To blazes with her! . . ." He walked several more steps and stopped again. "What in hell does she want? Why do they all make these terrible predictions? They hate me, that's the truth. Females hate every man they can't dominate and step on and that's what they call love. They are leeches. I'd rather have open hostility."

Sasha headed for the barracks. He stopped, picked up a stone, tossed it aside. Purposelessly, he strayed from the path.

He came to a swamp where frogs were croaking. He toed the slime aimlessly with the tip of his boot. The sun was setting in the west. Dusk began to fall. Gnats droned, chased each other in a whirl. Shadows skipped over the grass as if cast by invisible beings. "What is wrong with me? What torments me so?" Sasha asked himself. "It's gnawing at me so that I don't know which way to turn. . . . And what is the point of all this talk? What does she want of me? Something, after all, is tormenting her too. . . ." It suddenly hit Sasha that in the space of a short time he had lost his mother and father. "God in heaven, I am an orphan, I am all alone in the world!" he thought. "She is also an orphan. . . . We are all orphans. That's why we want to creep into one another. . . . That's why women want to hang on to someone, to cling. . . . Well, I won't have it! I'll spit on the whole lot of them! . . . I'll leave this whole mess, and go to the other end of the world! . . ."

Sasha had an impulse to throw himself into the mud.

"I'll simply kill myself. That will be my end! . . ."

23

I

Hannah, Zadok's wife, celebrated Rosh Hashana the way her parents did at home. Zadok insisted that it wasn't necessary: no one had yet been to heaven and seen people judged, the Book of Judgment open itself, the angels shiver, the good and bad deeds recorded. He argued that as long as Hannah had taken off her wig and broken away from Jewish fanaticism, she might just as well be consistent. But Hannah would not listen. It was no great sin to go wigless. Among the Litvaks, even rabbis' wives went around with bare heads. But Rosh Hashana was Rosh Hashana. Hannah had reserved a pew in the synagogue. She baked Rosh Hashana challahs, bought apples, honey, a live carp, carrots, grapes, and everything that was needed for the holiday. On Rosh Hashana eve she made a benediction over the candles in the silver candlestick her father, Reb Joshua Walden, had given her as a wedding present. Since they were celebrating the holiday, Zadok invited his Uncle Ezriel to join them. Hannah insisted that the holiday traditions be followed to the letter. They each took a wedge of apple and honey and said: "God grant us a good and sweet year." Then, before eating a spoonful of carrots, they recited: "God grant that our merits be many."

Zadok sat smiling at the head of the table, but from time to time he grew pensive. It seemed outlandish to be sitting here in an apartment in the Old City, while in Marshinov his father presided at the table. Thousands of Jews were assembled there. The court was full, the walls of the House of Worship were straining. No small thing, the Days of Awe in Marshinov! If Zadok had remained pious, he would at this moment be sitting at his father's right hand. Thousands of eyes would be looking at him, the heir-to-be. In his imagination, Zadok saw a forest of fur hats, sidelocks, beards. His father's following grew larger from year to year, but Zadok, his son, had joined the "enlightened." It was good after all that Hannah had insisted on celebrating the holiday. With candles lit and a white cloth covering the table, it was more pleasant even to read the *Courier Warshavsky*, or some German almanac. In the traditional holiday loaf, the fish, the chicken soup, there was some semblance of Marshinov. And his Uncle Ezriel was there with them discussing the Talmud. They were splitting hairs over laws, not for any practical purpose, but just to show that they still remembered.

From time to time Zadok imitated the chant and gestures of his former teacher. Hannah, who was busy carving the chicken, called out: "Don't make fun of Jewishness."

"I'm not making fun. Each nationality has its own nonsense. Take the ram's horn, for example. It undoubtedly stems from the Stone Age. It was originally used as a call to war. In the days when the Temple still stood, the mouth of the ram's horn was edged with gold and there were silver trumpets on either side of it."

Hannah opened her eyes wide. Her hair was bound up in a delicate scarf. "Trumpets? That's impossible."

"Yes, it's the truth. Ask Uncle Ezriel."

"Yes, that is so," Ezriel said.

"I never know whether he's fooling me or not. He tells me all kinds of stories. He can talk anything into me. But I know one thing: a holiday is a holiday. The Gentiles have their holidays too."

"Right as rain."

Hannah grew tearful. "Oh, Uncle Ezriel, I long for the way it was at home. At our house Rosh Hashana was beautiful! My mother had a gold dress with a train which she wore only on Rosh Hashana and Yom Kippur. When she put it on, the room lit up. She had a golden chain, so thick—an old-fashioned one, with a lock. It was a gift from Grandmother, may she rest in paradise. Papa prayed in the study house, but Mama had a seat in the synagogue, right near the east wall. She has a prayer book with a silver clasp. When I think of my sister Tilly standing near my mother, and of me here, all alone, in the city, I feel like crying—"

And big tears formed in Hannah's eyes. Zadok laughed. "Now she's bawling!" But he immediately grew serious.

Hannah went into the kitchen. They could hear her blowing her nose.

"Blood is thicker than water," Ezriel said.

"What should we do, Uncle Ezriel? How long must we hold on to this? There must be an end sometime."

"Zadok, it's not good."

"What is not good, Uncle Ezriel? The generations must go on. Epochs change; the Old Slavs had their religion too. They were idol worshippers. They served Baba Yaga, or some other idol. Now they are Christians. If everyone stuck to the old ways, there would be no progress."

"To the Slavs, Christianity is progress. But where is our progress? We had a spiritual life, now we are spiritually naked."

"Something else will work itself out. We are living in a changeable epoch. The times when we were the chosen people are over. Some of our laws are rooted somewhere in India. They have the same taboos about menstruation. Our system of kosher and impure foods probably stems from the African Negroes. Honestly, Uncle Ezriel, we have nothing to be so proud of. We have even borrowed the Ten Commandments from Hammurabi."

"According to the Bible critics, we have nothing at all of

our own. The entire Scriptures are one amalgamation of borrowed legends. Borrowed from whom? It's a big lie."

"It's the truth. They are borrowed, and why deny the truth?"

"And even if it is true? A cellar with poisoned air is just as real as a garden, but one suffocates in it. Second, since one cannot know *das Ding an sich*, and what we call reality is subjective, actually a dream—one can choose the kind of reality one wants. Why throw away gold and keep mud? Since a coal and a diamond are one and the same, why not remain with the diamond?"

"Because diamonds are useless and coals make factories run. Uncle is mistaken. According to Kant, reality is not a dream. Schopenhauer derides the second edition of the *Critique*, but actually the second edition is the true Kant. Kant is not Berkeley."

"Whatever he is, reality is not known."

"Why are you planning to go to Palestine? Olga has spoken to me. You're embarking on a disastrous path."

"Why is it so disastrous? I no longer believe that I can help the sick. I cannot swindle people. My father existed on six rubles a week and I can manage on the same."

"Are you serious about this?"

"Entirely. What is called nerves is a moral illness. I cannot forget what my mother, may she rest in peace, used to say: 'Satan has a new name: nerves.' Our grandfathers and grandmothers were not nervous, although they were hounded and tormented. Evil for them was not a sickness but a temptation."

"Would you call paranoia a sin and a temptation? Really, Uncle, I'm shocked. But why go to Palestine? If you want to become a pious fanatic, you can do that right here in Warsaw. And what will happen to Olga? She won't go with you."

"Is that what she said? She changes her mind every day. She's bringing Misha up to hate Jews and everything Jewish. I cannot allow this. Even if all religions are false, why reject one's own and accept somebody else's? Just because Ivan is strong and we are weak?"

"The world belongs to the strong."

"I cannot live in such a world. I cannot kiss the fist that hits me."

"They will beat you there too—the Turks, the Arabs. Are you going to leave Olga?"

"I cannot bring up children who will spit on me when they grow up. Plain and simple. They are already beginning to spit. Kolia keeps telling Misha that we are God-killers. When they quarrel, he calls him 'dirty Jew.' "

Hannah entered from the kitchen. "What are you two whispering about? It's a holiday. There is a God in heaven, there is. He is leading the world, not your philosophers."

II

A large crowd had assembled in Marshinov for the Day of Atonement. But only several score remained for the Feast of the Tabernacles. How many Hassidim could, after all, fit into a tabernacle? Although the rabbi was sick and constantly feverish, he spent the night inside the tabernacle on a bed made up for him there. The Warsaw specialists, who had long ago advised the rabbi to eat fatty foods and go to a sanatorium, had given up hope of his recovery. The Marshinov doctor, Ząbek, had let it be known that the rabbi's condition was hopeless. He was in the last stage of consumption. He had grown extremely emaciated and his face had a corpselike pallor. He coughed weakly, spat blood, had suffered several hemorrhages. His fingernails had split, his beard and forelocks had grown larger, thicker, a mixture of gray and white. His intimates knew the rabbi suffered from a catarrh of the intestines as well and that his urine was not clear. The rabbi drank half a saucer of milk each morning and ate nothing but an occasional spoonful of groats. But Reb Jochanan had remained Reb Jochanan, constantly refreshing himself in God's service. He continued to attend the ritual bath, maintained fasts, and studied holy books. When he recited the Torah, the rabbi's pale face flushed and his eyes grew brilliant. Even Dr. Ząbek admitted that divine powers kept the rabbi alive. His senses had become keener than ever before.

Although the rabbi had scarcely eaten all week, on the night of Succoth he made a benediction over the wine, tasted a sip of it, a bit of the bread, a bite of fish, a drop of chicken soup, a sliver of meat, a spoonful of carrot stew. He sang the table chants and gave a sermon. Hassidim remarked that such interpretation of the Torah had never been heard before. He revealed holy secrets. He seemed like an angel of God. The tabernacle was a permanent one, all that had to be done to use it on the Holy Days was raise the roof with pulleys, so that the worshippers sat under the ceiling of branches that replaced it. The boys from the rabbi's yeshiva hung lanterns constructed of melons; paper kites; clusters of grapes, apples, pears; a pomegranate left from Rosh Hashana; and birds made of eggs blown hollow from the branches. Marshinov maidens, daughters of the Hassidim, draped the walls of the tabernacle with blankets and embroidered throws. At night the table was covered by a festive cloth, on which was placed a braided loaf protected by a napkin, and a carafe of wine with a benediction beaker. And when Tsipele made the benediction over the candles in the silver candlesticks, the tabernacle seemed transformed into one of the mansions of paradise. The melodies of the Hassidim could be heard over half of Marshinov late into the night. The next morning, Kaile, Tsipele's maid, said to her that in the middle of the night she had looked out her window and seen a glow emanating from the tabernacle. By this time the candles had gone out. Afraid of fire, she had gone down to look through the draperies. There was no fire, but the light shining from the rabbi's face lit up half a wall. It faded as she stood there, and her knees had given way from fright.

The first two days of Succoth in Marshinov passed with great joy. The rabbi performed in a state of ecstasy: blessing the citrus fruit, waving his palm branch. There was dancing in the tabernacle too. The Hassidim who had been invited to the tabernacle were served wine. On the second intermediary day, Tsipele came to give the rabbi his medicine. The rabbi was not alone. He was studying with his youngest son, Gadele, already a grown boy. Now that Zadok, his elder son, had become worldly, Gadele was to be the rabbi's spiritual heir. The rabbi's son-in-law, Pinchus, Zelda's husband, the son of the Wysoker rabbi, was also there.

Seeing the bottle of medicine, the rabbi grimaced. "After the holiday."

"The doctor said you should take it every day."

"Not necessarily."

Suddenly the rabbi remarked: "Speaking of doctors, what's new with Ezriel?"

Tsipele was astounded. For years, ever since Shaindel had become insane and Ezriel had gone to live with a convert, the rabbi had not mentioned his name.

"Who knows?"

"His father, Reb Menachem Mendel, was a just and pious man."

"Yes."

"A pity. . . ."

Two hours later, as Tsipele sat reading at the window, a carriage drove into the courtyard and a tall man in modern clothes stepped out. Tsipele paled when she recognized Ezriel. There was a child with him. Mendel the beadle informed the rabbi that the doctor, Reb Calman's son-in-law (he did not want to call him the rabbi's brother-in-law), had come from Warsaw to extend his greetings.

The rabbi smiled. "Send him in."

Ezriel and Misha entered. Approaching him, the rabbi extended his hand.

"Peace be with you, Rabbi!"

"Peace to you. Welcome!" the rabbi exclaimed.

"The rabbi recognized me?"

"Yes, of course, Ezriel."

"This is my son, Moishele."

The rabbi bent down toward the child. "So, Moishele. Are you a good boy?" And the rabbi pinched his cheek.

Misha didn't answer him and the rabbi asked again: "You're a mischief-maker, eh?"

"Rabbi, he doesn't understand Yiddish," Ezriel said in a hollow tone.

"Well, one can serve God in any language."

"Rabbi, I brought him here. I want him to become a Jew."

Tears flowed from the rabbi's eyes. "Well, well . . ."

"Rabbi, I can't stand it anymore!" Ezriel cried out, his voice breaking.

Taking out his handkerchief, the rabbi dabbed at his eyes. "Did you see the truth?" he asked.

"Not completely. But I saw their lie," Ezriel replied.

"It's all the same."

III

During his student days and later when he practiced medicine, Ezriel had kept mostly to himself. The Christian students did not mingle with the Jewish ones. The Jewish students ignored each other to avoid becoming a segregated group. In the hospital and at the clinic, he had kept his colleagues at a distance, because, first, Shaindel did not want to know their wives, and also because they were not the kind of people with whom he could be intimate. They played cards, gossiped. Many of the doctors were involved in organizational activities, most of these supported by the assimilationists. Here in Marshinov, Ezriel felt for the first time in years that he was not alone. Addressing him in the familiar "thou," aged Hassidim recalled his father, Reb Menachem Mendel of Jampol. Reb Shimmon, the Stiktiner rabbi, had died and Mayer Joel, who had gone over to Reb Shimmon, and his sons-in-law returned to Marshinov. Young men and boys called Ezriel "Uncle."

Usually, a large crowd did not assemble for the last two days of the holiday. But this time a great number of Hassidim came. Some were curious to see the heretic who had returned to Judaism. It seemed odd that Zadok, the rabbi's son, had become an atheist, while Ezriel had repented. Tsipele wept when Ezriel came to see her. Her daughter gazed at him lovingly. Gadele trailed alongside Uncle Ezriel, eager to converse with him. Everywhere people went out of their way to greet him. Jews grasped his hands, reluctant to let go, gazed at him warmly. Each person wanted to hear for himself why Ezriel had forsaken the enlightened ones, the materialists, the philosophers. The women of the court took over the care of Moishele. They taught him Yiddish, pampered him, guarded him, kissed and petted him. Each day was filled with delight. Ezriel prayed in the study house, said the blessing over the citrus fruit, and helped Misha do the same. He ate with Misha in the tabernacle. The boy seemed to revive. He grasped the Yiddish words with unusual rapidity, played tag and hide-and-seek with the children.

Ezriel realized how isolated he had been all these years. He had formed no real friendships. No one had been interested in him. Here in Marshinov, he was at home. He could drop in everywhere, everybody spoke his language, had known his father, and even his grandfather, Reb Abraham Hamburg. He was treated like a prince who had returned from exile.

In recent years, Ezriel had grown accustomed to finding in everyone symptoms of neurasthenia, hysteria, or simply chronic dissatisfaction. Rage and pride showed everywhere. He read frustration, thwarted ambition, unfulfilled lusts in all eyes. People never seemed to have enough possessions, or they studied insatiably, or needed more and more love affairs. Ezriel had concluded that this was human nature, since he, too, was no different. He had accepted Schopenhauer's philosophy that human life oscillates between lust and tedium. The conception that everything was blind will, the result of blind forces, attracted him, although his reason rejected it. Every play, every novel, every chapter of history, every newspaper article led to the conclusion that all was futile and must end tragically. Even Olga's parties, the dancing, the drinking, the jokes, the flirting arose from melancholy. Everyone was trying to forget himself.

In Marshinov, there was joy. Eyes shone, faces glowed. The glory of God must have descended upon these Jews, the Talmudic scholars, the students of Hassidic study houses. Ezriel did not see in them the symptoms of uncertainty, overindulgence, impatience. He stood, on the seventh day of the Feast of Tabernacles, in the House of Prayer and looked around him. What he saw here was completely contrary to the textbooks. According to the sociologists, poverty was the cause not only of sickness but of crime. But these Jews were a living denial of all these theories. They did not enjoy fresh air, did no exercise, nor did they eat the food recommended by modern physicians. They stooped when they walked, shuffled their feet, spat on the floors, never used forks. Most of them wore patched satin capotes, ragged skullcaps, shabby shoes, torn stockings. They earned their precarious livings from half-stocked stores, tutoring, matchmaking, or brokerage fees. They sighed as they prayed. "Woe is me . . . Dear Father . . . woe and double woe . . ." This was no privileged class but an assemblage of paupers, less secure than the peasantry and the proletariat. They had been driven out of Russia, were the victims of pogroms; writers had vilified them, called them parasites; anti-Semites had manufactured false accusations against them. But instead of becoming degenerate, sinking into melancholy, drunkenness, immorality—they celebrated, recited the Psalms, rejoiced with happiness that could only come from the soul. No one here was in despair over the pogroms, as were the Jewish intelligentsia all over Russia. They placed their faith in God, not in man, evolution, or revolution.

IV

On the night of Simhath Torah, Misha carried a flag and a red apple with a candle stuck into it. He stood with the other boys on a bench and chatted in a mixture of Polish and Yiddish. For the first three years of his life, Misha had spoken Yiddish with his mother, and the language was not completely strange to him. Tsipele had bought him a skullcap and a sash. He knew how to make a benediction over bread, water, or a cookie. The procession of men carrying the scroll of the Law passed the boys and they stretched out their hands, touched its mantlet, and brought their fingers to their lips. Even girls had come into the House of Prayer. Simhath Torah is a holiday when rules are relaxed. After a while, Ezriel was called to carry the scroll. The beadle sang out his name in the traditional chant: "Arise, Reb Ezriel, son of our teacher, Reb Menachem Mendel," and the entire assembly looked toward him. When Ezriel walked past Misha with the scroll, the youngster jumped off the bench he was standing on and followed his father. Ezriel let him touch the Tree of Life, the post around which the scroll is wrapped, so that he too would be helping to carry the Torah.

Ezriel asked him quietly: "Do you want to remain here, or go back to Warsaw?"

"Remain here," Misha replied.

"For how long?"

"A thousand years."

The Hassidim sang and danced. The boys joined in with their high-pitched voices. The girls clapped their hands. The main festivities began on the following morning. Ezriel had forgotten that Jews could rejoice so heartily. Although it was forbidden to drink before the day's prayers were ended, Hassidim took a sip after the morning services. The beadle warned the tipsy descendants of Aaron that they would not be permitted to make the priestly blessing. But they paid no attention to him. Youths carried flasks in their pockets. They started playing pranks, tied together the ritual garments of two elderly Hassidim, hid someone's prayer shawl, or skullcap, or replaced the Succoth prayer book with the one used during the High Holy Days. Their elders scolded: "Pups! Ignoramuses! Tipplers! Where are you when there's no wine?" And the boys answered back: "What's so important about being old? A billy goat has a white beard too." "Heathens, you'll be thrown out of here!" an elderly Hassid said, smiling broadly. But even as they joked, not one of them missed an "Amen." When the reader, during the recital of the Eighteen Benedictions, made the mistake of praying for "dew" instead of "rain," everyone laughed. The rabbi smiled to himself. After the singing of "Unto thee it was shown," all the scrolls of Law were taken out of the Holy Ark. There were perhaps twenty scrolls both new and old. Some had ragged mantlets decorated with crowns and fescues; the coverings of others were unornamented save for the ancient dates embroidered on them. Because the Holy Ark was left empty, a lighted candle was placed within it.

Ezriel had forgotten these customs. Each prayer had its melody, its nuances and accompanying sighs. Holding the scrolls, the Hassidim danced, singing the chants of Marshinov. Too weak to carry a large scroll, the rabbi held a small one. He put his face to it, kissed it, buried his cheek in the velvet of its mantlet. Feebly, he began to sing. The Hassidim pushed forward to kiss his Torah. Dancing and swaying, he leaned down so the children, Misha among them, could reach it. Everyone watched, knowing the rabbi was in constant pain and that his days were numbered. Barring a miracle, he would never see another Simhath Torah. They smiled and wept. Singing, they wiped away their tears. They danced singly and in small groups. Holding up scrolls of the Law, two old men danced facing each other. What else did the Jews have beside the Torah? But what else was needed? After the procession, all but three of the scrolls were replaced in the Ark. There followed a kind of auction for the honor of being "the groom of the Torah" and "the groom of Genesis." "One ruble!" "Ten gulden!" "Two rubles!" "Two and a quarter!" "Three! . . ." The beadle banged on the reader's lectern and called out in a festive singsong, "Three rubles once, three rubles twice, three rubles for the last—" "Four rubles!" cried a hoarse voice. It was like a marketplace, but the House of Prayer needed money for the winter. The walls were peeling. Immediately after selling these honors, the reader began the recitation of "And this is the blessing." Each man and boy, all but the smallest, was called up separately to make the benediction. The smallest children were summoned and came running in a group. They were all covered by the same prayer shawl. Misha was among them. The reader made the benediction with them, in his deep voice, the children repeating in their thin, piping singsong: "Blessed be Thou who hath chosen us among all nations and given us the Torah . . ." "This is the true chauvinism," Ezriel thought, and smiled to himself. They had chosen themselves. In every epoch they had been roasted alive. In every generation there was another excuse for exterminating them and their holy books. Hadn't they crucified Jesus, used Christian blood in their matzos, defiled the holy water, desecrated the wafer? These Jews in the House of Prayer deserved destruction for many offenses: for being capitalists (wasn't that a joke?), they were strangers (merely eight hundred years in Poland). What were they not? Chauvinists, reactionaries, petty bourgeois, fanatics, jargonists, barbarians. Every "ism" spelled doom for them. But their real crime was that they tried to lead sanctified lives, without wars, without adultery, without mockery or rebellion.

But could their behavior serve as an example for others? Could their conduct become what Kant calls a maxim? Yes, it was possible. Humanity could abolish warfare, divide the land so that there would be enough for everyone. Each group could have its language, its culture, its traditions. But one thing all would have to have in common: a belief in one God and in free will; a discipline that would transform all man's deeds into serving God and helping one another. In a divine existence, there are no neutral activities. Everything must exalt, purify. But such things could not be brought about forcibly, nor could the Messiah be compelled to arrive.

V

There had been a time when Ezriel had assumed that he knew a good deal about the eccentricities of the human mind. He had been accustomed to hear his patients chatter irrationally, contradict themselves, accuse or justify themselves. He had also thought he knew intimately the workings of his own brain. But in the past weeks Ezriel had realized how plural man's thinking could be. The simultaneous existence within one of both an evil spirit and a good one, as described in the Holy Books, was apparently a profound psychological truth. Even while Ezriel was in Marshinov praying, studying, dancing with the Hassidim, and teaching Misha Judaism, something within him continued to worry about his patients, about Olga and Topolka. Something insisted that his piety would end with the holidays and his return to Warsaw. He argued with himself that a materialistic existence was bad and that religion was a remedy for all ills. But could he believe as these men did that every law, every custom had come down from Mount Sinai? Could there be anything more contradictory than a penitent who remained a heretic? Or even one who doubted? He was reminded of a passage in Proverbs: "None that go unto her return again"—which, according to the Talmud, referred to heresy. The essence of religion, as interpreted by Ezriel, was a wholeness, an unblemished faith. But could anyone who had read the Bible critics and understood the evolution of ideas revert to religious innocence? These Jews believed that the Torah came to them directly from heaven, but Ezriel knew it had been written by various writers at different times. In Genesis, light and darkness were two separate entities. The sun was apparently not the source of light but a lamp that added light to and brightened an already existent source. The stars were an addition to the moon. The sky was a dam or sluice that prevented the waters of heaven from inundating the earth.

In the same Torah that contained "Thou shalt not kill," there were commandments on how to liquidate entire nations, how to plunder, burn, even rape. Leviticus was full of magic and taboos similar to those found among savage tribes in Africa and Polynesia. Could Ezriel learn from the Torah the divine and absolute truth? What was he doing here in Marshinov? Why was he deceiving these people?

He had drunk wine with them and danced with them, but he had done so without real faith. "Am I a hypocrite? Have I taken leave of my senses? Am I simply a self-murderer, as Olga calls me?" He bit his lips. Perhaps among Jews he was an exception. But among Christians there were millions like him, after all. They studied Darwin and attended church. Not only had the church and state been separated in some countries, but within their own psyches the Gentiles had established a difference between religious and scientific truth. Was this possible? There could be only one truth: either the world was created in six days or it had developed over millions of years; either God had parted the Red Sea or he had not; either Jesus had been resurrected from the dead or he had remained dead. Was Ezriel capable of basing his life on contradiction?

Simhath Torah fell on a Friday. All day Ezriel went from one kiddush to another. He drank with the others, dry wine, sweet wine, mead with nuts, beer. He nibbled on strudel, flat cakes, tarts. At Tsipele's house he had partaken of cabbage with raisins and cream of tartar. He was sated, tipsy. But in some recess of his brain, he had remained cold-sober. No, he was incapable of building his life on revelations. He could not rely on the hearsay of religious authority. Perhaps there had been no Moses, no miracles. The Torah was merely a book. All religions were dreams. God was eternally silent. If He existed, was there a method for finding Him? How—a priori, a posteriori? Or should He once and for all be identified with nature, as in Spinoza's conclusions? So many had tried to show proof of His existence and had proven nothing. The Kantian elephant had borne a mouse.

Yes, for the Hassidim, it was Simhath Torah. Evening approached. At sundown the women hurried to make their benedictions over the candles. Kaile, Tsipele's maid, prepared the Sabbath stew and sealed the oven with dough. Soon they would see in the Sabbath, singing: "Come, my beloved." It was the Sabbath when the reading of the first section of Genesis comes round again. But did this have any connection with the outside world? Could Ezriel accept this life, forsake his career? He had fled because his life was not turning out well. Would it be more fulfilled here? What would he do when everybody returned home after the holidays? Why had he come in the first place? Had it been to escape estrangement, impiety, a daughter who hid a revolver under her mattress, a wife who arranged balls for lechers and oppressors, patients who deceived their husbands and wanted only to have more enjoyment at someone else's expense? Or to find the way to a mute God whose nature is unknown, whom one does not know how to serve, and even whether any service rendered Him is appreciated. He, the Almighty, had kept silent in times of idolatry, slavery, wars, plagues, tortures. He had disposed of all men in the same fashion: those who worshipped Him, and those who rebelled against Him. On the other hand, if God did speak, what would happen to free will? His father, peace be with him, had been right: God cannot reveal His purpose if good and evil, faith and denial are to remain hanging in the balance. Moral life depends on this doubt. Man must discover God through temptation and suffering, exactly as he had discovered that one could be poisoned by toadstools and that a serum distilled from cowpox could cure smallpox. Everyone sought God, every race, every savage tribe. Mankind could not exist without this constant search, as he, Ezriel, had so often pointed out to Zadok.

In the evening the Jews went back to the House of Prayer. Candles and kerosene lamps were already lit. The floor had been swept and strewn with yellow sand. The Hassidim chanted the Song of Songs. The reader stood before the lectern and began: "Oh, come, let us exult . . ."

VI

On Sabbath night, Ezriel went into the rabbi's study and remained there for two and a half hours. No one in Marshinov recalled the rabbi spending so much time with anyone before. Mendel the beadle, who placed his ear to the door, heard only mumbling. It wasn't like Ezriel to speak his thoughts to someone else, to reveal his torments, but this time he held nothing back. He sat opposite the rabbi and it seemed to him as if every word he uttered stabbed the rabbi like a spear. From time to time the rabbi grimaced as if in pain and clutched at his breast. Ezriel frequently asked if he should stop, but the rabbi replied: "Continue, continue!" Ezriel spoke frankly: What proof was there that the Law of Moses was true law? The other religions had their own laws. Where was there proof that God existed? And if He did exist, yet never indicated what pleased Him and what did not—why was there punishment? Could a king who did not issue laws to his subjects punish because the laws were not obeyed? From the rabbi's expression, Ezriel knew he was blaspheming. It was cruel to torment a saint who had given his life to his religion and was now close to death. What could the rabbi tell him that he himself did not know? Ezriel grew afraid lest the rabbi rebuke him, abhor him as a heretic, and drive him away. At times the rabbi's face grew mournful and baffled, at others there was the trace of a twinkle in his eyes. His sidelocks dripped perspiration. The candles in the holders grew smaller. Shadows danced on the walls. Several times Mendel the beadle peeped in, but the rabbi waved him away. From time to time, the rabbi had a coughing spell and spat into a handkerchief.

When Ezriel grew silent, the rabbi asked: "From whom are you descended on your mother's side?"

"Mother was a pious Jewess."

"I know. Was she also descended from pious men?"

"Yes, Rabbi, from Rabbi Yom Tov Heller."

"So? You are a grandson of saints."

"What shall I do, Rabbi?"

"Do no evil."

"Is that all?"

"It is much."

"What shall I do about my wife, Rabbi? I told you about her."

"Yes, I heard."

"Shall I leave her?"

"If you can."

"And if I cannot?"

"Then wait."

"What shall I do with Moishele?"

"Leave him here."

"Rabbi, I don't know what to do."

The rabbi smiled. "One does, nevertheless. At least don't cause anyone sorrow."

"Shall I put on phylacteries, live like a Jew?"

"Yes, as well as you can."

"Even though I don't believe in the Law of Moses?"

"The saints also doubted. As long as the soul dwells in the body, it can never be totally sure of anything. God willing, we will all see the truth."

"And meanwhile?"

"Meanwhile, don't harm anyone, or yourself either."

"Shall I remain a doctor?"

"Doctors are necessary."

"I have kept nothing from the rabbi."

"Everything requires God's help. Even with free choice, the grace of God is necessary. Even free will is mercy."

"What must be done?"

"One must pray for mercy."

"Even without faith?"

"There are no total unbelievers. The body is blind. But the soul sees, because it exists in this world and the other. Without the body, there would be no such thing as free will. That is its reason for being."

"It's good to hear this, Rabbi."

"Why worry? It's God's world. Everything comes from Him. The evildoer certainly harms—but there are remedies. There is no reason to despair."

"What shall I do to deserve mercy?"

"Perform kind acts. You have already done something noble in saving Moishele."

Ezriel wanted to say a few more words, tell the rabbi about his intention to visit Palestine, but the rabbi stood up, extending his hand. "Go in good health. God knows everything . . ."

"Thank you, Rabbi."

"The body is a vessel for pain, that is why it rebels."

Ezriel went to his room. Moishele was already asleep. Ezriel got into bed but could not fall asleep. The rabbi's words echoed in him. It was wonderful, that this saint who imposed such mortifications upon himself was so lenient with others. The real difference between a saint and a wicked man suddenly came to Ezriel: both weighed everything morally, but the saint made demands on himself, whereas the rogue made demands on others. Ezriel fell asleep and dreamed of Olga. He awoke trembling and lustful. Perhaps she no longer loved him.

He began to consider the reasoning behind asceticism. Why were there so many recluses, fakirs, monks, nuns? Why were the revolutionaries prepared to die for their beliefs? In this egotistical world, why were there so many candidates for martyrdom? He himself was about to renounce a woman who loved him, and a career, to assume an existence of suffering. Why? Because the soul yearned for as much power as the body. It craved freedom from material bondage, but could not achieve it. Even to acquire some freedom, the soul must struggle constantly. Jewishness is based on compromise between body and soul, not on war between them.

What the rabbi had tried to tell him was simply this: "Don't force yourself. It is better to do a little with good will than a lot by compulsion."

VII

Sunday morning, Ezriel went into the House of Prayer and put on his prayer shawl before praying. Many of the Hassidim had left the previous night or at daybreak, but several quorums still remained. Ezriel put a phylactery on his bared arm, and the other on his forehead, then wound the thongs around his fingers in the form of the Hebrew letter Shin, the initial of Shadai, the holy name, and intoned: "And I will betroth thee unto me for ever; Yea, I will betroth thee unto me in righteousness, and in judgment and in loving-kindness and in mercies. I will even betroth thee unto me in faithfulness and thou shalt know the Lord."

"What words! What a lump of auto-suggestion to swallow on an empty stomach!" Ezriel said to himself. Customarily in the morning Ezriel glanced at the newspaper. A pogrom had occurred, a flood, a strike, a demonstration. He would turn the page and read about murders, suicides, arson, thefts. In the House of Prayer, each day began auspiciously. He finished his prayers and went to say goodbye to Tsipele. Moishele had already eaten breakfast. Tsipele told Ezriel that she would engage a tutor for the boy for a few weeks before enrolling him in a cheder. Zelda, Tsipele's daughter, was staying in Marshinov and would help keep an eye on Moishele. Tsipele's children were already grown, and it would be a pleasure for her to raise another child, Shaindel's child, her father's grandchild. Ezriel wanted to leave her money, but Tsipele grew angry. "I don't need money!"

"It costs money to bring up a child."

"Pish-pash! He'll cost me a million. . . ."

"Moishele, do you want to stay here?"

"*Tak*. Yes."

"Mind your aunt."

"Yes."

Ezriel wondered why the child wished to stay. Olga had been like a mother to him. Kolia had played with him. But he'd raise a fuss if Ezriel tried to take him away. Moishele was holding a slice of ginger cake and drinking milk. He was at home with Tsipele already. They had bought him a gaberdine and a cap worn by cheder boys. He was mixing Yiddish words with his Polish. Ezriel left pocket money for the boy and rode to the train. The depot was filled with Hassidim. He should have traveled with them third-class, but he purchased a first-class ticket. He had to be able to think in the two hours it would take to get home. What was Olga doing? He had been away from home less than a week, but it seemed as if months had gone by. The train arrived. The Hassidim pushed forward with their packs and satchels. Ezriel watched them. They were almost all small, disheveled, with stooped shoulders, ruffled beards, and spoke with outlandish gestures. During the train's long wait, they shouted, ran about from one car to the next, became entangled in their long capotes, behaved so boisterously that the Gentile passengers laughed at them. Ezriel heard one Pole say to another: "A wild rabble, eh? . . ." Yes, here they were a rabble, but, only an hour before, they had been priests in a temple. Would the world ever understand this? They were completely lacking in that ornament the Gentile world called dignity or pride. Everything fine in them was concealed. Externally, they were almost caricatures.

The Hassidim came up to him, bustled around him, and for a while he was tormented by shame of his brothers. He was disgusted with himself! He was ashamed of Jews! This was what the Enlightenment had led to! . . . He decided to sit among them. He entered a third-class wagon. The bell rang for the third time. The train started. The benches were taken by

Gentile passengers who had gotten on at earlier stations, and the racks were filled with suitcases. The Hassidim stood in groups. Some tried to sit on their own baskets and traveling bags. They spoke, gesticulated, clutched their beards. One Hassid grasped another's lapel, trying to make him understand the rabbi's words. A yeshiva boy took a bottle of schnapps out of his basket and invited others to drink with him in honor of some rabbi's anniversary. Since there was no water with which to wash one's hands, the Hassidim wiped their palms on the windowpanes. Ezriel was also offered a sip of schnapps. He said the benediction, and they answered "Amen." They expressed the hope that he remain a Hassid and that he not, God forbid, be alienated from his ancestry. Two Gentile women began to giggle. A Gentile with blond mustaches spoke up. "Drinking, Jewboys, are you? You're drunks, eh? The Christian doesn't have a piece of bread to fill his stomach, but you scabheads, idlers, slurp vodka. They should do the same with you here as they've done in Russia: drive you out." "Where would you drive them to?" said a derby-hatted individual with black, piercing eyes. "Who would take them in, the vermin? The Prussians? They drop all their filth on us here in Poland. . . ." The Hassidim pretended not to hear, or perhaps they really didn't. They understood little Polish. Ezriel's impulse was to answer the Poles, but he knew that it was senseless. The Polish newspapers were growing more and more virulent against the Jews. Their wrath was aimed mainly at the Russian Jews, the Litvaks, who had been driven from the Russian provinces and were "Russifying" Poland. The Gentile in the derby continued. "They'll flood us, these devils! They'll do what they did to Egypt. They're chased like mice out of Russia, and here they spit on the Polish people and take away their bread. Create a food shortage. What are we supposed to do with this low rabble? Just look at them, folks: a wild horde! Worse than the Tartars! No manners whatever! . . ." "Hey, you, Jewboy, you've knocked down my satchel!" shouted a Gentile woman with a chirping voice.

"Pick it up, you lousy dog. . . . Oh, children, they're trampling my belongings! . . ." Ezriel picked up the satchel and put it back on the rack. "Yes," he said to himself, "in a first-class wagon I would have had rest, but this is the way it really is: we're a people without a home and we can't live with anyone. We remain alien, always the object of mockery and derision. Nothing has changed. Conditions are as bad today as they were a thousand years ago. Even worse: in those days, there was no 'enlightenment'. In those days, at least, Jews kept their faith. . . ." The conductor came in and began to search under the benches. Yes, a boy was actually concealed under one of them. The conductor pulled him out by his boots and one came off in his hand. The boy had long sidelocks, large black eyes. The bootless foot was wrapped in a rag.

"A thief, eh? . . . Where, you accursed ragamuffin, is your ticket?"

"I lost it."

"Lost it, eh? You'll sleep in jail tonight, you rascal! You leprous scab! . . ."

"Jews, we'll have to give him a hand," a young Hassid spoke up.

Ezriel paid the boy's fare. The conductor gave the boy back his boot. The Poles laughed, grew angry, twirled their mustaches. They whispered among themselves about Ezriel. With his European attire he did not belong to that crowd. Suspicious glances were cast in his direction. From time to time, Jewish correspondents from Western Europe came to Poland and wrote disparaging articles about the country for the European press.

VIII

Ezriel hired a droshky and was driven home. When he left the city, the sun was shining and it was still warm. Now, autumn had come. A mist hovered over Warsaw and from time to time a single drop fell from the overcast sky onto Ezriel's face.

The droshky reached the house. Ezriel paid the fare and started up the stairs. His name was inscribed on the brass plate over the door. At least he was still the master of this piece of metal. He rang the bell and heard footsteps. "Well, I mustn't be so nervous!" he said to himself. "I'll make my decision." Olga opened the door. She stood facing him—dark, slim, in a black dress and a new coiffure.

She smiled questioningly. "You're back?"

"I hope you recognize me."

"Well, come in."

He walked into the foyer and put down his valise.

"Where is Misha?" Olga asked.

"He's staying with the rabbi."

"Oh."

He opened the door to his office and glanced inside as if suspecting that someone had replaced him. In the living room, he hung his hat on the head of a little angel. It was a gesture to convince himself that he still lived here and could do as he pleased.

Olga followed him in. "You didn't even kiss me. . . ."

"From the way you spoke to me when I left, I thought everything was finished between us."

"What did I say? There were patients here, and I didn't know what to tell them. You're the talk of Warsaw."

"Let them talk."

"How does one just leave a child by himself?"

"He isn't alone. The rabbi's wife is his aunt. He has more relatives there than here."

"Well, I understand. After all, I'm a complete stranger to him. I only raised him. What will he do there, become a Hassid?"

"Go to cheder."

"Well, do as you see fit. I have nothing to say about it."

Olga stood near a rubber plant. As she spoke to Ezriel, she fussed with a half-withered leaf that was about to fall, as if trying to fasten the stem to its branch. She looked at him sidelong, smiling in a curiously embarrassed way. "Why don't you take off your coat?"

He kept it on and sat down, resting his head against the back of the sofa. A mood of tragic playfulness overtook him. "Olga, it's bad!"

"What is bad, dearest?"

"Everything. I want to be a Jew and I long for this home. I rode back in a third-class carriage and saw how the Poles feel about us. We're well hated!"

"Who is loved? Why did you ride third-class?"

"I wanted to be with the Hassidim."

"If you're going to associate with them, you'll always run into that sort of thing."

"Worldly Jews like us are hated even more. How are you?"

"Ah, I'm still alive. Did you think I'd commit suicide?"

"Why that, of all things?"

"You didn't even write one word."

"The letter wouldn't have come much earlier than I."

"Still—I hope you've decided what you want to do. If you're to remain a doctor, you can't treat your patients this way. You're not the only doctor in Warsaw."

"I know."

"Neither are you, as the saying goes in Yiddish, the only male in Moscow."

Ezriel tensed. "What's happened? Has someone made you an offer?"

Olga's face reddened. She paused a moment before she replied. "Yes."

"Who?"

Olga smiled, but her eyes remained sad. "I've told you about Dr. Ivanov, the lieutenant colonel."

"Aha."

"He was in Warsaw and paid me a visit."

Her words shocked him. He grew pale with jealousy. "He fell in love with you? Just like that?"

"Don't be so sarcastic. A man can still fall in love with me."

24

I

My dear Zadok (or do you prefer Zdzislaw?):

I know I promised to write you immediately, but six weeks have gone by since I left and I haven't until now been able to take time to write. What happened to Zina completely unnerved me. Perhaps I had no right to go and leave her in such a predicament. But, as God knows, I was unable to help her. I lowered myself before Sasha, when I finally located him, but all I got from him was impudence. He had sunk into deep gloom after the death of Clara and Calman. I had already liquidated everything and I had no alternative but to leave. I don't know what to write about first. I've been in Berlin, Paris, and have even seen the "Great Charcot," as he is called. I am now, as you can see, in Switzerland, in Bern. My sister Mirale is still in a sanatorium in Arosa, and I'm afraid that her condition is not good. She has sacrificed herself for the revolution, about which I hear talk here day and night. I cannot begin to tell you what is going on in the so-called Russian colony here, which consists ninety percent of Jews. A people that for four thousand years had lived with God and divine ideals has completely forgotten itself and its history of martyrdom. It has staked everything on a revolution that is likely to bring nothing but a blood bath. The tragedy of it all is that this handful of people are already divided into parties, groups, circles, all fighting and hating one another. Oh, how they hate! I don't deny that there are many idealists among them. My sister is one of them. And what drove Zina to all this? And what will happen to all of them when the guillotine begins to work? I was no less disappointed in the Western European idols. Charcot is a full-fledged tyrant. He screams at the doctors as if they were messenger boys. I saw his patients and God knows that neither he nor Janet can help them. They are the same unhappy people who came to me. One of them I actually recognized. They travel from Paris to Nancy, and from Nancy to Carlsbad or Baden-Baden. It is easy to hypnotize them. They are taken in by every fashion, every popular book, every new play, every blown-up scandal. We make too much fuss in Poland over this Western Europe! The Prussian governor is no better than our natchalnik. The stinginess and pettiness of the German hotel keeper is unbelievable. In Paris I encountered poverty and filth even worse than on our Krochmalna Street. The Alps are magnificent, but the philosophy lectures that I have heard here in Bern and in Zurich are just as tedious, pedantic, and false as the wisdom dispensed in Warsaw. In Germany, anti-Semitism is rife. Here, in Western Europe, I have seen what I have known for a long time: that the person who estranges himself from God seeks only an opportunity to hate. We hate in the name of patriotism, or class distinctions, party relationships, or simply because we live in different localities, or speak a different dialect. The professors make filth of one another. There is bitter combat concerning Kant in Germany. There is no greater accomplishment for the Prussian student than to drink scores of mugs of beer and fight duels. A youth who does not have a couple of dueling scars on his face is ashamed to go into a beer hall. Official Germany is permeated by an obsession for conquest, while France is consumed with a mania for revenge. Both are united in contempt and envy of England. Europe is full of plans, but all of them demand human sacrifice.

When I left Warsaw, I was still toying with the idea of settling somewhere in Western Europe. But here many things became clear to me. I am now fully determined to go on to Palestine. Do not think that I have any illusions. I know full well that the settlers there are no saints. How, in any case, can this or that part of the world solve human problems? Yet Palestine is for me the symbol of the return to my roots, the source of the ancient truths that for thousands of years people have tried to alter, emasculate, or drown in dogma. When I sat and listened to the celebrated Wundt, I realized that intellectuals would continue to present their philosophic, sociological, and psychological interpretations even if the whole world were to become Sodom. And how far are we from such a state? All this culture blunts moral feeling and destroys faith in the divine powers. Here, even more so than at home, megalomania is evident in every countenance. I mean, among the intelligentsia.

I have had moments when everything seemed black and I seriously considered suicide. But each time, as if by their own volition, my feet led me among Jews, the real Jews, the Jews who live with God. I found Hassidic study houses in Berlin and even in Paris. I cannot describe to you what a pleasure it was for me to encounter these Hassidim, to look at their faces, beards, eyes, to hear the words of the Torah. When one gazes at the Talmudic scholars, one actually sees eternity. What is Berlin to them? What is Paris? How wonderfully they have isolated themselves amidst all this madness! They do not even know that they are in Europe and that we are at the end of the "magnificent" and bloody nineteenth century. In their Houses of Worship, it is always the beginning. They do not boast of progress, nor do they build their hopes on a "new man" that this or that system will bring to the fore. These Jews are the true realists. They know that in all generations man is born bad and that he must work from the cradle to the grave merely not to become an evildoer.

I know, Zadok, that you don't agree with me, but I must tell you what I think. It is a riddle to me how men of my age, or even old men, can seek comfort in a future in which they will no longer be in existence. I have simply stopped understanding those people who hang their hopes on childish promises. I tell you, Zadok, that there is no worse nonsense than the optimism of the professors.

I don't have to tell you that I am going to Palestine with a heavy heart. Misha is with your mother. Olga and I are as good as separated. She is neither a Jew nor a Gentile. Like so many modern Jews, she has one desire: to forget her origin, to destroy her roots. I hope for her own sake that she succeeds. I am not in a much better position than she is, having no real faith and doubting everything, but at least I no longer have the illusion that our history can be obliterated. The power, whatever it is, that has kept us alive for four thousand years is still with us. I can deny God, but I cannot stop being a Jew—contradictory and strange as these words may sound.

I have heard nothing here about your father, and I hope it is not too late for you to go to him. I send you and Hannah my warmest greetings.

Your devoted, EZRIEL

25

I

Zadok was letting his beard grow. A shortened capote still hung in the closet and each time he opened the closet door he looked at it. His father, Reb Jochanan of Marshinov, was on his deathbed. Zadok was prepared to hear the bad news any day. But to go to Marshinov clean-shaven and in a jacket was unthinkable. It would be a disgrace for his mother. Zadok's beard grew quickly and he looked like a Hassid again. He sat in an armchair, smoking cigarettes and skimming the stacks of magazines he had bought. Since his beard had begun to sprout, he had ceased attending classes and paying visits to his assimilated friends. He was supposed to receive some assistance from the community, but he had neglected to ask for it and the stipend had gone to a more aggressive student. Hannah was pregnant and walked about with a pointed belly and yellow flecks on her face.

It was summer, and whoever could afford it was away in the country. The sun beat down on the roof of their attic room. Odors of rotting fruit, sewage, and fried onions from neighbors' cooking wafted in through the windows. The children in the street screamed, threw stones, and hit pieces of wood with makeshift bats. Zadok glanced through the magazines and knit his brow. When his Uncle Ezriel had been in Warsaw he had not been so wretched. At least there had been someone to talk to. Simply because in the last few years his Uncle Ezriel had denounced all material values, Zadok had argued for materialism. This summer Zadok had reached a stage where he had become resentful of the science that his Uncle Ezriel had compared to salt water: the more one drank of it, the less it quenched one's thirst. Every aspect of it was filled with detail, but one could arrive at no meaningful total. Zadok had long since discarded metaphysics. The philosophers played with words as children play with toys. Uncle Ezriel had been right about that, too: today's man worshipped words as if they were idols. Zadok could derive no true satisfaction even from the exact sciences. Mathematics—the language of nature, as Kant described it—was nothing more than a kind of chess game. The axioms were not axioms but accepted rules. Lobachevski's and Riemann's non-Euclidean geometries destroyed any illusion that mathematics was a basic truth. The more Zadok considered Darwin's theory of the origin of species, the less it appealed to him. Even if life should be millions of years old, the species could not have developed without a plan. Every flower, every bird, every animal contradicted this theory. And where had the first cell come from? And from where did dead matter come? And what were laws? What sort of thing was a law? The moment one stopped thinking about everyday matters, one was immediately faced with the eternal mysteries. Zadok pulled at the hairs of his chin and grimaced. He had escaped from the Talmud, the Zohar, from the Shulhan Aruk; he had wanted to depend only on facts, on reason. But facts led nowhere: reason was bankrupt from the beginning. Truth remained veiled. Abroad? What could one learn abroad that wasn't known here? He received literature from Berlin, Leipzig, Bonn, even from Paris and London. Sitting there in his armchair in the Old City, he was in contact with the greatest minds of the world. But how much, alas, did the greatest minds know of the world? Not very much.

Hannah came in from the kitchen with her hair disheveled,

in a spotted apron and battered house slippers. "Zadok, bring up a bucket of water."

Zadok picked up the bucket and went down to the pump. This fetching of water had become a nuisance. In the few years that Zadok had lived in Warsaw, he had literally seen the growth of anti-Semitism. Gentiles who used to say "Good day" and remove their caps had stopped greeting him. Children who had grown up before his eyes had begun to ape and ridicule him. Girls laughed impudently in his face. The Polish press grew daily more malicious, constantly inventing new accusations against the Jews. Even the assimilated Jews were no longer immune to abuse. In Russia, there was no end to the pogroms. Jews were driven out of the villages. The pale of settlement where they were permitted to live grew smaller from year to year. And who was in the vanguard of all this? Not the hoi-polloi or the ignorant, but educated people with university backgrounds. In Germany, anti-Semitism was rampant among the professors. If education was not a remedy against the ancient practice of human oppression, then what was?

Zadok pumped the water. Around him stood a circle of Polish boys, aping his motions with the handle. "Hey, Jewboy, that is a pump, not your fringed garment! . . ." Zadok picked up the pail, spilling the water and wetting his boots. He had ceased sleeping nights and he was weak. He could barely lift the bucket. Lately Zadok had begun to worry about another matter: the eating of meat. How could one be opposed to violence and at the same time consume the flesh of innocent beasts and fowl? Could there be a justification for this? It was simply a matter of power. Whoever held the knife slaughtered. But he, after all, was against the right of might. He had already informed Hannah that he would no longer eat meat, but Hannah had answered him with a lament. Hadn't he made her life miserable enough as it was? Because of him her mother, brothers, sisters, and sisters-in-law would have nothing to do with her. She had no Sabbath, no holidays, no life whatsoever. Now he wanted to deprive her of meat as well. She wasn't able to cook two kinds of meals, meat and dairy. She had neither the money nor the strength for it. She was in the last months of pregnancy and was barely able to stand on her feet. . . . Hannah wept, complained, and made such a fuss that Zadok gave in to her. He would eat meat, if only she would keep still! But the meat didn't agree with him. Hannah bought giblets, heads, feet, entrails, livers. He felt that he was actually swallowing blood and marrow. It would have been possible to kill him, and cook him, in exactly the same way. How can those who torture creatures talk of justice?

Hannah was fussing in the kitchen. Zadok riffled the pages of his book. Maybe it would be better to go to Marshinov now. True, his beard was still too short and he had no sidelocks whatever. But he could wait no longer. Suddenly he leaped to his feet. "What am I waiting for?" "Hannale!"

"What is it?"

"I'm going to Marshinov."

"Right now?"

"Right now."

"And you'll leave me alone?"

"Put on your wig and come along."

"I can't go running off like this. . . ."

Hannah promised that she would be ready the following day. Zadok went to the depot to inquire about the train schedule. During the trolley ride to the station, Zadok took account of himself. He had once been a devoted son. When his father had become ill, he had stained his psalter with tears. But since he had become a worldly man, he had become cruel. His father was spitting out his lungs and his son remained in Warsaw. He had not seen him in years. Days went by and he did not even remember that he had a father, let alone the state he was in.

II

Marshinov was quiet. The death of the rabbi had been expected for weeks. Two years before, Dr. Ząbek had said that the rabbi's days were numbered, but when God gave life, one lived. However, the rabbi was no longer able to rise. He saw only his intimates. He would glance into his Zohar, doze, awaken and return to the holy book. Still far from fifty, he looked like an old man. His beard was white and unkempt. His arm had become so scrawny it could scarcely hold the arm phylactery. He was white as a corpse and his eyes watered. It was no longer possible for him to tolerate a saucerful of warm milk, a spoonful of chicken soup. A sip of tea was all he could manage. Tsipele, not Mendel the beadle, served him everything now. Her face had become shrunken. Since Calman's death, she wore a kerchief instead of a bonnet. She had lost her sister Shaindel, and her father, and now her husband was dying. All she could do was to pray.

"Please, take a drop of milk! . . ." Tsipele bent over the rabbi. The glass in her hand trembled.

"Thank you, I don't need it."

"I beg you, drink."

"I can't."

"Woe is me!"

"Sh—there is a Creator."

"Why do I have so much misfortune?" Tsipele said, and burst into tears.

The rabbi wanted to console her, but his throat was too dry. What misfortunes? The soul was no man's property but an object left in trust. When the depositor wanted it back, one had no right to oppose him. And since the soul must return to the throne of glory, one must not damage or stain it. One must be confident that what God did was good. But the rabbi was unable to say this. He glanced fondly at Tsipele. When they were first married, she had occasionally shown some female vanity. She would laugh, joke, adorn herself with jewelry.

Blessed be the name of the Almighty, now that she was a grandmother she had cast aside all childish nonsense and her face was comelier, more Jewish, as her mother's had been, blessed was her memory. Yes, that's how it was: when vanity was gone, the fear of God took its place.

Tsipele bent lower. "Perhaps a sip of soup?"

"I cannot."

"Take your medicine!"

"I beg you, no."

Tsipele stood silently at his bedside. She muffled a cry, not wanting to grieve him. Then she left, wringing her hands. The rabbi closed his eyes. Although the shades were down, the light still bothered him. He had difficulty in praying. He lay there, yearning for silence. Even the chirping of birds in the garden disturbed him. He wondered if he had served the Creator properly. He had neglected his studies, had had evil thoughts, doubts about Providence. He was unworthy of being a Hassid and had been crowned a rabbi against his will. And how had he pastured his flock? He hadn't paid enough attention to the poor and to the children and the young men who had later been lost to the faith. He hadn't inspired the fervor of piety in them. His thoughts vanished for a long time: his attention slackened. Something bubbled in his breast, his back. He felt as if the last portion of his lung wanted to tear loose.

Fragments of thought passed through his mind, bits of Scripture raced by, disconnected portions of the Talmud, of the midrash, words in Chaldaic. Passages of the Torah, interpretations, holy names came to him. He feared that the devil was at work on him. Before a quorum of Jews, the rabbi had nullified the blasphemous words Satan might force him to say or think in his last hour. But who could know whether this nullification was valid? The rabbi felt a dull ache of the spirit. In all these years he had yearned for a vision, a sign from above. Saints had had revelations of the prophet Elijah. While still alive, they had ascended to the mansions of heaven, had seen angels, seraphim, cherubim. The saint Baal Shem-Tov, the miracle worker, had seen the Nest of the Bird and had spoken to the Messiah. Even less important saints, those of later generations, had been favored by visions. But he, Jochanan, was apparently not worthy of any grace from above. His sins blocked the way. If the eyes are not clear, they do not see. If the ears are stuffed up, they do not hear. If one is concerned with matters of the body, one cannot perceive the spiritual. He was even more afraid lest he find nothing later on. His soul might be incarnated in a cow, a wild animal, or a frog. Did he belong among those who were not worthy of seeing the face of the Shechinah? He thought of the arguments of the heretics: there is no judge, no judgment, no leader. A passage from the Book of Ecclesiastes came back to him: "The dead know not anything." How could Ecclesiastes have said this? And how was it that the immortality of the soul was not mentioned in the Scriptures? Perhaps the Sadducees, God forbid, were right? . . . "I'm losing my soul . . . I'm dying an atheist. . . ." Reb Jochanan began to mumble, "I am sinking —Father in heaven, have pity on me! Protect me! Not because of my merits, but because of my holy ancestors. . . ." Suddenly the rabbi smiled. "And what if I do sink into the abyss? Would this in any way lessen the glory of the Almighty?"

The rabbi opened his eyes. It was evening. There was a candle on the table. His wife bent over the bed. "You slept for a long time."

"Yes. . . ."

The rabbi remained in a dreamlike state, praying inwardly for the truth. Someone had entered and left. The candle went out, or was extinguished. The rabbi thought about darkness. It is nothing but the lack of light, the concealment of His face. Then what was there to fear? He was still there. Evil spirits? Let them be—they were necessary! Incarnation! So be it. Rabbi Jochanan saw his father, his face emerging from the ritual bath. Everything dripped, his beard, his sidelocks. Were there ablutions on high, too? His father spoke, but without a sound. The rabbi listened. So that's the way it was. Suddenly something fluttered. Opening his eyes, the rabbi saw a great light. What was it? Sunrise? Lightning? He lay there, his limbs numb. It was neither of these. It illuminated every beam of the ceiling, every corner of the room, the windowpanes, the bed cover. "And God said, 'Let there be light.' " "And God saw that it was good." The rabbi was witnessing Creation. Within one moment everything had become clear, all questions had been answered. The rabbi closed his eyes, but the light was still there: a radiance that shone neither outside him nor within him, but filled all space, penetrated all being. It was everything together: revelation, surcease from all earthly turmoil, the profoundest joy. "All is right, God is perfect!" something in the rabbi cried out. It was all so simple that he could not grasp why he had not known it before. How long had it all lasted? A minute? Seconds? Time itself had vanished. He had merged with eternity. He had only one wish left: to let those who had sunk into doubt and suffering know what he had seen. He stretched out his hand to knock on the wall, but his hand made no sound.

He lingered in this state until sunrise. He seemed still to be in his body. The stars dimmed. The morning star rose and faded. Opposite the bed, the wall turned purplish, but it could not interfere with that other brightness. This now was a reflection of fire. What the flesh saw appeared hazy: the sky, the sun, the trees outside, the walls of the chamber. The door opened, and Tsipele brought in a glass of tea, but she seemed to be enclosed in shadows. A young man entered. The rabbi knew that this was his son, Zadok, but it no longer mattered.

A few minutes later the rabbi rattled, the death throes had begun. The Hassidim tore their way in, to be present at the departure of the soul. The warden of the Burial Society placed a goose quill near the rabbi's nostrils, but it did not stir. Tsipele wailed. The rabbi's daughter, Zeldele, came running up with a cry. Pinchus, the rabbi's son-in-law, wept with a piercing sound. The rabbi's youngest son, Gadele, had fallen asleep, and Mendel the beadle went to wake him. Zadok spoke to no one and no one spoke to him. He just stood there. They opened the windows and said the Justification of the Law. They raised the body and put it on the ground. It had almost no weight. There was a smile on the rabbi's face. He was covered with a prayer shawl and two candles were lit at his head. His intimates went out to telegraph the Jewish settlements that Jochanan, the Rabbi of Marshinov, had died.

Stanford University Libraries
3 6105 002 575 574

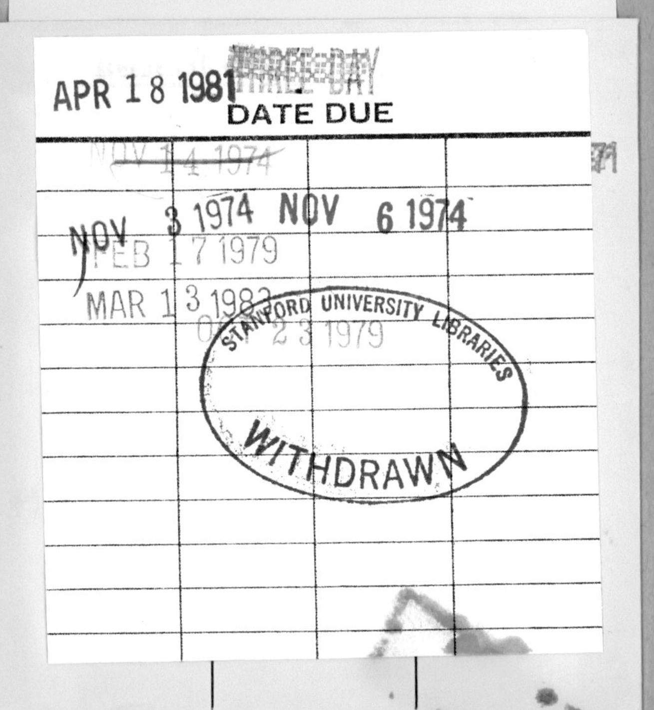
APR 18 1981
THREE DAY
DATE DUE
NOV 14 1974
NOV 3 1974
NOV 6 1974
FEB 17 1979
MAR 13 1983
OCT 23 1979
STANFORD UNIVERSITY LIBRARIES
WITHDRAWN